1.

Consciousness coalesced, and his ticket memory a
fleeting indulgence. For barely a heartbeat, he was free. Opening
his eyes collapsed the fragile superposition of knowing and not
knowing, and physical pain seeped through him. Day after day,
week after week, year after year, he performed this feat of
resurrection, and he longed for a freedom he feared he would
never rediscover. He turned his mind outward, and the now-
familiar ceiling came into focus, its painted surface almost flawless,
washed with the artificial daylight that he chose to wake to. But
the real world shuns perfection, and his eye catalogued each tiny
familiar flaw. He shut out the present and summoned an image of
long ago. That remembered ceiling was rendered immaculate by
his curated memory, a backdrop to her hair across his face, her
weight at his centre, and her hot skin against his. The indulgence
was too painful to sustain, and he opened his eyes, heart racing,
his chest tight. His tears were long shed, sorrow diluted by time; if
he allowed them now, they would be from self-pity, which led
nowhere.

Last night! He sat up against the bedhead, unaware that he was
gently shaking his head. It was banal, but had felt so complicated
and upsetting. Before he kissed her, he had not touched a woman
other than in simple greeting for over a decade, and it had become

a dangerous, debilitating need. A single kiss on the lips had proved too intimate. He closed his eyes again, attempting to untangle the emotion. Her reaction as he drew back, the look of bewilderment on her face at his curt apology as he turned and walked quickly away. The embarrassment returned to him now, and he felt his face flush and his breath quicken. He had no idea then why he had panicked, and no idea now.

He spoke out loud. "OK, enough! Get up; yoga and meditation."

The sun rising behind his building threw a band of light across the flats opposite. He could see the river along the street, the water choppy and dark but gilded with the morning light. He rolled out the mat in the middle of the floor, glad, for once, for the lack of furniture. Spartan. The word was apposite for much of his existence, but he was no warrior; his body was softening, and he was beginning to dislike it in a way he never had. He held the soft flesh of his stomach in both hands, resolving to exercise more, knowing he would not.

Two decades of practice and deep muscle memory soothed his body and mind, and twenty minutes later, sitting cross-legged with his eyes closed, he had calmed the storm.

He stood at the island worktop watching the morning headlines without seeing them, absentmindedly eating a slice of toast and drinking a cup of tea. It was Friday; he liked Fridays and arranged his workload to be back in London for the weekly meeting at Cyber Futures. Seeing Paul and Sania had assumed a disproportionate importance. He pictured them and wondered if they were aware of his growing dependence on their emotional as well as technical support.

Callum always walked the mile from his flat to the office,

THE LANDS OF THE BLIND SERIES

1. THE LAND OF THE BLIND

"In the land of the blind, the one-eyed man is king."

Dutch philosopher Desiderius Erasmus (1466-1536)
"Collecteana Adagiorum".First published in Paris in 1500.

whatever the weather. He did not own a car, but he would have walked anyway to immerse himself in the river of people flowing along the capital's arteries. Each person carried a little of the energy and ideas that fuelled the city. When he joined them, he absorbed a little of their vitality, allowing him to believe both that anything was possible and that he might remain invisible.

This morning, he was earlier than usual. It was barely seven-thirty when he stepped from his apartment block into New Globe Walk on the south bank of the Thames. From the large expanse of glass that walled much of his three-bedroom penthouse, four floors above, he overlooked the adjacent Globe Theatre and could see the iconic dome of St Paul's Cathedral across the busy river. The flat belonged to one of the many companies he owned, and he had transported all his possessions there in two large suitcases over a year ago. Paul and his wife, Lisa, had persuaded him to move, to change his life, and leaving his old claustrophobic flat was the first step. It was a vast improvement. Lisa had decorated and furnished the apartment but, so far, had failed completely in the next stage of what she considered her mission to save him from himself. Unfortunately, their concerns for him were well-founded. His life then and now was consumed by his convoluted, dangerous work; he thought of little else and had time for little else. When, years earlier, he had planned all of this and visualised his future, none of this messy, emotional detail had occurred to him. The unanticipated, self-inflicted, corrosive isolation was proving more than he could manage. It had been obvious to Paul and Lisa that he was slipping towards depression, living almost entirely alone in the tiny flat since they had known him. Their intervention had prevented him from drowning, and he certainly had a purpose and agency that sustained him, but his life remained joyless.

This morning, he walked the short distance from the apartment door to the embankment and leaned against the cold stone parapet for a moment. Today was summer in name only; clouds cloaked the early sun and lidded the tall glass buildings of the City of London and the colossal constructions at Canary Wharf to the east. Lifting his face to the fine, soft drizzle, he smiled and absorbed this small pleasure, remembering once again where he had come from. He watched the river boats knifing across the choppy, slate waters for a few minutes and glanced up at the sound of an invisible aircraft hidden in the oppressive cloud.

His phone rang as he was crossing London Bridge; the ringtone told him who was calling.

"Morning, Armando, how are you?"

"Good morning, Callum; I am well, thank you."

Callum smiled at his accent. Both men spoke fluent Spanish but habitually conducted their business conversations in English. Callum had stayed with Armando, his wife Constanza, and their twin daughters on several occasions, and it was only on his third visit that Constanza discovered he was not Spanish. Having lived there until he was 10 years old, Spanish had been his first language, and it held a strangely romantic attraction for him; the feel of the words in his mouth connected him to that unencumbered early childhood.

"We need to discuss our next funding round, Callum. Would it be possible for you to come over next week?"

"Of course, I could come tomorrow if it's urgent." He had nothing else to do and would have been happy to avoid the inevitable sense of isolation yet another lonely weekend would bring.

"Oh no, it's fine; Monday will be fine."

"At the restaurant, as usual?" Callum asked.

"Perfecto, I will see you then. Chao, Callum."

Callum returned the phone to his pocket and continued in the stream of bodies moving north across the river. At Monument Street, he slipped out of the flow, down to the monument and the quiet at the base of the stone tower. He stood as though reading the wooden memorial to London's great fire, but his thoughts were on what Armando's call meant. They were burning through money at an astounding rate. The only business that currently washed its face financially was Cyber Futures, where he was headed this morning. The laboratory in Berkeley was not designed as a profit centre; it was a research facility that would always require funding. However, their joint ventures and battery fabrication plants needed to start turning a profit soon, or they would be in trouble. They were close to financial self-sufficiency, and as soon as their novel battery technology went into production and they could license it to others, they would be free of the need for external investment and the risks associated with the way they acquired their funds. It was pointless worrying; Armando had said Monday was fine, so it could not be an emergency.

Their proximity made him realise afresh how much he was looking forward to seeing Paul and Sania. Along with Armando in Switzerland, they were his confidants and had become the precarious emotional foundation of his world.

2.

Vivien Cazinski stared at one of the large computer screens on her desk. Like everything in her laboratory, it was the best money could buy. She loved the freedom to concentrate solely on the research without worrying about money. There were no grant applications to produce, no quibbling about buying the best equipment available, and, best of all, she was directing the research. Her mind drifted back to the first meeting with him. This stranger had phoned her out of the blue and asked to meet to discuss setting up a laboratory with her as director. It had seemed unlikely that anyone would make her such a grand offer, but when she searched the company he represented, they appeared to be serious about their technology investments. At the time, she was reluctant even to consider his approach, feeling that she would be betraying Jennifer and Emmanuelle, with whom she was working as a senior researcher in their lab.

Callum had been persuasive and persistent, and eventually, she relented and agreed to meet to hear what he had to say. What harm could that do, she had told herself, knowing full well the self-deception she was entertaining. She only realised when they met at the restaurant that he had flown from London to California specifically to see her. He was charming and attractive, which was irrelevant given that she was happily married with young children, but ? that emanates from attractive people is seductive. It was d meeting in a good, but not flashy, Italian restaurant off Street in Berkeley. She remembered the excellent food and verted warehouse building, which was loud with young peo ying themselves. It could not have been less like a bu eeting. Over dinner, Callum explained about the private eq npany he represented and how they were building a p of start-ups or buying young businesses in specific te y areas. He seemed to know a great deal about her re mentioning several papers on which she was a lead a d discussing the potential direction of their research. She ered. He repeatedly told her she could have carte blanche g up the laboratory, could have any equipment, and hire she wanted. At least for the first three years, the budget tty much whatever she reasonably wanted it to be. She a little too much wine with the meal and remembered ; in the taxi with her head spinning. His offer was wildly us; she could stay in Berkeley, could run her own laboratory, oney was no object. She told him she would think about it, fore she left the restaurant, she had already decided to accept fer.

allum was as good as his word; he hired the administrative she needed before she even found an office for them and ed hard from the outset for her to start her research as quickly ossible. People often use the words, but in this case, money ly was no object; whatever she asked for, she got. She owned per cent of the laboratory; he had offered this before she asked, d the rest of the employees, at the end of the first year, shared other ten per cent. Genetic Futures, the company that owned e laboratory and for which Callum worked, was the majority

7

shareholder but did not interfere with her work. Q
opposite. In the early days, Callum attended a monthly
with the team and soon began to make suggestions
direction they might take with some of their work. The te;
his suggestions on board without ever questioning his kno
but she remembered the first time it happened, her flash o
and surprise at his apparent depth of knowledge.

The progress they had made in such a short tim
astonishing, and what she was looking at on the screen repre:
another giant leap forward. But she was troubled. She remem
the meeting with her team leaders and Callum about nine m
earlier, during which they had discussed the use of the
nuclease. Callum claimed to have read a blog about it from a
in Japan, but the promised link to the article had never arr
One of her groups had looked more closely at Cas19, and
resulted in this recent breakthrough. Callum was not a biologi:
a chemist, but once again had made a suggestion, slightly 'ou
left field', which had led to this latest breakthrough. From the
Callum expressed his ideas, it was clear he was repeati
something he had heard or read elsewhere. When they prob
him, he could not provide any detail, simply indicating the gene
direction he thought they should explore. Given that Callu
effectively paid for everything they did, but more important
because his suggestions immediately seemed promising to t
team, they tended to pursue them. Vivien's disquiet had be
growing, and now she was convinced Callum was getti
intelligence from somewhere, and that could only be
competitor's laboratory.

Here it was again, the evidence splashed across the screen
front of her, too good to be true. The fidelity of the changes to th

RNA they had attempted in their latest protocol was perfect; faultless. If further tests confirmed these results, they would have overcome one of the fundamental issues with the CRISPR/Cas gene editing process: the presence of undetectable off-target edits. If true, she knew she might well get a Nobel prize, as everyone assumed would her mentors Jennifer Doudna and Emmanuelle Charpentier, in whose laboratory she had been working when Callum recruited her. She could barely imagine the thrill of receiving that ultimate science honour, but she did not want it based on the theft of someone else's work. If it seemed too good to be true …. She had to speak to Callum; she needed to look him in the eye and ask for the truth. It was the middle of the night in London, but she phoned anyway and left him an unambiguous voicemail message.

***

Callum knew why Vivien had phoned and asked for the meeting. Flying five thousand miles from London to California was not something he wanted to do, but it had to be done face-to-face. He had expected this from one of the companies; if he was honest, he was expecting it from all of them at some point. It was perhaps unsurprising that Vivien was the first. He had pushed hard for the advances in gene editing. Given the choice, he would have started this program years ago, but that was outside his control. The need for rapid progress meant he had not tried to disguise his direction of travel by throwing in any blind alleys for Vivien and her team. As a result, all their resources had been directed, from the start, along the path he knew would succeed. But you can only be lucky so often without raising suspicion, and his hot streak was just a little too hot. He stared out of the window at the white blanket of clouds below, thinking about the conversation he would have with her. He would lie; he had no choice, and he was once again trying to decide what would be the most effective way. He liked Vivien and wanted her to believe that she and her team owned the discoveries they had made. After all, he had not told them how to do the science; he did not understand the chemistry or biology nearly well enough to do that; they had made the breakthroughs themselves; he had simply pointed them in the right direction, passing on details he had learned by rote. Wasn't most human progress a combination of intelligence, hard work and luck? He had just stacked the odds in their favour. Had he not done so, a European team would make the same breakthrough in a little under a decade, but that would have been too late for him and outside his control.

He hated these trans-Atlantic crossings. He would not be in California long enough for his body clock to adjust and was resigned to forty-eight hours of disorientation. The British Airways flight from London to San Francisco landed on time, and with just hand luggage, he was quickly in a taxi, heading for the laboratory on the outskirts of Berkeley. The evening traffic was heavy, and they joined the crawling metal. Most cars carried only a single occupant. Objectively, it was beyond crazy. He gazed around in wonder as he always did when he visited the United States. Such unbelievable affluence and profligate waste. From his perspective, it was sickening; he knew where this led, but for the majority of the population, it was just the way they lived their lives. Easy come, easy go. He could not change the minds of billions of individuals, most of whom gave no thought to, or did not know about, the damage they were inflicting on the planet. He had to provide them with a less destructive way to live their lives, and only if his way was cheaper or easier would they choose it. His plans relied on the fact that, at some level, humans are rather simple and reliable animals.

It took ninety minutes to cover the thirty miles to the laboratory, an unremarkable-looking building on Hearst Avenue close to the university and downtown Berkeley. The security guard at reception knew Callum, a regular visitor, but would not let him in unattended. Callum waited in reception for Vivien to descend in the lift to collect him.

"Hello, Callum; how was the flight?" she asked. "A flying visit, it would seem." She eyed his small bag.

"I'm only here to see you, Vivien." Callum smiled, and they kissed on each cheek.

In the lift, Callum asked casually, "So, how's everything going?"

Vivien turned her angular features to him, her pale blue eyes watching him carefully. "How do you imagine we are doing, Callum?" She asked evenly.

Callum just nodded gently, returning her gaze. "Ok." He said softly.

The lift doors opened. "Any chance of a cup of tea?" Callum asked as they walked towards her office. The office floor was empty at this time; anyone still working would be in the laboratories below.

"Sure; you Brits and your tea." Vivien smiled and led him towards the small kitchen. "If you're lucky, we might even have some milk, which I know you like to adulterate your tea with," she teased him.

She seemed relaxed despite what he knew was the reason for the meeting, and Callum was having difficulty reading her. They chatted about the weather while she made his tea and ran herself a glass of water from the cooler before leading him to her office.

She sat in her large chair, and he dropped his bag by the door and sat across the desk from her. The screens along the wall to her left were all turned off, and the papers were neatly stacked on her desk. Order and precision. She got straight to the point.

"You won't be surprised to hear that the results from the new cas19 protocol are rather good." She paused. "When I say rather good, I mean they are remarkable, astonishing even. But I suspect that's not news to you, is it Callum?"

"That's excellent," Callum responded carefully. I'm not surprised in the sense that I know how good you and the team are."

Her eyes bore into him, "Really. So why do you think I'm feeling so uneasy; why don't I believe you, Callum? Why are you here?"

He needed to be sure; he wouldn't make it too easy. "There's no one doing this sort of work; not even Doudna and her team are as good as you are, Vivien."

Her annoyance was growing. "OK. You roll a couple of sixes one after another, a one in thirty-six chance; lucky, but no big deal. Then you throw a couple more and a couple more. Eventually, you need to take a close look at the dice because they seem to be loaded." She pinned him with her pale eyes and waited.

"Well, I get that analogy; I'm the dice here, I assume?"

"And every pointer or idea you suggest we pursue, well, jeez, guess what, we keep on rolling sixes." She watched him, unblinking. "How, Callum? You're not a biologist; you don't even understand this stuff at the detailed level."

Despite the hours he had spent anticipating this moment, he still did not know what he was going to say. He trusted her and wanted to tell her the truth, but there was no way he could cross that line; not yet. He reached for his tea and sipped it, splicing in just a few more seconds before he had to commit himself."

She said, "I wondered about you having someone in another lab feeding you with their developments, but I've done a quick sanity check with my contacts, and I'm pretty sure no one else is even close to where we are."

"Think of it as a kind of second sight." Callum heard himself say.

Her eyes narrowed briefly as she processed this and then widened in incredulity. "Divine intervention?"

"Not exactly." He was visibly nervous now; this was not going well. "It's not spying or anything underhand like that. I've not stolen these ideas from another team or anyone. I just know how to make this work, at least theoretically."

She jumped at his response, "Rather more than theoretical, Callum, you've given us some specific pointers to Cas proteins and protocols, which we might have found in five years. This is not some grand vision. I think you've seen this working somewhere, and you're smart enough to learn a few key details, and we've been smart enough to figure out how to make it work."

She was spot on, and Callum felt cornered but stuck to his line, "Vivien, this stuff does not exist anywhere in this world; I've not ..."

"In this world?" She pounced again, "What exactly does that mean? Next, you'll be invoking alien technology."

He shook his head, smiling bleakly, wondering why he had used the phrase, "No, no, nothing so exotic. OK, look." He made his decision and took a deep breath. "I am afraid I'm not going to be able to tell you how I know this stuff, Vivien. I would prefer to tell you because I like you and I trust you, but there's something much, much bigger going on than just this. I'm stuck in the middle and have to see it through. So that's all I can say. One day, perhaps in a few years, you will find out through something that happens, or I might be able to tell you. But it should not undermine what you've achieved or will continue to achieve here. You're going to have as much impact on human medicine in the next few years as things like vaccinations and antibiotics have had. This is history, Vivien; you are making the world a better place for millions of people; I just hope you can accept this and carry on with your work."

She was seething and could not respond, staring at him, her jaw clenched. After an ocean of silence, she spoke, her voice shaking slightly, "This is unfair, Callum; you are putting me in an impossible position, professionally."

He nodded his agreement. "Some people claim divine intervention when they make great breakthroughs. Perhaps if you think about it in those terms"

"Don't patronise me! That is not remotely what's going on here." She was furious, and he was only making it worse.

He held his hands up, "I'm sorry, Vivien. I shouldn't have said that. It was stupid of me. I just don't like to see you upset. It's not what I wanted. It's not what I intended."

They sat in silence for almost a minute. It was pointless for him to say anything else, and they both knew it. They also both understood that the scale of the progress made in the lab over the last few years meant that she would not walk away from the work based on whatever she thought Callum was concealing, provided she believed him when he said the ideas were not stolen from someone else.

The silence continued until she had to speak, but it was only to tell him she had plans for the evening and could not spend it entertaining him. She had invited him to her home in the past, but tonight, it would have made for an uncomfortable evening with her husband and two children. He left her in the office, at her desk, from where she bid him a curt goodbye without rising from her chair or looking at him.

Callum calmed himself in the taxi to the hotel, breathing away the stress. He reflected on how, even after so long, he still found confrontation so upsetting. She would make her peace with his evasion; she had no choice, and when, one day, she discovered the truth, it would be obvious why he had lied, and perhaps she would forgive him. Whatever happened, she would have to learn to accommodate the idea that the plaudits inevitably heading her way were in some way devalued. It would cast a shadow which she was unlikely ever to escape. Callum regretted this, but he had no choice; what he was doing was too important.

3.

Equatorial Guinea is, by African standards, a small country and potentially a wealthy one, given the substantial gas and oil reserves that lie beneath its wetlands and verdant islands close to the coast. Nearly three decades of partnership with one of the world's largest energy companies had made billions of dollars for the energy company and the Guinea National Oil Corporation. As so often happens in Africa, most of the wealth now belonged to the oil company's international shareholders and the country's President and coterie. The once pristine landscape had been comprehensively trashed, and the considerable and ongoing cost to the environment was the cause of a decade-long protest by Friends of the Earth. In the last few years, peaceful protests had escalated into armed insurrection by three of the tribal groups that had for centuries lived on the vast river delta and archipelago of islands dominating the country's west coast. The wealth of species that evolved over millennia had created an environment that supported the tribes sustainably for centuries. The people had lived in balance with their environment across countless generations. Now, in a single generation, their world was visibly dying around them. Their fishing grounds were polluted through careless oil spills, the air foul with escaping hydrocarbons and flared gas that the company burned, unwilling to invest in the technology to trap and use it responsibly. The fish that survived the ecological vandalism carried a heavy burden of toxic chemicals, which they passed on to the people who ate them. Deformed foetuses were common, and cancers proliferated. The people had nowhere to go and no way of defending themselves. Eventually, after decades littered with the broken promises of their politicians and their President, they did what people eventually do as a last resort: they turned to violence.

Sabotage of the pipelines and the processing facilities had become a weekly occurrence, and President David Kigale had to deploy an increasing number of troops to defend the infrastructure to ensure that the hydrocarbons flowed out and the US dollars flowed into Equatorial Guinea to his and his loyal Generals' private bank accounts. To begin with, the 'terrorists' had been stupid and easy to kill. But they were growing smarter every day, both in evading the army and creating a nuisance on the internet with pictures of a ruined environment and the bullet-ridden bodies of their young men and women.

The President was having a particularly bad day. He had spent almost an hour shouting at General Bissouna, the head of the army, berating him for allowing yet another pipeline to be blown up. His valuable crude oil was once again spilling into the River Delta. The poisoned fish, fouled sea birds, suffocated animals and the people breathing the carcinogenic fumes did not even cross his mind. For the tenth time, he was telling the General to make an example of the terrorists and their families to make sure it did not happen again.

The General stood stiffly, immobile, in the middle of the President's private room, his uniform immaculate, his perfectly polished boots nestled into the fine Persian rug on the polished marble floor.

"Go now. Get out of my sight and do as I say, or I will find another who can." The president barked.

With overwhelming relief, the General saluted, turned and marched to the door. He had been kicked, and it was his turn to kick someone else.

The President stood at the large plate glass window looking over the perfect lines of the lawn, the geometric flower beds and the elaborate fountains in the Palace gardens, allowing the anger to subside. His private secretary knocked and entered quietly.

"Sir, I have the Finance Minister waiting for you. Would you like me to show him in?"

"No, Jacob, I would not. I am tired now and need to eat and relax; I have done enough for one day. Tell him to come back tomorrow morning at ten o'clock."

Jacob turned and was closing the door when he heard the President add, "I need to relax a little after dinner. Can you arrange something for me?"

Jacob understood exactly what the President wanted, "Of course, sir. Is there anything particular that you would like?"

"Just one and young."

"Of course, sir."

This was, for Jacob, the most unpleasant duty he had to perform for his President. Like many men of his age and with absolutely nothing to constrain his desires, the president enjoyed having sex with young girls, sometimes several at the same time.

Jacob had daughters, and he had witnessed the distress of the girls who were driven from the palace most nights. Some were clearly in physical pain, some cried silently, and some buried whatever had been done to them behind an expressionless mask, which he found unbearable.

"And Jacob, a large Gin and Tonic."

Twenty years earlier, while studying at Oxford University, the President had acquired a taste for Gin and Tonic. He still enjoyed the feel of the cold crystal glass in his hand as he stood in the warm evening air, looking over his palace grounds.

The serving girl arrived with the Gin and Tonic, and the president noticed she looked unwell.

"You have a cold, girl?"

The girl stopped dead in her tracks and looked at the ground, shaking in terror.

"Don't be so worried. Go home; I do not want your cold."

She nodded, placed the glass on the table beside the president and scurried away.

After dismissing the Finance Minister, Jacob phoned one of his aides and passed on the message. He had no idea how the girls were acquired or who they were and would ensure it stayed that way.

***

A few miles and a world away across Malabo, the capital city, Wonkehmi Conteh sat at the single table in the tiny one-room shack, quietly sewing with her mother. Wonkehmi was seventeen, smart, poor and angry. The fury she carried within was well buried, and everyone who knew her felt the gentle, irrepressible force of calm surrounding her. Her mother knew nothing of the friends she had made in recent months. She would not have approved of their radical and often violent aims, and she would not have understood how they used their computers and phones to talk with like-minded people across the world.

Wonkehmi's friend Akachi had told her about the Western

man who had somehow connected with their small group of dissidents. The man had messaged them to explain that he knew about their President's corruption and the blood on his hands and warned that worse would come if he was not stopped. The man wanted him removed from power. It seemed like science fiction, but Akachi told her that the Western man had already sent a large amount of money to them as a sign of goodwill, and he had told them he would demonstrate his power by bringing the traffic in the city to a standstill. Akachi could barely contain himself in telling her that the recent failure of all the traffic lights across the city had been his doing. He had told Akachi that it would happen, and it had. He had brought an entire city to a standstill by controlling the computers that ran the road systems. She had seen this for herself, assuming it was just one more power failure, but if Akachi was telling the truth, perhaps this man really could force justice on a pig like Kigale. Wonkehmi wondered at the ingenuity of the Western world, desperate to believe that this man could do what he said.

The mobile phone vibrated gently in her pocket, and she answered and listened for a few seconds, nodding imperceptibly, "Yes," she said and disconnected the call.

The man she had first spoken to on the phone a few days earlier had told her exactly what would happen. She had been shocked to hear that she would be strip searched and internally searched before being taken to see the President. She would be given a robe and would have nothing with her. The president was fanatical about personal safety; it was not paranoia for a man with as many enemies as he had. Behind the curtain that divided their one room, out of her mother's sight, she stripped naked, took the tiny perfume bottle from her bag and sprayed a fine mist into the air.

President, David Kigale

She breathed the cool droplets deep into her lungs as instructed, exactly as she had done earlier that morning. This time, she sprayed herself carefully from head to toe until the bottle was empty. She was still dressing when there was a heavy knock on the flimsy door of the shack. Wonkehmi synched the traditional skirt around her and went to the door without hesitation, a word, or a glance towards her mother. She followed the man in the suit along the dirt road towards the huge Mercedes glinting like a malevolent black beetle between the dust-covered shacks. People watched her, curious but not staring; you did not question or look at the men who arrived in these cars.

The journey across the tiny capital was swift. Few could afford cars in the impoverished city, and what traffic there was quickly moved aside for their limousine. Wonkehmi sat for this brief time, feeling the cool, smooth leather seats but seeing nothing outside the tinted windows. She focused all her energy and attention inward, constructing a fragile wall between herself and the world.

The ornate gates swung open, and seconds later, she was escorted through a side door into the palace. She registered the cool, bright marble and the thick, richly coloured carpets, and as she mechanically ascended the sweeping staircase, she felt the fabulous crystal chandelier above mocking her with its bright, sparkling innocence.

After several minutes of walking through the empty palace, her escort opened an unmarked door for her, and she was looking into a dressing room, clearly a man's room. Dark wood panelled the walls, and two uniformed men sat on either side of the door at the far side of the room. They straightened, looking at her closely, but remained in their seats. A hand gently pushed her into the room, and the door closed behind her. She flinched as she heard it lock.

President, David Kigale

The two bodyguards were leaning forward eagerly, and Wonkehmi dragged her eyes from them to the door ahead of her. She didn't move, but her heart was pounding, and she felt lightheaded.

"Clothes on there, " one of the men said, pointing to a chair beside a wide floor-to-ceiling mirror in a gilt frame. She looked at the chair and willed her legs to take her to it, but she could not move.

"We can do it for you if you like." One of the men said.

It was enough to release her from the fear that almost overwhelmed her. She moved unsteadily, the few paces to the chair. Focusing just on the buttons and clips of her skirt and blouse, she removed them and placed them on the chair.

She paused momentarily, long enough to elicit "And the rest." from one of the guards.

She took a deep breath, and it was done; she was naked, trembling, staring at the wall.

"Stand in front of the mirror and place your hands on it."

Both men stood and moved towards her. She looked forward and, in the reflection, past the flawless dark skin of her vulnerable body, saw them approach before she shut her eyes.

She felt a booted foot tapping the inside of one ankle, then the other, and she moved her feet apart until it stopped. She bit her lip, fighting to control her shaking body. She did not hear the second door open slightly; the murmur of a low voice reached her but not the words, and she sensed something change. One of the guards made a dismissive sound and slapped her naked buttock hard.

"Get dressed, you fucking whore."

She did not understand their anger or what had just happened, but she opened her eyes and quickly grabbed her clothes, fumbling to dress as they watched her.

"Our great president does not need you, you little whore so go back to the hole in the ground you came from." He knocked hard on the door she had entered, and it was opened instantly by the guard who had delivered her.

"Come, be quick." He said, shooing her out of the room and along the corridor as she struggled to fix her dress. She would not be driven home, just far enough from the royal palace to ensure no one saw her leaving the grounds. She would have to walk the rest of the way across the city.

The president was feeling unwell. He had enjoyed a pleasant family meal with his wife and three children before they all retired for the evening and left him to his diversions. He had been looking forward to getting his hands on the young girl. Like all the girls, she would have been lucky to have a man as important as he was taking an interest in her. He never tired of the feeling of power he felt as he forced himself inside their perfect bodies. But tonight, he did not feel that familiar, thrilling anticipation; he felt strangely weak, a little breathless as he climbed the stairs to his presidential bed chamber. By the time he had undressed, he was feeling worse, and reluctantly, he had sent the girl away. There would be plenty more days ahead and many more virgin girls.

The flu virus suspended in the liquid in the perfume bottle was now being carried on and in almost every part of Wonkehmi's body. She was not yet feeling its effects, but as she walked home, she felt a deep sense of disappointment in failing to deliver whatever poison the bottle contained. Wonkehmi was unaware of the others who, like her, hated the president enough to risk their lives and infect him with the same virus. The young woman who had served the president his evening drink and the family their breakfast that morning carried the same cleverly engineered virus. Flu changes all the time, and this was yet another version altered, not this time by evolution, but by someone who knew how to make very specific changes. The result was a moderately virulent and highly infectious strain; easily passed between humans. It was now busy invading cells in the president's body in exactly the same way as it had the cells in Wonkehmi's body for almost thirty-six hours and the serving girl's for over forty-eight hours.

Thousands of people would soon be infected with the virus, and in all of them, it would behave in the same way that all viruses do. The virus inserts itself into the target cells of whatever organism it infects, and once inside a cell, the DNA or RNA in the virus hijacks the cell's natural machinery to create copies of itself; thousands of copies in each compromised cell. About six hours after the virus enters a cell, the copying process is complete; the cell is destroyed and literally bursts, releasing the myriad copies of RNA into the body. Each new copy finds its own host cell, and the avalanche of viral replication sweeps onward, inducing flu symptoms.

For Wonkehmi, the waitress, and almost everyone else who was now infected, this process would result in a slight cough, an irritation of the cells in their throat and lungs. The discomfort would grow for a few hours and then subside over the next days to disappear with no long-term effects. Everyone except President Kigale. Inside his cells, something very different was happening. The modification to the original flu virus included the addition of a section of RNA that matched a sequence in all the President's cells. Of the more than seven billion people in the world, its sequence was unique; it matched only the President's DNA. His DNA had been acquired without his knowledge at an international conference more than a year earlier, and a small section was used to provide the unique RNA key. Now it was unlocking a series of complex reactions in his infected cells. In addition to creating the virus copies as it did in everyone, his cells were also producing a special protein in huge quantities and sending this tiny molecule out into the bloodstream along with the replicated virus. As complex as it sounds, creating a specific sequence of RNA and inserting it into a virus is routine. For the scientists and researchers at Genetic Futures, it was done all the time in their experiments on live cells. Callum had provided the sequence of RNA letters to a lab technician as a data file; the technician followed a series of steps, a protocol, to modify the original virus RNA and to insert Callum's sequence.

Proteins are at the core of animal biology, a fundamental part of the machinery of the body. We know a lot about some and nothing about countless others. Our ignorance is impressive; estimates of how many different human proteins there are vary from 100,000 to more than 400,000. They are complex molecules, but in the end, it is usually their physical shape that determines the function they perform. Callum had inserted an RNA sequence that produced a tiny protein currently unknown to science. It would one day be identified as dangerous and its genetic sequence stored for reference in a global database, along with many thousands of others, which should never be produced. This novel protein was now doing its work in the President's body. As each molecule was created, it folded naturally into its characteristic shape, which, in this case, made it a perfect fit for another protein found in all humans. Haemoglobin occurs only in red blood cells, and it has one purpose: to carry oxygen from the lungs around the body to where muscles and other cells use it. When there is a high concentration of oxygen, as in the lungs, the oxygen molecules slot into haemoglobin and are carried around the body to where they are needed. The oxygen is ejected and carbon dioxide replaces it and is carried back to the lungs. Callum's protein was slotting into more and more of the haemoglobin molecules, and once there, it could not be ejected.

The president woke only an hour after falling asleep and immediately felt unwell. He was breathless, panting, and the effort of swinging his legs out of the bed and raising his large torso to a sitting position was almost beyond him. No matter how hard he breathed he seemed unable to get enough air into his lungs. Gasping, he bellowed for help. Instantly, the bedroom door opened, and two guards, weapons in hand, advanced into the room.

"Doctor, doctor," gasped the President between torn breaths as he rolled back against the pillows. One guard holstered his weapon and ran from the room. The remaining guard stood helplessly looking from the President to the open bedroom door for the few seconds it took the Doctor to arrive carrying his medical bag. One of the president's doctors was never more than a few meters from him, ready for any emergency. The stethoscope was out and on the President's chest in seconds, and a light shone down his throat, but there was no constriction of his airways, no reason at all for the look of panic that suffused his face.

The doctor pulled open the silk pyjamas to look at the great barrel chest, searching desperately for any sign but finding no external symptoms. He would have to give the President something to calm him; he was hyperventilating, the breaths becoming fast and short.

"Panic attack," said the doctor, more for his own benefit than for those around him, "Do you have a paper bag?" He looked to the two guards. They looked back, uncomprehending.

"Go and get me a paper bag—or any bag! " the doctor shouted at the two guards.

One of them ran from the room.

"Sir, sir, try to slow your breathing; try to calm yourself."

Inside the President's body, the modified flu virus continued its blind production of the clever little protein molecules, pouring them in ever-increasing numbers into his bloodstream. Hundreds of thousands were being released every second, and each one found a home in a haemoglobin molecule in his red blood cells where an oxygen molecules would otherwise have been. The oxygen in his lungs simply streamed in and out with each desperate breath while his body carried less and less to his muscles and his brain. Before the doctor could do anything to save him, the President suffocated.

4.

Paul Croft was meeting a friend for a drink in a large pub in Wimbledon town centre. It was evening in London, and the silent television screens which adorned the walls of the pub chain were playing a news clip of the Hollywood 'A' list actor Matt Denver's drive down Hollywood Boulevard in his revolutionary electric car. Rob had been Paul's colleague and the only one he had stayed in touch with after leaving his previous job. They had always got on well and, once or twice a year, made time for a few beers to catch up and gossip about the staff at the call centre where Paul used to work. The beer and food in the pub were cheap and acceptably good for a low-key Tuesday evening. Early in the working week, the pub was relatively civilised; neither of them would be visiting on a Friday or Saturday night when the cheap alcohol guaranteed a young, unsophisticated and noisy crowd.

Like Paul, Rob was a technology nerd, and he nodded at the screen, "That tech is from one of your group of companies, isn't it?"

Paul was mildly impressed, "You keeping across battery technology?"

"Sort of. I just happened to read something about their aluminium cells a while ago; it sounded interesting, so I followed them."

"Yes, a joint venture based in Africa somewhere I believe," Paul said.

Rob knew that Paul worked for one of the companies in the same group as the battery manufacturer. "Pretty low-profile, the people behind Green Futures. Do you get to see any of them?"

"Only their technology guy, really. The companies are all owned by the group, but there's no interaction."

"What's he like, rich American?"

Paul smiled. "No, he's English, lives here in London. Nice chap, actually; he's sort of become a friend of the family."

"What? The technology director of Green Futures, a family friend? Surely, he lives in Monaco or the Isle of Man or another tax haven."

"It's not his company," Paul laughed, "He's just a technology consultant." It was a lie, but the truth about who really owned Green Futures would not have been remotely credible.

"So you work with him?"

"Not exactly," Paul dissembled, "He's in the office every week or so, but we don't exactly work together. We have a meeting each Friday and he spends more time with my boss, Sania."

Rob smiled, "Yes, I read about her; smart woman. She was a hacker, according to one of the articles I read."

"Blimey, you're stalking us."

Rob laughed, "Nah, just an interesting company, and these days, I keep seeing the name and logo popping up all over the place. We're even using your apps in the call centre now."

"That's cool," Paul said. "Yeah, the basic small business package is pretty competitive, and to be honest, there's no one better than us out there, so why would you not."

Rob drank a mouthful of beer before responding, "Well,

someone in that organisation is on the ball because I also read about the new gene therapy from Genetic Futures."

"Woah, you really are stalking us."

Rob rolled his eyes, "Just one of those slack days at work recently and me ending up too far down a rabbit hole. But seriously, their new gene editing therapies look like a game changer. It's way too complicated for me to understand, but apparently, the woman who runs that operation and her team are going to get Nobel prizes. They're not regular house guest, too, are they?"

"Very funny. No, never met any of them. They're based on the US West Coast, I think." Paul reached for one of the cartoon-colourful menus. "Want to grab a bite? The burgers are actually remarkably good."

"They have beef?"

"Apparently so; they happened to have a deal with a British supplier, so they can still get it, I think. One sec." He rose and walked across to the bar, chatted with one of the young staff for a moment, and returned, shaking his head and smiling. "OK, so yes, they still have three burgers left tonight, eighteen pounds each."

"What the …"

"Yep, it's two and a half times more expensive than a month ago, and they think this delivery may be the last. Want one? It might be your last for a while."

As they waited for their food, they chatted about the recent questions in parliament and the news coverage of protests about the price of meat and dairy products. Even lamb, fish, and other seafood, unaffected by the recent livestock pandemic, had become unaffordable for most people as demand and prices soared.

Rob observed, "It's funny how little protesting there was, given how big a deal this seems to be."

"Did you see the news a couple of nights ago?" Paul asked. "One of the politicians, for once making sense, saying that in the absence of anyone to blame, no obvious solution on the horizon and the fact that the whole world is affected means that protest is completely pointless.

Rob was nodding, "Yeah, you can't turn the TV on now without seeing a cookery program about how to cook vegetarian food."

Paul smiled, "I guess the sudden fall in cheap protein for people to eat must be causing serious concerns about health services around the world. But there are lots of crops now that won't be going to animal feed, so I guess we'll work it out."

They were still discussing how the world would adjust to the lack of animal protein, wondering whether the talk of breeding insects for food would ever happen when their burgers arrived. As he ate his last ever beef burger, Paul wondered what Rob would say if he knew how this outcome had been so carefully planned years ago.

5.

The private jet rolled to a standstill at the west side of Linate airport alongside the row of low, utilitarian buildings that handled private flights. As the whine of the twin engines died, the driver in the black Mercedes opened the rear passenger door and waited. The aircraft steps swung down, and Emanuele Bontempi descended and walked briskly across to the waiting car. The sky was clear, the Milan sun already warm on his shoulders.

"Good morning, Gino." He smiled at his driver.

"Good morning Signor Bontempi." Gino replied. "I hope you had a good flight."

"Yes, thank you." Bontempi slipped his briefcase onto the cool leather seat and slid in beside it, folding his jacket carefully beside him.

As Gino drove smoothly away from the stand, he looked in the rearview mirror. "San Damiano?"

Bontempi nodded and was already dialling her number on his phone.

Francesca Mondi had just enough time to prepare the apartment and make herself presentable for her boyfriend's arrival. She consciously designated Bontempi's role as 'boyfriend'. On the rare occasions when he referred to her at all, he did so as his mistress. He was more than twenty years older, and her chosen label served to quiet the dissonance the relationship caused her and to reduce his importance in her life. The flat she was living in was paid for by Signor Bontempi, as were most of the expensive clothes and jewellery she wore. It was a simple trade, as old as time, a share in her youth for a share of his wealth.

"Lele, darling." She greeted him at the apartment door, wearing only her silk dressing gown, undone, and her black stilettos. It made her laugh that he thought her red shoes were a little 'cheap' and preferred the 'classier' black ones.

In no time, they were both naked; he was lying, as he preferred to, on his back on their big double bed. She straddled him and slid herself slowly, but with surprising ease, down onto him while he kissed and fondled her breasts. She was considerably taller than him, and the geometry was effective. As she continued her smooth mechanical movement, she held the bed head and increased the appreciative noises she was making. It had not always been like this; she could remember, not so long ago, her thrill at the fact that he could barely keep his hands off her. Now she was thinking instead of the young man who had been fucking her on the kitchen countertop when her phone rang. The remaining two minutes she had given him after the call was plenty of time for him to express his anger at being thrown out. He knew the score, but that did not disguise the fact that he was so easily usurped. He had turned her around and had been as rough with her as he dared. She dealt easily with the slight guilt and had enjoyed the feeling of his young, hard body driving into her until he came, almost oblivious to her. He had been dressed and out of the door in another minute, slamming it loudly behind him. Francesca quickly showered him from her and tidied away any sign of his presence. She had just enough time to compose herself with a cigarette and an espresso before she heard Bontempi's car pull up in the street below her veranda.

Her orgasm was a pleasant surprise, even if it owed more to what had happened just before Bontempi's arrival than after. There was a subversive thrill in having a second man inside her in minutes, and it was nice for once not to have to fake it.

They showered together, and despite Bontempi being in reasonable shape for a middle-aged businessman, Francesca could not avoid comparing his soft, yielding flesh with her young lover's lean, hard body and flat stomach. Bontempi arranged dinner with her for later in the week. Tonight, he had to fly back to Rome to be with his family, having been away on business, but he would be back in Milan in a couple of days. That he could not wait to see her again, she did not doubt; the problem was that she was starting to dread these evenings. Her modest salary as a sales assistant in the nearby boutique did not come close to paying for the apartment and her current lifestyle. She loved living in central Milan on the Via San Damiano, but as she saw him out, standing by the door, she wondered how much longer she could do this, knowing she had no way out.

Bontempi enjoyed the short ride from the apartment to the office in central Milan. He was pleased with how easily aroused Francesca had been as soon as she had seen him and how much she clearly enjoyed the sex with him. He stared at the city around him, but his thoughts were of the body of his young mistress. The car pulled up outside the office some twenty minutes later, and he said good morning to the two thickset men with their inscrutable, hard faces, who, between them, managed the reception area. His driver joined them, and they settled down to drink coffee and smoke and do whatever it was they did all day while Signor Bontempi was in his office. The men all liked their boss, who was fair and generous, and they had never seen him lose his temper in all the time they had worked for him, a rarity in their line of work. They were also impressed that he had a mistress, a goomah in their slang, as attractive as Francesca Mondi. She was the subject of many of their conversations, and driving the couple to evening engagements when her cleavage was always on show was considered a perc of the job.

Although it was only his regional office, which he visited one or two days a week, it was large and expensively furnished with wood panelling, a big desk and a luxurious leather chair, as befitting his status as the chief accountant for the 'Ndrangheta. Like their better-known neighbours in Southern Italy, the Sicilian Cosa Nostra, they had been involved in crime for centuries and had grown to be one of the largest criminal organisations in the world. They were part of a wider network that spanned the globe, each organisation based on close blood ties to reinforce the loyalties that their line of work demanded. Their annual profits were rumoured to be around fifty billion euros. In common with all modern organised crime groups, the origin of the money they made had to be quickly obscured. This was done through the complex web of businesses owned by the group, many of which appeared to be completely clean, divorced from any criminal activity. Nevertheless, each had its role in laundering the proceeds of crime. All these companies kept accounts, and all their accountants reported to Emanuele Bontempi.

Bontempi, known to all his friends as Lele, had been born in nineteen sixty-nine in a small village in Calabria, just as the 'Ndrangheta were starting to expand out of their parochial stronghold. His family were tied over many generations to the organisation, and he had been a small boy when John Paul Getty

III was kidnapped and held in another village close to where the family lived. A good student, he had done well at school, particularly in mathematics, but also in science and languages. The 'Ndrangheta was starting to see the value of expanding their influence into the governing class in Italy, and he was sent to university in London, where he went on to qualify as an accountant. On his return to Italy, he worked for two years in one of Italy's main accountancy firms. All the partners knew who he was and who his family were, but he was an excellent accountant, and his affable nature belied his background. To the unspoken relief of the partners, his return to the family business was inevitable. For the 'Ndrangheta, the contacts he made in the legitimate world of accountancy and business in London and Rome proved extremely useful as they expanded into northern Italy and the increasingly lucrative drugs business.

Selling illegal drugs is a cash business, and every organisation in that world has the same problem: how to deal with the vast quantity that it generates. The cash is moved through businesses in order to obscure its origins, and Bontempi had set up dozens of companies and their management teams, all to ensure the river of dirty money flowed smoothly through each one, transmuting it to clean, pure digital credit in the international banking system used by all the world's legitimate enterprises.

Bontempi began setting up companies in Northern Italy in the late nineties, and for many years, the business grew almost without constraint. Italy was blessed with morally flexible politicians and law enforcement officers, many of whom enjoyed a profitable relationship with the criminal organisations they were mandated to prosecute. But crime-friendly regimes usually have a shelf life, and the hypocrisy and blatant corruption, evident to most Italians, eventually had to be addressed. Over more recent times, hundreds of 'Ndrangheta had been arrested, and in 2014, even Pope Francis denounced the organisation for its 'adoration of evil..'.

Emanuele Bontempi had never questioned his role in any of this. It was all about family and the blood ties that held the sprawling organisation together. His father and two brothers had died for the cause, and he never questioned his loyalty or considered another way of life. This was how his people made a living, and he welcomed the new drugs trade. It felt to him much more like a legitimate business than the original extorsion and protection through which his parents and grandparents had made a living. The violence required to maintain their pre-eminent position in global trade, the reason the Mexican and Colombian cartels trusted them, did not cause him sleepless nights. It was just one facet of this particular vertical market. He counted himself lucky that almost all the world's governments were so blinded by their own hypocrisy and fear of taking hard decisions that they effectively sustained a stable global market in illegal drugs. His one regret was that he did not have a son. His wife had produced three beautiful daughters but no son, and he knew their time had run out. Sofia had made it clear that she had no intention of having another child despite the pressure she knew this brought on her husband. She had performed her part in this saga and now was more than happy to allow one of the young girls she knew he spent time with to provide him with a male descendant if they wished. More fool them. It kept Lele amused and away from her, and she had made her own arrangement in that department. The young tennis coach who taught her eldest two daughters was a more than adequate replacement.

Despite all the killings and arrests of family and friends and largely through his strong links with legitimate business leaders and politicians, Bontempi had never been arrested. He had for some time now wondered if his luck would one day run out. So far, his cohort of businessmen and politicians still held sway in Italian politics, and of course, the organisation continuously recruited more. Nevertheless, if they ever came for him, he had made his plans. Hopefully, he would never have to use them, but he and Sofia had talked about it when the last rounds of arrests were made in 2017 and then again in early 2018. They no longer spoke about it, but they were prepared.

Bontempi powered on his internet router, computer and monitors and asked through the intercom for an espresso. He opened the large safe behind his chair and took out the ledgers that contained the account details for each of the businesses he was responsible for. It ran to hundreds of accounts with names and numbers, far more than he could ever remember. He would never entrust this information to the digital world. No matter how secure it purported to be, no matter what level of encryption was advertised, no password manager would ever be secure enough for him. His life and that of his family literally depended upon the contents of these ledgers, copies of the ones he held in his Rome office. Two security guards, sgarrista, or soldiers, as they are known in the 'Ndrangheta, were always outside the office door, day and night, twenty-four hours a day, every day. They and the hardened steel of the AMSEC fire safe were the security on which Bontempi's safety rested.

He took his diary and the SecureId device from his briefcase and interpreted the first entry in his diary. He superficially coded all his entries. It was a trivial system that he used just because writing the actual business and account names and amounts was uncomfortable for him. It would provide no practical utility in the event that the ledgers fell into the wrong hands, but it eased a little his constant preoccupation with security. The first entry was a transfer of funds from one of their manufacturing businesses to their central clearing account, both of which were held at the Gruppo Bancario Banco Di Napoli. He typed the first few letters of the bank name into the browser, and the frequently used address auto-completed. He clicked on the link, and the bank's login page appeared. Out of habit, he glanced up to check for the 'https' address before he typed in the username. The password was not one that he could remember because he used a random generator to produce them and changed them periodically, so he typed the twelve letters and numbers written in the ledger. The page refreshed, prompting him for the One Time Password, and he reached for the SecureId. Repeating the six numbers on the small LCD screen to himself, he typed them into the authentication screen before the digits changed again, continually weaving their random trail through the million possible combinations.

The list of account names scrolled down the screen with the balances to the right, and he was about to search down the list for the company account he wanted when his eye caught the balance of the main clearing account at the top of the list. The spike of adrenalin caused his hands to jump up from the keyboard. He stared at the screen, his eyes scanning back and forth between the account name and the balance of a little over one thousand euros. He did not remember the exact figure that should have been in the account, but he knew that it was close to seventy million euros. Except that it wasn't. As clear as day, the number on the screen read 1,234.56.

Emanuele Bontempi

When his conscious brain confirmed what his eyes had first seen, more adrenaline was injected into his bloodstream. His hands were shaking, and beads of sweat formed on his forehead. He glanced at the door and forced himself to breathe slowly, gradually regaining control.

"Bank error." He muttered to himself and reached for the desk phone. His hand rested on the handset, but he did not pick it up. His eyes were no longer focused on the screen; he was in control again and rapidly calculating what might have happened.

There was a knock, the office door opened, and Giovanni, one of the soldiers, came in with a coffee and a small biscuit on a tray and walked towards him.

Bontempi involuntarily pulled his hand away from the phone, and Giovanni, reacting to the abrupt movement, scanned Bontempi's face.

"Signor Bontempi, are you OK?"

Bontempi ineffectively wiped the sheen of sweat from his forehead, causing it to drip on the desk. Giovanni continued up to the desk, placed the tray on one side and passed the napkin from the tray to Bontempi. His jacket swung open as he leaned forward, and Bontempi saw the shoulder holster and pistol butt under his arm. He had seen it innumerable times; it was always there, but on this occasion, its presence unsettled him. He wiped the sweat away from his forehead with the napkin, closing his eyes as he did so.

"Thank you, Gio. I don't know what came over me."

"Perhaps you were a little too energetic with your.." Giovanni started and trailed off.

Bontempi looked straight at him, regaining his composure. He could see that Giovanni was wondering if he had been disrespectful in mentioning his visit to Francesca on his way to the office. The boys had obviously discussed it, and Bontempi could imagine the sort of language they would have used.

"Perhaps Gio. She can be demanding, that one. The energy of youth, and perhaps I am not as young as I used to be." He smiled up at him.

Giovanni made an appreciative noise and smiled. "But you are OK now?"

"Yes, thanks, Gio. Who knows, maybe something, probably nothing, I'm fine now, thanks." He reached for the espresso and took a sip, pulling the tray towards himself across the desk.

Giovanni retreated and left the office.

Bontempi replaced the cup slowly and leaned back into the chair, allowing his logical mind the space to work. After a while, he resumed at the computer, now searching the transaction list for the main account. There it was at the top, the most recent transfer, yesterday at ten twelve in the morning. He had been at the conference then, drinking coffee with the Italian trade minister. A transfer of sixty-nine million, eight hundred and thirty-two thousand, two hundred and seven euros, forty-six cents, to an HSBC account he had never seen before. He did an internet search on the SWIFT code and found it was HSBC in Bermuda. The chance that this was a bank error was receding, but the alternatives seemed too unlikely. He wondered if the balance meant anything, why leave such a distinctive amount, "one, two, three, four, spot five, six", he whispered.

Now, he picked up the phone and called the direct line of the manager at Banco di Napoli.

The phone was answered on the second ring.

"Luciano, good morning."

"Good morning, Signor Bontempi; how are you today? How

can I be of service."

"I am well, Luciano, but I need some details of a transaction we made yesterday from our principal account. It was made at ten twelve AM; you will see the one I mean."

"One moment, Signor Bontempi, let me find the details."

There was the intermittent, soft rattle of a keyboard, and Bontempi waited for about thirty seconds.

"Yes, Signor Bontempi, I see the transaction you are referring to. It was flagged in our systems, of course, but it was identified as your computer, and the two-factor transaction authentication was made. Is there a problem with the transfer?" Obsequious concern edged his voice.

"Could you confirm the originating IP address?"

"Of course it is, one moment." More tapping of keys and a pause. He read out the four numbers of the IPv4 address.

"Thank you, Luciano. That's all I need." Bontempi wrote down the numbers and hung up.

He pressed the intercom, "Gio, who was in reception yesterday morning?"

Giovanni's metallic voice came straight back, "I was here all day with Carlo."

"Was there anyone at the office yesterday morning, at around ten o'clock?"

"No, Signor Bontempi, nobody was here all day, and we changed shifts at four o'clock in the afternoon from six in the morning. Is there a problem?"

Bontempi paused before replying, "I thought I left my pen here, but it's gone. I must have left it somewhere else."

Bontempi finally made the planned transfer between accounts at Banco di Napoli and moved on to the next transfer in his list.

He was managing his growing panic as best he could, determined to maintain the semblance of normal activity, at least for the moment. Over the next hour, he made fifteen transfers in all and discovered seven more accounts at different banks, which had effectively been cleared, leaving all with the same remaining balance of 1,234.56 euros. Every transfer had been made within a few minutes to the same account at HSBC in Bermuda.

He was certain now that they had been hacked. No one else had access to the accounts and passwords, so if he had not made the transfers, it had to be hackers. The transactions all appeared to have come from his computer, the same one he was using at the moment, as identified by the unique IP address recorded against each transaction. He had not bothered calling the other banks to confirm this; it had to be the case; otherwise, the transactions would not have been authorised. Except, that was impossible. The office internet connection was on a fixed IP address with their Internet Service Provider, the address permanently allocated to his router. That was a pre-requisite, allowing the banks to implement the IP address checking at their end to confirm that it was his computer and no other to which the connection was made. Because his internet router was always switched off when he was out of the office, he knew for a fact that the transactions had not come from this office. He was by no means an expert in cybersecurity, but he was well-informed and understood the main ways in which bank accounts were compromised. This seemed to him to be a sophisticated hack. It was complicated, but he could demonstrate that he was innocent. He sat in silence for some time, forcing himself again and again to examine the options and what he should do next.

He pictured the conversation he would have, sitting in front of

La Provincia. They would not understand the subtleties of the security measures he had taken to protect their money. Talking to them about fixed IP addresses would be like talking to them in Mandarin. They would simply ask him how much was missing and where it was. So far, he was aware of well over four hundred million euros that were missing, and he had not yet checked all the accounts. He would soon be able to answer the question of how much; as to where it was now, that would be harder.

He used his mobile to make an encrypted call to Dragan Jotic, a Director at HSBC in London.

"Hello, my friend, how are you?" Dragan answered almost immediately.

Bontempi could hear him moving and the sound of other voices in the background. He waited, and then he heard a door close, followed by silence. "Well, Dragan, I'm well; how are you? How are those boys of yours?"

"Growing fast. But so naughty, it's exhausting."

"Dragan, I have an unusual request for which I need your utmost discretion."

"Lele, my friend, that goes without saying."

"I need you to look at some transfers to an account at HSBC Bermuda. I'll message you the account details in a moment. There are a number of high-value transfers which I did not make, but which," he hesitated, "which, well, I'm a little concerned about, and I need to know who the payee is?"

"Send me the details now, and I'll find out and come straight back." Jotic knew not to ask any further questions. He sensed the urgency of Bontempi's tone.

Seconds later, Bontempi messaged the SWIFT and IBAN account codes; then, he sat and waited. The next seventeen minutes were some of the longest he had ever experienced, but he forced himself to sit in the chair, willing himself to remain calm. There was still the possibility of retrieving the money. They had huge leverage across many of the world's banks. If the money could be traced, he was confident that it would be returned.

His phone vibrated, and he jumped despite expecting the call. "Dragan."

"I am sending you a list of twenty-three transactions, all to the nominated account and all within a few minutes of each other yesterday morning at a little after nine o'clock London time. The total value is a little over six hundred and fifty-five million euros."

Bontempi closed his eyes, trying not to react. "Beneficiary?" he asked quietly.

Jotic hesitated, "Mmmm, this is odd. The account belongs to a European division of Apple."

"Apple Computers?" Bontempi was astonished.

"Yes. But there's more." Jotic continued. Immediately after the last credit transaction, there was a single debit to another Apple account for a little over eight hundred million US, the exact equivalent of the total euro credit value."

Bontempi knew there was more and waited as Jotic paused.

"Then, there was a series of credit transfers from the dollar account to various other banks and accounts. Over two thousand transfers, all within two minutes and totalling the exact dollar value of the original credit. I have never seen anything like this before, Lele, it's …."

Bontempi was stunned and fought the wave of panic as he absorbed what he had just heard. He could not begin to address the fact that what he was being told sounded impossible. The implications for him were profound. "So Dragan, if I've understood you correctly," he said, with exaggerated calm, "Our funds are now distributed across several thousand bank accounts somewhere in the banking system through principle accounts owned by Apple Computers."

Jotic said simply, "Yes."

There was silence for a few seconds, and then Bontempi took a deep breath, "Thank you, Dragan."

"Lele, is there anything you would like me to do?"

"Thank you, Dragan, no. We'll speak again soon."

As he spoke the words, Bontempi simultaneously thought how unlikely it was that he would ever speak to his friend or see him again.

The enormity of it settled on him like a physical weight inside his chest. He was fighting blind panic; he was a dead man, his children were dead, his wife was dead. He was unable to prevent images of other murdered children he had witnessed forcing themselves into his consciousness. He tried not to see their small defenceless, contorted, bloodstained bodies. For once, he failed to hold in place the veil behind which the brutal horror of their world was always kept. He pressed his palms over his closed eyes in a vain attempt to escape the horror that he knew with absolute certainty would be visited upon his wife and daughters.

Time ceased to flow. He sat, shocked into submission, resigned to his fate until, eventually, the panic started to subside. The image of his wife came to him; they had a plan. But it was like stepping off a cliff. They had talked about it so many times, but the words, so easy then, seemed impossible now in the blinding light of this reality. Perhaps he could find evidence to explain to La Provincia that it was not his fault. Perhaps he did not need to make this irrevocable choice, this act of blind faith. Perhaps his 'family' would protect him and his family. Even as he clung to the idea, he knew it was complete fantasy. The 'Ndrangheta did not need an accountant who had misplaced more than six hundred and fifty-five million euros. The fact that this huge amount of money would not materially affect their business was irrelevant. Someone had to pay, and there was only Emanuele Bontempi.

He sat for a few moments to arrange his thoughts and check he had considered everything he could. Then he made the call.

"Sofia, my darling, how are you."

"Lele, Where are you? Back in Rome, will you be home for dinner?"

"Of course, my love, I will be home this evening. I'm still at the office in Milan, but I'll leave soon." He paused, rehearsing the words they had agreed and was almost unable to speak.

"Lele, are you there? Is everything OK?"

"Yes, fine. Actually, it's been so long since we had langoustine at Mario's. Shall we take the girls tonight?"

This time it was Sofia's turn to be silent. The words took a moment to land. "Are you sure, Lele?" she said softly.

"Yes, darling, let's take the Girls."

There was silence from his wife.

"We'll take the car, just us tonight, no need to have Stefano drive us."

"What time should I expect you?"

He could barely make out his wife's voice, and suddenly he was fighting back tears. "I'll be home around eight and we can go straight out when I've changed. OK?"

"OK. I'll get ready; I mean… See you later."

They hung up.

Bontempi behaved as normally as he could on his trip from

Milan to Rome, projecting external calm while fear and mayhem roiled inside. Stefano, his driver in Rome, collected him as usual from the private terminal at Ciampino airport after the brief flight. Bontempi told him that the family were eating at their favourite restaurant, Mario's and that they would drive themselves. Stefano would, of course, accompany them, but at a distance. Rome was as safe a place as one could find to live if you were a senior member of any organised crime group in Italy. There was now a long-running agreement between the competing Mafia organisations that Rome and Milan were considered off-limits for violence and the settling of scores. For the last few years, the organisations had maintained lower profiles, having decided that if they stopped fighting over territory, the cake was large enough to feed everyone. Despite the cessation of in-fighting, the organisations were cautious, and having a heavily armed sgarrista close by was just how life was lived. On certain family evenings, the agreement was that the soldier could remain at a distance, in this case, a small terrace at the front of the restaurant, watching the street while the family were inside.

The family Range-Rover and the black Mercedes were parked directly at the kerb outside Mario's exclusive restaurant. The family were inside, welcomed like old friends, as indeed they were, and Stefano sat alone on the terrace, flirting casually with a couple of young women at another table. The food was, as always, fabulous. There was no menu, just one delicious course after another; the girls ran around the restaurant, playing with the other children and being indulged by everyone. The adults drank wine and talked increasingly loudly. A close observer of Emanuele and Sofia Bontempi might have wondered why they were so subdued. They spoke to each other quietly, only occasionally engaging with the other families in the restaurant, and because he was driving, for once, Emanuele drank little, and their bottle of expensive chianti was barely touched.

They left after protracted kisses and goodbyes and loaded the children into their seats in the back of the Range Rover. Bontempi casually told Stefano that he would be right behind him and took sufficient time in starting the car and preparing to make a U-turn in the street that Stefano was through the lights and had turned, momentarily, just out of sight into the next street as the Range Rover pulled away from the kerb.

Instead of turning around, Bontempi drove rapidly in the opposite direction. Through the small streets, he headed across the Tiber River without giving it or the fabulously ornate façade of the Supreme Court on the North bank a second glance. They headed steadily West across Rome to the A90 ring road and then North, all the while watching nervously in the rear-view mirror. The girls slept in the back of the warm, safe car, and Sofia and Emanuele talked quietly in the front. Their phones were off, the batteries removed, and they navigated using the in-car system. The display had originally shown nearly 1,700 kilometres, and the number was gradually decreasing as they drove North, always North.

Behind them, still in Rome, a bewildered Stefano had returned quickly to the restaurant only seconds later to find no sign of the Bontempi family. Concerned enquiries on the restaurant terrace elicited an uncertain idea that the Range Rover might have gone in the opposite direction towards the river. An increasingly anxious Stefano sped in that direction, vainly phoning his boss, whom he had seen for the last time.

6.

Paul had taken Sania a cup of tea and chatted about a couple of their staff members who had recently become engaged. Now he was back at his desk in the corner of the first-floor, open office, where no one could see his screen, doing what he did at the start of every workday.

Joining Cyber Futures had been his idea. In the months after their first bizarre meeting at Leith Hill, he and Callum met frequently, sometimes several times a week. Then, Paul worked at a call centre, managing all their information technology. He had been gently bumping along without any great ambition, happy with his life and the family. Callum's abrupt inclusion in his life had come without warning. The story Callum shared with Paul that day, and his unbelievable plans, seemed like fiction, but one step at a time, it started to happen. Very quickly, momentum built, and events began to move at a dizzying pace as Callum and he set up the corporate structures needed. They founded companies and hired the key people to deliver Callum's plans. Callum was good at delegating; he had little choice, but nevertheless, he was working ridiculous hours on things only he could handle, clearly not getting enough sleep. Paul's own life had changed; the family had moved home, the children were growing fast, and at the start, he and Lisa still had their old jobs, but while Lisa seemed to be thoroughly enjoying hers, his heart was no longer in his; the excitement and rapid progress of Callum's project throwing his mundane work into sharp relief. Callum had liked the suggestion immediately, not least because employing Paul at Cyber Futures meant they no longer had to meet at inconvenient times outside their daily schedules. It also provided Callum with another set of eyes across everything going on; it was as much emotional support as practical.

Paul worked directly for Sania, the CEO of Cyber Futures, but she never asked what Paul did for Callum from day to day. He worked for her on small development jobs for the company, he created process flows, dealt with basic network issues, and generally oiled the wheels that allowed the other employees to do their jobs efficiently and the organisation to run more smoothly. Callum told Sania that Paul was an old friend who needed a job and asked her to fill about half his time; the rest would be spent doing projects for him. Sania had expected little, initially, resenting having 'a friend' foisted upon her. But Paul was far more useful than she had anticipated, mopping up the small admin jobs that otherwise would have required time from other staff members. He was also easy to work with and somehow leavened the rather geeky, childish edge that could creep in with a group of young, highly technical employees. She could not put her finger on what he brought to the company, but he made her feel valued without ever saying or doing anything explicit to that end. He frequently made her tea and always asked if she needed anything when he left the office. When her time allowed, she found herself chatting with him about anything and everything. He quickly became a friend who did useful things for her in the office rather than an employee. When Callum joined them for the weekly progress meeting, Paul's commute on Friday mornings often involved meeting Callum at his flat and walking together to the office, chatting. They had been doing this on many Fridays for more than four years, and it was the only window Paul had into the impact on Callum of what they were doing.

The other benefit of Paul's new role was that it gave him a pretext to bring Callum into the family socially. After their first meeting, Paul had tried to engineer this for months, but Callum had resisted. Paul never asked about Callum's social life but knew there was no significant other person, and that worried him. Callum's misgivings about his effect on the family had proved groundless; Paul had been right; the family accepted him as a friend and, perhaps unsurprisingly, liked him from the moment they met. Callum visited often in those early years, at times visiting most weeks, and the children had come to think of him as an uncle in the way that families adopt close friends.

***

Sometimes, his start-of-day routine took only a few minutes, and other times he ended up spending half the day scouring the internet for articles, press comments and anything on social media that might be relevant to their wider plans. As Callum's various companies progressed with their work, he collected the press notices about each of the technologies, not because Callum had specifically asked him to, but because it gave him a sense of where they were headed and their progress. He kept the articles and links in encrypted files on the encrypted disk of his work computer. These files, one for each of the technology strands, now contained information covering a period of almost six years. There was a file for each of the companies: Cyber Futures, which he worked for; Renewable Futures and Genetic Futures, as well as one for the private Equity company Green Futures, which owned the group.

There was also a separate file labelled 'Nuclear' unconnected to any of the companies.

The Cyber Futures file covered articles from the company's original incarnation, the first from a technology journalist reporting the purchase by a private equity company of the niche cybersecurity firm Sentinal Technologies and the installation of Sania Hussein as CTO.

Unknown Hacker Hired to Head Up Rebranded Sentinal

She was described as a reformed black hat hacker who had worked for the UK government's security service at Government Communications Headquarters, GCHQ, as it was known. There were many other links to increasingly prominent publications with stories of Cyber Futures' stellar growth and cutting-edge technology. One of the recent article profiled Sania as the UK's most successful Muslim female within Information Technology.

Is This The Modern Face of Cybersecurity?

It was a 'feel-good' piece in the Sunday edition of one of the broadsheets, the traditional British print media, but similar articles had appeared around the world, and Sania and Cyber Futures were touted as global leaders in their field and an example of ethnic and gender diversity in technology.

Another of the early links referred to the company's decision to set up a cryptocurrency mining operation. Paul had been surprised when this information appeared publicly until he spoke to Callum about it. Callum had, anonymously leaked it. They had a massive server farm in Iceland, where the availability of geothermal energy and the cold climate allowed them to cool the football field-sized building they owned more responsibly. The building housed a vast array of graphics processing units, which the article said were being used for cryptocurrency mining. 'Crypto' and the blockchain were everywhere now, but few people had even heard of them at the time, and no one knew which crypto-currency the company was mining or how profitable it was. The reality was so much more interesting, and Callum needed the presence of the server farm to be known and for its apparent prosaic use to be taken for granted. The massive array was indeed occasionally used for mining crypto-currency, but this was a cover for its clandestine purpose.

Paul remembered the evening when he and Callum explained to Sania what the server farm was really for. He smiled at the memory of her reaction and shock, a replica of his when Callum revealed this same secret to him. It was by far the most useful weapon in their technical arsenal, and it related to encryption. In the future, this technology, on which the entire digital world now relies for security and secrecy, would change when quantum computers develop the capability to defeat the current encryption algorithms. But that would not be for decades. Callum, using their clandestine server farm in Iceland, could break encryption now, and this ability was fundamental to their plans, and it was why Callum had bought the company that was now Cyber Futures. Provided nobody was aware of their capability, they could decode and read internet traffic, which the sender and recipient believed to be invulnerable.

Despite Callum's explanation as to the real purpose of the server farm, Paul did not believe him until he saw it work for him. At Callum's request, Paul created a simple interface for the servers with a very basic messaging system. It had only taken him a day to develop. Entirely disbelieving what Callum assured him this interface would do, he tested it with a copy of an encrypted message from their office network. It was a random setup message, a request to a website for a trivial search, but in its original form, it appeared as a seemingly random string of letters and numbers. With Callum watching him, he copied this long string of characters into the simple interface he had built and sent it, along with the public key from the website, which anyone with basic technical knowledge could find. He hit the enter key, but nothing happened; the cursor blinked. After about five minutes of staring at the unchanging screen, he went to get them a drink, just for something to do. After twelve minutes and seven seconds, the website's private key appeared on the screen. He copied it and used it to decrypt the original encrypted message, and the plain message contents appeared; it worked. Paul vividly remembered his heart racing as the plain text appeared on his screen, and he tried to understand what this meant for them. Still barely believing what he had seen, he repeated the exercise with three more encrypted messages. Then, the server farm comprised around forty thousand graphical processing units or GPUs. Now, they had more than one hundred times that number, and the same algorithms returned the private key and the decrypted message in under a second. None of this information was stored on any computer, and the interface and the application running in the data centre in Iceland were known only to Paul and Callum.

That breakthrough and their demonstration to Sania occurred nearly three years ago. The three of them had been in Sania's office one evening when Callum explained what they could do. He had started by talking to her about his idea to target criminal organisations through their connections with the global banking system and, in particular, the online systems of the big banks, many of which were clients of Cyber Futures. Paul remembered being surprised at how easily Sania aligned herself with the idea. It was not until some time later, when talking with Callum, that he understood how carefully he had selected her for the job. She actively wanted to do whatever they could to damage the organisations Callum spoke about, knowing they were beyond sanction, often operating with the tacit agreement of the states where they were based. As Callum explained this idea, she was enthusiastic, but she understood the limits of what her technology could do and assumed they would have to insert malware into their clients' systems to get the data they needed. At this point, Callum explained that this was unnecessary because they could break encryption. She refused to believe them, assuming it was a joke or test. No amount of explaining would persuade her, of course, and when they demonstrated through Paul's interface that it worked, her initial incredulity and excitement had been spectacular. She understood all of the implications instantly and was like an excited child. Paul remembered that as they parted several hours later outside the office under the street lights, she kissed them on the cheeks and left them saying, "We can change the world. We will change the world."

Other than that first evening, Paul only spoke to Sania about their new secret capability once more. It took a little over two weeks for her to work out how to best use their new tool, and when she did, she was desperate to explain the process to someone, and there was only Paul. He knew little about how the banking systems worked at the level of detail she was describing, and she had laid it out for him as simply as she could. The task Callum had set her was deceptively simple: to find the account details and passwords for several accounts at a specific bank, a client of Cyber Futures. He had provided her with only the name of a company already in the press because they were the subject of a police investigation into corruption. The enormous pool of information she was working with came from the bank's network logs. These contained vast quantities of data, 'packets', which their legitimate monitoring software inspected, checking for malware or unusual activity to protect the bank's systems. These packets and the data they contained were copied from the bank's network and stored temporarily while the Cyber Futures applications did their work. If nothing untoward was found, they were deleted.

It took Sania several days to create the software to automate the process of finding the password data Callum needed, but with the tools she had, nothing was hidden from her. She explained the process to Paul as a way to sense-check her logic. Paul questioned her about two-factor authentication, something high-value commercial clients routinely used as another layer of security. Again, she had dealt with this. It was simply more encrypted data, trusted by everyone and now completely transparent to her.

From that watershed, Paul's archives began to reflect reports from the financial press about regular investments in the Green Futures group. A Financial Times article from 2017 opined that the group appeared to be headed for significant growth over the coming years, as long as their luck held in picking the right technologies. The headline was:

Private Equity Green Futures Back Winners… So Far.

The article contrasted the high-risk approach of a narrow portfolio of technologies versus a more broad-based investment strategy. Green Futures' high-risk tactics were criticised. The FT acknowledged that they seemed to be delivering spectacular returns in the short term but that this approach was unlikely to lead to sustained success. More recent articles charted the group's steady and continuing rise based on the limited information released by the individual group companies. However, to even the most sceptical analyst, their future looked increasingly bright:

Can Green Futures Overtake Apple

It was still speculation, but the article made the case that, valuing each of the group's companies in the same way as their publicly listed competitors, all were on track to become the most prominent players in their sector.

In academia, Vivien's Laboratory in California produced a steady output in publications such as 'Cells and Nature'. Their activity initially received little attention from the wider biotech press until their first targeted gene therapy was announced. It was portrayed as a cure for a rare disorder which only afflicted an estimated two or three thousand children worldwide. The disorder resulted from a single nucleotide polymorphism or SNiP, one letter 'misprints' amongst the three billion letters of a human genome. In principle, the cost of treatment for so few people would have to be huge for the company to make a useful financial return on its development. Genetic Futures agreed to provide free treatment. Many lauded this philanthropic model, but it seriously annoyed others in the Pharmaceuticals and Bio-tech world, who pointed out that if there were no financial returns to be made, then people would not invest in new treatments. A little of the noise spilt out into mainstream media, simplifying the story to suit whichever angle they decided to take. One example headline that Paul had saved was:

Progress

Genetic Futures A Threat to Bio-Tech Sector

Of course, the 'miracle cure' was anything but. At the time, it worked well for some patients, and for reasons no one understood, it worked less well for others. There was also the constant risk of 'off-target' effects, where the modification to the patient's DNA did not work as designed, and another section of DNA was altered. Across the whole sector, their understanding of the biological and chemical mechanisms at work and the development of new techniques and protocols was changing rapidly and nowhere more quickly than at Genetic Futures. Technical articles were being published all the time, but for the typical lay reader these were too complex to understand. One of the more recent headlines, however, was not.

Cazinski & Genetic Futures Team - Shoo In for Nobel Prize

The picture of Vivien and three of her senior researchers was anything but celebratory, just the hint of a smile from the three and a straight-faced Vivien on the office steps, the Company Logo behind them catching the Californian sunshine. The article explained that they had refined the CRISPR editing process to prevent off-target effects. The simple analogy was that they could now cut DNA with a laser rather than a chainsaw. It was being hailed as a massive breakthrough by everyone in the industry, and those who had carped most vociferously about Genetic Futures not commercialising their Intellectual Property in the past were conspicuously silent now that they were allowing anyone to use the technique for a nominal sum.

Within the same file were links to the increasingly serious nature of the global livestock crisis. On every continent, the same set of novel viruses were decimating livestock production. Infections of this kind had happened periodically, but their effects had always been limited and short-term, usually mitigated by a combination of culling the infected animals to prevent the spread and, in time, a vaccination. Now, three separate viruses affecting cattle, pigs and chickens were spreading across the world. The scientists had discovered that all three were reverse zoonotic; they were being carried by humans and infecting these three animal species. This, in itself, was novel and accounted for the fact that animals in every part of the world were affected. People were spreading the virus but were unaffected by it.

Paul's links documented the spiralling outrage and speculation up to the point, only days earlier, where the United States government had concluded that this was a terrorist attack. Farmers across the world were protesting and demanding that their governments 'do something', but the infection had stumped the scientists. All the infected animals were perfectly healthy; they simply failed to become pregnant. Something, a different protein being produced by each virus, was preventing them from reproducing.

Terrorists Decimate Global Livestock Production
US Warns of Food Shortages and Starvation

The most recent article from the US Department of Homeland Security explained why this could only be a concerted attack by an unknown actor with considerable resources. However, scientists were still unable to understand how the novel proteins worked, and no one had any idea who was behind the release of the virus.

The only people who were sanguine about this disaster were the environmental groups. They pointed out that there was ample protein to feed the world if you didn't feed it to animals first.

Paul searched for the latest news on the story, but there was nothing material to add. Nations security services were collaborating to search for whoever was responsible, but they seemed to be getting nowhere.

More mundane was the progress being made by Renewable Futures. Their work was initially focused on solar panels and typically took the form of joint ventures or collaborations with existing companies. Solar cells had been getting incrementally more efficient for decades, and the research that Renewable Futures had further improved the rate of improvement. The trade articles referred to the improving efficiency of the silicon cells and panels and rarely mentioned the company's involvement. Their work on battery storage got more attention. The early articles were predominantly in trade journals, but this switched to the mainstream and financial press with the announcement of their fabrication facilities in India, South Africa, and Mozambique.

Claims New Aluminium-Ion Battery Charges 60 Times Faster Than Lithium-Ion

At the time, there was a finance round for the company, and according to the rumours, they managed to secure upwards of two hundred million dollars, valuing the company at around two billion dollars. Most analysts thought this was a crazy valuation given that they had produced only small-scale prototype cells so far. Most analysts were wrong, and when the first full-scale production batteries appeared, estimates of the company's valuation doubled overnight and then continued to double. There was a large photograph accompanying the article about Matt Denver with his half-a-million-dollar car on Hollywood Boulevard.

All this progress represented one side of Callum's strategy; the other had no public face and was, in Paul's opinion, far too dependent upon the activities of the highly unreliable Carlsen Olson. Initially, Paul did not understand Callum's preoccupation with nuclear energy, but Callum steered him to the data, allowing him to understand its critical importance. From a quick internet search, Callum found a simple graphic showing global energy use broken down by energy source. Like many others beginning to focus on renewable energy, Paul had been seduced by the reports of increasing electricity generation from solar and wind and the uptake of electric vehicles; it felt like good progress. But it was easy to forget that electricity generation represents only about 1/5th of total energy use. In reality, after decades of focus and public excitement about renewables, they represented a little over five per cent of global energy production at the time, a shockingly thin slice of the energy pie in the graphic. For the first time, Paul understood the true scale of the problem, and that despite all of the work Callum had done so far, without nuclear power, there was simply no viable way to prevent catastrophic climate change. Was it possible that so much rested on the actions of Carlsen Olson? Paul had to trust Callum, of course, but the absence of tangible progress was like an open wound he could not forget or dismiss.

There was nothing to add to this file as usual, so he closed it and grabbed his pad and pen. It was time for more tea and to ask Sania what she needed from him today.

Progress

7.

In one of their early conversations, Callum had described how he planned to use the biotech weapons they would be developing. His intervention in the global livestock industry was shocking but made sense. But Callum also suggested that a version could be made to target a single individual. Paul remembered him being reticent about discussing this, almost as though it had been a slip, that he regretted mentioning. The context had been an unnamed African dictator, but it was at odds with his other plans, and telling that Callum, ordinarily so pragmatic, would not discuss it. Paul had not pressed but, ever since, had kept an eye out for news of the death of a dictator, and one day, it appeared. When he searched further, he found two others which bore striking similarities, all reported as deaths by natural causes. Paul did not know for sure that this was Callum's doing, but it worried him.

Some weeks after the third death, searching for others, he came across a strange website claiming that a mysterious organisation had killed all three dictators because of the way they had treated their people. The 'All-Seeing Eye' was apparently watching other dictators, and there was a list and a threat to remove them from power if they did not improve the way they were treating their citizens. The internet domain was private, and there were no contact details. Paul was torn; if he dug and found that Callum was behind this, how would he react? He vacillated for days but eventually decided he had to know. He asked Sania to get one of her people to find out who was behind the site. Two days later, one of the young penetration testers handed him a note with just an email address. The young man also confirmed that the physical address for the domain was a post office box in Lusaka, Zambia. Could this be someone working for Callum?

Paul's email, from an anonymous server over a secure network connection, read, 'All-Seeing Eye? I know it was not you who killed these men.'

The following day, there was a reply, 'Who are you? I would like to talk.'

If it were Callum, it would simply be an embarrassing expose, but if it was not and someone had discovered what he had done, then what? Aware of the potential for this to go dreadfully wrong, Paul checked with Sania that, in principle, he could remain undiscovered if he took some simple precautions; she knew not to ask for details. He bought a cheap Android phone with a new SIM, loaded the Signal App so that they could have a secure, encrypted call and emailed the number to whoever was responding to his emails. Despite these precautions, he was nervous about making contact, and at the agreed time, he took a tube train to the end of the district line to ensure he was nowhere he would typically be when he made the call. Just before the appointed time, he inserted the SIM, turned the phone on and paced along the tube station platform. He was a long way from his comfort zone, and attempting to remain calm, his hands were forced into his pockets.

He started as the phone vibrated and stopped walking, his hand shaking as he accepted the call. A woman with a South African accent spoke. "Hello." She was straight to the point, "You could only know we did not do this if you knew who was responsible."

"I found your website and wanted to see who you are and what you are doing." Paul's immediate reaction was relief; it seemed unlikely that Callum was involved, and this woman did not seem to know how the killings had happened, although she had connected them, but so had he.

She assumed he was involved. "So, tell me, why did they do it? Why these three men? There are others more deserving of their fate, whatever that was."

Paul played along, "I didn't do anything."

"You contacted me, why? You know something about this." The woman said.

Paul was stuck; why had he done this? "Perhaps they deserved their fate." He said.

"Of course they deserved their fate, all of them." She replied instantly, "But you know something about this; I know you do."

She had no means of identifying him or finding him. "I'm not sure this is helpful," Paul said.

"You contacted me for a reason." She was adamant. "You know something, so I think you must know who did this."

Paul was shaking his head, about to disconnect the call.

"Why stop at these three?" He was unsure how to respond, and she continued in the pause, "What did you gain from this anyway? I think nothing. So I believe you are doing it because you can."

"It is not me; I'm not responsible."

"You disapprove?" she asked, but it was more of a statement than a question.

"I can understand why someone would do this."

She seemed unimpressed with his equivocation, "So if we made an ultimatum to other dictators and demonstrated that The All-

Seeing Eye is watching, would you punish someone else like those three, worse even?"

"I've told you I'm not responsible and don't speak for them, but I don't think this is a good idea."

"What," she snapped back, "making the world better?"

"If you continue with this, someone will come looking for you. I found you easily enough." Paul countered.

"You have no idea who I am. We are talking only because I responded to your email. You would never have found me otherwise."

She was infuriating, why was he still even talking to her?

"Speak to who is responsible and get them to call me. Use a new phone and new number when you contact me next time."

She cut the call abruptly, and he was left at the end of the tube station platform, staring at the phone. After a moment, his hands still shaking, he removed the battery and the SIM, snapped it in two, and discarded the tiny pieces onto the tracks before boarding the empty, waiting westbound tube.

***

The call had taken place two days earlier. Now, just the two of them in the office boardroom, Paul haltingly told Callum what he had done, summarised the conversations with the South African woman, and showed him the All Seeing Eye website.

"Was it you?" Paul asked

Callum took some time to reply, staring impassively at Paul, "Yes."

"You were always going to do this, weren't you? I remember you once said something …"

"Yes."

"But you didn't want anyone else involved, did you?"

"No."

"Are there more, or just these three?"

"Just these three."

Callum betrayed no emotion. After a few moments of silence, he stood and said, "This is interesting. Let me get another tea. Do you want one?"

Paul stared at Callum's retreating back. Whatever reaction he had been expecting, this was not it. He waited while Callum went away to process what he had just learned. Three or four minutes later, he returned with their teas.

"I'm trying to see this from the perspective of whoever set up this website and the idea of the all-seeing eye concept," Callum said as he retook his seat. "You'd have to be pretty sure there was a pattern, that these three deaths were related to go out on a limb like this, don't you think?"

"Either someone had investigated the deaths, or it's just a whim. But I think we should probably ignore it, let it die away; they don't have any way to link it to us." Paul said.

Callum didn't react, staring off, thinking about what they had found. Paul drank his tea and waited.

Eventually, he said, "So tell me again exactly how you contacted her and why."

Paul did so, emphasising the details about the new phone and SIM card and where he had made the call from.

"So how likely is this woman to be able to identify us, do you think?" Callum asked. "It sounds to me like she couldn't."

"You're assuming this is just a single person or a small group; what if it's not? What if it's one of the security services, a trap?" Paul said.

Callum was nodding. "That's possible."

"I spoke to Sania about making the call," Paul registered Callum's instant unease, "I didn't tell her anything about the context. Don't worry; I just checked to see how traceable I might be and how to protect myself." Before Callum could speak, he continued, "And I definitely got the impression that whoever I spoke to was an idealist, not some state actor or group."

"But we don't know, do we?"

"So I think we steer well clear of her," Paul said.

Callum equivocated, "Or if this contact method is secure, we try to find out who is behind this and what they want."

Paul was shaking his head, but the logic was hard to refute.

***

Callum phoned the woman from the lakeside in Geneva a few days later, following the same process as Paul had for the first call.

"Hello."

"Who is this? You are not the same person." The Woman replied after a brief pause.

"No, you are talking to the person responsible for... well, you know."

"So you want to help us?"

"Us? Who are you?"

There was a prolonged silence, and Callum was about to speak again when the woman finally replied, "We are people who believe that these men need to be stopped, and somehow you have the capability to reach them in a way that nobody, before, has been able to."

"What you are suggesting is very dangerous."

"It is interesting you phoned to tell me this when you did not need to."

"I just wanted to hear your story and to understand how you

think this crazy idea could ever work."

They ended up speaking for over fifteen minutes. The woman outlined her plan to continue to flag up human rights abuses, and only after the International Criminal Court had indicted someone would they threaten them and give them six months to begin reforms. They even ended up discussing how she would deliver the DNA of the targets to him. Callum explained that he would need three samples taken at verifiable times and places. He did not want to be responsible for killing the wrong person. They were plotting murder, but in the detailed practicalities, it seemed too abstract, too distant to think of it as that. Callum had done this three times, but the self-delusion so far had been relatively easy; sending perfume bottles to an unknown destination had never felt like murder.

At no point did the woman ask how he had killed the three men, and when he asked her whether she had moral concerns about doing this, she laughed at him. "My friend, my concern, my fear, is that I do not act when I know I can. We have endured too much already at the hands of these people. If I were religious, I think I would feel like the hand of God." There was a short pause, and she added, "But then that would make you God, I suppose."

After the call, Callum stood on the lakeside footpath, staring across the calm, clear water to the mountains beyond. This woman, whom he was now convinced was acting alone or with the help of very few others, was driven by the identical motivation he had been in killing these men. She might not have the same certainty he had in knowing what horrors they would go on to perpetrate, but the patterns of behaviour and offences of their predecessors amply justified her conviction.

The following day, Callum walked the Embankment in London

with Paul for an hour, explaining his decision and the parameters he had agreed to with the nameless woman. Paul was deeply unhappy with the decision but understood Callum's reasons and the lengths he was going to go to to ensure that they could not be connected with the very public position she was taking.

Two weeks later, the next communication was an anonymous email to Paul pointing him to the website. The landing page of 'The All-Seeing Eye' had a paragraph with a picture of Joseph Onjwen, the head of state in South Sudan. He had been indicted by the ICC a year earlier for crimes against humanity, but they had no prospect of arresting him in South Sudan, and he would never visit a country where he could be arrested. The website for TASE now had an explicit ultimatum giving him six months to return hundreds of millions of stolen dollars and to begin reforms in education and social support for his citizens. If he did not, according to the site, he would suffer the same fate as the three leaders whose photographs were below the ultimatum. There was also a link to an article about the site published in the Sunday Times of South Africa; otherwise, almost no one would have found it. Paul and Callum looked through the biographies of the staff at The Times and found one with a picture of Poppy Xaba. Based on her work, this had to be the woman they had been talking to. When they found an old video recording of her conducting an interview, they were sure.

Paul continued to make clear to Callum that he thought this was a bad idea, but Callum would not be dissuaded. He agreed there were risks but believed they were manageable and would not change his mind. They both believed that Onjwen would ignore the ultimatum, so if Poppy managed to produce DNA samples, as Callum had stipulated, they would be taking a big step in an unknown direction.

The first DNA sample arrived at the parcel forwarding service six months and three days after the article in The Times indicting Joseph Onjwen was published. Callum had a strong 'firewall' between himself and Poppy, and this started with a mail forwarding service to which Poppy had addressed the parcel. The small, innocuous-looking box was delivered to the company in New York, and their contract required them to readdress it and to mail it by any route they saw fit to a Laboratory called Advanced Bioscience in Houston, Texas. The company provides many services, including genetic sequencing. They received a small plastic bottle containing some human hair labelled with a customer account number. Their service was to sequence the DNA of whatever the container held, load the results on their web portal and destroy the sample and the packaging. Other than the company which had set up and paid for the contract with them, the ownership of which Armando had carefully hidden, they had no way to contact their customer. Their web portal would record that someone had logged on and downloaded the results, but the encrypted link would obscure the connection's origin.

In practical terms, Callum received a message from Poppy via an anonymous email. When it arrived, he checked the Times of South Africa website for an article about Joseph Onjwen's activities. He found one, unattributed, just a short paragraph and a social media link to some photographs of Onjwen attending a public event. Poppy had placed this to corroborate the arrival of the sample. In a few days, the genetic sequence data for the sample would be posted on the laboratory's database, and Callum could download it whenever he chose to. When the time came, he would do this through a secure Virtual Private Network, but for now, he would wait for two more samples, the arrival of which would determine the fate of Joseph Onjwen.

8.

Grace woke to her alarm. She rolled from her back to reach for the phone, and her foot slid across the large bed and touched warm flesh. She recoiled and was awake in a moment as the fragmented images returned. The musty smell of an unfamiliar body triggered the memory of a large blond man beneath her on the bed, inside her, his hands on her breasts. He was lying on his side, facing away from her, beginning to stir, his straight, sandy-coloured hair all she could see. She must have fallen asleep immediately after the sex; why else would he still be here?

Silencing the alarm, she stood beside the bed, looking down at an unfamiliar, sleep-crumpled face blinking up at her.

"Oh wow, yeah. Hi," he said and shut his eyes as if remembering something unexpected.

"Grace." He said, having dredged her name from somewhere. He was one up on her already.

He opened his eyes again, squinting up at her naked body, his eyes seemingly unable to choose between her breasts or pubic hair.

"Sorry, who are you?" she asked with a slightly resigned tone.

"Karl", replied the young man, clearly offended. "You know, we …" his eyes flicked again to her breasts and back to her face.

"So it would seem," said Grace evenly, not moving, apparently unaffected by his interest in her naked body.

"Well, you were rather more enthusiastic last night." He offered, and whatever thoughts were replaying in his mind caused him to have to free the duvet from his groin. He blushed as she glanced down to where his hands were.

"Are you an athlete or something?" he asked, apparently unable to hold eye contact. "You're body is … hard, I mean fit, you know, strong." He stumbled.

"Something like that." She finally graced him with a small smile. "Look, sorry, but I have to be at work, and I need a shower." Turning to pick up a towel draped over the chair by the bed, she prompted him, "So you need to be gone when I get out of the shower. If that's OK," She added as if remembering a distant lesson in manners.

"Oh yeah, sure." Karl sat up, keeping himself covered with the duvet, waiting for her to move.

Grace did not move. "Go on then." She said, encouraging him to get up. She glanced at his hands covering the duvet and his erection. "Show me."

Karl looked mortified and didn't move.

Grace held his gaze, the towel in one hand loosely at her side, the other hand on her hip. "I don't remember you being shy last night, so don't start getting all coy now."

Karl closed his eyes briefly, in resignation and blushing slid from under the duvet to face her across the bed, holding his rapidly fading erection in one hand.

"There's a pad in the kitchen on the worktop," Grace said, "You can leave me your number before you let yourself out if you like."

In the shower, Grace washed herself quickly in the hot water. When she emerged, there was no sign of Karl or his phone number. She dressed and tied her hair back. Instant coffee and a slice of toast later, she was out of her flat door.

***

"Morning, Polly." DS Andrew Morris greeted her as she sat down across from him and tapped her computer alive. Almost everyone in the police force had a nickname, many derogatory, and this was Grace's. Hers was more of an affirmation, a recognition of her ability to know when she was being lied to.

"Morning. Get up to anything interesting over the weekend?" she asked while logging in to check her email.

"Just the usual. Won four-two on Saturday against Reigate, though. Scored one myself for a change. You?"

"No, not really. Too much vodka last night in the pub."

"There's a surprise. I bet you scored, though." He winked at her.

DS Morris was in his late twenties, married, expecting a child in a few months and completely infatuated with Grace. On occasions, she was indiscreet about her sex life, and the two of them had evolved banter around this.

"Fuck off."

Morris grinned, "Fuck off, sir, you mean."

"Yea, fuck off, sir."

She was scanning her email list, looking for anything interesting, when the phone rang. "DC Sommers.", she answered, listened for a few seconds and nodded, already half out of her chair, "On my way, sir."

DCI George Bailey was seated at his desk, and across from him, sitting in the only other chair, was a woman Grace did not recognise. The woman, dressed in a suit, had an air of authority about her. She was a little older, perhaps forty and looked, Grace thought, rather formidable. The woman appraised Grace impassively, and Grace kept her attention on DCI Bailey, who got straight to the point with none of the verbal niceties that she could have expected had they been alone in the office.

"DC Sommers, we have someone arriving shortly in our custody suite who we would like you to interview. This man is part of an OCN operating across Europe, mainly drugs and prostitution, and he has some interesting information regarding the finances of their organisation. In particular regarding a significant amount of the organisation's proceeds that have recently disappeared."

"Disappeared, sir?" Grace queried.

"There is something approaching a war that has kicked off between this OCN and another. Until recently, they had managed to co-exist relatively peacefully, but this issue is too big to allow business as usual, it would seem.

"How much?"

"Best part of six hundred million."

Grace looked surprised.

"There's more. The man in question came to us for protection, so he's desperate. He's an accountant, and he tells us this is not the only incident of this kind that has happened recently. He claims he heard a rumour that the Sinaloa Cartel lost over eight hundred million US Dollars. Even for them, it's a sizeable chunk of cash, so as you can imagine, people have been killed. We've asked our Mexican contacts for anything they have that might be useful. They confirmed the accountant's basic story, but we have no details. What we do know is that the Mexican cartel's accountant and most of his extended family are missing."

"Any intel as to who's be behind the thefts, sir?"

"Nothing. We don't even have conclusive evidence that the money, in either case, was stolen. As I say, we do know that the accountant in the Mexican cartel and his family have disappeared and that he was high up in the organisation."

"Does our man have a family?"

"Wife and children, three girls, they all came together and are currently being housed somewhere secure."

"So why do you need me, sir? How can I help?"

"That amount of money cannot just disappear, DC Sommers. You know better than me that these organisations hold their funds in accounts all over the world, usually in the same places as legitimate businesses, so the idea that the money has just gone is obviously nonsense, but that's his story."

The woman spoke. "We have been aware of your particular combination of skills for a little while, DC Sommers."

Grace shifted her gaze to the woman and looked her up and down. Many people found this uncomfortable, but if she did, the woman hid it well and continued speaking.

"Your knowledge working in cyber-crime and fraud is relevant, and I'm led to believe you are particularly good at assessing when people are lying." Grace looked impassively at her, waiting for a question.

"Is it true that everyone calls you Polly?"

Grace suppressed the impulse to roll her eyes, "Yes."

"Assuming that you can't actually read minds, how is it you seem to be so good at telling when people are lying?"

"I don't know," Grace answered evenly. "Sometimes I can tell, sometimes I can't. But when I can, I'm usually right." She shrugged, "Honestly, it's just as much a mystery to me as it is to everyone else."

"That must make relationships difficult for you?"

Grace failed to prevent the flicker of surprise, but she held the woman's gaze and said nothing.

Reaching into her briefcase, the woman handed her a folder marked Confidential.

When Grace had left the room, the woman turned to DCI Baily, "I see what you mean, Derek. She's rather … disconcerting, isn't she?"

Grace sat at her desk for about ten minutes, reading the background on Emanuele Bontempi. Forty-eight years old, born in Southern Italy, he had, until recently, lived in Rome with his wife, Sofia and three daughters. He studied at a London University and had a spell with the accountants GWC before returning to Italy in his mid-twenties. She thought it was probably an unusual education for a child of an organised crime family back in the eighties and nineties. Then, just over a week ago, he walked into reception at Scotland Yard carrying a briefcase, the contents of which seemed to prove that he was, as he said, the chief accountant for the 'Ndrangheta. Unusually for someone with his background, his only close family seemed to be his wife, daughters and his elderly mother. Their research had confirmed his account that his two brothers and father had all been killed in the last decade, or at least presumed killed because they had disappeared and no bodies ever found. Bontempi was claiming that the money, held in more than twenty different accounts across multiple banks in many jurisdictions, had been there one day and gone the next. Each affected account had been left with the same balance after the transaction. Someone was sending a message, but who and what was unclear. What all this suggested, she did not know, but at least it was interesting; she read on. When Bontempi had tried to trace the funds, he had discovered transfers to many different accounts, all of which were to HSBC in Bermuda. Grace had no idea what to make of the fact that the money, according to Bontempi, had been washed through an account owned by Apple Computers. She had the account details listed but no way to verify them. The idea that Apple would hack the 'Ndrangheta was obviously nonsense, but the implication that Apple had themselves been hacked in such a comprehensive way was also implausible. The possibility that HSBC had been compromised was worth a question mark in Grace's notes. Their problem was how to follow the money trail to determine how plausible Bontempi's account was. They would be denied access to the Apple account, of that she was certain. The money had been transferred into the Apple account and then, according to Bontempi, out to a huge list of destination accounts. It would take months to investigate and trace even the few accounts to which they might be granted access. The money really had for practical purposes disappeared; where it was now and in whose possession was anyone's guess.

Senior management at the MET were quietly beside themselves with excitement. The prospect of having such a high-ranked member of a large criminal organised network walk in, with apparent reason to co-operate, was an event which had promotion written all over it. Huge quantities of cocaine ended up in the UK from Italy, and the prospect of being able to make substantial, newsworthy seizures meant that this was a high-profile case. Grace was smart enough to read between the lines; she had not been at the MET long, but it was enough time to know that practically no one of senior rank thought the whack-a-mole game they played with the suppliers of popular drugs was anything more than that, a highly dysfunctional game, and ultimately a political one. They had been winning the 'war on drugs' for decades, with the amount in circulation consistently growing despite the billions spent on pretending otherwise. That side of the case was of no interest to her, and as she walked across to the custody suite, her thoughts were focused on Signor Emanuele Bontempi.

Bontempi stood when Grace entered the room, which made her smile. He was a short, reasonably attractive man who clearly took pride in his appearance. He was wearing what appeared to Grace to be an expensive suit. She thought he would once have been good-looking, but even the beautifully cut suit could not hide his expanding waistline.

She stepped towards him, "DC Sommers."

He shook her hand, holding it firmly for a little longer than was necessary.

"I did not realise the Metropolitan Police had such attractive officers." He said with only a trace of an Italian accent.

She extricated her hand slowly, but rather than move away, leaned towards him, feeling the material of his lapel between her thumb and fingers. She was nearly a head taller than him in her modest heels. "I don't see many suits like this."

"Caraceni. Do you like it?" he turned slightly as Grace stepped back to look him up and down, nodding imperceptibly.

"So, Signor Bontempi, thank you for coming in today." Grace indicated for him to sit, placed the closed file in the centre of the table and moved around to sit across from him. "Although, I guess you were not given much of a choice." She continued, fixing him with her gaze as he sat down to face her.

"How are your family coping with their new circumstances? I believe Mia is only four, isn't she? This must all be rather upsetting for her."

"We accept the world as we find it," Bontempi said evenly, turning his hands palm upwards before returning them to his lap. "You obviously know why we are here in the United Kingdom. This is not our preference, you understand, but as you say, our choices have narrowed."

"You are fortunate that your extended family is small. Do you think your mother will escape retribution?"

Bontempi shifted slightly in the chair. "Honestly, I do not know. I have tried to communicate, through an intermediary, with some of my colleagues, explaining that this really is not my doing and that I do not have the money. She is rather old, so I hope they will not… be unreasonable."

"Unreasonable. I hope for her sake you are right, but I'm glad it's not my mother."

"I pray for her, but that is all I can do now."

"I'm surprised there are so few people you are close to, Signor Bontempi, an attractive, wealthy, powerful man like yourself. I'd be surprised if there were not one or two other significant people in your life, younger women perhaps? After all, your wife is not as young as she was."

It was a rather crude attempt to unsettle him, and Bontempi shrugged and said nothing, watching her warily.

"Collateral damage is the phrase everyone uses these days when they don't want to admit responsibility for killing innocents."

Bontempi remained silent, clearly irritated.

Grace watched him closely, calibrating his reactions, "I'm sure you'll find plenty of other similar diversions in this country, easy come, easy go, as we say."

He was now visibly annoyed, "Miss Sommers, do not presume to know things about me which you are ignorant of. I have not

82

been told why you are here, but I think it is not out of concern for me or my family situation."

"I'm here, Signor Bontempi, because my colleagues are finding your story hard to believe. There is, of course, a lack of evidence as to where all this money has gone. So they are unsure about your value to us and therefore unsure of what to do with you."

Bontempi was about to speak, but Grace continued without allowing him to interrupt. "I work in our Cyber Crime unit, and they are hoping I can find a way to explain what happened to such a large amount of money. Now, I'm sure you've told my colleagues this many times already, but perhaps you would indulge me and go over it one more time." It was a rhetorical question, and she flipped open the file to the back page and the closely typed list of account numbers, names and currency amounts.

"It appears that all the money was transferred out of these accounts over a period of just a few minutes. And this was," she indicated the date on one of the transactions, "Ten days ago. Where were you at ten o'clock on Tuesday twelfth when this happened?"

"I was away at a conference for only twenty-four hours, and all the transfers happened while I was away."

"I'm guessing there's evidence of you attending the conference," Grace continued, "So, let's assume for now that there is a third party and that it was not you stealing from your employer, and -"

Bontempi interrupted, "No sane person steals money from my employer. You must understand this would be suicide. What possible reason would I have for this? I'm a rich man."

Grace smiled at him, "Well, except the money has disappeared, and you are not dead, not yet, at least."

"Ridiculous. Everyone knows this."

"OK, let's assume for now it was not you. Whoever took the money clearly knew you would not be at work."

He calmed down and smoothed his trousers straight over his thighs, "So it would seem."

"Where do you keep the details of all these accounts, the names, numbers, security details." She indicated the list on the desk.

"I keep them in my safe in my office."

"I imagine it's a rather good safe, given what it contains."

"Actually, it is an American safe, and although it is secure, it does not really need to be so secure because my office is guarded all the time, every day, whether I am in the office or not."

Grace nodded, watching him. "Explain to me in detail what would have had to happen for each of these transfers to take place. She pointed to the first account in the list. So how would you have transferred nearly seventy million euros out of this account at the Gruppo Bancario Banco Di Napoli if you had done so?"

"It's the same as any account; I would log on to the bank in -"

Grace interrupted him, holding up her hand. "Do you know the account details without going to the list in the safe?"

"I know this account; I use it frequently, so I go to the bank site on my computer. And log on to see the balances and so forth. We have many businesses in Italy and many more accounts, some with Banco Di Napoli, many with other banks also."

"You know the password?"

"No, I know the user name for this one because I use it frequently. The password I change every few months, and it is just some letters and numbers from a generator program."

"You use a password manager for passwords?"

"No, no, never. I do not store passwords on any computers; it is not sufficiently secure."

Grace nodded again, "Does this bank use multi-factor authentication?"

"Of course, my phone receives the code and … no, actually," he corrected himself, "for Banco Di Napoli, I have the SecureId device, you know, RSA."

"Sure. And for other accounts, you get codes on your usual mobile phone; you have only one?"

"I have two phones. These codes come to my work phone, and I enter them into the computer. Just like you do, I would expect, Miss Sommers, when you use your internet banking. But in this case, as I said, I used SecureId."

Grace nodded, indicating he should continue.

"Then I find the details of the other party for the transaction and enter these into the system and authorise the transfer."

"And do you have limits on the account, values above which additional authority is required or where the bank would require verification?"

Bontempi shook his head, slightly contemptuously, "Our banks do exactly as we ask them; they work for us. But they do validate the IP address, and we have a fixed address in both of my Rome and Milan offices."

"So, it would appear that you could legitimately transfer millions of euros from any of your accounts without it raising any alarms anywhere?"

"Our business and our partners deal with large value transactions, Miss Sommers."

"I'm sure you are highly valued and respected by the banks you use, Signor Bontempi. I don't doubt that it could be a grave mistake not to respect an organisation like yours."

Bontempi nodded slightly, acknowledging her jibe, but did not respond. Grace continued.

"How would you know if your computer had been compromised?"

"It has not."

"Easy to say, but huge sums have been stolen with the help of malware on people's computers; what makes you believe yours is so secure?"

"I use a dedicated computer only for banking transactions. We are not naïve Miss Sommers. I do not have email on this machine, and it is not connected to any network. It is secure; I can guarantee this. Also, do not forget that the machine and my router were switched off when these transactions took place. It was not my computer, " he added emphatically.

"So secure, in fact, that you are the only person who could reasonably have authorised these transactions." Grace paused, watching him for a reaction before adding, "I'd be interested in any theories you have about how this could have happened without you being complicit."

Bontempi shook his head slowly. He clearly had no other explanation but offered lamely, "Perhaps someone at the bank is corrupt."

"Really?" Grace was unimpressed, "You think all these banks are somehow colluding to take your money?" She tilted the list towards him.

He controlled himself and simply replied, "I am sorry, Miss Sommers. I do not know how this has happened, and I have no explanation for you. You are a detective, I believe, so perhaps you are clever enough to work this out. But I do not think so." He looked away from Grace, feigning disdain. "Do you have any more questions, or are we finished?"

Grace smiled broadly at him, "Signor Bontempi, we're just getting started. Can I get you a tea or coffee? You might as well make yourself comfortable."

He shook his head curtly and stared away.

Grace pulled out the printed list of transactions that had been used to move the funds out of the Apple US dollar account; it ran to many pages. They had put names to a few, but so far, all appeared to be the accounts of private individuals, and they had no access to details or any obvious way of identifying the owners.

"How did you get this list, Signor Bontempi?" she asked.

He turned back to her, "A close contact at HSBC."

It would obviously help us corroborate your story if you were able to put us in touch with this contact."

Bontempi had obviously been asked this question before, and he was about to respond in the same negative way.

Grace continued, in a slightly more sympathetic tone, "We understand how your organisation works, Signor Bontempi. I know that this individual and any family they have would be at considerable risk if their involvement with you was revealed to the 'Ndrangheta. I've seen photographs of their work, so I appreciate the possible consequences. But if we are to find out who did this and to believe your story, speaking to this individual would be enormously helpful."

Bontempi was subconsciously shaking his head, just the slightest movement, but Grace sensed an opportunity. She had sat across a table or a bar from so many men and women, deciding, drawing them in. It was not the same at all, but she sensed his underlying attraction to her as well as his fear. She was enjoying both. Leaning slightly towards him, she watched him watch her.

"If you were to allow me to meet with this man," she guessed it would be a man, "I would be discrete, and I would meet him personally, alone and in a setting that would not arouse suspicion in the event that he is being watched."

He was now unsure, considering her offer. She was asking him to trust her.

Grace allowed the silence to lengthen before adding, "I have no wish to get anyone killed, Signor Bontempi. He may be a father with children and a wife. I know the cost and would not want it on my conscience."

"You would meet him yourself? You give me your word?"

'Yes!' She remained outwardly calm and nodded gently. "Yes, you have my word."

He reached for her pen and wrote down a first name and mobile phone number on her pad.

She was slightly surprised, "He's in the UK?"

Bontempi Nodded, "Dragan. Yes, in London."

"Thank you, Signor Bontempi; I think this will help both of us a great deal."

Grace spent another hour asking further detailed questions about his physical and computer security, about his daily work habits, how he handled transactions when he was on holiday and about many other aspects of the accounts he managed. Most of it was just her being thorough; she had her answer. Finally, she thanked Bontempi for his help and said that they would speak again, wishing him and his family good luck. There was a spring in her step as she walked back to her office. She was certain he was telling the truth, but knowing that left her with a deeper, much more intriguing puzzle. She had no idea how these crimes had been committed; they did not fit any current exploits she was aware of. Far from that worrying her, she was excited; she loved a challenge and could hardly wait to throw this one at the other members of her cybersecurity team. Then there was the phone number and Dragan, whoever he was. She was enjoying her day, and it promised more excitement to come.

9.

Dragan Jotic had been reluctant to meet Grace, but the implied threat that it could be on or off the records had given him little choice. They met at a café in The City of London, and as she had anticipated, she learned nothing useful about the exploit. But, having met him face to face and listened to his account, it matched exactly with Bontempi's. She was confident that both men were telling the truth and that the list of transactions was real. Someone had stolen a great deal of money from the 'Ndrangheta, and Jotic had been paranoid about meeting her, convinced that they might be able to link him with Bontempi and might be watching him. Grace thought his paranoia was a little far-fetched, but nevertheless, knowing Bontempi's wife and children were also at risk, she was as discreet and careful as she could be. Arriving at the café well in advance of the meeting, she had recognised him easily from his online pictures and had observed him and the other people in the café for almost twenty minutes before approaching him.

During their conversation, hearing him explain how he had printed the transaction details so quickly after Bontempi's call, it occurred to her for the first time that the perpetrators of the hack might be unaware that it had been exposed. They might legitimately have expected Bontempi to be killed when the losses came to light. The fact that he had been so well prepared and had managed to escape, with what appeared to be real evidence, was a highly unlikely outcome.

Walking to Liverpool Street station after the meeting, her subconscious mind had been doing the heavy lifting, and suddenly, the ubiquitous HSBC logo had acquired a new context. Jotic had insisted, repeatedly, that HSBC were confident their systems had not been hacked, citing their use of Cyber Futures software to monitor and protect all of their networks. Suddenly, there was the name again, along with the arresting image of Sania Hussein. Grace stopped for a moment and looked up at the huge display at the road junction. The advert promoted Cyber Futures and their paradigm shift, anti-virus technologies and AI threat mitigation. The HSBC logo, their largest client, was prominent, and they were obviously also polishing their equality credentials. Sania Hussein, CEO of Cyber Futures, was a young, very attractive woman, clearly not of white ethnic origin. Grace would call Sania Hussein. If, as she now believed, the list of transactions was real, then HSBC must have been hacked, and Cyber Futures might know about it, whatever Jotic's opinion. Whether they could discuss it with the MET was a different matter, but she would ask.

Grace loved the power that even her lowly rank bestowed; how else could she have ended up, within an hour, on the phone with the CEO of Cyber Futures? The Geneva office had, of course, asked what it was about but had provided Hussein's mobile phone number when she used the magic words, 'Detective' and 'Metropolitan Police in London'. It was, to her surprise, a UK number. The mobile was busy, and Grace left a short message, betting that their head office had called Hussein at the same time. She signalled to DS Morris, also on the phone, and was barely got out of her chair to make them tea when Hussein returned her call. Two minutes later, she had arranged to meet her at their office in Shoreditch later that same day. Grace had assumed her only option would have been a phone conversation with Hussein in Geneva, but today, at least, she was working in their London office.

The office in Shoreditch was a classic tech start-up; table tennis and pool tables, but no reception. Grace surveyed the space after she was buzzed in. In seconds, a small, dark woman appeared from a corridor across the room. Sania Hussein was immediately recognisable from the advert. She was wearing a plain blouse that looked like silk, a well-fitting black shin-length skirt, and black boots. The word 'classy' came to Grace.

They shook hands, and Grace produced her warrant card, which Hussein looked at closely. She gave no sign of discomfort in the unexpected presence of a MET detective.

"Thank you for seeing me so quickly, Ms Hussein."

"Please, call me Sania. Can I get you a drink?"

She was about to demur when it occurred to her that Sania might make the drinks herself. She liked questioning people when they were multitasking, so she asked for tea. Sania led her across the room to a drinks area. It was spotless, as if no one had ever used it.

"How many people do you have here, Sania?" Grace asked casually, watching her take two mugs from the cupboard.

Sania did not reply immediately, just pointing to the wide array of teas on a rack.

"Oh, just builders," Grace said.

She watched Sania drop the individual breakfast tea and green tea bags into the cups and fill both from the boiling water tap and, in the process, learned several things about her. Despite her dark, almost black eyes and Middle Eastern appearance, she was a native, probably also from London, based on the few words she had spoken. She was fastidious, realigning the individual tea bags in the rack after taking the ones she wanted and carefully dropping the wrappers in the nearby bin. She was composed, not feeling the need to answer a Metropolitan Police Detective's question immediately, and she was not at all intimidated by Grace towering over her.

"There's usually between a dozen and twenty of us on this floor; the offices are back there." She indicated where she had entered. "I assume you're based in Central London, DC Sommers, given how quickly you were able to get here."

"Please, call me Grace. Putney and Wandsworth, mainly, but the work takes me all over."

Sania was slight and all angles: prominent Cheekbones, fine, curved nose and small ears, her black hair in a neat bob. As always, Grace wondered what she would look like naked. It was a classic way to strip people you met of any power, although far more effective with men, whose bodies were inherently rather ridiculous. It was inappropriate in this setting, but had become a habit for Grace with almost everyone she met.

"Are you just visiting London? I assumed you worked in Geneva; that's where your main office is, isn't it?" Grace asked.

"I go over now and again, but I've lived in London for years now; I moved here when I took the job, and I like it here. Milk?"

"A splash."

Sania carefully added milk, handed Grace the cup and unhurriedly placed the milk in the fridge and the teaspoon in the dishwasher.

"Sania, I'm sure you are a busy woman as CEO of such a

prestigious company, so I don't want to take up too much of your time."

Sania turned to Grace, "Late afternoon is my thinking time. I always take the last hour, from about five to six, to step back and consider what has happened during the day. So there's no rush."

Grace was momentarily mesmerised by the velvet darkness of her eyes, but caught herself; this was work, and the interview was already intriguing. This precise, evidently clever, and poised woman was dictating the pace, and it seemed she was not about to be thrown out of her routine by a visit from the MET.

They took their teas, and Grace followed her through the doors to the main office space, most of which was divided by low partitions, with a few glass-walled offices along one side. This was a high-tech environment. A huge screen, which Grace knew was showing a global threat analysis display, covered one wall, and everyone had multiple large screens in front of them. A few heads turned as they walked through, but no one really paid them much attention.

Sania had the mandatory double screens and inevitable snake of cables, but her office was tidy, surprisingly comfortable, and personal. Several photographs of family and friends were on the desk and shelves. Two low chairs were on either side of a coffee table to one side of the desk. Grace removed her jacket before sitting in one of them, retrieving her phone, pen, and notepad from the pockets.

"So, Grace, how can I help? You mentioned something about some fraudulent transactions?"

Grace lowered herself into the chair, muted the phone, left it on the table, and opened the notepad on her knee.

"We have recently come into possession of a list of

transactions from a bank which I understand is a major client of yours. We strongly suspect them to be fraudulent, and if that is the case, it seems likely that you will be aware of these transactions, too."

Sania raised her eyebrows. "That's interesting."

"The bank in question is HSBC, and the transactions were made at a branch in Bermuda."

As she said, Bermuda, there was no reaction from Sania. Not the tiniest flash of recognition, and a new possibility occurred to Grace. "I had assumed that you would be aware of this exploit, but perhaps that was …."

"Sometimes our clients feel it's best not to advertise failures in security, assuming that's what this is. It could be a disgruntled employee and nothing to do with digital security. Do you have details of the account that you believe has been compromised?"

Grace leaned forward for her tea and sipped it slowly, deciding where to go next.

"Sania, what would your reaction be if I told you we had solid evidence and witnesses to the illegal transfer of funds, hundreds of millions of euros, across several thousand accounts all at the same time and almost all requiring two-factor authentication."

Now, Sania was clearly surprised and took a moment to digest this. "I'd be surprised if that was true. An employee accessing a few accounts is possible, and a bad actor acquiring account credentials for a few accounts is possible, but not thousands at the same time. No, that's… well, I'd be very surprised."

"OK. Well, imagine for a minute I could prove it was true; what would your reaction be then?"

Sania nodded slightly, obviously running scenarios through her mind, staring off into space. Grace sipped her tea and waited.

The Land of the Blind

"The only scenario I can envisage is someone internally at the bank with direct access to their IT systems. Getting the credentials for thousands of accounts, including two-factor, is impossible; that data just does not exist in one place, well, only encrypted, so effectively it's not accessible to anyone. But if someone in the bank had access to the back-end systems, they could programmatically move the funds anywhere they liked, and all at the same time, it's just code."

"Could you check that? Could you find out whether that's what happened? Presumably, you have access to the bank's systems?"

"Not that level of access, not to the internals of individual systems, no. And it would need a programmer working directly in those systems to code something like that. That's just not what we do."

"So there's no way to find out if that theory is correct."

Sania shook her head slowly, thinking, and then, "Let's see… If it's an employee running code, it would be in their server logs, but we've no access to those logs; we only deal with network traffic. If it were an external actor, we might see the activity in our network logs. If the transactions were consecutive or at least in a tight time frame, they would be flagged as unusual activity. Actually, our AI might have already picked it up and flagged it, but if it did, then we will have already checked it and passed it as legitimate. We see traffic patterns," She explained, "but it's just network messages, and they are all encrypted, so we wouldn't even be able to read them to see if it was the transactions you are interested in."

Grace knew enough to realise that what Sania was saying was true. There was no way to decrypt network traffic between secure endpoints. The whole world relied on encryption being unbreakable; it was the bedrock of the digital world. But matching the activity was at least something. "So, are you saying that if I gave you a list of the transactions, you could probably tell whether they were in your logs and whether it was an inside job?"

Sania nodded and then equivocated and shook her head. "Possibly, not probably. We'd need the exact timing of the transactions to even stand a chance, but if you have that …"

"We do." Grace nodded and then continued, "Where does this go then?"

"How do you mean?"

"If there's no network traffic for these transactions, as you're predicting, then do you tell your client they have a rogue programmer? Makes you look pretty good for finding something the client was not even aware you knew about."

Sania smiled, "Maybe that decision would go to our account manager in client services. If it's an internal matter at HSBC, then it's not in our remit. But that assumes they don't know already. Transactions of the size you are talking about would raise a flag in their internal systems, although a programmer would know that and perhaps that's why there were so many transactions, keeping the individual amounts below a threshold."

"The pattern was one large transaction in and thousands of balancing transactions out."

"Net zero?"

Grace nodded

Sania frowned. "So neither the bank nor the client accounts have lost money?"

"Money Laundering, plain and simple, it would seem. Although on an unprecedented scale."

"OK, in that case, to be honest, I don't know. Someone else's call." She paused for a second, "Hang on, you said hundreds of millions of euros in one transaction. Surely, the bank or client is going to spot that. You have to assume they've seen that. Then it all balances out and just goes away." She was thinking it through. "So someone transfers millions of euros into an HSBC client account, and then a bank insider transfers it all out to other HSBC client accounts."

Grace nodded.

"Sounds to me like you need two parties, one outside making the initial transfer and one inside doing the laundering." Then she added as an afterthought, "Do you know the client that owns the main account?"

Again, Grace nodded, this time wondering how much detail to surrender. It was the account of a global tech firm, a big one."

"Do you think that was chosen at random?"

"No." Grace replied, "It had to be an account with limits that would not be triggered by the initial credit, and possibly it needed to be a company with sufficient clout that if anyone comes to investigate, they can just tell them to go away. Simply state that they have not experienced any loss through fraud, which is true."

"Neat," was Sania's somewhat surprising summary.

"Yes, I guess it is. It was certainly well-planned. OK, assuming I can get the evidence released, I'll email a copy over. From what you've said, you just need the timestamps or IDs for the transactions; the actual content is of no use. Is that right?"

Sania nodded. "Yes."

"I probably don't need to add that this is confidential, but more than that, some people's lives may be in danger, so this must be done discretely. We only have hard copies of the transactions, so you'll get an image or PDF, and it will be encrypted. Can I

WhatsApp a password to you? Or better, Signal or Telegram?"

Having agreed on a plan, they finished their teas and chatted for more than an hour. They were both women working in male-dominated domains, and while their backgrounds were very different, they had an instant rapport.

Finally, Grace stood up, "Sania, it was lovely to meet you. Thank you so much for your time. I've probably overstayed my welcome. I don't know when to shut up."

"Not at all, Grace; it's not often I meet someone so charismatic and, actually, just as nice as you."

Grace laughed, slightly embarrassed, "Woah, few people meet me and think I'm nice, I can assure you."

The office was almost empty now, and as they walked through to the entrance and approached the front door, it opened, and Callum almost collided with them.

"Oh. Sorry." He stopped the door still in one hand and surveyed the two women. "Hi, Sania." He took in the other woman. She was tall, and he involuntarily glanced at her feet to see her shoes were almost flat, making her at least 6 feet tall. She was wearing a suit, her hair pulled back, and she was watching him very carefully. He looked at Sania.

"Callum, This is detective Grace Sommers, Grace, Callum Moorcroft."

He let the door swing closed and offered his hand. She took it, and hers was warm, soft, and strong. Her eyes had never left him, and he felt his eyebrows rise. Without thinking, he said, "Oh, I wasn't expecting…" He stopped himself too late and felt her gaze intensify.

"Wasn't expecting anyone so tall?" she offered with a raised eyebrow, and then, before he could answer, added, "Or female?"

The Land of the Blind

He was shaking his head, "No, I mean -"

"Why were you expecting anyone?" She asked, interrupting him and relentlessly holding his gaze.

With surprise, he realised her eyes were exactly the same colour as his. His eyes flicked to her lips, and he registered the slight pout and the delicate pink, her mouth slightly open.

She did nothing to fill the silence.

"Sania mentioned that there was a detective visiting, and I assumed that would have been earlier, so I wasn't expecting anyone still to be here."

Somehow, she communicated that she did not believe a word of this, and Callum desperately needed to escape. But all he could see was her strong jawline and flawless skin, while his peripheral vision taunted him with the curve of her jacket and the flare of her hips. He willed his eyes to hold hers.

Finally, she released his gaze and turned to Sania. "It was lovely to meet you." As she said this, it was her turn to be surprised to find herself still holding Callum's hand. She looked down, and they quickly released one another. For a moment, Callum glimpsed something other than a dangerous predator.

Callum and Sania did not move after she left, looking at one another with concern.

Callum said. "Wow, she was fast. One tiny slip, and she pounced on me. My pulse is still racing."

"Our meeting was nothing like that," Sania said. "We got on really well. That's why she was still here; we were just talking for ages."

"She feels dangerous to me," Callum said, staring at the door through which she had just left.

"Does she?" Sania had a slight smile.

"What?"

"Pretty, isn't she?"

"What?"

"I mean really pretty. And did you know she was once a first-class sprinter? World ranked?"

"How do you know that?"

"I searched before she got here, obviously."

Callum was staring at the door again.

"You know, Callum, that's the first time I've ever seen you react like that to a woman."

He turned. "Ok, hold on, like what?" He was blushing.

Sania just raised her eyebrows and smiled. "I think she liked you."

"Don't be ridiculous! She was interrogating me. I'm staying well away from Detective Sommers." Callum said. He moved across the office, changing the subject "So what did she say? How much do they have?"

She fell in beside him. "Sorry to call you. It was probably an overreaction, but I could not get hold of Armando. I assumed you would be out of the country anyway; I wasn't expecting you to come over. I just wanted to check there had been nothing untoward in our recent 'funding round'."

"No, it went by the book." He replied, or at least so we thought. Clearly, something happened."

Sania nodded, "They have the transaction list."

"What? How?" Callum held her office door for her; he was clearly concerned.

"I don't know how they got it, and I don't know for sure that it's accurate, but they have the bank and branch, so we should assume it is our transactions."

The Land of the Blind

They sat in Sania's office, his chair still slightly warm from Grace's body heat.

"How bad is this?" he asked.

"It's a concern that they have it at all, but they have no idea how it was done, and I don't think they will be able to find out. I think we're fine."

Callum breathed out heavily. "Ok, good."

"She's sending me the transaction list, and of course, I'll let our analysts check it and find nothing unusual."

"So I can go back to worrying about the other hundred things I usually worry about." He said

She nodded.

***

Grace sent Sania the transaction list that same evening, and two days later, having heard nothing, she phoned to see if Sania's team had made any progress with matching the transactions. They had not. The working assumption was now that it was an HSBC insider, and it was no longer something for Sania to deal with. Grace did not examine too closely what had then made her suggest, at the end of the call, going for a drink one evening after work. She had been surprised but pleased when Sania agreed.

10.

As usual, Sania had done exactly the right thing after the detective's visit: to react as if she had no idea how the hack had happened. She set her best analysts on the job and let them discover what had happened. Now, one of her senior intrusion detection analysts explained their analysis to Callum. He had the list of transactions that the detective had given Sania, and he and his team had crawled over the logs looking for anything that could mark any as fraudulent. It was, of course, one of their actively monitored client sites, and the surprising thing was that they could find no sign of malware or obvious activity despite having their sophisticated software embedded in the client's systems. Their AI had detected a bump in activity when the transactions happened, but all had used two-factor authentication, and all were flagged with a low-level warning, which had subsequently been checked and cleared by the admin team.

Callum's and Sania's concerns about this incident were very different to the analysts who worried that malware might have been installed without detection in their client's systems. Cyber Futures was arguably the best in the world at what they did, but even for them, there was no way to completely guarantee the security of a network as large as one belonging to a global bank. Four people knew the source of the hack. Three of them were at the meeting room table in Sania's office, and the other was

The Land of the Blind

Armando Castilliano, the group accountant. There had, in fact, been three similar exploits over the last weeks, all following the same pattern, and until now, the four complicit in the hacks believed all were buried forever beneath a mountain of corporate paranoia. The secondary targets were all banks, and none of their clients had been adversely affected; their accounts were simply used as stepping stones to steal and conceal the funds from the targeted organisations. For each hack, the main clearing account was selected because it belonged to a global blue-chip company which cared a lot about its financial reputation and was large enough to rebuff an investigation even from state regulators. This, along with the fact that the organisations they had robbed would never air their dirty laundry in public, meant they were confident the hacks would go undetected by everyone other than the victims.

Somehow, details of the 'Ndrangheta hack had emerged, which was potentially extremely dangerous. They had to find out how much was known and how far this would travel, which meant getting access to the MET investigation, which was impossible without significant risk. Callum and Sania flew to Geneva two days later to meet with Armando beside the lake in Morges. Sania was adamant that the detective did not suspect Cyber Futures; she was just looking for information and had no reason to distrust her. But to rely on that interpretation was not something they could do; inaction was not a smart response; their hand was being forced.

Despite the advantages Callum and Sania enjoyed and the formidable tools at their disposal, any organisation with security at the heart of its culture is difficult to penetrate. Sometimes, it requires a return to the basics. Getting malware into a network such as the MET's would be difficult, possible only through the weakest link, their employees. Hacking a person, that is, finding actionable information on them without their knowledge, takes time and often luck. But one piece of ubiquitous technology makes the hacker's job more straightforward: the mobile phone. With the right tools, the devices themselves are not difficult to hack, and when you own a person's phone, when they have been 'pwned', in the jargon, they completely surrender their privacy.

Despite having the best tools available, the twenty-three targets that Callum identified in the Met Ops division and their Digital and Technology group took nearly two weeks to research. Three people from the penetration testing team at Cyber Future were allocated to the project full-time for as long as it took. Most of the targets had very little personal data online; all were careful about dealing with email at work and had phones that were difficult to access. However, three were a little more relaxed about their personal email, two had phones that could be compromised, and one had a second phone that the team were fortunate to find. As usual, the list of viable targets grew slowly.

Twelve days into the project, Maarten Decker, one of the penetration test team leaders, provided Sania with access details to the phones of the designated targets, Five, Twelve, and Nineteen, as well as links to surveillance software now installed on the home computers of targets Twelve and Sixteen.

The type of data the team had gathered, and the process they followed were the same as for any of their projects. Sania had briefed Maarten exactly as she always did for these types of projects. A business, and sometimes specific individuals within it, are identified as potential targets, and the team then deploys a range of tools, both digital and physical, if that is within the project scope. As with this brief, the aim is to access the targets' personal devices and digital accounts that could potentially reveal details of their private lives. They always acted as 'white hats', which the team believed they were doing on this occasion, and the end product was a report to their client detailing the robustness of their digital and personal security systems. In this case, Callum and Sania had no contract with the client to establish the rules of engagement. They needed the information for their own reasons and subverted their business process to obtain what they wanted.

One aspect of the job that Sania disliked and, in normal circumstances, would avoid doing was assessing the value of recordings taken from people's phones. In this case, she passed them straight to Callum. He had no choice but to listen, with obvious discomfort, to as few recordings as possible to assess the value of the compromising material, the 'kompromat'. In the normal course of their work, the staff at Cyber Future never went this far; establishing that a target's device could be accessed by a 'bad actor' was usually the end of their remit. In this case, Callum listened to sufficient audio and read enough private messages to know that he had two candidates through whom he might gain access to the Met's internal computer systems. Sania was unconvinced that either would betray the trust of their employer. In the end, she told Callum, "Leave it with me, and I'll decide which to pursue."

***

Sania met Grace on Friday evening at a wine bar in Covent Garden after work. She did not tell Callum. The venue was Sania's choice, and the two women timed their arrival for the exodus of the theatre-goers. Sania was still waiting for a table when Grace arrived.

"Sorry I'm late."

"No problem, I got your message, and I've literally just got here; perfect timing." Sania invited a brief kiss on the cheek, relieving Grace of having to choose an appropriate greeting.

The waitress cleared a table and invited them over, and they draped their coats across the backs of their chairs.

"Busy week?" Sania asked.

Grace blew out heavily, "The usual, I guess. They all seem to be busy these days. You?"

"Pretty average. We had the excitement of that thing we met about …" Sania checked the proximity of the staff and other customers. "… but there were plenty of other things going on. It's digital warfare, really; you wouldn't believe how many bad actors there are out there constantly probing, always on the make. Well, actually, you might in your line of work."

"Good for business, for you, I guess." Grace picked up a menu and asked, "Drink?"

Sania nodded, "Definitely."

Grace hesitated, "Do you drink alcohol? I mean, I assume you are Muslim; I probably shouldn't assume, but you know."

Sania smiled, "It's a minefield; no one knows what to say about anything anymore. No, I don't drink alcohol, but it's more cultural now than religious, but you go ahead. I'd describe myself as a non-practising Muslim. My mum is religious, and my dad isn't, which, believe me, created some pretty serious tensions when I was younger. I took the easy option as a teenager; I mean, how many kids want to be praying five times a day."

In the end, they both ordered mocktails and then drank water and were soon chatting animatedly. Grace quizzed Sania about some of the black hat hacking she had done before she was caught and recruited by GCHQ. The food arrived, and they had to stop talking to avoid it going cold.

Just before they left, Grace asked Sania, "Callum Moorcroft, he's an interesting chap; what's his story."

"Oh, he's such a delightful man," Sania said.

"Interesting, that was not what I was expecting you to say. He's 'the money', isn't he? Green Futures?"

"Well, their representative on the board, yes."

"Did he hire you?" Grace asked.

"Sania nodded.

"So, are you and he in some sort of relationship?"

"Oh good gracious, no, Grace." I'm married.

"People have affairs. He's not unattractive."

"He's not, is he?" Sania was smiling at her. "I think you'd like him."

"You can forget that. I don't date old men." Grace said with a laugh.

"Old. He's only late thirties."

"Absolutely not my type," Grace said.

"And your type is …?"

"Younger, not a banker."

"He's not a banker, he's …" Sania paused, thinking. "He's smart and kind." She watched Grace carefully throughout this exchange.

Anyone watching the two women as they left the restaurant that evening might have thought they were lifelong friends. It was the definition of serendipity, the intoxicating joy of discovering someone so outwardly different and yet a fellow traveller in the world. They hugged, kissed, and parted, each feeling their lives would be a little brighter for knowing the other. A casual observer would also have been unaware of which woman had the hidden agenda.

The Land of the Blind

***

Ten days after agreeing to compromise, one of the MET's employees, Sania, asked Callum to come to her office. She told him she had compromised the phone of someone on the investigation and that she was gathering information.

"Which one did you choose." He asked.

"Neither, it's the detective."

He frowned at her, "How on earth …"

"I've seen her socially and –"

His look of alarm made her smile, "Don't panic. She's actually really good fun. A bit …" She searched for a description for a moment, "Anyway, I messaged her and managed to pwn her phone."

"Pegasus?" he asked quietly.

She nodded.

"And?" he asked.

"It's early, but I don't think they have anything. There's only one brief, relevant conversation so far, and she seems to be working on other cases."

"OK, so we think we're good?"

"I think so, but I've set up some watches on the data, so if anything comes up, I'll let you know. Of course, it could be she's not in the loop on the investigation; she's only a detective constable; I'm not sure how close she would be to it."

.

11.

A little more than a month after her first meeting with Sania, Grace was summoned to Scotland Yard. She had seen Sania again socially, but Cyber Futures' investigation of the 'Ndrangheta hack had revealed no additional insight, and her department's fraud investigation had stalled, clearly going nowhere. The only party out of pocket was not about to go to the police for help and there was no way to gain access to any of the long list of accounts they had. Getting a warrant was impossible in the circumstances. She and the other members of the MET cyber team were concerned but quietly impressed with whichever group had perpetrated the hack; they could not determine how it had been done. Now Grace was on her way to The Embankment to New Scotland Yard for a meeting with her Borough Commander and the MET's Solutions Delivery Director, David Luckins.

She had tuned out from the conversation between the Commander and Director. She was in the Director's office completely by chance, simply because everyone wanted a piece of the OCN case, and Luckins was no exception. Grace and the Cybersecurity team did not report to the IT Solutions Director, but their worlds were enmeshed, and so the cyber angle gave him a thin pretext for getting involved. In fairness to Luckins, there could have been network security issues as a result of her following up on Bontempi's evidence, but she really didn't need to be in the room. The fact that it would be good for her career was not lost on her, but it felt like politics, not policing. Her boss, DCI Bailey, had been asked to provide someone 'technical' from the investigation to accompany borough Commander Susan Dillon to the meeting. Grace was the best they could find at short notice, and her prior involvement allowed them to limit the number of people who knew about Bontempi's presence in the UK.

Just in time, Grace surfaced from her thoughts to hear Luckins' ask for her assessment of any potential threat to the MET's systems.

It was a stupid question, there were clearly no implications for their internal systems, "Hard to say, sir; it's possible. As you probably know, we've been unable to find out how the hack was perpetrated, so that's a concern. I've spoken at length to Sania Hussein, the CEO at Cyber Futures, and I'd say that if they can't track this at one of their clients, then it will probably be beyond our capabilities."

"Assuming our mafia friend is who he says he is and didn't just make this banking thing up."

Luckins was, Grace thought, talking out of his arse.

He addressed Commander Dillon "Am I right in thinking we're going a little cold on our mafia friend, Susan?"

She shook her head, "No, I don't think so. We have since been made aware of what appears to be a very public and, we believe, related homicide in Milan. The 'Ndrangheta are extremely upset about Bontempi's disappearance and are searching for him. Also, the Italian police have informants in the OCN, and they are hearing a consistent message, so I think it's safe to assume that he really is who he says he is. As DC Sommers says, it's intriguing, perhaps slightly alarming, that we've had nothing useful from

Cyber Futures. Although, to be fair, what's in it for them? We don't officially have a crime to prosecute, so this is unlikely to go anywhere."

Grace was not about to mention her subsequent social meetings with Sania; she had not thought them relevant, but there was always the possibility that Hussein or someone else at Cyber Futures was aware of the hack and had decided not to pass this on to the MET. The fact that Cyber Futures was not part of an ongoing investigation meant there was nothing to prevent Grace from meeting Sania. Although, Grace reflected, her interpretation of 'no conflict of interest' might not survive close examination. Grace was lost, thinking about this when they dismissed her.

"Thank you, DC Sommers. I think we need to get our Digital Defence people to talk to them as a matter of urgency. Perhaps NCSC and GCHQ need to be in the loop?" Luckins suggested.

"Way above my pay grade, sir," Grace responded superfluously as she stood to leave. "Sir, Ma'am, I have, I believe, established some rapport with Sania Hussein, and I had no sense that she was being evasive or hiding anything; in fact, she seemed to be doing whatever she could to help. But if you think it's worth me pushing them a little harder I could re-connect with her and see if I can find out anything more?"

Luckins was not interested, but Commander Dillon considered it briefly: "I'll talk to DCI Bailey and see if he thinks that would be useful. Thank you, DC Sommers."

Walking to the Embankment underground station Grace wondered about the 'related homicide' that Commander Dillon had mentioned; she would find out.

***

Grace walked into the office three days after her visit to

112

The Land of the Blind

Scotland Yard to find a group gathered around one of her colleagues' desks. DC Jane Hinkley lived in Kent and commuted through central London. She was holding something silver about the size of a smartphone in her hand.

"No, of course, it won't work with a normal charger, you moron." She said to someone. "Those are five volts and, like, a few amps or something."

"Well, I don't know about electricity, do I." DS Morris responded lamely.

"What's that?" Grace asked looking over Morris' shoulder.

"Some fancy battery that Hinkley got at Waterloo this morning. They were giving them away." Morris said.

"What's the big deal?" Grace asked. "Looks like a power bank. You can buy them on the Web for a few quid."

"Not one like this, you can't; well, not yet," DC Hinkley said, passing the device to Grace. "It has about double the capacity of a typical power bank. This one is twenty amp hours, so it would charge your phone about five times. But that's not the big deal. If you have one of their special chargers," she indicated the slightly larger than usual charger on her desk, "you can fully recharge it from empty in about fifteen seconds."

The faces around the desk all looked at Grace as if somehow she would validate this claim.

"Bollocks. J, you've been conned." She handed the device back to Hinckley.

"Hardly conned, it was free, but watch this, you disbelievers." Hinkley plugged an adapter cable into the small battery. Rather than a standard plug at the other end that would have charged the battery, it had a standard plug socket. With this little transformer cable, which converts it to mains voltage, it will run my computer screen for about an hour and twenty minutes or so, but we've not got time. Andrew, have you still got that manky old fan heater under your desk?"

DS Morris retrieved it and plugged it in to the tiny battery pack. The fan whirred and the smell of burning dust filled the room. They all recoiled. "Fucking hell Morris, you plonker" someone shouted above the laughter and loud complaints as they all covered their noses.

They coalesced around Hinkley's desk again, and she continued. "So, this is a one-kilowatt heater, which means it will drain the battery pack in about four minutes. Look." She held up the battery pack, and on the side visible through the casing, they could see a display of numbers showing the percentage charge figure. It was slowly counting down. They all watched it, mesmerised, for about thirty seconds until Grace broke the silence. "OK, guys, some of us have work to do; that's enough.

Hinkley unplugged the fan heater and laid the battery on her desk with the pale glowing numbers showing a charge of seventy-one per cent. She handed the charger to Morris, who plugged it in under her desk, while she connected it to the battery. The display on the pack cleared and then showed two plus signs for a couple of seconds and then the charge state of the battery again. The numbers cycled upwards to one hundred per cent in about five seconds and then blinked at one hundred per cent.

"Wow!" Grace was impressed, as were all the others. "What's in that thing?"

"No idea," Hinkley replied, "but search, it's all over the internet already. It's that tech company Renewable Futures. Some sort of aluminium-based chemistry instead of lithium, the article said, big deal apparently."

There it was again, Grace instantly caught the link. "Renewable Futures? Part of the Green Futures Group?"

They all looked at her blankly. "Never mind," she said turning towards her desk and slipping her jacket around the chair, "just something I came across the other day."

12.

The link from Paul appeared in Callum's Signal app and he stared at the headline for several seconds as a feeling of dread seeped through him. The New York Times article was headed:

In The Bloody Footsteps of his Father. The Violent Kigale Dynasty Continues.

He knew from the headline that this meant he had probably killed David Kigale to no end. The visceral churn of guilt he experienced was exacerbated by the fact that only days earlier, he had sent three small packages, each holding an innocuous bottle of what appeared to be perfume, to the addresses in South Sudan that Poppy had given him. There was no way to retrieve these lethal weapons. The fate of Joseph Onjwen had been sealed, but to what end?

Five minutes later, having read the article, his worst fears were realised. The new president, Kigale's son Teodor, was violently suppressing calls for legitimate democratic elections after his overwhelming victory in the sham election that followed his father's death. In the most recent clash, hundreds of protesters had been killed, a bloodbath in the streets of Malabo. Callum had, somehow, convinced himself that the people would rise up and that Western oil interests would press for a more democratic regime, which would drive out the endemic corruption. He sat at the kitchen worktop, head in his hands, staring at the small screen

116

without seeing it. His overwhelming emotions were guilt and embarrassment. He had murdered people, and the world was not the better place his naïve optimism had promised. He was dreading seeing Paul at the meeting on Friday. Paul would not make him feel guilty; he didn't need to, but he had been right all along, and Callum would have to acknowledge this and apologise for being so intransigent. Now, he had a flight to catch and two days of meetings ahead, and he had to attempt to put all of this to the back of his mind.

***

Early Friday morning, Callum finally responded to Paul's message two days earlier; he knew no response was expected, but they needed to talk before the weekly meeting. They met on the embankment, as usual, to walk to the office. They began slowly, in silence, side by side in the steady flow of commuters.

"You were right, all along. I'm sorry, I should have listened." Callum said, speaking quietly.

There was a pause. "So you've not seen it yet?"

Callum turned. Paul was watching him. "Seen what, the article?"

"No, the Eye website." Paul pulled out his phone and loaded the site as he walked.

"Oh, God no." Callum breathed heavily when he saw the new front page. "Have you spoken to her?"

"No. This just appeared last night."

The site held links to reports of the death of Joseph Onjwen from 'natural causes'. The president of South Sudan had died in his sleep the night before, and the website was explicitly claiming that this was a result of their ultimatum. Below these links was a new ultimatum. Beneath a picture of Teodor Kigale, there was a statement to the effect that unless he instigated a proper democratic election, he would suffer the same fate as his father and now three other African dictators."

"Enough," Callum said. "We need to tell her this is over."

Paul glanced at him.

"OK, I need to call and tell her this is over," Callum said, grimly.

"You tried," Paul said, heavily.

There was nothing more to say and they continued in silence.

13.

Sania and Grace had arranged to meet at a very expensive restaurant in the centre of town. Sania had been a little mysterious, saying that it was her treat, it was worth dressing up, and that she had a surprise. Grace arrived on time, but Sania messaged her, saying she was running a few minutes late and that she should order a nice bottle of wine for herself. Sania was behaving strangely, but Grace played along.

Grace had been unable to make herself spend more than £50 on a bottle of wine, but she had chosen one twice the price she usually would. She was sipping the wine, wondering what Sania would drink, when a man was led to her table. He stopped short when he saw her.

"What the fuck." Grace said, quietly, but not quietly enough and a few heads turned.

Callum reluctantly approached, thanked the waiter, and stood with his hands on the back of the empty chair.

He was frowning and smiling. "Sania looks so sweet, doesn't she."

"What did she tell you?" Grace asked.

"That she had a surprise and that it was time I treated her to dinner somewhere nice. I thought it was odd. It's not like we ever socialise, so I assumed it was business."

Grace pulled her phone out and typed, 'You duplicitous cow!

I will never trust you again.' And added a happy and an angry emoji.

"Just sit down, " she ordered him, and when he hesitated, she added, "I really don't want to drink this whole bottle on my own, and I'm hungry, and I promise not to bite. Also, your employee promised me dinner, so you need to make good on that promise."

Callum heard the words, but his mind was elsewhere. Her hair was neatly tied, and this time, she was wearing a dress. His eyes flicked to her cleavage and back to her lips, now adorned with an amused smile, and then to her eyes, which were waiting for him.

"Like what you see?"

His look of surprise made her laugh. "You don't need to answer; I saw your responses."

He felt the weight of her uncompromising gaze and he realised his mind was searching for an excuse to leave. 'I saw your response'. She was so aggressive and self-confident; why did he find that challenging and, at the same time, so powerfully attractive? The silence lasted several long seconds. A part of him might have wanted to leave, but the words he spoke were, "You look lovely, actually."

Four words, and he disarmed her, and he watched it happen. "Oh, interesting." He said, smiling broadly; it felt like she had let a secret slip. He looked more carefully at her now, a riposte, openly inspecting her in a way he would never usually do to a woman he did not know intimately. She appeared to be wearing no make-up or, if she was, it was done too subtly for him to see, just a little lipstick. His eyes traced her lips, and then he could not prevent them from flicking to her breasts, and suddenly, a memory came to him from years earlier. He remembered looking at a female cyclist in her skin-tight suit and realised that today was the first time he had looked at a woman and wondered what she would look like naked.

He returned to meet her enquiring gaze. She had not flinched in the face of his overt assessment, but she had softened. "What happened there?" she asked gently.

He hesitated, wondering how much to reveal. "You reminded me of someone."

"Someone no longer alive?" she asked.

He was taken aback, "No." That was not it, but she had intuited a basic fact about him that he did not want to reveal. He sensed how dangerous this woman might be, but despite his growing misgivings, he removed his jacket and sat as she poured him a glass of wine.

They touched glasses. "To dangerous liaisons." She said with a smile that made his heart race.

They talked about her working in the Metropolitan Police and whether there was as much misogyny and racism as the press reported. She told him stories that made him realise the reality was as bad as the press made out. He kept watching her lips as she talked about the groups of officers who hid themselves from scrutiny, and held views that belonged to an earlier age.

She quizzed him about Green Futures and their work and talked about the battery her colleague had been given and how astonishing it was to see.

Behind the bravado and confidence, she was not what he expected. They got on well, but at the end of the evening, he gave her no opportunity to extend their time together, saying he had to be home for a conference call with a colleague on the West Coast of the United States.

They pecked one another on the cheek as they left the

restaurant, and she said, "You can call me."

There was that arrogance again. His attraction to her and wariness of her were in perfect equilibrium. As he told himself he should avoid her at all costs, he imagined kissing her, smelling her, and feeling her against him. "I will," he heard himself say, adding, "If you give me your number, that is."

She recited her number, and when he nodded, memorising it instantly, he caught the slight surprise and turned away with a smile.

Walking home, he rehearsed all the reasons why it would be a bad idea to have anything more to do with Detective Grace Sommers. Despite his misgivings, he found himself smiling, walking energetically while wondering what this Tuesday's Child was filled with; it did not feel like grace. At least, he realised, he had not thought once about Poppy and the All-Seeing Eye, so the evening had not been a waste of time. As he arrived home, thinking of her the whole way, he decided, on balance, there was no way he could risk calling the very dangerous detective Grace Sommers.

14.

Callum phoned Grace the following morning.

"That's nice," She said, "I like a decisive man."

They arranged to meet at a pub on Clapham Common on Sunday evening. Looking back on the conversation, Callum realised she had simply told him where to meet her and when.

He was distracted all day Saturday, reading reports, staring out of the flat windows and then wandering the Embankment. The image of her lips, slightly parted, kept returning, intruding, heavy with what he acknowledged was his visceral attraction to her. Eventually, he acknowledged it was the same intoxicating feeling he had had when he met his wife, Maria, so many years ago. The swirl of emotions was dizzying: guilt at feeling like this about someone else and the thrill of feeling like this at all. He was a teenage boy again; his emotions so easily captured by a pretty face.

Sunday dragged, cloudless and too warm. He could not sit and walked to release the coiling anticipation, wandering aimlessly amongst the tourists in the centre of London, willing the time away. Once more, with an excess of time on his hands, he fought to bury the circling thoughts of self-reproach, his failure with Kigale and his too-easy seduction by Poppy and her All-Seeing Eye. But now, even that felt like a distraction from examining his unexpectedly troubling attraction to the woman he was meeting later. By the time he walked across Clapham Common in the early evening and into the busy pub, he had convinced himself that she would prove to be narcissistic and disinterested in him and that a couple of drinks would disabuse him of any romantic thoughts. His nerves surfaced as he approached the door of the busy Windmill pub. Loud voices spilt out to meet him, and his heart suddenly beat uncomfortably fast and strong.

The wall of heat and sound that enveloped him as he entered the bar swamped his introspection. He stopped, eyes accommodating the darker room. Her hair was tied back as before, and he caught her distinct profile first, the natural, tiny pout of her lips drawing his eye. She was exactly where she said she would be, sitting on a stool at a corner of the bar chatting with one of the bar staff, a scruffy, pale-looking girl with piercings along both ears and through one nostril. Grace stood, leaned over the bar, and pulled the girl towards her, kissing her full on the lips for a couple of seconds. Callum wondered if this was for his benefit; she must have seen him come in. He froze for a moment, thrown, wondering whether to leave. Then she turned and saw him watching her, and the momentary unconscious look that crossed her face made his heart leap. He pushed through the bodies, mostly people buying drinks in plastic cups to take out onto the common and the warm evening sunshine.

She smiled at him as he approached and undid everything he had constructed for her in a moment. She seemed smaller, less formidable than he remembered. It all happened in slow motion. He would endlessly replay the timing and movements, but in his every remembering, the bar was out of focus, the sound muted, and there were just her eyes and her mouth. He reflected her smile as she approached and watched her hand rise as though to shake his but then continue upwards to reach behind his neck, and her nails were on his nape. Her face was flushed, her skin glistening. She drew him gently towards her and kissed him, her tongue touching his fleetingly. It was so unexpected, so fabulously electric.

How long they kissed, he had no idea, a few seconds, half a minute. She pulled away and watched him recover. "I wanted to do that on Friday." She said, "But it didn't seem appropriate."

He could not speak; she seemed to actively enjoy his disorientation, almost thrilled by it and her effect on him. Smiling broadly, she brought him back, "Drink?"

"What's that?" Callum managed, looking across at her half-full glass on the bar.

"Gin and Tonic."

"OK, why not."

Grace turned and raised her voice above the hubbub, "Cyn. Two more. For outside"

The girl appeared to have been watching them while serving another customer along the bar. She nodded, pursing her lips at Grace in a kiss.

"A friend of yours?" He asked.

She watched him closely, "You could say that, yes, a close friend. Does that worry you?"

"What, because she's a woman or a close friend?" he asked, attempting to answer the question for himself before he could tell her.

"Either, both?" She replied.

He didn't know and did not reply but it did not seem important. They waited, looking at one another, neither feeling the need to speak, surrounded by bodies, noise and heat. His eyes kept returning to her lips. They were so astonishingly soft, the edges dark. As though drawn, shading to vulnerable, erotic pink, and always, just slightly parted. The girl returned with the two gin and tonics. "Thanks babe." Grace said and handed her a credit card.

She steered them through the bar, and suddenly, they were outside in the common's relative quiet and gentle evening warmth. They scanned the busy space, searching for a place to sit amongst the people scattered beneath the trees. There was still sufficient heat in the lowering sun for people to be comfortably on the threadbare earth in t-shirts and shorts. Weaving through the random groups of bodies, they found space at the periphery and sat and, for a few moments, just watched others around them, drinking and chatting, eating picnics or throwing frisbees and playing ball games.

A football rolled toward them, and Callum scooped it up and threw it with both hands over his head back to the young boy racing after it.

"Do you play football?" she asked.

He laughed, "God no, well, not for …"

He wondered for a moment how even to make that calculation; how long since he had been at school.

"You're not that old, surely. You must have played at school, or were you one of the posh rugger boys?"

"Oh yeah, very posh." He rolled his eyes. "No, not posh at all, but yes, it was a rugby school, so we just played football on the field at lunchtime. I was never particularly good at it; not that skilful with a round ball, but I was quick." He turned to look directly at her, "But not, it seems, as quick as you."

She nodded slowly, "You've been doing your preparation for this evening, I see."

"Hardly Poirot." He countered, "Tell me about your running."

He was genuinely interested, and Grace told him about school and discovering her speed as she grew. "It was one of those classic stories of a child finding something they are good at when the world around them seems intent on limiting what's possible. I grew early, and they said I was too tall to be a sprinter. To be fair, the other girls were all of a type. Compact, muscular. But somehow, I was still quick, and since then, of course, we've seen that the greatest sprinter the world has ever seen, Usain Bolt, has a body like mine." She smiled.

Callum laughed, "Usain Bolt, the male Grace Sommers. Does he know?"

She laughed. "I'd been classically lazy at school, more interested in my hair than history, and boys rather than biology. But something happened when I was fifteen, and my little brother was nearly killed. He was fine in the end, but I had this sense of us being trapped, Zeph and me. All our friends were caught in the same world, our chances narrowed, our futures pre-ordained."

"I can't imagine anything less like the woman I see here than that description," Callum observed.

She nodded, "She's long gone, that frightened, angry girl."

"How? How did you escape?"

"Luck, in part, but all the usual things, I guess. A couple of inspirational teachers who saw something in me, in many of us. The spark caught in me, but mostly because of my running; I was starting to win things. I won the hundred at London Schools, and then that year at the UK under sixteens, I was second, by a few centimetres."

She held up her thumb and index finger to measure the loss, and he noticed her bright silver nails. He laughed at her irritation at the memory of the distant defeat.

"Yeah, Carla pipped me at the under eighteens as well. I was never the fastest out of the blocks, so if it had been 105 meters, who knows? But honestly, even then, she was starting to be in a different class, and Olympic medals don't lie. And that bitch was the nicest person you could ever meet. I was training at E&H by then, Enfield and Haringey," she explained. "Then I got the scholarship to Stanford, which was a game changer. All the doors that had been closed in my face were suddenly open; people were pushing me, begging me to go through them. I majored in psychology and American jocks."

Callum looked confused.

She laughed, "The world of serious athletes is just an ocean of testosterone. The most exquisite, young, fit bodies in the world, together in the same environment. Oh my god, I got so much cock."

Callum did not know how to respond to this.

She saw his face, "Sorry, there's the other Grace. I didn't mean to be crude."

"Oh, I'm pretty sure you did." He replied, holding her gaze.

"Fair cop." She acknowledged after a moment, breaking the eye contact to sip her drink and then continued more seriously.

"I see now it wasn't all great sex and joy. It was mostly just young people fucking one another. Nobody knew what they were doing."

She seemed about to continue the thought but stopped and smiled at him. "But that was a while ago; I was a kid then."

As she talked, he lay back, flat, watching her against the sky, and she felt him looking up at her, "What?"

"Do you always tie your hair back?"

"Work hair." She looked down at him, paused, considered, and then reached up and pulled the bands from her hair. Leaning

128

forward, she shook and teased it free. Unbound, it framed her face above him in a halo.

Callum lay on the grass and closed his eyes, struggling to process what was happening and the unexpectedly powerful emotions which had assailed him. She had talked openly about her childhood; did she expect to know the same about him? If so, she would be disappointed; his life and history were too complex and incriminating to be shared. He was caught in a cleft, pinned between his almost unbearable attraction to her and his wariness of her and the lies that intimacy would entail. A couple of times, she had given the impression of being able to see straight through him. He had no idea where that feeling originated, but he felt it keenly, and the stakes, for him, were too high. She was a detective; even if she were not investigating him, her instinct to dig and ask questions would never be far from the surface.

He answered a few questions about the company and the technologies they were developing, as well as how his life was split between London and Geneva and the fabrication plants they were building in Africa and Asia. He avoided, without, he hoped being too obvious, questions about family and friends. As he was doing so, he was reminded again how sparsely populated his life was with anyone close to him. He was digging holes all over the place, but hopefully small enough that he would be able to extricate himself. When she challenged him, he put the lack of anything other than work in his life down to the intense pressure of a rapidly growing global business and his belief that they needed to do something about the climate emergency that was already being felt everywhere. He talked to her animatedly about their new technologies and their effect on energy use if they managed to get them to market. His passion was real, and although the subject held no interest for her, she saw it. He eventually steered her to her own work to discover how, as a Stanford psychology major, she had moved through marketing and corporate communications to land in the Metropolitan Police, where her psychology background and her ability to read people were a perfect fit for a detective. She hinted at, but skirted, her own counselling that had tuned her natural intuition into a genuinely useful set of skills. Callum probed out of genuine interest, and she acknowledged a difficult relationship with her father and some other men in her life.

They had been quiet for more than a minute, and he was still lying on the ground on his back, looking at the sky with her sitting beside him, people-watching. She was wearing jeans and trainers with no socks and just a T-shirt. He could see the curve of her breast against the darkening sky and her nipple evident in the lack of a bra; the halo of hair above contained her precise features. He felt dizzy and closed his eyes. Callum, Callum, what the hell are you doing? He thought to himself. She looked like a goddess. He marvelled at her poise and physical confidence, understanding now where it originated. Her body was her weapon; it had carried her physically and metaphorically from a hard, closed London childhood to where she was now, and she clearly understood its power.

He needed to break the spell. "Shall we walk?" he asked.

She pivoted elegantly onto her feet and faced across the common towards the setting sun. "I live over this way", she said.

Callum avoided analysing any implicit meaning and started walking, dropping their plastic cups in a nearby bin.

She took his hand. It was such a natural, simple gesture that he didn't react for a moment, and then it hit him. He snatched his hand away and shut his eyes. His heart was hammering in his chest, the image in his mind of walking with Maria and Rachel, and it was her hand, his beautiful daughter's tiny hand, he felt at that moment. The last hand he had held in that way.

"Are you OK?" he heard Grace ask quietly. "What happened there?"

He was unprepared and overwhelmed by the wave of emotion that, locked away for so long, now burst over him. The defensive wall he had constructed and tended for so long toppled. He saw Rachel. His child looked up at him, and finally, he looked back at her and remembered the feel of her in his arms and her arms around his neck. The tears were streaming down his face, forced through closed eyes, and he was sobbing. Grace instinctively pulled him to her and held him. He had no perception of time, and when the shuddering emotion had passed, he opened his eyes and eased back, and Grace's concerned face swam into focus.

"I was married once, we had a daughter, and they were both killed in an accident. Her's was the last hand I held, like that. I'm sorry." He closed his eyes, and the tears returned, hot on his face.

"Oh, Cal." Grace wrapped her arms around him, his distress infecting her.

They stood there for a while, Callum's tears falling silently into her T-shirt. At some point, Callum became aware of her again, her smell and the heat of her body pressed against him. The well of pain and loneliness he felt thinking about Rachel and Maria was replaced by guilt as he reacted to her breasts against his chest, her groin against him. He went to push her gently away, but suddenly, they were kissing. He was drowning in her smell, her taste and his overwhelming desire for her. He had rarely felt an emotion so powerful. She felt it, too; how could she not? It was radiating from him. When he pulled away, shocked at the intensity of his raw lust, the emotion burst forth as uncontrolled laughter. She took a step back, shocked, too and folded down onto cross legs. He lay on his back, on the still-warm ground, her hand on his chest. He could feel his heartbeat reflected back from her palm, and she was calming him with this intimate contact, and his breathing slowed.

"What the fuck." Grace said, wiping the tears from her eyes.

"Sometimes there's no way to keep it in," Callum said quietly, sitting up to scan her face. He took her hands in his, and they were quiet, both wondering what was happening, unnerved by the unexpected emotional landscape they had stumbled into.

The dark was edging in now, and street lights began to circle the common. The traffic, until then unnoticed, suddenly encroached. Grace stood from her cross-legged position, seemingly without effort, as if levitating. She took his hands and raised him too. They held hands as they walked in silence across the common and through the quiet residential streets to Wandsworth, where Grace lived.

"Tell me about them." Grace said, "If you can."

Afterwards, Callum had no recollection of the route they took. He talked about meeting Maria, their wedding, the birth of their daughter, Rachel and how hard it had hit him when they died. He described always having had the image of himself as mentally robust, someone who would survive a tragedy. The reality of how desperate he had felt after losing them, how helpless he had been in the face of irredeemable loss, reawakened the barbed memories, and for the first time, he made no attempt to conceal his distress. The contact of her hand in his became an emotional sluice through which the dammed pain and grief could flow, and it poured from him. He described his search for meaning in his life and his determination to change the world and make it a better place. Grace absorbed all of this, setting it into a context that made sense to her, framing his obsession with work and the single-minded vision she had felt deep in him. There was no way for her to imagine the knotted reality behind his words as the first roots of their entanglement slipped unseen into her.

***

Her fourth-floor flat was tiny. He glanced around the space: a living room and kitchen combined, a small table, a pair of bright plastic chairs and a two-seat sofa facing a large television screen. The intimate bedroom was barely twice the size of her large double bed, with a wall of built-in wardrobes and a door to an ensuite shower and toilet. She switched on the low bedside light and slipped out of her jeans. In silhouette, the soft, warm glow of the light refracted through her halo of hair and glanced golden off her elegant, impossibly long thighs. She turned and deliberately held his gaze as she crossed her arms and slowly lifted the T-shirt over her head.

It was blatant, fabulous exhibitionism, exhilarating. Callum watched as she slowly and deliberately revealed herself to him, now wearing only her pale knickers, barely concealing the mass of dark hair. He was, in equal measure, stunned and intimidated by her body. They had talked about her athletics career and that when she could, she still trained, but he was totally unprepared for the physical reality. The mute light glanced off her skin, and shadows emphasised the contoured muscles beneath. She was an amazon and, without the slightest doubt, the most physically impressive human he had ever been this close to.

"Oh, my god!" he heard himself whisper and saw the tiny reaction flit across her face.

The Land of the Blind

She stepped across to him and, sliding her index finger into the waist of his chinos, drew him gently towards her.

Suddenly, there was an exquisite smell. He could not have described it, but the urge to immerse himself in it, in her, was overpowering. She did not shave her underarms, and spontaneously, he did the strangest thing. He took one of her wrists and gently lifted her arm high, pressing his face into the damp, pungent hair.

"Woooah." She whispered.

She stepped back, and she regarded him with a curious gaze. "Well, that's a first."

He leaned forward and kissed her, his lips returning the coercive aphrodisiac.

Her lips were impossibly soft, and her tongue was strong and insistent. After a moment, he had to pull away, breathless.

He knew what was coming and suddenly felt the embarrassment flood through him anticipating his rather average and recently slightly flabby body being revealed. He had invested no time in his physical appearance for years, and here was his comeuppance.

She lifted his T-shirt over his head and dropped it keeping her eyes on his as she undid his trouser button and fly. She pushed the material gently down, and he completed the graceless removal of trousers and socks. She pulled him against her as he stood, one arm around his waist and one around his neck.

Pulling back from the kiss, she took his hand and watched him as she pushed his fingers gently between her legs.

He felt the soft, yielding heat and the wet material, and she smiled as he reacted.

"When was the last time?" She asked.

His focus slipped away.

"Your wife, Maria?"

"Yes."

She smiled, apparently deciding something and then eased him gently back onto the bed on his back and, kneeling astride him, pushed him flat. He felt her peel back his underwear and the cool air and then her warm hand. He closed his eyes and heard himself groan.

"Better slow the pace, I think."

He could hear the smile in her voice as she stood, and he watched her step easily and elegantly out of her knickers.

"I'm sorry, this is all a bit overwhelming." He said.

She hushed him with her index finger in front of her lips and then stood surveying him, hands on hips, her feet slightly apart.

At the arch of her inner thighs, he could see tiny, bright droplets of moisture in the dark hair and lay back, breathing heavily; this was way too much and much too fast.

He felt her sit alongside him and heard the bedside drawer slide. He opened his eyes to see her holding a condom.

Birth control had not even entered his mind. "I had a vasectomy, so …" he said.

He watched her consider this and, after a moment, toss the condom onto the table. He had no idea what she was thinking.

She stretched out beside him, her hand stroking his chest gently, allowing his arousal to ebb from its so obviously fragile peak. He attempted calm, but when he opened his eyes, her face and hair filled his vision, and he wanted her so badly he could barely breathe. With one slow, graceful arc of her leg, she straddled him and leaned forward, one palm flat on his chest, their faces close, her eyes searching his as she reached back and slid herself easily onto him. She sat up, moving slowly, and despite every effort to dissociate himself from the unendurable pleasure, it was impossible. The complex harmony of emotional sound that escaped him filled the room, and she pulled her hips tight against him as he came.

"Wow, that's a record, " she said, but her words and intent were warm, carried on a wide, almost delighted smile.

"Oh my god, I'm sorry. That was just …" His mouth was open, and he was breathing heavily, his eyes devouring her.

It was so blatantly, fabulously clear what she wanted, and she carefully, skilfully used him for her pleasure, and throughout, he could not take his eyes off her. After her first orgasm, he attempted to lift himself forward, but she pressed both her palms onto his chest and firmly held him down. It was not aggressive; it was simply what she wanted, and she watched his reaction impassively. His easy acceptance seemed to please her, and they kissed for a long time, her hair brushing his face, his hands moving slowly along her back and thighs.

Time dilated, and his world contracted. For some time, he was a willing spectator witnessing her physical pleasure, and as hers grew and filled her, so did his. She closed her eyes, her hands on his chest, hails holding his skin. He watched a bead of sweat run from her collarbone to a nipple and hang for a moment, a trembling jewel of liquid, golden light, before it dropped in slow motion onto his stomach.

Time could not be measured, but at some point, he came again and clutched her tightly against him. As she felt his warmth fill her, and the shocking intensity of his need, she opened her eyes and looked at him as if seeing him for the first time, and a low hum escaped from deep within her. Her eyes glazed, and she continued her slow rhythmic movement, lost in a sensory world so deep that she was unreachable. Her second orgasm was longer, more intense, and forced tiny high-pitched noises from her, her head arched back, mouth wide. Afterwards, she opened her eyes and blinked him into focus.

"That was nice," she said unemotionally, but her smile told a wildly different story.

She put her hands behind her head and stretched, and her abdominal muscles moved and patterned beneath her skin, tracked with lines of sweat. He realised then that she had, apparently effortlessly, kept her weight off him throughout. He ran his hands slowly up her muscled stomach through the sheen of sweat to her breasts. She watched him and then covered his hands with hers, pressing tight.

He had expected her to lie with him afterwards, but instead, she stepped away, leaving him naked, feeling very exposed. She stood beside the bed, considering him thoughtfully. After a moment, she moved her feet apart and cupped her hand as his semen spooled out. She ran her fingers through the frictionless, immiscible mix in her palm and then looked up at him, "That is the first time I've had unprotected sex for years, since …, I can't remember." She picked up her T-shirt and wiped her hands thoughtfully.

"Tea?"

"What?"

"Do you want tea?" she asked.

She had her hands on her hips, watching him again as he scanned her body. His gaze might have been a warm breeze for its effect on her. Had all of that been a performance of some kind, some demonstration of her power? Perhaps, but there was so much else there, glimpsed. He had never encountered anyone so emotionally strong and confident. It seemed impossible, and if he carried on seeing her, he sensed he would eventually reveal another side of her. He understood himself well enough to know how dangerously appealing this was.

"What?" Her acute, dangerous perception again.

He wanted to explain to her what he was feeling, but that was impossible; he didn't know himself. He managed only, "Yes, tea."

He lay on the bed, his sweat cooling, listening to her moving in the kitchen, water running, the kettle popping and boiling and a spoon ringing the cups. He suddenly felt his nakedness and climbed off the bed and removed the top sheet, patched, translucent, with their sweat. He was about to cover himself when she returned.

"Don't." She instructed gently. "I love these warm summer nights. Can we just enjoy being naked?"

He lacked her apparent absence of self-consciousness and thought not, but nevertheless dropped the sheet and propped himself on the pillows, legs extended, grateful that the full-length mirror on the bathroom door was facing away.

"I just made it with milk; there's sugar if …"

"That's fine."

She placed a mug on his side table, and he watched the muscles and tendons in her thighs move beneath her skin as she traversed the bed. The length of her legs disguised their size and strength. He glanced at his legs, and it felt like she belonged to another, more impressive species.

"Can I ask you something?" He said.

She placed the mug on the bedside table and, amused, replied. "I think we're past the 'can I ask you' stage, Callum."

138

The Land of the Blind

She arranged the pillows and sat shoulder to shoulder, hip to hip, her foot resting on his. The earthy smell of her laced faintly with an acrid thread of semen drifted up to him.

They were facing forward, and he glanced sideways at her, but she did not turn. "I was wondering whether you cared what I thought about you physically. It's just that I've never met anyone who appears to be so unselfconscious about their body. It's more than that; it feels almost like intimidation."

There was a long pause, and he wondered if she would answer but held the silence, sipping his tea. She turned to look at him for a moment, but he could not read her, and she looked away, and the silence lengthened.

"About five years of therapy. That's what it took." She said quietly as if stating a simple fact.

"I assume you're going to explain that."

"Do you?" She was not smiling.

He twisted and faced her, "I'd like to understand what that means, Grace; I'd like to understand you better."

Again, he failed to decipher the look that passed behind her eyes as she glanced at him, turned away and sipped her tea.

"If we get to know one another better, then perhaps I will. For now, Let's just say I once had a very different and far less healthy relationship with my body and how I used or abused it. I needed help and found it. And in answer to your other question, no, I don't care what you think about my body. Well, that's not entirely true, obviously, but your reaction to it is pretty unambiguous. But, in the end, only one opinion matters, and that's mine."

"OK. That's …" Her self-confidence was astounding.

She turned to him, "You asked." But she was smiling.

They drank their teas in silence and then slid down the bed, legs entwined, almost facing one another, his arm across her hip, his other arm between them, the back of his fingers gently teasing her pubic hair. He closed his eyes, listened to her breath whisper, and felt her warm skin, sheer as silk, against him. He remembered feeling this overwhelming peace so rarely and was old and wise enough to lose himself to it. An unexpected thought came to him; at no point had the intense pleasure caused him a moment of guilt. He had not betrayed his wife or her memory.

"What are you thinking about?" She asked.

"Why, what did you see?" he asked.

Their faces were close, her eyes the same colour, a mirror of his.

"Something." She said.

He chose to tell her the truth, "I was thinking of Maria."

Grace slowly placed her hand on his chest. "She's still here; Cal always will be; she's part of you forever; they both are."

His eyes filled, and a tear escaped, and she stroked it gently away. Once more, he could not speak.

They lay in her bed for the rest of the night, talking, touching, intoxicated in the warm, safe monochrome, until the colour crept from the lightning sky through the tiny window. For a time, they kissed and caressed, aroused but not needing to go any further than recognising the pleasure each was giving and taking, the universe momentarily confined to the space of their two bodies. Finally, well after dawn, they slept briefly. Callum woke with a start to find Grace standing at the foot of the bed, sipping tea, watching him. She was wearing a short, open dressing gown, falling mid-way down her long thighs, and her hair was wild.

A momentary wave of lust coursed through him, but as quickly as he felt it, it passed, and although it was trite, possibly predictable, and almost certainly untrue, he knew she was the most beautiful woman he had ever seen. Again, there was no pang of guilt.

"You're so beautiful." He said.

She laughed softly and blushed, smiling. "I bet you say that to all the girls. But thank you. "Do you know you talk in your sleep?" she said.

He watched her register his over-reaction. "Really, what did I say?" his affected nonchalance was brittle.

She watched him momentarily before replying, "It seemed like a nightmare, perhaps about the car crash. You said, no, no, stop, and other stuff I couldn't make out."

They did not speak about what had happened over the previous twelve hours. Twelve hours, Callum thought. That's just crazy; it felt like days, concentrated into something thrilling, intoxicating, valuable, and forever his. She affected nonchalance, but he had seen past the mask. He had glimpsed hidden shades of her as they talked late into the night, and he was in equal measure awed and terrified by what he had seen and the feelings she had created in him.

Grace showered, brought him tea and toast in bed, left him there and went to work like any other Monday. He was unaware she had never left a man alone in her flat. He did not see her standing on the other side of the door, one hand resting on the handle, her head tipped forward, eyes closed, and he did not hear her whisper to herself, "Oh, girl, what was that?"

He heard only her staccato steps riffing down the stairwell. In the warm bed, Callum sat, staring, sightless across the small room. He would replay the sex in his mind hundreds, possibly thousands of times. Thinking about it now, the overriding sense was of being completely powerless and dominated. He had not felt the need to assert himself in any way; she was so clearly in control of the choreography, and he had loved every moment. Now, his chest was tight with conflicting emotions. She was so very dangerous for him and all the secrets he contained; did he really talk in his sleep? He knew that to continue seeing her would be reckless and stupid. She seemed to have flashes of insight into his inner thoughts, and a careless slip could undo everything he had spent years working for. He also knew with absolute certainty that he would continue seeing her for as long as he could. He told himself that time would dilute the madness and lust, knowing he wanted it to last forever.

He fell asleep and woke after eleven; for a moment, with no idea where he was.

Out on the street, the world seemed different as he walked through the busy centre of Wandsworth. The sky was cloudless, the sun hot on the pavements, everything a little brighter, the sounds clearer, everyone looked happier. He marvelled at the capricious nature of time. Could it really have been only hours since he walked into that pub on Clapham Common?

His thoughts turned to work, and Sania and her brilliantly effective ploy to bring him and Grace together. He wondered momentarily at her motives and then had a shocking thought. Sania had pwned Grace's phone. How had he not remembered? Hardly surprising, perhaps, given the sensory overload of last night. Where had her phone been? He could not remember and felt his face flush at the thought of Sania listening to them. He would not be in the office again until Friday; he would call Sania, get her to remove the software from Grace's phone, and ensure that Grace never found out about it. What had he been thinking? That image, possibly the most erotic single thing he had ever witnessed, a golden droplet of light trembling on her nipple before falling onto him, answered the question, and he groaned audibly at his stupidity and the fabulous joy and the void of longing that filled him.

15.

The water was black and freezing cold, and he was soaked to the skin, surrounded by other bodies in the frigid darkness. The clouds parted, and the moon seemed to spotlight the vast craft bearing down on them, a physical manifestation of the deep throbbing sound that he had not even registered until that moment. There were voices around him, women and children screaming and men shouting, but he could not understand them. He shouted for them to escape the crowded boat to save themselves as his own panic rose. Why was he the only one who could see what was about to happen? Why were they ignoring him? There was no time; the water bulged upwards as the bow wave reached them, their boat tipped, and the hull of the monster vessel obliterated the moon. As he hit the freezing water, he could sense the other bodies all around and knew that the thrashing blades of the propellors would hit them and slice through them. He watched his leg drift away, ink-black blood somehow visible in complete darkness, and there was silence as he drifted to the surface. It was always the same; he knew he would look as he always did. His eyes were clamped shut, but he always saw the severed limbs bobbing around him in the boat's wake.

Drenched in sweat, he woke to the sound of his own breathless fright and waited for it to ebb. This nightmare had started years ago while he was researching the history of the migrations and had stumbled on the report of the appalling incident. In the scheme of things, it had been insignificant, a few dozen people killed out of so many, but the images would not leave him. Now, its periodic visitation provided a reminder, if he ever needed it, of what he was attempting to prevent.

Another sleepless night. Callum knew that was not true, but it felt that way as he abandoned the bed to perch on the stool in the kitchen and wait for the kettle to boil. His mind, usually so obedient and rational, would not be quieted or controlled, swinging between nuclear reactor schematics, DNA sequences, footage of police violence against protesters in Buenos Aires and now pornographic images of Grace Sommers' arched body, slick with sweat running between her breasts. He felt a decreasing guilt in obsessing about her, and the fact that they were too busy to see one another often heightened the intense anticipation. Part of him was amazed at the depth of his physical attraction to her, simultaneously frightened that it would wane and that it might undermine his judgement about all of the practical issues he had to deal with.

She had plucked him from the spiral of loneliness, the depth of which he was only now, as he emerged, beginning to understand. She had replaced that deeply corrosive monochrome unhappiness with such intense physical and emotional pleasure that he was struggling to hold any useful perspective on the relationship. Some nights, as he lay in the dark, unable to think of anything but her, his whole body ached at her physical absence; it felt like a debilitating weakness shocking in its intensity. They had seen one another five times over the five weeks since that first night. Their mutual physical intoxication had dominated each evening, and he had felt like a teenager anticipating the sex. They ate quickly, each time in a different restaurant and afterwards went to her flat. He was almost embarrassed at the memory of them kissing in the back of a black cab, his hand up her skirt. They managed only a few hours of sleep each time, spending most of the night in thoughtless, hedonistic pleasure. Her total lack of self-consciousness infected him. She had quickly understood his excitement at seeing her aroused and surfaced her lust for their mutual gratification. This feedback quite obviously intensified her pleasure. He had never experienced anything like the rapture this produced in both of them, a symmetry that had grown with each encounter, like seeing oneself in a mirror yet in another's body and mind. Now staring, unseeing, out of the window, he replayed their last encounter, wallowing in the sensory avalanche she always precipitated. He also knew their mutual obsession was changing. She always dominated physically, and the submissive role he took was easy to adopt, but it was not him. During that previous night, lying on their sides, kissing, touching one another, he had instinctively moved across to be above her, and she had stopped him. She placed her hand against his chest. She did not speak, and he could not tell what was behind her steady gaze, but it was a glimpse of another side of her, carefully concealed and the first time he had sensed vulnerability. The cocktail of emotions was far too complex for him to disentangle then or now.

He was aware enough to know that all of this was profoundly good for him, provided he could control it. As the word appeared in his mind, he smiled to himself. The idea that one could control Grace was beautifully self-delusional. Tea in hand, he headed for the study and his computer, determined to banish her from his mind until he was in the shower later, when he could indulge his memory and imagination.

The Land of the Blind

***

He began with the output figures at the battery fabrication facility in India and the two in Africa. They were now producing generic batteries for the automotive industry and larger grid-scale storage. They could not make them fast enough and had licensed the technology to dozens of other companies who were also making them to satisfy the huge and growing global demand. A number of large mining companies suffered when Renewable Futures' latest aluminium and carbon cells had proved reliable and safe. Along with the owners of the huge mining operations, governments in Indonesia, Australia and South America, all with reserves of nickel and lithium, saw the value of their natural assets crash.

Both Ferrari and Maserati recently launched electric vehicles that outperformed their internal combustion engine predecessors in every respect for the first time. Range anxiety was almost forgotten; with the right charging equipment, the new batteries could be fully recharged in less than the time it took to buy an espresso, as the Ferrari advert stylishly demonstrated. This strand of their plan had worked as well as Callum could have hoped, but it had unintended consequences they had not anticipated.

While many now touted global warming as the worst threat to man's continued enjoyment of a benign planet, the move from fossil fuel to electric transport was proving double-edged. People believed the problem was almost solved, ignorant of how small a proportion of global fossil fuel use, electricity generation and private transport represents. The highly visible developments in solar and wind conjured the delusion that enough was being done. The fossil fuel companies were laughing behind their hands and continued to make vast financial bets in the form of new extraction projects worth hundreds of billions of dollars. Their plans were based on an expectation that the world would continue to burn copious quantities of fossil fuels for decades. Callum knew how to change this doomed trajectory, but the technology he needed to make this a practical reality was still not ready. The only way to stop fossil fuels from being extracted and burned was to provide a cheaper, or at least comparable, alternative. His plan relied heavily on 'green' hydrogen, produced without releasing carbon dioxide. Hydrogen, as a fuel, works like natural gas in many respects. It is not as energy-dense and, like natural gas, has to be compressed for storage and transportation, but in liquid form, it would be a competitor for the fuels distilled from crude oil.

Water, H_2O, is composed of Hydrogen and Oxygen and is extremely stable. You need a lot of energy to split it into its constituent parts, and the 'green' way to do so involves using electricity to force apart the water molecules into their constituent elements. Another way starts with natural gas through a process that requires steam. Either way, you need a lot of energy, and unless this is generated without producing carbon dioxide, the whole process is self-defeating. Callum knew how this could work and would work at some point in the future, but the energy had to come from nuclear reactors at the scale required for his plans. There was simply no other way to generate the quantity of electricity where it was needed in the time scales that they had to work with. The clandestine project with Carlsen Olson was his way of making this happen. It was taking time, and the reports he received from Olson were promising, but it remained a frustrating missing piece in their plans to usurp fossil fuel use. The complementary project involved developing the devices that split the water, and Callum studied the experimental results from the

The Land of the Blind

latest test of their polymer electrolyte membrane developments. They were part-funding three joint venture projects with the most promising hydrogen generation companies. Finally, the numbers were closing in on the efficiencies he knew they needed to produce hydrogen at a price that would compete with gas and oil.

He read an online article from GulfCo, a consortium of oil-producing states in the Middle East that purported to invest heavily in hydrogen generation for a 'sustainable future'. Callum wondered at the sheer hypocrisy of the company. Anyone who understood the industry and scale of the problem knew it was greenwash, but they were never called out. He sat back and stared out the window, considering how GulfCo and the other petrostates would react when his nuclear plans became reality. They would resist change, that was certain, perhaps violently. With the amount of money already on the table for future extraction projects, they had little choice. Despite the growing amount of renewable electricity, the global economy still depends almost entirely on cheap energy, and governments everywhere subsidise the extraction and production of fossil fuels to ensure their energy security. Callum understood both the scale of the problem and the possibility of unrest and conflict that could result from his intervention, but all he could do now was implement their plans. It appeared to be working, with the Chinese close to commercialising the reactor prototypes, which, through Olson, Callum knew they had already built. "Worry about the things you can control," he said aloud, turning back to the keyboard to read Vivien's latest report.

It was almost midnight in Berkeley, California, and Vivien Cazinski would be sleeping. He pictured her and vividly remembered her anger in their meeting several years earlier. Since then, she had never trusted him, and he could do nothing to change that. She knew he was lying to her then and that he continued to do so, but not in the way she supposed. Her team had already made breakthrough discoveries, which made her a shoo-in for a future Nobel Chemistry prize. Enhancements to the CRISPR/Cas gene editing process, which she had designed and overseen, were revolutionising genetics, and the first effective treatments were already appearing. She had taken a highly sophisticated yet still rather crude gene editing technique and had turned it into a precision tool. Now, specific sections of DNA, down to a single letter code, could be altered reliably without causing 'off-target' effects. The fact that Callum had effectively pointed the team to the key molecule that made this possible was simply what he had had to do to develop the technology in time to disrupt the global livestock trade, amongst other things.

Vivien's latest update charted their continuing progress with the research but raised no flags for him. He moved on to looking at the accounts for Cyber Futures and then to those from Armando, summarising the finances of the Green Futures Group. They counted their legitimate group revenues in the hundreds of billions now, almost all of which was being re-invested into production and research facilities worldwide. He would review the numbers in detail with Armando tomorrow, but they were in robust financial health. One benefit of their commercial success was that they no longer needed to hack various illegal organisations, as they had once done to provide their early development capital. One less thing for Callum to worry about.

Finally, as he did several times each week now, he checked the websites of The Times of South Africa and the All-Seeing Eye; it was emotional torture he seemed unable to resist. On the one hand, the site promised a fairer world where brutal dictators like David Kigale would no longer be able to act with selfish impunity; on the other, the continuing deaths of protesters in Equatorial Guinea at the hand of Kigale's son portrayed a different reality. When the death of Joseph Onjwen in South Sudan hit the global press, the International Criminal Court condemned how the All-Seeing Eye was claiming responsibility for what was, according to the doctors, a natural death. They stressed the need for the international criminals they indicted to be brought to justice through a legal process. They stated unequivocally that they considered it irresponsible to advocate for vigilante retribution. As with any outlandish idea easily accessible on the Internet, some people were drawn to it. The All-Seeing Eye reported well over a million followers across social media platforms, and there had been calls for the major social media platforms to suspend their accounts. Despite all of the 'noise', no one in power was taking this seriously so far. Most were sceptical about the claims of the website. Callum wondered whether Roger Musike, the president of Cameroon, was as sanguine about his ascent to the top of the All-Seeing Eye's list alongside Teodor Kigale. A similar demand for political reform made of Onjwen had been made of Kigale and now Musike. Otherwise, the site proclaimed, they would suffer the same fate as the four dead men pictured on the website.

Callum had briefly considered getting Sania to take down the All Seeing Eye site, but Poppy would have just resurrected it on other servers. It was better for him to ignore her. It might take a while, but when her latest targets did not die, people would abandon the idea that they had any agency.

The sixth-month period for Musike to act would end in a few weeks, and there was no chance he would comply. Callum had seen the recent BBC news item reporting on this and the simple line-drawn All-Seeing Eye that was appearing across Yaoundé, the Cameroon capital city. The BBC, as usual, did a good job of setting the context, explaining that the 'Eye' was an old and viscerally appealing idea common to many societies, from ancient Egypt to modern times, including the United States, where it adorns the one dollar bill. Often referred to as the Eye of Providence or the All-Seeing Eye of God, the image was the subject of any number of conspiracy theories, and it was easy to promulgate. Callum had rarely found an issue so hard to deal with. He had the power to stop these people, and a part of him still believed that if he continued, whether it took the death of one, two or three more dictators, at some point, everyone would realise that the All-Seeing Eye was exactly what it purported to be. But he had so clearly miscalculated. Creating the space for change mattered little if the fundamental conditions remained the same. In retrospect, his idea of removing these 'evil' people was so obviously misguided that it verged on embarrassment. Poppy and her 'All-Seeing Eye' idea might have had an impact, but it would not dissuade people like Teodor Kigale.

Although there had been no contact with Poppy for months, Callum had seen the two email messages she had sent about the test samples for Musike. He had not acknowledged them and knew that when the third arrived, as it surely would, he had to ignore that too; he should never have engaged with Poppy and her dangerous idealism. Impulsively he checked the news in Equatorial Guinea and read reports of ongoing protests and killings, badly beaten bodies found in gutters, and women raped and killed. One report showed the same All-Seeing Eye image appearing in Yaoundé, the Cameroon capital city, also being drawn on walls throughout Malabo, the Equatorial Guinea capital. He felt little guilt over what now appeared to be the pointless death of the dictators, but the appalling wave of guilt at the futile hope he had created for their countless victims caused him real distress. He had to shut his eyes, his hands trembling above the keyboard. This was a lesson; he needed to understand the limits of his power and listen to those around him. He stood abruptly; he had to get out and walk to gift his mind the time and space to process the tumult of emotion. He knew nothing would be resolved by doing so, but the simple movement, the physical distraction, would ease the weight of this egregious miscalculation that so often settled on him.

16.

Grace walked into the bar, her white denim jacket over one arm. Heads turned and pretended not to look at the striking woman by the entrance. The waiter checked her reservation as she waited, feeling out of place. There was no basis for her discomfort, a tall, attractive, outwardly confident single woman in a smart London bar. Hardly a rarity, but, in common with so many women, she always felt watched, and despite her unshakable indifference to their opinions, she was incapable of losing that sense of being prey in someone else's world. She slipped behind her sunglasses, following the waiter through the bar and onto the terrace. Many eyes glanced at her elegant, athletic limbs moving beneath the light summer dress.

The table was empty; she was early. She ordered a Gin and Tonic, and before sitting, she took in the familiar view across the Thames before turning towards The City and Canary Wharf in the distance to sit with the gentle evening heat on her shoulders. Soon, no one paid her any attention as she sipped her drink.

Callum could feel his pulse quickening as he rode up in the elevator to the bar and restaurant. He knew exactly what this feeling was, but he had never experienced it like this before. Objectively, he knew it was circumstance conspiring to prime this overwhelming desire for her, but it was a gorgeous, dangerously powerful feeling. It took only a moment for his eye to find her even though she was outside on the terrace. He saw her turn slightly and see him, too. The thrill at the simple act of their eyes meeting meant he missed the waiter's question and had to re-focus.

It had been less than three months since that first delirious night in her flat. They had seen one another only ten times when their choked calendars aligned. Callum had lied several times and moved trips to ensure they could meet. She was as busy as he was and could not control her commitments in the way he could.

She rose as he approached the table, placed her sunglasses beside her drink and he reached out and took both her hands.

"Grace."

"Callum."

They leaned in, eyes open and kissed for long enough that everyone on the terrace knew that this was still new.

"God, you look so …" he said, leaning back to look at her closely.

She arched her eyebrow, and his smile broadened. Despite the tanned skin and light beard, she was sure he blushed.

"Lovely, no, gorgeous." His eyes took in her hair, and he smiled broadly now. "Wow, impressive." He nodded his appreciation.

She shook her mass of hair, "Go big or go home."

She ran her hand gently down the front of the smooth, cool silk shirt he was wearing, "This is rather nice; special occasion?"

"I bought it today, in a larnie place in the middle of town. It's a bit of an extravagance, but I seem to have a wardrobe full of rather functional clothes."

They sat, and the waiter arrived to take his order. He eyed her gin and tonic in the large goblet studded with condensed, refracting droplets. "That looks delicious. G and T? I'll have the same, thanks." And then, remembering the bar in the Windmill and their first date, he added, "The last time I did, it ended well."

Callum was squinting into the lowering sun and pulled his chair beside hers so that they could face away from the other people on the terrace, looking out across the river below. He placed his hand, open, palm upwards on the arm of the chair and turned to see her looking at him, inscrutable. Carefully, she mirrored each of her fingertips against his and gently pressed their palm together and then watched the effect this simple act had on him as his eyes danced around her face. They sat, quiet without moving, watching the river traffic, the sound drifting up from the people on the embankment below, conversations babbling around them until his drink arrived.

Callum twisted in his chair, looking into the restaurant behind them, "I think I've been here before, a long time ago. I remember being at someone's birthday, maybe when I was a child."

"Really? Has it been open that long?"

He gave a little laugh, "Might have been somewhere else."

"You grew up in London, didn't you?" she asked, "You never say much about your childhood."

"Yes, near Wimbledon; I must have told you."

She was shaking her head slowly.

"We didn't eat out that often. I can't remember whose birthday it was. Memories, so unreliable."

She was somewhere else for a moment and he asked her what she was thinking about.

"Sorry, what?" She realised he had asked her something.

"Where did you just go?" he asked.

"I was remembering us on the common that first evening when we were walking to my place. After we held hands."

He looked away, remembering the moment and felt her watching him.

She covered his hand with hers. "We haven't talked about it much since that night but I sense you're dealing with it now. Are you?"

He picked up his drink and took a sip, giving himself time, replacing it with exaggerated care. "Sort of, yes. It's been more than a decade now, and I'd never dealt with it. Time blunts the pain." He stared out across the skyline, "Perhaps I'm just distracting myself." He turned and smiled at her."

"That might explain why most of our time together is spent fucking." She said quietly, mirroring his smile.

He considered this, "Are you getting bored with it?"

"Not in the slightest." Grace said quietly, "But if you want to talk about them, we can, whenever."

He took her hand.

They turned again towards the river and listened to the conversations around them until he asked, "OK. Tell me about your day, DC Sommers."

"Same old, same old, chasing bad guys, saving the world, you know."

"You seem to really like the job; I'm guessing you're good at it."

She looked at him thoughtfully for a moment, "What makes you say that?"

"You seem to understand people, and you believe in the truth." He answered casually, reaching for his glass.

"You're right; being a detective is a good fit for my skills, and it turns out I am good at it. Better than most of the 'suits' I work with. And, as for the truth …" she looked at him now and drew his gaze.

He had seen this just a few times since their first meeting at the Cyber Futures office, and his pulse ramped. He waited.

"You lied to me." It was a statement of fact delivered quietly, without emotion. The alarm on his face was reflected in her eyes. "There is one thing which might undo us, Cal, and that is you lying to me."

"What did I lie about?"

"How Maria and Rachel died."

"What. No, I didn't. Why are you bringing this up now? What makes you think I lied."

She watched his strong reaction closely.

"Yesterday, I had to check something about a suspect involved in an RTA, and I probably shouldn't have, but I searched for their accident in the database."

Callum was watching her uneasily, realising what he had revealed in telling her about their deaths.

"Nothing that matched over the last two decades anywhere in Cambridgeshire." She paused before adding, "I'm as sure as I can be that they existed and died, or you should get an Oscar for your performance, but why lie?"

He registered her apparent lack of emotion; she was interrogating him. He looked away and breathed out heavily, scrambling to decide how to attempt the evasion.

"You are right; I lied about part of that. It did not happen where and when I said, and I can only ask you to trust me when I say I have my reasons."

"Trust."

Her expression was impossible to read; again, the word carried no emotion. She stared into the distance, lost somewhere momentarily, and then faced him. She spoke quietly, "My job is not always pleasant, Cal. We deal with some appalling humans, and I need a place outside where I'm safe, and I can put my trust in good people."

His realisation that she needed this from him triggered a cascade of alarms, but before he could react, she continued.

"How was my day? Well, you remember how we first met?" Her gaze was suddenly so intense it burned his face.

He nodded, unwilling to say anything.

"Organised crime. I found out that the organised crime group killed the mistress of the man they assumed had stolen the money, which, as it happens, he did not. They cut her breast off while she was conscious and dropped her from a fifth-floor balcony onto a Milan street."

The rush of blood overwhelmed Callum for a moment, and his vision dimmed, and all he could hear was the sound of blood in his ears. Why was she telling him this now?

"Oh, Jesus." He managed in a choked voice.

He could barely breathe, struggling to compose himself and conceal the churning emotions.

"Are you OK?" she asked. "I wasn't trying to upset you; I just wanted you to understand the sort of things I sometimes have to deal with."

He knew his reaction was disproportionate. As far as she knew, this was an unrelated random death for him, but the violence of her words and the image they conveyed had sliced through him, taking him completely by surprise.

"That's just so dreadful, " he said. But alarms were blaring in his head, and he was watching Grace, willing her not to see past his reaction.

"Cal, are you OK?" she asked again.

He attempted to speak, but the rising panic turned this into a cough. He leaned forward and rose, saying, "I need the loo. I'll be right back."

Concerned edged into her voice now, "Cal, are you OK? What's going on?"

He confected a smile and touched the back of her hand gently, "I'm fine. I'll be right back."

He could feel her eyes on his back as he threaded the tables into the restaurant, where one of the bar staff pointed him towards the toilets. He stepped into a cubicle and closed the door, his hands fumbling the latch. He stood, leaning his head on crossed forearms against the wall. There was just the sound of his carefully controlled breathing. It took nearly a minute to still his mind and to order his thoughts. He was infatuated with her; it was an undeniable fact. He also sensed her feelings for him were more profound than she had anticipated. He knew from things she said that she had a very low opinion and deep distrust of most men and that to deceive her in any way would be both dangerous and cruel. And yet, here he was, deceiving her in the most fundamental way. He was lying about who he was, and it was only a question of time before this fabulous gift blew up in their faces and destroyed part of each of them.

He had been away from the table for almost ten minutes, and when he returned, she stood, looking unnerved. They sat, and she gave him a moment to compose himself and then fixed him. "Cal, I need to know what's going on."

He met her gaze, "Grace, there's …" he hesitated, "there's stuff. It's so complicated. There's so much I …. but …."

He saw her panic as plain as day. "Grace, no, no, whatever

you're thinking, I can absolutely guarantee it's wrong. I promise you."

The waiter, returning to see if their empty glasses needed filling, wheeled quickly away.

Her eyes teared, but she blinked them away, her jaw set. Callum waited for her to compose herself, his hand gently on her wrist.

Before she could speak, he started talking quietly, "These last few months, the time I've spent with you, have been the happiest I can remember for so, so long." The context caused a small, abrupt laugh, "To be honest, that bar was pretty low." He leaned closer, speaking slowly and quietly. "There are no skeletons, no one else in my life, nothing like that."

She brushed a tear away before it could run down her cheek. They sat for nearly a minute, looking past one another without speaking, and gradually became aware of the tables nearby listening, furtively observing the domestic drama being played out, thrillingly close by.

"Grace."

He could see the panic had receded but could not read her as she shifted in her chair, twisting to watch him more easily.

"There is some stuff connected to my business life that is …"he paused again, "I don't know how to put it because it's pretty crazy. All I can tell you now is that I would like to share it with you, but I can't."

He was watching her closely and realised how much hinged on what he was about to say. He thought she might walk away, and the feeling of panic that notion produced in him was shocking. He was breathing heavily, barely controlling himself. "I'm older than I look, Grace, at least in terms of things I've seen and done, people I've known and loved and lost. So I'm an old head in a relatively young body. That means I've learned what's important in my life the hard way. I've played emotional games, tried to second-guess people, and been afraid to allow people to see me. It's hard to do. And I know from what you've told me in our time together that somehow, in your short and exciting life, you have managed to understand some of the same things. So I'm going to make you a promise. It's one that I don't even know for sure, that I can keep, but I'm going to try."

She was watching him, curious now, unsure where he was going with this.

"It doesn't sound like a big thing, but it is." He continued, lowering his voice, "I promise that where we are concerned, the two of us, in whatever relationship we have now and in the future, I will always be completely honest with you. If I want something, I will ask for it; if I need something, I will tell you; I will not play games with your emotions or mine. I don't mean this to be an obligation, so I will accept your response if I ask you for something you can't give me. I will always tell you the truth about my feelings for you."

He registered her surprise and continued.

"We all play games and worry about what the other person thinks; we spend too much time in our own heads. I've never suggested this to anyone before, not even Maria, and I realise how dangerous it is to be completely emotionally honest with someone. I'm not entirely sure I can do it, but I sense you need that from me."

He watched her digest this. She looked at him, distracted and then stared into the distance, unfocused.

"I would like you to think about doing the same; to always tell me completely honestly how you feel and ask for whatever it is you want from me, whether you believe I can give it to you or not. And never lie to me."

She turned to him, holding eye contact, and he could see that she understood what he was offering and asking.

"You are an odd man, Callum. I don't know if you're smart or delusional or how dangerous …"

He smiled. "When you find out …."

"I want to say yes, but I don't think I can. I would have to trust you in a way that I just don't do with men." Her mind was obviously racing.

Callum stood up and picked up the glasses. "Take a moment; I'll be right back."

She watched him walk away again towards the bar. Heads all around followed him, and people twisted to look at her. She kept her eyes on him and ignored them.

She was sitting, eyes closed, hands palm up on her knees when he returned.

"Are you OK?" he asked.

She opened her eyes and nodded, "Yes, I am."

He placed the drinks on the table, sat and turned to her, waiting.

She spoke quietly, "I'm going to struggle with the idea that there are things about your work that you can't tell me, and that thing about the car crash has …."

She paused, shaking her head and held him fast with her beautiful gaze. "I think you are a good, honest person, so I will try. On my side, I don't know if I can do what you're asking. First, it requires a level of self-knowledge that I probably don't possess. But it's also one of the most exciting and provocative things anyone has ever asked of me. So I'm inclined to try."

The Land of the Blind

The words appeared as if she had no control over them, "I'm going to start by saying that I am unable to untangle my feelings for you, but they are real and …" She breathed out heavily and looked up and then back to him, "… and important. But I am also absolutely shit scared, and you have to know that what you are asking would give you a power over me that I have resisted giving anyone for my whole adult life. It feels like I am cutting out my heart and placing it in your hands. You have to know that if you are careless with me, it will do damage, real, proper, serious damage." She paused, "So, in summary, I'm in, but if you fuck with me, I'll probably kill you."

Callum had not planned any of this and had no idea what her response would be. He realised he had been holding his breath as she spoke and he slowly let it out. Why had he made that promise to her? It felt spontaneous but he sensed a deeper connection to the total deceit he was living in the rest of his life, lying to almost everyone all the time. He desperately needed something honest and wanted this unbelievably fabulous woman; he wanted Grace. She had not smiled as she delivered the last line, and the piercing intent in her voice had an edge which made him believe she might be capable of killing him.

His intoxication in the moment owed little to the alcohol. He leaned forward, fixated on her beautiful eyes until they were too close, and kissed her lightly.

They sat, fingers loosely linked, sipping their drinks, each lost in thought, unable and unwilling to say anything more. She turned to look at him several times as if searching for something and then looked away again across the London skyline.

They had almost finished their drinks when the waiter came to tell them their table was ready. As they stood, they could feel all the eyes watching them. Callum wondered what they saw. Objectively, they watched a tall, tanned, handsome, well-dressed man following a slim, athletic, black woman, only an inch or two shorter than him, in her bright summer dress, long bare legs and sandals. They saw a couple move easily, almost gracefully, between the chairs. Heads turned towards them in the restaurant too and from somewhere drifted the words, 'attractive couple'. Callum spoke quietly to the waiter, who walked quickly back to the bar, leaving them facing one other in the centre of the restaurant a short distance apart. The people watching them ceased to exist. For a moment, it was just the two of them, wrapped in their mutual intoxication, oblivious to everything else.

The waiter returned, "If you'd follow me please, Sir, Madam."

They walked through the brasserie and into the restaurant across from the bar.

"There's no way we could talk in there," Callum said as they were led to a quiet table in the far corner of the restaurant. "No view, I'm afraid," Callum said, "but on the plus side, no one will be able to hear you threaten to kill me."

They sat, and a waitress brought menus and water while Grace fiddled with her napkin. Callum wondered how one started a conversation after what they had just said to each other. Would each word that they now spoke have to be considered as if written in stone?

"Ok, she said, there's something I'm going to tell you now which you need to understand because it's created my behaviour towards men. I can see that you already understand this at some level. You know my friend Cyn, Cynthia, the waitress at the Windmill."

"Of course. Funny; I remember thinking you called her sin, as in original …"

"I've never spoken to you about this, but she's important to me."

"Did you see me arrive at the pub that first time? When you kissed her?" He asked.

"Ha, No. You saw us kiss?"

"I assumed it was for my benefit."

"Oh, really, well, don't start getting above your station, mate. No, it was for my benefit and hers. Anyway, you might, therefore, guess we once had, well, sort of still do have a relationship. She is my closest friend and occasional lover. We tell each other everything and don't have any secrets."

Callum looked apprehensive

"Don't look so worried; it's not about my relationship with her now; it's about how we met. You know from some of the things I've told you that in the past, I had issues with sex and my behaviour. I went through a period of being extremely promiscuous and sometimes with men who mistreated me. The usual shit, looking for what I thought I deserved, low self-esteem, blah, blah, blah. Anyway, I met Cyn in A&E after some shit-bag wanker broke my jaw. One of her piercings had got infected, and she was …."

"A man broke your jaw? How." Callum was horrified.

"Punched me unconscious and then had sex with me, well, had sex using me while I was out."

"Oh my god." was all Callum could offer, open-mouthed.

She brushed this horror away as if it were nothing, "Anyway, Cyn rescued me, and she's gay, and at the time, I had never even considered that I might be attracted to women. It had just never occurred to me. But, seems I am, sometimes. We became friends, and one day, she kissed me, and where I was expecting to feel nothing or maybe worse, I was instantly aroused. I then discovered how much nicer sex was with someone who likes you rather than views you as a cunt on legs."

Callum closed his eyes and made a noise, "You don't have to do the profanity thing, you know, Grace."

"It's for my benefit, Cal, not yours. I need it not to be sugar-coated, euphemised away. It was what it was."

He held up his hands, and she carried on, "The sex with her is irrelevant; it was the contrast between a physical relationship with someone who really cared for me and the ridiculous ones I kept subjecting myself to. In a real sense, Cyn saved me from myself and made me get help. She put me in touch with a therapist friend, who wasn't the right person, but I finally ended up seeing Louise, who probably saved my life again after Cyn had saved it before. I was a bit of a mess then, if I'm honest. You'll be pleased to know that I'm not going to go through the details of five years of therapy with you, as fascinating as that would be. You really needed to be there."

He was straight-faced, "The bloke who raped you, what did you … "

She shook her head, "I'm not going to talk about that other than to say he won't do it again."

He was too close now to have any perspective, and he could no longer see who she might be. He wondered what she had done to the man. It could have been anything from sliding him into a dark corner of her mind to sliding him into a hole in the ground.

"All you need to know is that I could see that I would be fixed one day. I say one day, ignoring the previous thousands it took to get there."

The Land of the Blind

He nodded, "I see it in the mainstream media everywhere, the effects of constant social attention to young people's appearance, but I suppose I thought that someone as attractive as you…."

"It's everyone, and I was dealing with this way before social media exaggerated it and sent it spinning out of control. No matter how objectively attractive they are, you won't find any young people, girls or boys, who 'truly believe' they are attractive and have the confidence to act it. And don't forget the racist element of this, too; it's real. I used to look in the mirror at the gangly young black woman and see dark, ugly skin. That girl had tits that were too small, her arse and thighs were too big, her mouth too wide, her lips too big, her hair too frizzy, her nose too small and pointy; you get the picture. That's not easy to undo."

"But you've done it."

"Yes, I have, but it was difficult, and sometimes I feel that steep slope close by and wonder if I could slip down it again."

"Can I help?" he asked.

She was clearly not expecting this, and he saw the emotion flit across her face, and she reached out and covered his hand with hers. She thought for a moment, "You are doing; I see how you look at me, Cal." Then she smiled, "But I also see how little perspective you have on this. Lust is the drug; boy, you are so fucked."

This was said with a gentle smile, but Callum knew it was true, and she so clearly understood the strength of her emotional hold on him. Until this evening, he had discounted the emotional hold he might have on her.

He was about to speak when she added, "And maybe reflect on how easy it is for a middle-aged white bloke to get away without any of this angst, even when he doesn't look after himself, physically, the way he should." She held his gaze until he broke it.

"Wow, that's harsh."

"You think?" She said, raising an eyebrow.

"That's …"

She smiled, "A new challenge then. Let's order."

They ordered their food and chatted. She described her diet and how poor it had been when she was competing as a sprinter, contrasting it with how top athletes now integrate good nutrition into their training, along with attention to sleep and general well-being.

They had finished their meal and were waiting for the bill when she said, "And please don't use endearing terms, like sweetie, sugar pie; I really dislike that shit."

He sat back. She clearly did not want romance in any guise, or at least she needed to see their relationship differently. She only ever talked about them having sex or fucking. He was more than happy with their current arrangement, but he also knew that they couldn't make the kind of connection they had without this, at some point, becoming more than just sex.

"What?" She asked.

"I can see the other Grace, you know." He said quietly.

She was very still. "Yes, I know."

He did not respond; he just took her hand.

"In which case, you may understand why you frighten me."

"Frighten you?"

"I've made my world safe. I've had to, and now, for the first time, I come across a deluded sap who seems to like me for exactly who I am, no more, no less, despite my attempts to hide myself. If you understand that, then you'll understand my fear."

***

169

The Land of the Blind

They descended the lift and walked hand in hand onto the embankment beneath the OXO tower. It was a clear evening, just the waning light washing pastel the western sky. A gentle breeze plucked at the water on the river. It was high tide, and water slopped against the stone embankment just meters away.

"My flat is about five, ten minutes that way," Cal said, indicating Blackfriars Bridge just east of them. "It's still early. Should we walk along past the Southbank first?"

They walked slowly, arm in arm, saying little, each of them content to digest the events of the evening. People milled around leaning on the embankment wall, drinking, talking too loudly, some even sitting atop the stone parapet, closer to the water than they needed. They walked and talked, ending up at Westminster Bridge as the brightly lit face of Big Ben approached ten thirty. They returned slowly, stopping to kiss like teenagers on several occasions as people walked around them.

They were almost back at the OXO tower, walking beneath the trees where the embankment narrows. People had started to drift home, and the earlier crowds were gone. A few people still lingered; some had been drinking all evening, and that's when the words reached them.

What Callum heard was "… fucking gollywog." Carried on a derisive laugh.

He turned to see where the words had come from and felt Grace stiffen and pull against his arm around her waist. She stopped walking.

"Grace." Callum said quietly.

She turned to him, her face like stone. "Stay there, do not intervene!"

She firmly removed his arm and pivoted slowly towards the

river, just a few meters away, and the source of the offensive words. Reaching into her inside jacket pocket, she transferred something into her left hand without taking her eyes off the two men leaning, smoking against the stone wall.

"Did you say something?" she asked evenly, not moving.

One of the men spoke quietly to the other, "Leave it, mate, not worth the hassle." The first man ignored his companion and said loudly enough for them to hear him but not loud enough to attract the attention of the other people nearby. "You heard me, bitch." And then to Callum, "Like a bit of that, do you?" sneering at Grace.

The men were wearing 'T' shirts, both white and heavily built, short, slightly overweight, with tattoos visible on their necks and arms, probably about forty. Callum saw all this without fully registering it through the fog of adrenalin that had assailed him. His heart felt audible to whoever was near them; he could hear nothing else.

Grace started to close the gap between her and the two men, moving slowly, both hands by her side. Callum did not know what to do, rooted to the spot, commanded by her. She directed her attention at the more aggressive of the two, and when she was about three meters away, she slowly raised her left hand and held something out for them to see as she continued to close the gap between them.

"Do you know what this is?" She asked quietly.

They looked at what was in her hand. But before they could see properly, she said, "I'll tell you, in case you can't read, it's a warrant card." Her voice was tightly controlled, and she paused to let this sink in. Then, she continued, "I have this because I am a detective with the Metropolitan Police."

The Land of the Blind

"The bitch is a pig, big deal." the first man said, slurring his words slightly.

"Billy, leave it, mate", said the second man, pulling at his friend's arm.

"I'm not worried about this fucking stringy bitch." Said the first man, pulling his arm free. As he did so, Grace made a slight movement with the Warrant Card, which she was still holding just to one side of the man's eyeline. His eyes caught the movement, and he involuntarily started to turn his face. Grace leaned forward, and Callum, still rooted to the spot a few meters behind her, saw her right arm flash forwards and upwards and heard a sound somewhere between a slap and something hard, snapping. The sound was the heel of Grace's hand hitting the bridge of the man's nose. He had just enough time to register the movement and start to raise his hands, but his reactions, dulled by alcohol, were too slow.

The man crumpled to his knees, holding his face, blood gushing between his fingers. He howled in disbelief, rage and pain, and the noise made everyone nearby turn to see what was going on. They saw a slim, tall black woman with large afro hair in a patterned dress, wearing a white denim jacket. They saw her turn smoothly away from two men in 'T' shirts, one kneeling on the ground. There was blood dripping from the man's hands covering his face, and he was now screaming, "You fucking bitch, I'm going to fucking kill you." But he stayed on the ground, and the man beside him seemed unsure what to do; he just stood there, looking bewildered and shocked. The tall woman walked to a man standing nearby, took his arm and led him away along the Embankment towards the OXO tower. In a few seconds, they were gone.

Grace and Callum walked along the footway as quickly as they could, turning beneath the OXO building to the deserted area away from the river.

As soon as she was out of sight, Grace half-collapsed against the wall and was violently sick. She had one hand supporting herself against the brickwork, one holding back her dress, her feet splayed back, away from the splashing vomit. Callum had to turn away momentarily to stop himself from being sick as the smell and sound of her retching hit him. He choked it back and moved to support her, holding her waist.

"Grace, Grace, are you OK." Callum repeatedly asked but she was still retching, unable to respond.

Gradually, she regained control and wiped the vomit from her face, flinging it from her fingers, now crying.

Callum turned her around and held her against him. His racing pulse slowed, and he finally started to process what had just happened.

"Those bastards, how dare they; what's the matter with them? Why, why? I hate them." She shouted.

A couple, perhaps local residents, walked into the small square and stopped at the sight of the two people. They hesitated, unsure of what to do and then quickly walked on, looking back at the drama in progress.

Grace gradually controlled herself and wiped some of the tears away with the arm of her jacket.

"Are you OK?" Callum repeated.

She nodded, and he saw her containing the anger, suppressing it tight inside her. He suddenly felt the same anger rise in him, his concern for her replaced with outrage and a visceral sense of what it must be like to have something like this always just out of sight, a constant, silent unseen threat. An overwhelming sense of impotence swiftly replaced his anger. He had done nothing to help, and even if he had, how many other drunken, ignorant racists would she face? For a moment, he glimpsed the world where she and every other dark-skinned person must live. The emotions were too strong to process, and he just held her, desperately wanting to protect her in the full knowledge that there was absolutely nothing he could do.

They calmed themselves, standing together until Callum started to shake gently. She was familiar with a shock reaction and quickly broke free, taking his hand. "Take me home, Cal, come on, let's go." She led him through the short walkway back onto the embankment and towards Blackfriars. She didn't know where she was going but needed to move. After a few steps, Callum began to regain control and lead her towards his flat. They walked past the few people still out enjoying their evening without seeing them, barely aware of anyone else. Turning past the Globe Theatre into New Globe Walk, they were suddenly at the door of his block. Callum fumbled his keys, dropping them, before holding the fob to release the door. A minute later, taking the lift to the fifth floor, they were safe in Callum's penthouse flat.

They stood inside the door without speaking, wrapped in the sudden, safe silence. The acrid smell of vomit reached both of them at the same moment; there were flecks of food on Grace's dress and sandals, and she grimaced, surveying herself. "Sorry." She said.

"Do not say sorry, Grace," Callum said more forcibly than he intended.

"Can I shower?" she slipped her sandals off.

"Of course, here." Callum indicated a half-open door along the entrance corridor and walked to show her.

174

The Land of the Blind

"Would you wash me?" she asked.

They stood together under the deluge of warm water in the large open shower until the condensation ran. Callum did as she asked and washed her. Under the water, her mass of hair collapsed, and she seemed, at first, smaller and more vulnerable. As he ran his hands gently over her, he marvelled at how beautiful her skin was, glistening in the strong bathroom lights as the water streamed over her. The idea that anyone could use this to hate her seemed utterly ludicrous to him. He wrapped her in his arms in the large bed, his hose against her nape and held her until her breathing descended into asleep. So strong, so vulnerable; he held onto her with the desperation of a man drowning.

17.

Grace and Cynthia walked with their coffees, chatting about one of Grace's cases. She was working a week of lates, and they had both been at the sports centre in Wandsworth, Cynthia swimming and Grace in a yoga class. The weather was fine, cooling as autumn transformed the trees around them, the gusting breeze foretelling winter. They had time, so they were walking to Clapham, where Cynthia had a regular shift volunteering at the Ascension Church, close to Clapham South Tube.

Grace complained about the quantity of paperwork and how her colleagues frequently wanted her with them when they interviewed suspects. She could persuade people to be more open at a time when they were rarely predisposed to be. They sensed, in her, an empathy with their predicament and bearing the gift bestowed on all attractive people, despite the circumstance, they instinctively wanted to like her and be liked in return. She could sense when there was something unsaid, just out of sight, and steered people to reveal more than they had intended. In those moments, she had no conscious understanding of how she knew, but she always knew when they were lying, at least with the men. So her reputation for getting results had grown and despite the extra demands on her time, she quietly enjoyed the nickname they bestowed on her as their living polygraph.

"And are you still seeing that posh bloke from the pub?"

Cynthia asked a little too casually.

"Posh bloke? He's not posh. Just because he doesn't dress like a tramp."

"So that's a yes then."

"That's a yes," Grace said with a smile.

"How long have you been seeing him?"

Grace hesitated, doing the maths, "Four months."

"That has to be a world record." Cynthia said quietly, "By about three and a half months." She smiled. "About time."

Grace said nothing for a few moments, sipping her coffee thoughtfully before she asked, "Are you OK to talk about him?"

Cynthia punched her gently on the arm, and Grace smiled her gratitude.

"You're right, he's … well, he's different. He's older than the children I'd been molesting before him, I guess, so perhaps that's it, but I think there's more to it." She looked at Cynthia as if deciding how much to tell her.

"Come on, girl, you can tell me."

"I don't think I've ever been with anyone so completely and utterly besotted with me. He cannot get enough of me, and the sex is really good, I mean, given how …"

There was a pause before Cynthia asked, "Do you still find it difficult to …"

Grace looked at her and nodded, "Yes, I still have to be in control all the time, and he seems to be OK with that, I can see he likes it. But he's not like the others; it's different with him."

"Sounds like he actually gets you."

Cynthia caught Grace's slight glance, understood her need to tell her, and took her hand.

"When he comes, he holds me so tightly sometimes that I can

barely breathe. It's frightening and wonderful and …"

"Intense."

Grace nodded, "I can see how deep he's in, how much he needs me and the sex, but the rest of the time he doesn't behave like that. There's none of the needy phoning or messaging; he doesn't try to wheedle endearments out of me or test me. I'm just not used to having someone so …, so I'm just going with the flow."

"It's not as though all that sex was making you happy before." Cynthia looked up at Grace, who held her gaze for a moment and then looked forward but said nothing.

They walked on, and after a moment, Grace said, "I know, it had become a habit. I always enjoyed it in the moment; you know that's always been a bit of a thing for me, a bit addictive …"

Cynthia waited. She sensed that Grace wanted to share more: "Maybe my expectations were too low. Perhaps he's just a nice man who likes me, and I've got used to, well, you know, you've met a couple of them."

"Let's just say you didn't always choose people who would make you happy. But he certainly seems to. That must be nice for a change." Cynthia hugged Grace's arm against her.

"It's nice just to be accepted as me, rather than someone else's idea of who they want me to be."

Cynthia looked at her sideways, "You're really into this guy, aren't you?"

"I just don't have to pretend about anything."

"Sounds too good to be true. How old is he?"

Grace made a deep hum that morphed into "Older, nearly forty, maybe. There is certainly some stuff he's not telling me; he's got a bit of history, but who hasn't at his age, and his work is complicated. I had no idea, to begin with, but he has his fingers in so many pies." After a moment, Grace added, "He was married with a daughter, and they were both killed in a car crash."

Cynthia stopped walking, "Oh, how awful, poor man. When, how long ago?" Cynthia instinctively took Grace's hand.

"A while, ten years or so, I think. He got pretty upset about it that first night after the pub."

"He told you that on your first date?"

Grace looked at Cynthia thoughtfully. "Odd, I never really thought of it like that. It just came out." She stared off into the distance, remembering. "It was a pretty intense night all around." She was talking to herself.

They walked on with their own thoughts and were soon on Wandsworth Common.

"So, are you his first proper relationship since they died?" Cynthia asked.

"Yes. First relationship of any kind since …"

"Heavy. So what happens when he gets bored with the sex?"

"Zero chance of that; he's so deep in, he's underwater." She laughed but was immediately serious. "Who knows? There's certainly no sign of that at the moment, and you know me, I like to push a bit, keep it exciting, see what happens."

"You don't have to tell me, babe."

A little further on, Grace said, sounding almost mystified, "Last week, he almost begged me not to wear lipstick."

"Why?"

Grace looked ahead, and for a moment, Cynthia thought she would not answer. Cynthia watched her and saw a slight frown as she eventually replied.

"He said I couldn't make my lips more beautiful."

179

The Land of the Blind

Cynthia's smile lit her face, "Ooooh, shit, hon, you're in deep trouble."

Off Wandsworth Common, they found their way into the grid of roads leading towards Clapham South, and the conversation moved on to the idea of them getting away for a few days and staying somewhere outside London while the weather was still reasonable.

As they were about to part, Grace asked. "Would you like to meet him?"

"Of course," Cynthia replied instantly.

Grace left Cynthia with a hug and a long kiss outside the Ascension Church and walked along Malwood Road to loop across the common for the bus back to Wandsworth.

18.

Callum was watching the evening news alone in his flat when the phone on the sofa beside him buzzed Paul's ringtone. He answered, keeping his eyes fixed on the evening news story.

"Hi, Paul, Are you watching this?"

"Watching what?"

"The news, South America."

"No. I've just spoken to our friend, the one nearer to our time zone, and there might be a problem."

Callum took a moment to realise what Paul meant. "Worth chatting about over a beer?" he asked.

"I think so. An hour? Waterloo?"

"Fine, see you then."

Callum continued to watch the special reports, from Buenos Aires and Brasilia, showing the violent clashes with the police in both Argentina and Brazil. People were obviously being badly injured and after three days, the protests were close to riots. The cause was the collapse of the beef industries in both countries. The report showed before and after images of cattle in Argentinian pastures and feedlots; once huge herds, now just a few animals scattered across the landscape. Current estimates were that the number of head of cattle in Argentina was less than two million compared with over fifty million less than a year earlier.

It was an economic disaster for the ranchers, and despite being only a few per cent of the country's Gross Domestic Product, there was a national pride in the quality of the beef they exported around the world. The ranchers had waited for the promised vaccine, which they had been told would save their cattle; it never materialised, and their time had run out. There were calls for the government to support the whole industry as they would do in any natural disaster. The country was not wealthy and the absence of around thirty million tons of beef for export would be uncomfortable economically, but it was clear that the government would have to act. The story was the same in Brazil, where around thirteen billion dollars worth of beef and chicken, around six per cent of the whole economy, had simply disappeared. The news presenter trailed an exclusive report from China, which would be shown the following evening, about the collapse of their livestock industries, and there was a short piece from the Netherlands, where angry farmers had blocked one of the main motorways.

Callum hit the off button and turned to stare out of the window. He was directly responsible for their suffering, and it was unpleasant to watch, but his plan was working almost exactly as he and Graham believed it would. As far as he was aware, none of the world's security agencies had made any progress in finding the source of the infection. Various competing rumours had been flowing through social media for some time as to whether this was a natural virus, a form of terrorist threat to Western lifestyles or, gaining credibility, something discovered by one of the ecology groups and released to reduce meat consumption and reduce global warming. Of the many things Callum worried about, the discovery of their involvement in this livestock 'disaster' received little of his attention. He wondered momentarily whether this assessment was justified, but as quickly as the thought arrived it was displaced by what Paul had said. Poppy and the All-Seeing Eye was something that he frequently worried about.

The bar at Waterloo station is impersonal and utilitarian, frequented mainly by travellers subject to the vagaries of the train timetable. It had none of the atmosphere of a typical London pub or bar, and Callum encountered different staff on each of his irregular visits. He arrived a little after seven o'clock. Fewer than ten other people were dispersed around the large, uninspiring space, sitting alone at tables reading or flicking at mobile phones. He bought two over-priced beers at the bar and, as he was deciding which table to choose, saw Paul arrive. They settled in a corner.

"How's the family?" Callum asked.

"All well. You should come over; we don't see you nearly enough."

"Yeah, I know, busy, busy. So tell me about our friend."

Paul scanned quickly around, and lowering his voice, he replied, "She thinks she's being followed."

"That doesn't surprise me, with all the fuss about the Musike deadline, then the two more people she added to the list. It was only a question of time. She's been campaigning about these things for decades and her newspaper always leads the stories. It was inevitable. But it's irrelevant now. It's over."

"You seem surprisingly calm about it," Paul observed.

Callum shrugged, "Not calm exactly, but there's a lot of distance between us."

"But who do you think might be following her?"

Callum shook his head, "Hard to say, one of the security agencies, or maybe more than one if they are collaborating. I would guess the South African State Security Agency, in which case China might be involved."

The Land of the Blind

"They can't have any real evidence against her, can they?" Paul asked.

"No. They will probably just arrest her, interrogate her and let her go. She's always known this could happen and knows she's playing with fire, but she has a profile over there, which I imagine will keep her safe."

Paul clearly had more to say and leaned in, "It might be over as far as we're concerned, but have you seen social media?"

"No, and I'm not giving it any more attention."

"Well," Paul responded, "I check most days, and the site is still reporting millions of hits, and people believe … well, they believe what they want, of course. Some are convinced it's divine intervention, and the deaths being reported as natural causes plays to that."

"Why are you giving this any of your attention? I understand I have to let it go; we all do, and eventually, Poppy and the millions of deluded followers will, too." Callum tried to end the conversation.

Paul sat back for a moment and sipped his beer before asking, "I'm guessing you've not seen any of the reports from Equatorial Guinea?"

Callum wanted to ask but said, "No."

"You may have given up on the idea, but the people being killed every day by Teodor Kigale's regime certainly have not."

There was a long silence. Callum looked at Paul for a moment and then away, registering, all too easily, the implicit suggestion and wondering whether Paul could be considering this.

"You think I should deal with Teodor Kigale?" Callum asked quietly.

Paul's face was grim, jaw tight, and then he blew out his cheeks,

"It's an option, and given how many people are dying …"

"Unless we stop them now it will never end." Callum completed the thought, without conviction.

"I know it's dangerous, Callum, but you just said there's no way for them to get from Poppy to us."

Callum shook his head. "There are already four people out there dead through our virus technology. Someone may have blood samples and may be able to trace the virus. If we did kill Kigale, given how well this has all been trailed, they will be on their guard, and someone could easily get a blood sample from him."

Despite what he thought was his implacable aversion to resuming their involvement, Callum found himself thinking aloud, "The deadline passed weeks ago now, so they may believe it's an idle threat. But even if they are wary, I don't believe they have the skills or technology to find the real cause. Plus the technology is now widespread. Hundreds of labs, probably thousands of labs, around the world, have the capability to do this. They can't investigate them all and connect it back to us."

Paul was blunt, "Really; I think they could. It's thousands, not millions. And if they do, how would your people, how would Vivien deal with it? You know she's suspicious of you as it is."

This is ridiculous; we're both arguing both sides of the argument. Callum observed. He drank a mouthful of beer, staring out across the almost empty bar. After a while, he said, "You think we have an obligation to see this through?" He held Paul's gaze.

"As do you, Callum." Paul observed, quietly, "Whatever you've been saying recently."

"You've always been so against it," Callum said.

Paul nodded grimly, "Yes, I've always thought it was a mistake, but we're past that point, aren't we? Hundreds of people are now dying for a cause we've created. I don't think you …, we can stop."

Callum knew there was a dreadful truth in Paul's argument, evidenced by the recurring guilt he continued to experience. He had given all those people the most dangerous thing of all: hope; could he really do that and now walk away? Poppy's words and the disdain dripping from them in their last conversation forced a grim smile. "Do you think it's safe to talk to her again?" he asked.

Paul equivocated, "Well, if she's being followed they will know she's communicating with someone, but she's very, very cautious."

"They could certainly eavesdrop on her side if they can get physically close enough, and they might get to the phone before she can dispose of it." Callum mused.

"They still won't know who we are and, encrypted over VPN, even we would not be able to find us."

"You're getting to be a proper secret agent," Callum said.

"This is not my idea of fun, Callum." Paul shot back, "It's not just a game."

"Sorry. I know. With everything that's going on, I have to sort of distance myself from reality. Otherwise, it all gets a bit much."

"I can imagine." Paul replied, "I don't mean to criticise; I want to do something, but I'm just concerned that this will …. Well, you know."

"Yes, I know." Callum replied quietly." And sipped his beer, staring off into space.

The idea arrived in an instant. One moment, it did not exist, and then it did, conjured from the ether. He examined it for a moment. Paul could see something happening and was watching, waiting.

"So, here's an idea. What if we get ahead of this, what if the All-Seeing Eye lets everyone know that the security services are now investigating the deaths?"

Paul looked puzzled, "Why would we do that?"

"Make it visible, ask the millions of people who visit the site to vote for continuing or stopping."

"Citizens' democracy." Paul drank from his glass and sat back, "Now that's an interesting idea."

"It would have no legal standing, obviously, but if enough people voted, then whatever the outcome the All-Seeing Eye would follow it. At least then, we're not judge, jury and executioner."

Paul seemed impressed despite his reservations, "Was this your plan all along?"

Callum laughed, "No, I'm nowhere near as smart as you seem to think, and don't forget the All-Seeing Eye was not even our idea. We have our friend to thank for that."

"The question is, will our friend go along with the idea?" Paul asked and immediately answered, "As if she had any choice."

"Set it up, make the call, see what she thinks about the idea of a global Citizens' Assembly. Your Sortition friends will be very excited about this."

19.

Yet another taxi from Heathrow, late, he wondered where she was and what she was doing.

He messaged her, and a minute later she phoned. "Hello, what are you up to?"

He smiled at the sound of her voice. "Evening, detective. You still at work or out on the town?"

"I wish. Yes, in the office. Why?"

"Nothing. Just wanted to hear your voice."

"Where are you?"

"On my way home from the airport."

There was a pause, "I'll come over when I finish. Don't wait up; I'll be late, but I'll come."

***

Callum woke in velvet darkness to the sound of the flat door being closed, gently. He always slept in pitch darkness, having fitted blackout blinds to the bedroom windows; the city was never really dark. He opened his eyes but saw only the occasional artefact of his brain creating light where there was none. The opening bedroom door drew pale light around her silhouette and silently wiped it away. He made no sound, listening to her undress, willing her to be quick, to be beside him. He visualised her movements and heard the soft whisper as she shook her hair free, followed by her bare feet on the rug receding towards the bathroom. Her nails skittered across the wall as she searched for the door frame and then the sound of the toilet seat lifting and her weight settling. Silence and then the sibilant splash of her urinating. It was outrageously intimate, and he stilled his breathing to better hear her. The toilet paper's soft staccato tear was followed by the sound of the seat being closed. He smiled to himself when she did not flush; the sound would have been too intrusive. The tap was silent but he heard the water issue gently into her hands and imagined them moving against one another. Silence and then the sound of brushed teeth, spitting and more water and the final gentle scratch of towel against skin. She tutted as some part of her caught the door frame, and then the slow tread of her feet on the hard floor, muted as she slowed, feeling in the darkness across the large rug towards the bed. He felt the lifted duvet and the cool air invading as the mattress yielded beneath her. And then she was there, fitting against his body, her strong, cool flesh against his warmth. Their arms found their way gently around each other's necks, and he felt her nipples against his chest, her pubic hair against his pelvis and thigh and her feet between his. They lay together in silence, their cheeks touching, impossibly close in the darkness. She had not showered, and the familiar musty smell of her was intense and, for some reason, calming. He had the urge to push his face under her arm, to taste her as he had on that first night. He inched back until their noses were touching, their breath shared in the blackness, and their lips met gently, and they kissed. After a moment, he had to stop, easing away from her, fighting some emotion he could not fathom, close to tears. He had no idea why. He turned his back towards her, and she wrapped her arms around him, and in no time, they were both asleep.

***

The Land of the Blind

Insistent vibration and a rectangle of light suspended in the darkness woke them.

"Oh Fuck. What time is it?" She yanked the duvet away and fumbled across the black to the floating light.

"Oh Jesus." she groaned squinting at the phone's dazzling screen.

Callum heard the sound of a man's voice

"Sorry, boss, I'm on my way. Lost track of the time. Yes, forty minutes, yes, yes, I'll see you there."

An expletive escaped before she killed the call. With the illuminated phone, she hurried across to the wall switch and flooded the room with light. She grimaced and squinted back at the bed, where Callum had raised himself on his elbows, watching through half-closed eyes.

"Time?" he asked.

"Eight fifteen, I should have been somewhere at eight and it's across town." She started pulling at the pile of clothes on the floor looking for her knickers. "You and your dark thing, I could have slept until noon."

He watched her hop on one foot, trying to hook the other into the tangled black knot of material. "Thanks for coming over last night, " he said simply.

She twisted to see him still fighting with her underwear. "You ok?"

"I'm fine. Sometimes things get a bit, you know… heavy."

"Oh, I know." She smiled at him and then "That darkness thing, that was quite intense. I'm coming back for more of that when I have time."

She focused on dressing, wearing the same clothes she had arrived in. When Callum commented on this, she stopped, slowly turned, and stared at him, daring him to continue. He held up his hands, laughing. Less than five minutes later, face and armpits washed, and teeth brushed, she blew him a kiss. The flat door slammed, and she was gone.

Callum lay back and attempted to plan his day. He had so many things that needed his attention, so much to do, and so many dangers ahead. It would be days before he saw Grace again; he needed to focus.

20.

For Grace and Callum, the rhythm of their lives had returned, but the tectonic plates of their relationship were shifting. They were both keenly aware of their new reality, slowly coming to terms with emotions neither had expected nor anticipated. As these inner foundations strengthened, their physical relationship began to change.

Kept apart by their unyielding commitments, it was more than a week until they were together again. It had been in their calendars for a while and they saw 'Much Ado About Nothing', literally on his doorstep at the Globe Theatre. Grace was late, sprinting along the embankment, dodging people to collide with him for the briefest of breathless kisses. They just managed to slide into the back of the standing area at the Globe and held hands or leaned against one another for much of the performance, their minds clamouring for what they knew was coming. It took them all of a minute to walk to his flat, and in that brief time, their mutual desire could barely be contained. Lying together, facing one another on their sides, they went in moments from a simple caress and a kiss to being deeply aroused. Grace lay beside him, her hand at the base of his spine, holding him gently against her, kissing him. She flowed onto her back and drew him on top of her and, as she did, whispered to him, "Slowly, Cal. Gently"

She had her hands on his shoulders, and whether she was

conscious of it or not, she was holding him away. For a moment this was their only physical point of contact. He held himself clear above her, his knees on the bed between her legs, his hands on either side of her. She had her eyes closed and she was trembling.

Her pulse, clearly visible in her neck, was racing, and he sensed something in her he had never witnessed. It took him a moment to realise it was fear.

As quickly as his desire had flared it ebbed, "Grace, what is it?"

She did not reply, but moved her hands around his waist and very gently drew him down. Slowly, he laid his body against hers, taught beneath him, tense and unyielding. He held the gentle contact, now from chest to pelvis, soft and warm, and they were completely still for a long moment. The only whisper of sound was her quick, shallow breath, gradually slowing. Her palms moved slowly down his back, and as they did, he felt her softening, yielding, and their combined warmth began to drive out whatever was possessing her.

With exaggerated care, as if she were fragile, he allowed all his weight to rest on her until she held him. He completely relaxed, their cheeks together, his face against the bed and she slid one hand up to his neck and held him. Her heart hammered against him. He waited as it began to slow and he could sense her returning. He began to lift his torso, but she held him and he relaxed again.

So immersed was he in the powerful tide of emotion she was being carried by he had been unaware of their bodies. Now he felt her heels across the backs of his knees and was suddenly aware of lying between her open thighs. His involuntary response was almost instantaneous despite his conscious sense that it felt inappropriate. She felt it, too, and gently released him, laying her arms straight out at each side so that she was splayed beneath him. He had no idea what to do and raised his chest to look at her. Her eyes were open, but there was no expression on her face; she was simply watching his reaction. He leaned forward and kissed her gently, the softest touch and he felt her hips tilt imperceptibly. He drew away again and lifted himself clear of her, and he felt her rise to meet him, and somehow, effortlessly, he was inside her, and her gaze dissolved.

She was completely still, almost in a trace, while he barely moved against her, his arms straight, just that deep, intimate contact. He made barely a sound as he came, but it was strong, almost overwhelming in intensity and he had to close his eyes. She barely reacted. Her mouth opened wider, and she sighed and closed her eyes as the tension dissipated outwards from her core.

After a moment, she pushed him gently down her body, and he slid his torso between her legs, his head cradled in her pelvis, arms around her thigh, one of her hands caressing his head, moving her fingers slowly through his hair. They lay like this for minutes, absorbing what had happened, and gradually, his peripheral senses returned, and he could feel her pubic hair damp against the back of his neck.

He woke in the same position sometime later. She had pulled the duvet partly across them and was awake, waiting for him. As he slid up beside her, she curled her back, and he folded himself against her, holding her tight.

"Do we need to talk about this?" He asked her quietly.

"Soon."

When he woke, she was gone, and he panicked, wondering what had happened and whether, somehow, he had hurt her, knowing that was not how it had felt. On his phone was a single heart emoji, sent at 05:48. She was online, and he typed, 'Are you OK?'

A moment later, she responded, 'I am. It's just work.'

He returned her heart emoji. Sometimes an image was so much better than words.

***

The complex mix of desire, fear, and euphoria of that night lasted days. Callum was distracted at work, almost mystified at times by what had happened. He desperately needed to talk to her, but once again, they could not be together for over a week. During that time, Callum visited two manufacturing plants on two continents and flew to meet Carlsen Olsen in Dubai.

They met in Olsen's hotel room, the first time they had seen one another for over a year.

Olsen answered the knock on his door, and Callum had to smile at the man who greeted him. Olsen had lost weight, was tanned, and was wearing an expensive silk shirt and casual trousers.

"Carlsen, you look well; your new jet-set lifestyle seems to suit you."

Olson held out his hand, smiling broadly. "Callum, how nice to see you. Yes, life is very exciting at the moment. Thank you. Come in."

There was a tray of tea and biscuits on the small table in the suite, and Olson indicated for Callum to sit. Beside the tray was an electronic device, and after a moment, Callum asked, in surprise, "Is that a bug detector?"

"Can't be too careful, old boy."

"I'm pleased to see you're taking this seriously, Carlsen, I was concerned that you might be getting complacent by now."

"Certainly not, Callum. My rooms in Shanghai and Moscow are

always bugged. I just like to know where they are and get a sense of who I'm performing for, as it were."

"Here?" Callum asked.

"Clean as a whistle. And unlikely to be observed." Olson indicated the beach and ocean way below them, the clear blue sky, artificial islands and azure water filling the unobstructed view through the tinted glass.

Olson poured them tea and talked Callum through the progress he was making with each of the research and engineering groups he was in contact with. It was clear that he was enjoying the personal attention the Russians were lavishing upon him, but his professional respect was invested in the Chinese, who were racing ahead with their development. They already had prototypes of a second-generation design, and he was fairly sure working versions of their original deployed somewhere in China. They were tight-lipped about the exact progress and would not divulge where the reactors were sited, but he showed Callum new schematics which he had worked on with their design team and which he would soon, unbeknownst to them, be sharing with the Japanese, Europeans and Russians.

They talked for several hours, and Callum left the meeting hugely encouraged by what Olson had achieved and with several photographs of a Chinese second-generation reactor under construction. He agreed to meet for dinner at an expensive restaurant Olson frequented on his regular visits. In the time available, Callum went for a swim and managed to sleep for three hours.

The dinner encounter left Callum less certain about how well Olson might fare in the long term. He was clearly far too enamoured of his playboy lifestyle. The table was for four, and when Callum arrived, Olson was chatting happily with two extremely attractive Middle Eastern women, clearly prostitutes. He talked openly about the Russian women he had met and who he knew were provided to ensure he was chaperoned day and night while there. He seemed blasé, possibly even impressed with the fact that they were filming him with the women. After dinner, Callum made his excuses and bid Olson and the two women farewell as the three of them left together for a nightclub. Callum was interested only in his hotel bed and a good night's rest.

Most of the following day was consumed in travelling back to London. He spent the evening alone in his flat planning a strategy to force into the public domain all the clandestine nuclear developments that he and Olson had fomented. He was still months away from confirmation that the Chinese reactors had been successfully deployed and were reliable, but on the grand scale of these developments, it was tantalisingly close. When he woke the following morning, disoriented, he realised, to his delight, that it was Friday and his heart lifted. He had the weekly meeting with Sania and Paul and he was seeing Grace that evening.

That afternoon, after walking home from the morning meeting at Cyber Futures, he was back at his desk, and his thoughts were chaotic. The meeting had been uneventful, business as usual on all fronts. He had felt detached from the details, and afterwards, Paul and Sania had checked separately that he was OK. The evening was still hours away, as his thoughts could not be stilled.

Whatever was happening with Grace had unbalanced him, he replayed that night endlessly. It had been so physically and emotionally powerful that he was beginning to doubt his memory, and he could not understand her reaction. Thoughts of her dominated so much of his mind, but there were so many other tiny scabs which he continued to pick at, so many ways for all of his convoluted plans to run aground. Callum could do nothing now, and when he was not tired, his rational mind downed the intrusive thoughts, but fatigue often dogged him, and then they flocked, orbiting in the gravitational well of his fear.

***

He had arranged to meet Grace at Waterloo station and, impatient to see her, arrived early. He waited on the concourse, standing beneath the central clock. He stood content, watching the mass of commuters heading towards their weekends. He saw two young men meet and embrace and kiss and walk away arm in arm. Such easy pleasure, he thought. Suddenly, she was beside him, her hand on his arm and he had not seen her. He turned and the unbelievable rush of pleasure was fabulous. She saw it instantly and they held one another.

"What do you want to eat?" He asked.

"I thought we might go to a little tapas place on The Strand, one of my friends mentioned. You can't book, but the theatre crowd will be leaving now so we should be fine."

He smiled. She always had a plan. Arm in arm, they walked without speaking through the station and joined the throng heading towards the South Bank, along and over the Hungerford footbridge.

There was a twenty-minute wait for a table, so they perched at the bar and drank large, bright goblets of gin and tonic. The barman, Phillipe, was an attractive Spanish man, and he and Callum chatted in Spanish for several minutes while Grace watched them attentively.

When he moved away to serve another customer, Grace said, "I didn't know you spoke Spanish so well; you sounded Spanish."

The Land of the Blind

"I like languages and Maria was Spanish."

"Oh god, of course, I'm sorry." She put her hand on his arm. "What other languages do you speak?"

"French, Italian and a smattering of some others. I was born in Spain, it was my first language."

She looked at him, surprised, "I thought you grew up in London. So we still have our secrets."

"Not exactly a secret, just things yet to be discovered. I left Spain when I was 10, so, yes, I did grow up in London."

Their table on the first floor was at the end of the room, in a small alcove, and they sat across from one another, shielded from the other diners. The space felt intimate, the dark, panelled wood holding them safely. Waiting for their food, Callum turned his hand, palm up on the table. It was an invitation. She had been quiet all evening, uncharacteristically so, and he wondered what she was thinking. She placed her fingers on his, and they linked them, and after looking past him for a moment, her eyes unfocused, she came back to him and began, very quietly.

"There's something I need to tell you." Her tone made him lean in, and she registered his concern, "Something I want to tell you, Cal, something you need to know."

"Ok."

"A long time ago, when I was a student in America, there was this man. He was an American Football player, what they call an 'offensive lineman'. Which means he was big; enormous actually, Six seven and built like a fucking …"

She looked up, took several breaths, and looked back down at their hands again, gathering herself before she continued.

"He was a nasty piece of work; went on to abuse his wife when he was in the NFL, but at that time, in College, nobody knew what he was like. Anyway, we ended up having a night of very non-consensual sex."

She had her eyes closed now and he covered her hand with his.

She looked up at him, tears in her eyes, and said, very quietly, "He held me down …"

Callum waited as she closed her eyes and then very quietly said, "There was a moment when I thought he might kill me."

The pain in his chest felt like a hand squeezing his heart, "Oh Grace, I'm so sorry." Tears slid down his cheeks, too, and dropped to the table as they sat in silence.

She held his gaze, "I never want to speak about this again." She said.

He nodded and she gave him a grim smile that sliced his heart. "Thank you, Cal."

21.

The weeks and months passed with a rhythm that shortened time. All of Callum's businesses continued to grow. Their aluminium batteries were being produced in factories worldwide, initially in their thousands, then millions, and now hundreds of millions each month. The company took a royalty from each one sold and reinvested it. The group was now the largest company, by annual turnover, on the planet, having passed Saudi Aramco and Walmart, with annual revenues exceeding one trillion dollars. Paul and Armando had shared a bottle of red wine one evening on a visit to Switzerland when Armando told him about this landmark. They had smiled and, by the end of the bottle, laughed at the idea that they were running the world's largest-ever company. The scale of their celebration, which also included some delicious, aged Swiss cheese, amused them further.

Callum was almost ready to begin the next phase of his wider plan. It was separate from everything else, and he had not discussed this with Armando or Sania; only Paul was aware of his work with Carlsen Olson. The Chinese Communist Party had done as he hoped they would and, out of fear that the Americans and Europeans had stolen a march on them, had poured resources into developing the modular nuclear reactors. He was expecting confirmation any day now that the reactors were operating, but all he could do was wait for Olson to send him proof.

The Land of the Blind

***

Grace was gradually allowing Callum into her social life, and the emotional barriers she had constructed were falling away. He discovered she had a surprisingly wide group of friends. He had thought all her time was spent at work, but she managed an erratic, varied social life when her job allowed.

Seeing her with others, her peers, altered his view of her again. They went to dinner at people's houses, to restaurants, birthday parties, and all of the normal social interactions that Callum had foregone for over a decade in his self-imposed exile. He was a little older than most of her friends but close enough that the difference did not matter. He always played down his work, describing himself as a technology investor in renewables, which, for most people, allowed for a brief conversation about solar panels before he quizzed them about their lives.

Grace was, without fail, the joker in the group, telling stupid jokes and scandalising them with her somewhat embellished stories about her work. She made fun of everyone, including herself, and it was clear that they adored her. Several of her female friends took him aside at various times and ensured he knew how happy she seemed to them and how nice it was for her to have a 'normal' boyfriend. Each time he heard this, the joy at her happiness was threaded with a deep-seated dread that this pleasure, this joy, could not last. Time and again, he put the negative thoughts away, happy to live in the moment and to pretend to be the 'normal' boyfriend they all saw.

One weekend, she took him to watch her train at her athletics club, Enfield and Haringey. She had jibed at him a week earlier about his less-than-athletic profile when the two of them were naked in his bathroom. He laughed it off, but the words wormed their way in. Given how little time he spent exercising, he realised the pleasure he took from her fabulously functional body could not be reciprocated. He resolved to make an effort. Watching her train made him realise how far he had to travel. She left him to jog around the track and watch the athletes go through their routines while she worked with the other sprinters. Watching her run was thrilling. She moved with such astounding elegance, and when her movement was combined with the explosive strength he had only glimpsed in their intimate physical contact, he was astonished, unable to take his eyes off her.

Her flat was too small to entertain more than one other couple, and Callum offered her his so she could entertain her friends for dinner. She had seemed strangely unenthusiastic about this idea until he probed, and she, embarrassed, revealed she could not cook. It had never occurred to him; they almost always ate out, or he cooked for them. She invited her friends, and Callum cooked for ten. He noticed how she reacted to how all her friends were impressed by her boyfriend's beautiful apartment. The joy he experienced in the simple pleasure of that evening, in having them all gathered around the kitchen island, talking loudly, music playing, and then sitting around the large dining table drinking and laughing, was profound, and she saw it clearly; as she did every emotion he experienced in her presence. The sexually aggressive, provocative woman he had first met was barely recognisable as the calm, sensual woman he spent time with now. He knew only too well what was happening to them and the dangers this posed, but the pleasure they were both taking from it was a blessing. He knew just how unusual this was and how lucky they were, and there was no way either would willingly surrender it.

22.

Jamie Jones was sitting at his desk at the BBC when the email arrived. The subject line: 'Chinese company develops first commercial travelling wave reactor'. As the BBC News technology correspondent, he regularly received updates from technology companies. The company email address this mail purported to come from was not one he knew, and there was an attachment that he was not about to open without knowing the source. He phoned the IT team and asked them to check the mail attachment for him, and while they were doing that on the mail server, he read the rest of the email text. The gist was that this unknown Chinese company, which had existed for less than five years, had taken the travelling wave model, which some American companies publicly backed, and had developed a working reactor. The device, about the size of a shipping container, was completely self-contained and, according to the email, could continuously generate about four hundred megawatts of electrical power for two decades without refuelling. This was intriguing because Jones, who was well versed in the current state of most major technologies, knew that the American companies were years away, even from a prototype. It seemed unlikely that the Chinese had successfully developed the technology so quickly and secretly. The questions piled up in his mind and multiplied when he read that they were working with a second Chinese company using their hydrolysis technology to produce hydrogen with the new power plant as an energy source. The eye-catching number that leapt at him was the cost, ninety-five cents per kilogram of hydrogen. Jones knew the numbers and knew this was not credible. The best American and European companies were reaching the two dollars per kilogram mark for compressed liquid hydrogen and aiming for the one-dollar mark with future technology enhancements and cheaper renewable energy. When the price reached that level, the consensus was that hydrogen could out-compete fossil fuels. But even the most optimistic green hydrogen advocates believed this was a decade away. Ninety-five cents, if true, would have a seismic effect on energy markets and the standing of the oil states in the world economy. He was being played somehow, but to what end, he had no idea. He needed to check the source.

Two hours later, he was more convinced than ever that this had to be a hoax. He had tentatively sounded out his extensive web of contacts. On the off chance he had something newsworthy, a scoop even, he did not want to tip off the competition, so he had been circumspect. He had confirmed that both Chinese companies existed, and they appeared to be state-owned. What the companies did, he could not determine, and no one he spoke to in the energy sector had ever heard of them, either on the research front or from a financial perspective in the energy markets. Now, he was staring at the email on the screen and at the attachment, which he was not going to open, his mind poking around for a reason why anyone would send him this. His reply to the email had bounced. Whoever had sent it was covering their tracks, creating an account and deleting it after sending the email.

His desk phone rang, and one of the IT team confirmed that the attachment contained no malware, just some images and a

The Land of the Blind

PDF document. Jones immediately opened the compressed file and extracted the contents. The images were taken inside a large factory. In one photograph, there was a complex-looking piece of machinery, taller than the men working on it and perhaps two meters wide across one side and four or five across the other. The workers, he counted twelve in one photograph, were dressed in white overalls and arrayed at various points around the device, clearly assembling it, whatever it was. They appeared to be Chinese. He did not know what they were building, but there were photographs from multiple angles, looking slightly down on the construction and the workers, but none close up. In one image, the edge of a walkway was visible at the first-floor level around the building, from where the photographs had been taken. They appeared to have been taken covertly, but there was no way to verify this. He needed someone expert in nuclear reactor design, if that's what it was, to tell him what he was looking at. He browsed through the technical document before thinking more about who to contact. It was in English, but he understood almost none of it. There were some obvious references to pumps and containment layers and a fuel feed, which plausibly could be related to nuclear energy generation, but it could have been a spaceship for all he knew.

He encrypted the archive file and sent it to someone who used to work for Rolls Royce in Derby as an engineer in their nuclear reactor division. The man had retired a few years ago, and his son sometimes played tennis with Jamie. He was happy to look at the photographs and the document to provide a more expert opinion, for the fee of a good bottle of single malt. Jones had just finished talking to him when his mobile rang. There was no caller ID, but that happened frequently to journalists.

The Land of the Blind

"Good morning, Mr Jones. Did you get my email?"

"Hello, who is this? Which email?"

"About the TWR."

It took him a moment to recognise the acronym, "Ah, yes, I did. Who am I talking to?"

"Who I am is not relevant, Mr Jones. I am just calling to try to convince you to take the contents of the email seriously. I know what you've just read seems implausible, but I can assure you it is real. This reactor, or I should say, these reactors, exist and are working at two sites in China."

"Did you take the photographs?"

"No, a colleague of mine took them on a recent visit to the facility."

"That would be a secure facility if what you are telling me is true, and I can't imagine they would let anyone take photographs. And then there's the technical document. How did you manage to get hold of that, assuming it is what you suggest?"

"You could say we are a trusted partner of the Chinese state in this enterprise. They did not want photographs taken, so these were obtained covertly, but we are trusted to visit whenever we like. The design document ultimately belongs to us, at least the intellectual property does. We gave it, or a simplified version, to the Chinese government, and it is the design of the reactor in the photographs."

The man spoke slowly and confidently and was completely convincing. Jones was momentarily at a loss for what to say, but then the obvious questions arrived: "Why would you give this technology to the Chinese Government? Can we meet?"

"Because they need this technology the most and can put the most resources behind its development. And no, we cannot meet.

You will not hear from me again at the end of this conversation."

"So why call me? What do you want from me?"

"In the little time you have had with the information so far, I assume you are already checking its veracity. When you find out it is real, you will have an interesting but serious problem. I'm certain you understand some of the ramifications of this in terms of the global energy market and its effect on all the petrostates and the large oil and petrochemical companies. The information is, shall we say, market sensitive. I have sent it to you because you work for the BBC, and I hope you still possess a moral compass. For now, you benefit by being the sole recipient of this information; a scoop, I think, is your term. Of course, it's double-edged. This information will upset many people, and in some quarters, it will inflict considerable financial damage. So you will have to tread carefully. What I can tell you is that no one else is likely to have these details for several weeks, perhaps even a month and then the Chinese will go public with it."

"They could potentially short the whole fossil fuel energy sector and make a colossal financial killing, couldn't they? Perhaps they already have." Jones observed.

"One of the conditions of us bringing this technology to them was that they would not do that. But they are the Chinese state, so they will do what they do. However, we own the intellectual property, and while they do not always play by the rules with these things, we are not without leverage."

"Was the technology stolen from someone else? How did you get this information? You don't sound like a physicist."

"What does a physicist sound like, Jamie?" there was amusement in his voice, and the man had used his first name. Jones thought he seemed too relaxed for such a portentous call.

"You sound like a businessman. One destined to be extremely rich, I would guess."

"You should stick to technology, Jamie. No, it's not stolen, and the rest of the world will soon have access to the same designs the Chinese have vigorously pursued over the last few years. They will enjoy a brief period dominating this technology, but their internal energy requirements are vast, and they will spend that grace period replacing their coal-fired power generation with this less polluting and significantly cheaper alternative. It will make them competitive globally, but the United States, Europe and others are closer on their heels than most people realise."

"And what about the Gulf states and Russia."

There was a pause before the response this time. "The Russians, too, have access to this technology, but this will create difficulties for some states. They know this change is coming, and with hindsight, they will realise that they should have acted more quickly. You're about to reveal to them that the future has just arrived, and the honest answer is that we don't know what they will do."

"We?"

"I am hardly one person orchestrating all this, Jamie. Exactly who we are is not something that you need to know or are likely to find out any time soon, but perhaps one day, we can sit in a bar and have a beer and chat about this conversation. Until then, you have, let's say, three weeks to get this out there with as little collateral damage as you can. Good luck."

The call was disconnected.

Jamie briefly looked at the phone screen as if to reassure himself that the call had happened. His head was swimming, and he was on his feet as if to go somewhere, but he had no idea where.

The Land of the Blind

He slipped the phone into his trousers, pocketing both hands to stop them fidgeting. He needed time to think, so he did what he always did and set off for the BBC restaurant to get coffee. Several people nodded their greeting to him as he walked and were surprised to be completely ignored by the normally affable and gregarious correspondent.

He was staring without seeing at the rolling news screens on one wall of the restaurant and occasionally drinking from the mug of coffee while already composing some of the lines he would deliver in the special report. His mobile phone vibrated in his pocket, startling him, and he fumbled for it. It was Bob Cramer, the retired Rolls Royce engineer. Jones listened to him for several minutes and, after thanking him, asked him not to talk about this with anyone until the story broke. Cramer was excited in the way that real engineers are when they find something new, and he said he was looking forward to seeing more details when Jamie published. They both had a sense that this could be a huge story.

Reassured by the call from Cramer, Jones was again staring into space; why had the man contacted him? What did he gain by having the BBC break the story just before the Chinese went public? Was he and the BBC being used to tip the Chinese into going public against their will? If the man owned the intellectual property as he claimed, why not just go to other companies and consortia working on next-generation nuclear; there were not that many of them. There was much that he did not know. His effort needed to be focused on creating the most compelling narrative, and the ideas were already starting to flow; he needed his notepad.

***

Jones' next two weeks were characterised by bouts of exciting activity and frustrating lacunae waiting for others to respond. He spoke to the energy ministers of most of the top ten oil-producing nations, asking them for their comments on the idea that a sub-dollar hydrogen price was imminent. They more or less laughed at him. A couple, whom he had spoken to more often in the past and with whom he had a little rapport, conceded, off the record, that it would present serious problems when that day came, but they were all working on a ten to fifteen-year time horizon. None would engage with the idea that it was imminent and what the effect would be. He tried the oil industry analysts he knew, but they all told him the same thing. Changing tack, he approached an economist and an energy market analyst he knew, telling them he was writing a novel where this technology was being developed and about to break into the market. He wanted their ideas about what was plausible as a reaction by the top oil and gas producers. The analyst speculated, rather flippantly, that if Russia knew where the technology was being developed, they might bomb it out of existence if they could.

He persuaded the economist to meet for a few beers and a longer chat. After some prompting about the plot for his fictitious novel, the economist indulged Jones and eventually painted a more measured scenario of a market shock, good for some and bad for others. Energy in the form of liquid hydrogen, at that price, in sufficient volume, would be good for most nations, and, of course, the tree-huggers would be in seventh heaven if the hydrogen was produced from renewable energy. Their optimistic speculation was tempered by the knowledge that this was currently impossible in the face of too little renewable energy. Jones explained that the energy would come from new nuclear technology in his novel. They agreed that the effects depended greatly on who owned the new technology, how fast they could deploy it, and at what cost.

The Land of the Blind

You don't replace around a hundred billion barrels of oil a day over a long weekend, so even if that technology arrived tomorrow, scaling up would still take years. Many nations would drag their feet, of course, but there would be a new world order in energy in the end.

This conversation occurred late on a Friday evening in a pub, and in no time, the economist and Jones were on their fourth and fifth drinks, respectively. Their calculations, actually on the back of a beer mat, took much longer than they would have had both been sober. They did several internet searches for information but insisted on doing the maths long-hand, eschewing the simplicity of the calculators on their smartphones. They found that the ballpark efficiency of hydrolysis, that is, turning electricity into hydrogen, is about eighty per cent. About four-fifths of the energy you put in comes out as liquid hydrogen. So if one of Jones' fictitious new power plants could generate energy at four hundred thousand kilowatts in twenty-four hours, it could create hydrogen containing about seven thousand seven hundred kilowatt hours of energy. It was a meaningless number in isolation, but it sounded like a lot of Hydrogen. Perhaps unsurprising if you are converting four-fifths of the output of a nuclear power plant for a day. Having searched for how much energy is in a barrel of oil, they discovered that the accepted average is one thousand seven hundred kilowatt hours in each barrel. So one of these nuclear reactors would produce the equivalent of about four thousand five hundred barrels of oil daily. For some reason, this number disappointed both of them, and they tried to imagine a row of barrels from a day's nuclear energy generation. Eventually, they estimated that side by side, they would stretch nearly three kilometres, making them feel a little happier about their efforts. A beer stain on one of the mats rather sabotaged the next step of their calculation, as did their inability to get the correct number of zeros in the global number of barrels of oil produced each day. Their Wikipedia search revealed that daily global oil consumption was around one hundred million barrels, with nearly half of that production coming from the United States, Russia and Saudi Arabia. With a dry beer mat and on the third attempt, they decided that the world needed twenty-two thousand of these new nuclear reactors to replace the world's supply of crude oil with hydrogen.

At this point, the economist pointed out that this only dealt with about a third of the world's fossil fuel use because they had not considered coal and gas, so the same calculation needed to be done for these, too. More beer and more internet searches ensued.

A different way of looking at the problem revealed that the world uses about one hundred and forty thousand terawatts of fossil fuel energy every year. Although the two men worked in this space, neither had a handle on this amount of energy and how it might relate to these new small nuclear plants. Working out how much power generation you needed to produce this amount of energy in a year defeated the beer mat method, and, finally, they resorted to a calculator. They discovered this meant a constant generation of fifteen point six terra watts. In simple terms, this would require about fifty thousand new nuclear plants, all generating hydrogen twenty-four hours per day every day, for the rest of time, more or less.

Over their final pints of beer, they lamented that these devices did not exist. But what had seemed to Jamie Jones a ludicrous idea several hours earlier suddenly seemed, if not plausible, then at least possible. Sure, fifty thousand nuclear reactors was hardly a trivial matter, but after another internet search, he discovered that the world produced about two and a half thousand commercial aircraft every year. He did not imagine that a nuclear reactor was much like a large commercial passenger jet, but based on the image of the machine in the photographs and the highly complex jet engines in modern aeroplanes, it did not feel so completely different. On the train journey from London Waterloo to Surbiton, he tried but failed to find out how many jet engines were operating worldwide. He reflected on how quickly humans can make huge numbers of devices of almost unimaginable complexity when needed.

Finally, his intoxicated thoughts turned to the list of oil and coal producers. Some of them, the United States and China, for example, had the resources to do something on this scale. But for countries like Saudi Arabia and Russia, there was no way they would aggressively 'eat their own lunch', as the saying went. So, China and the US would start building these devices for internal use and become ridiculously competitive. In the case of the US, they would likely carry on selling oil and gas to the rest of the world. Jones thought the new nuclear energy world order might not look so different to the existing one. But what would happen when the public realised there might be a practical alternative to burning fossil fuel? After the short, very unsteady walk home, he collapsed noisily into bed to the severe admonishment of his wife. He eventually fell asleep, his mind swimming in numbers of barrels of oil.

He had drunk too much alcohol for a good night's sleep and woke far from refreshed to the now mild censure from his wife about his pathetic inability to control himself. He sat in bed with his eyes closed, sipping the tea he had been brought with the sound of Radio Four issuing gently into the bedroom, unheard, as he tried to imagine the scene in the Kremlin when they delivered the content of his report to the president. He was hung over, but nothing could disguise the rare, thrilling sensation of having the bones of a globally important news story to unearth.

23.

Grace was exhausted and at her wit's end. Her job was killing her, and she adored it. She had missed training for almost a month and knew she needed to reset the balance. Easier said than done. It was almost midnight, and she was at her kitchen table with a cup of tea, mechanically working her way through fish and chips.

On top of everything else, three days earlier, Cynthia discovered a young girl at the church where she volunteered. The terrified child was hiding under a tarpaulin amongst building materials and was forced out only when her hunger exceeded her terror. Sensing the girl's desperation and fearing its cause, Cynthia persuaded Grace to talk to her at the church. With the help of a translator, they ascertained that the girl's name was Elira; she was sixteen and had been trafficked from Albania. The story was horribly familiar to Grace; she knew from her colleagues about the London-based gangs that were bringing over thousands of girls like Elira, usually for prostitution. Grace had never been close to one of these investigations, but based on what the distraught girl had told them and entirely in her own time, with a combination of dogged, angry determination and good luck, she had managed to trace the girl's route to the church and to find the house and the man who had last paid for sex with her. Grace had hidden Elira in her flat for the previous three days and, earlier that afternoon, had finally persuaded her to go with one of Grace's colleagues to a shelter where she would be cared for and protected. Only an hour ago, using the pretext of a house-to-house search based on the concerns of a neighbour, Grace had been talking to the man who had raped her. She had walked away seething, powerless to do anything to make him pay for what he had done. Her anger and frustration were only now eclipsed by the weariness steadily enveloping her.

The man could claim he was unaware the girl was underage and deny he had paid for sex or that she had ever even been in his flat. It would be impossible to prove otherwise. Prostitution takes place all over London, all the time, and Grace was under no illusion about the police's ability or even motivation to prevent it. Beyond the visceral anger, she was not interested in this loathsome man; she wanted a way up the chain to those who were exploiting all these girls. She also knew that the only link between the two would be a phone call or, more likely, a secure encrypted message. People's privacy needed to be protected; she felt strongly that what people did, legally, was entirely their own business. However, that right to privacy meant the only legal way for her to pursue this further would be to arrest the man and attempt to get access to his phone. If he had a competent solicitor, she knew, she had no chance. In a perfect world, a responsible, competent and moral police force might be allowed to access a citizen's phone to determine if it contained any helpful evidence and, if not, to keep no record. No such police force exists, and few citizens trust their state to be forever honest and competent. In common with every other detective she knew, Grace had resigned herself to impotence and frustration.

Grace had always been intolerant of colleagues who were more morally flexible in how they did their jobs than she believed was reasonable. Now staring, unseeing, across her kitchen, she wondered what technology Sania and Callum had. Just having the thought frightened her. Despite all the bold moral lines she believed sketched her self-image, what if Callum could help? Bone tired, and unwilling to deceive herself any longer, she phoned him. Despite the late hour, he immediately agreed to come over, as she had known he would.

"Was that your evening meal?" Callum said, looking at the beers on the table.

"No. Fish and chips." She pointed to the loosely wrapped detritus, "Help yourself. I need to talk to you." She retrieved a beer from the fridge and passed it to him.

He sat at the table, took a mouthful, and scanned her face. "You look tired, really tired. What's going on?"

She dived straight in, "I've spent the last few days dealing with a young girl from Albania. Short version: sixteen, trafficked to the UK and forced into prostitution, a sex slave for months, somewhere in London. She escaped by chance and, desperate, goes into the food bank where Cyn works, and Cyn called me."

Callum was confused but followed her lead, "You rescued her?"

"Yes, I didn't know any of this to start with, but she spent a couple of nights here with me before I could work out what was happening and how to help her. Now she's at a shelter being properly looked after." Grace stopped, suddenly fighting tears. "I'm a fucking detective, I know this stuff happens. But she's a child, and the men who did this to her. I just want to fucking kill them."

She fought to control herself. "Anyway, I managed to find the flat she escaped from. She was taken there for sex, and I found it

218

and the man who raped her."

"A gang member?"

"No, a punter. Just another sack of shit excuse for a human being who paid a few quid to fuck a child."

The rage boiled off her, infecting him. He knew instantly, "And you want the gang?"

She nodded. "But we have nothing that a competent lawyer couldn't unstick, and we can't get to his phone."

"Does he know you have the girl?"

"No, I don't think so. I just did a little house-to-house asking about burglars. He and the pimp were heard shouting in the back garden after she escaped. She buried herself in a compost heap."

"Oh god, the poor kid. She must have been terrified."

"Scared witless, barely a word of English, starving. We were so lucky to find her before someone else did."

"Why are you telling me this?" he asked.

She closed her eyes briefly as though steeling herself, "The only way to get to the gang will be if the punter contacted them by phone. That's how they usually run these things. It could be the dark web, but chances are, it was just a phone call or, more likely, encrypted messaging, WhatsApp or Signal. He's just a punter to them, so I'd guess nothing sophisticated."

"And you want help accessing his phone or computer?"

She nodded. Such a small thing to step across that invisible line.

"Do you have his phone number?"

"No, just a name and his address."

"That's probably fine; unless he's a competent professional criminal, his data will be easy to find."

Grace tore off a piece of the chip wrapper and wrote down the name and address. "How long will you need?"

"Hard to say, but if he is just an ordinary bloke, then only a day or two."

She nodded, folding the paper on itself, wanting it closed, unwilling to invest any more time and emotion for now.

"Grace, I thought you were an athlete. You can't live on takeaways. You need to look after yourself if you're going to cleanse the world of evil."

She smiled half-heartedly at him, "Perhaps, but tonight, I'm going to finish this beer, and as soon as I have, I need sex and sleep."

He laughed, "Ah, the real reason you called me in the middle of the night."

She was as good as her word, and barely ten minutes later, she was asleep in his arms.

***

Six days later, Callum provided Grace with a full copy of the secure messages from the Signal communications app on the man's phone, along with a similar and much larger set of messages from a second phone, one of many used to arrange the delivery of the girls. It belonged to one of the gang members and was still being used. She had dozens of physical addresses, the linked Signal accounts, and phone numbers, but no names. Grace now had a dilemma; she had information from a gang member's phone but had obtained it illegally and could not get the phone traced without a plausible reason. To have a chance of catching and prosecuting the gang, she had to bridge the gap between her illegal data and a real-world target the MET could pursue. Callum brought her a laptop configured with the appropriate surveillance software and real-time access to the Signal accounts that Sania's team had hacked. She could effectively eavesdrop on the messages, almost in real-time and listen to the call recordings. Grace knew enough about the technology to wonder how this was possible and how Sania could access this encrypted data. That woman was smart; just thinking about her made Grace smile.

Conversations with the clients were mainly in English, and others, she assumed, were with other gang members in Albanian. Just reading some of the text messages was distressing. References to very young girls, men asking for teenagers and complaints from the gang member about the state of one of the girls and having to get a doctor for her, for which there was a surcharge. It was sickening.

She made her plan. It was far from ideal, and it would undoubtedly attract attention, but people at work knew she had become obsessed with the trafficking gangs. Elira was now a case in the system, and Grace was confident they would put her breakthrough down to perseverance and luck. She listened to the messages in every spare moment and waited for an arranged 'delivery' of one of the girls to an address in South West London. It took less than a week, and one early evening, Grace contrived to be driving in the street as the girl was delivered. She managed to get two photographs on her phone, which she claimed to have snatched to avoid being seen. They showed the young girl and her handler clearly enough to identify them as they approached the house door. The second was of the handler returning to his car. If her colleagues suspected her of anything, it was only of being too emotionally close to the case. A face and a vehicle plate were a start; where she plausibly could, she would point the investigating officers in the right direction. The police investigation would take many months to infiltrate the gang's activities, but she hoped they would catch most of them eventually.

The Land of the Blind

Based on her photographs, the MET formally opened the case against the trafficking gang, and DCI Bailey congratulated her on her good work. Grace was euphoric. She left work on time for once and ran across South London to Callum's flat. She crashed through the door, slamming it behind her so hard he thought the plaster might come off the walls. She could not stay still, literally jumping for joy, punching the air, unable to contain the energy bursting from her.

"We're going to nail those fuckers, we are. We fucking are."

She wrapped her arms around him, holding him tight, and he could feel her energy flowing into him, along with her sweat through his shirt.

He waited until she broke away, "That's what I call job satisfaction." He grimaced and pulled at his now sweaty shirt, "Thanks, by the way."

She laughed and rested her hands on her knees, still breathing deeply. As she calmed down, he saw her excitement was real but barely a veneer.

"It's the girls I keep thinking about," she said eventually. "I think we'll get the bastards, but it's going to take months and every day it goes on … It breaks your heart. I spoke to the translator earlier; she's in touch with Elira most days. That's the girl Cyn found, and she says she's doing fine in the refuge. They get a little counselling, and she's started the process of applying for asylum with the Home Office. But some of the girls there have been waiting nearly two years for a decision as to whether they can stay in the UK. It's cruel keeping them in this limbo, another form of imprisonment; they can't work, they are just stuck."

Her euphoria had evaporated, and Callum put his arms around her. They just stood for a while. "You're helping, Grace, making a difference, and that's all you can do."

She leaned away from him, thoughtful, "It's intoxicating, isn't it? The power to change things."

He smiled, "It is a bit, yes. Or at least it would be if there wasn't so much to do and so much you realise you can't fix."

"You look tired." She said, running her hands through his hair. "I hadn't noticed, sorry." She kissed him lightly. "Let me shower, and I'll make you dinner."

Grace cooked them risotto, copying one of the recipes Callum had made her recently. He sat on the stool across the worktop and pointed her in the right direction as required, and they shared a bottle of Chardonnay.

"look at me." She said, twirling the wine glass, "Turning into a posh girl, risotto and chardonnay. Fuck me sideways."

The risotto bubbled, and Grace removed the towel from her hair and dried it vigorously.

"I've been thinking"

Callum looked wary.

"You know what I was saying about the refuge and the girls waiting months or years while the Home Office dick about doing whatever it is they do?"

Callum nodded.

"Well, I thought it would be a good idea if someone set up a proper refuge with lawyers to help the girls find casual jobs, support them while they volunteer, or help them get their lives back. A charity or something."

He noticed she was suddenly nervous, her hands doing that thing they did on the rare occasions when her confidence ebbed. He made it easy for her.

"That sounds like it would be a good thing to do. You need

someone who knows their world enough to understand what's needed and someone with more money than they need."

"Don't take the piss."

"Grace, I'm not. I think you should do it and one of our companies could sponsor it. We're doing well; it wouldn't even be a drop in the ocean for us.

"Really?"

"Really."

"Wow. Thank you."

She concentrated on stirring more stock into the rice, her eyes blinking rapidly. The risotto was delicious and she seemed almost as pleased about that as she was about the idea of setting up a refuge for trafficked girls.

Lying in the dark with his arms around her in bed, listening to her steady breathing, he did what he often did and allowed her scent to fill him. He preferred her not to shower, sharpening the olfactory pleasure, a simple Pavlovian arousal that had, so far, never failed. When tired, she could sleep within minutes of an orgasm while he lay and immersed himself in the feeling of her body in his arms, the texture of her skin and the clump of wet pubic hair, which he stroked if she was sleeping deeply enough not to wake her. It was a profound, secret pleasure. Tonight, she had, impossibly, contrived to fall asleep facing him, his thigh between hers and her arm thrown across him. She would doubtless wake in a moment and move to a more comfortable position. He remained as still as he could, attempting to delay that moment.

Grace's need to control their sex life had lessened ever since that night in his flat, but it required an effort of will for her to suppress the memory of whatever that thug had done to her. Sometimes, she exercised that will, and Callum sensed that she found the gentle sex that resulted deeply pleasurable, as did he. She was a different person on those occasions, and the two versions of her were edging towards one another.

His thoughts returned to the conversation earlier when he had offered her the funds to set up the hostels. It was a pleasure to be able to help, but a small part of him worried at his inability to resist her entreaties, or did he mean manipulation? He always did her bidding and knew she recognised the extent of her power over him, although they had never discussed it. His desire for her was undimmed, and he still had no sense of the half-life of his carnal infatuation. Now lying there, luxuriating in the feel and smell of her body against his, her warm skin beneath his fingertips, he wondered how much control she really had over him.

***

The following day, sitting alone at his desk, removed from the sensory dislocation of her physical presence, he re-examined his recurring disquiet. He had no balanced perspective and no way to make an objective decision about her, but he needed to create a way to do so. After more fruitless introspection, he abandoned the train of thought and phoned Armando to talk about setting up a company to fund the refuge. For once, Armando pushed back on the administration of setting up another entity when they already had many UK businesses. He asked why not use Cyber Futures; it was a good philanthropic story. As Armando asked the question, Callum realised he had the perfect solution, staring him in the face. He immediately phoned Sania and told her about the plan to fund the refuge. When he told her that she would be working with Grace, there was silence.

"What?" he asked, and then. "When I spoke to you about her phone, you did remove that software. Didn't you?"

"Of course, but before I did, some words were triggered, which …."

He shut his eyes and shook his head, "You didn't listen to any of the …."

"No, Callum, of course, I didn't listen to any of it. The automated transcript told me what I needed to know, which was that my little plan had succeeded."

The smile, all too evident in her voice, told him she was enjoying this. "That was mean."

She laughed. "I've seen the difference she's made to you over the last months, and I know you see one another whenever you can, given how little time both of you have."

"How do you know that? Do you talk to her?"

"Of course, that's what women do when they are friends, Callum."

He did not know what to say for a moment, wondering how much of their relationship Grace had shared. Then he asked, "Were you aware of her idea about the refuge for the trafficked girls?"

"No, she never talks to me about her work."

"And did she say anything else about that hack, ever?" Even he thought he sounded hesitant.

"Where are you going with this, Callum? No, she has never mentioned it."

There was silence, and Callum knew he was being paranoid.

"Do we need to talk?" She asked.

"No, we're good. Just give Grace whatever she needs for the refuge project. It's just…. We gave her the software she needed to break that case, and she's too smart not to wonder how we did it, so tread carefully."

24.

Callum had to deal with the new reality of Sania working with Grace on her refuge project. Knowing the two women were friends—and much better friends than he had realised—pleased him more than he could explain, but he sensed danger, too. He asked Sania how much they should tell Grace about their technology.

"No, Callum. I assume you mean encryption?"

He nodded.

"She's a Police Detective. Have you lost your mind?"

He looked at her steadily before answering as truthfully as he could, "Yes, a little."

She was watching him closely "Of course, I can't believe I missed this. You're completely besotted with her, aren't you?" She sat back and might as well have added, 'you pathetic man.'

She was shaking her head, "This is my fault. I should never have hooked you two up. What was I thinking?"

"I've never asked you about that; what were you thinking?"

She stared at him and he could not tell which of them she was more annoyed with. "Do you remember how miserable you were, Callum?"

He looked at her with a frown.

"Seriously?" She said.

"He looked away. "I suppose so, yes."

"So personally, it was a smart thing to do; I could see from that first chance meeting here how you looked at her. It was so blindingly, searingly, beautifully obvious."

He looked at her in astonishment and blushed.

But she was shaking her head, "What was I thinking? I love Grace, but she's a dangerous witch, and I mean that as the highest compliment. She can make people do almost anything when she puts her mind to it, and she has completely done a number on you."

He was a spectator at his own trial for emotional incompetence and knew he would be found guilty.

She was thinking fast, "Why tell her? How can you even be considering it? For one thing, it puts her in an impossible position and …, oh, of course! How have I not seen this? It's so obvious; I just didn't recognise it until now." Sania was shaking her head, eyes closed for a moment. "She's almost as besotted with you as you are with her."

She opened her eyes and sat forward. "This is such a dangerous game, Callum; we could all so easily end up behind bars."

He watched the thoughts fly and her eyes moving and had no answers.

"And what happens when you both come to your senses? When you stop thinking with your dick."

He had never heard Sania use anything approaching foul language; she was angry.

"That's when I end up in jail for the rest of my life."

Then he understood. He had completely forgotten her brush with the law and incarceration when she was just a teenager. "No, Sania, absolutely not. I won't let that happen; whatever else happens, I'll go to jail, not you. I promise I'll never, never let that happen."

He knew she liked and trusted him and desperately hoped this would persuade her to listen now. "She won't turn us in, Sania. I'd bet my life on it; I will bet my life on it," he said quietly.

She was calming down, watching him, her dark eyes no longer blazing. "How can you be so sure? Her infatuation won't last forever, you know." There was a long silence before she asked quietly, "Are we in any danger?"

There was another long silence. Are you buying her off with this refuge thing?" she asked.

Callum frowned, but it fit the evidence, and after a moment, he gave a hollow laugh. "That's not how I thought about it, no. But I can see how it might look. No, Sania, it's not a bribe to keep her quiet. But I do have a problem saying no to her; I know that."

"You and everyone else, Callum."

The others would arrive soon for the weekly progress meeting, and Callum asked, "Are we OK, Sania?"

"I'm not sure. I think so, but …"

The connecting door swung open, and Paul walked through and saw them in her office.

"Morning." He called cheerily, heading for the conference room.

***

Callum messaged Grace and asked what she was doing later. She was having drinks and something to eat with work colleagues but would come over afterwards.

Grace tasted of wine. She was not drunk, just a little mellow, reflective. They sat on stools at the kitchen worktop and drank tea, and when Callum started to talk to her about the refuge project and Sania, Grace stood and moved between his knees and hushed him with a finger against his lips.

"Not now, tell me later."

They both knew that their relationship had shifted, but it suited each of them to avoid explicitly acknowledging the depth of the change. Their busy lives continued to preclude anything other than sporadic evenings together and the occasional weekend. Frustratingly rationed, their mutual desire usually held centre stage, except that recently, it had been very much more than desire assuaged through sex. Callum waited for her lead; it made life simple, and she was never ambiguous. Tonight, it was the new Grace again. They lay on their sides kissing and touching one another, but her mood and movements had a legato feel. She ran her hand slowly along the contours of his thighs and back and pulled him on top of her, opening herself to him. It was slow, quiet, and beautiful, and they watched one another throughout. She held him against her, nails gently insistent as he came, and she orgasmed immediately afterwards, waiting for him. As so often, her pleasure was physically powerful but she held it within, making no sound, simply losing herself, eyes glazed, totally immersed. Afterwards, he saw a tear escape her eye and slide across her cheekbone.

"Are you OK?" He asked.

She managed a trembling, brittle smile, nodded, and closed her eyes but did not speak. A little later, she slid away to go to the bathroom but was gone for too long. He walked to the door and could hear her breathing.

"Grace, what's going on? Can I come in?"

She was sitting on the toilet, eyes wide, silent tears sliding down her expressionless face.

"Oh, Grace, what's the matter? Come and talk to me; come

back to bed."

He led her to the bed and curled around her, and she asked him to turn out the light.

"Talk to me, Grace."

She said nothing for several minutes.

"I'm sorry, Cal, I'm being stupid."

He could barely hear her. "Oh, I doubt that, Grace. Whatever this is, it's not stupidity."

She pulled in a deep, shuddering breath, and he was suddenly aware of her size, physical presence, and strength in his arms, so at odds with this unaccustomed vulnerability. His hands soaked in the warmth of her skin, their bodies pressed together.

"That wasn't just sex, was it Callum? Like that time in your flat, the first time I …"

There was a long silence before he could trust himself to reply. "No, Grace, that was something else." His heart was beating against her back. "What changed?" He asked.

She was almost inaudible, "I know you're lying to me, Cal. I don't know what about, but I know. The accident that killed Maria and Rachel and whatever you and Sania are involved in. I know that usually, I would have walked away by now. I can't live with people lying to me. She was struggling to hold back the tears again, dragging in broken breaths.

Eventually, she said. "You can call it what you like, Cal, but I know exactly what this is, and I want it so desperately to be true, and I'm frightened. It makes me feel vulnerable and pathetic."

"You think I don't feel it?" he asked, almost in a whisper.

She turned, and they interlocked their legs and held one another tightly. After a moment, they kissed, and her lips were like velvet, and his tears were so close.

The Land of the Blind

They were both breathing to calm themselves, clutching one another cheek to cheek. It was exhausting, and eventually, they eased apart, the tips of their noses touching.

"I know about loss, Grace …."

He had to stop again, breathing to regain control in the darkness. "I know about loss, Grace, and it's unbearable. I've never said this to anyone, but I won't leave you, I promise."

He could barely hear her, "Oh, Cal, you can't say that. I know there's another world you are involved in, and it's that world taking you, I fear, not you leaving. I know how this always ends."

"No, you don't, Grace; nobody knows how this ends."

He could feel her fighting the tears. After a vast silence, Callum said, "I think you already know, Grace, but I'm going to tell you anyway. This, what we have, is the most beautiful, rare gift. It's serendipity, time and place, and circumstance. We have to live in the moment and accept these pleasures: Clapham Common, that first night, discovering someone new and fabulous. That time in my flat when you first … and, … " He was fighting to control his breathing, "… and tonight and the many days and nights we've had and the many I hope will follow. Whatever happens next, these things are part of us; they can never be taken away. These moments, these memories, are jewels strung on the necklace of time."

She was crying again, but now she was calm and quiet. They fell asleep, the deep, dreamless sleep that follows profound emotion.

25.

Callum did not ignore the final hair sample that Poppy somehow managed to acquire and send him. The DNA profile matched the previous two, and her newspaper articles and photographs confirmed she had been in the exact location as Musike on all three occasions; she had fulfilled her side of the bargain. Callum ran the software to find unique strands from within Musike's DNA and selected the longest usable one to include as part of the viral DNA he needed. The company he used to synthesise the sequence provided frequent plasmid DNA preparation for Genetic Futures. He sent them the request from a Genetic Futures email account, ostensibly for a small pre-trial experimental viral sample. It was a run-of-the-mill request, and the DNA sequence he requested triggered no alarms in the global GenBank repository of pathogens. A week later, he had the small flasks of innocuous clear liquid delivered to a courier in Yaoundé, the Cameroon capital. Poppy simplified the hardest part of the process, which was finding, anonymously, the people in the target's city who could spread the virus. Callum did not know how she was doing this, but she had contacts in the countries where these men ruled, and she provided him with the details of a small pharmacy in Yaoundé that, if well-paid, would accept and safely store the viral samples. It took her another two weeks to identify someone who claimed they could access Musike. More money was required, and Callum had

Armando send half of it to the account she gave him, the second half to follow the successful delivery of the virus. It was easy to verify.

Roger Musike's death finally changed how people across the world viewed the All-Seeing Eye. Poppy, all too easily linked to the site because of her history and the way her newspaper constantly reported its activity, was immediately arrested again, by the South African Security services. They held her this time for four days, but the paper's lawyers established, once again, that they had no evidence linking her to the site and certainly not to this most recent death. She was released but knew that she would now be heavily surveilled and that communication with the people who were killing the dictators would be dangerous. She decided to sit tight and let things die down.

Immediately following Musike's death, the website was overwhelmed, and it crashed repeatedly. Heated debate raged worldwide as to what to do with the site and whoever was behind it. Despite no state having been identified as culpable, public opinion varied from accusations of state-sponsored murder to it representing a new model of international justice. Inevitably, many still believed that it was divine intervention, beyond the control of mere mortals. The five men who had been assassinated were overwhelmingly thought to be both evil and guilty, and this played well in people's perception of The All-Seeing Eye. The global news cycle is fickle, and without more fuel, interest soon waned. Even so, for weeks after Poppy's release, there were millions of visits to the website each day, presumably all waiting to see who would be the next high-profile individual to be targeted. Eight current or former leaders of countries had been indicted by the International Criminal Court but remained beyond the court's jurisdiction.

The Land of the Blind

There was no prospect of these men being arrested and standing trial, and people were now openly speculating as to which of them would next attract the gaze of The All-Seeing Eye.

What happened next took everyone, including Poppy, completely by surprise. She heard about it one morning as she walked across the office floor towards her desk. A colleague asked if she had seen the new site, and when she loaded it in her browser a moment later, she barely recognised it. Someone had taken control of the site and had taken things in an intriguing direction. She read the new manifesto several times to make sure she understood it, and as she was reading, one of her colleagues, a political correspondent, came and stood by her desk.

"What do you make of that?" She asked Poppy.

"I'm not sure. Do you think it is for real?"

"It's hard to tell, but whoever is behind the killings has to be taken seriously whether you agree with their methods or not. I know you do, Poppy, and as you know, I do not. But even so, this is interesting; whoever these people are, they certainly know how to get everyone's attention."

Poppy agreed, but her thoughts were already drifting to how she could contact her partners in justice as she thought of them. An hour later, Poppy logged on to her secure mail server, intending to ask for a call and was surprised to see an email already waiting for her asking for a conversation the following day. Her partners would be seeing this new site, too, of course, so perhaps it was not surprising that they wanted to talk. They would probably assume that this radical idea was her doing.

At three o'clock the following day, Poppy sat quietly in a cubicle in one of the ladies' toilets at Pretoria train station. She was waiting, her phone on silent, for the call she knew would come.

The phone lit up within a few seconds of the agreed time; it was the older-sounding man.

"Hello Poppy."

They had made it clear some time ago that they knew who she was, doubtless to ensure she understood the balance of power. "This was not me, this new idea." She began without any pleasantries.

"We know. Let's just say it's a new partner."

"So you know about this?" and then, before Paul could answer, "Did you decide to do this?"

"We did."

"It is ambitious. Do you really think it will work? Do you think people care enough?"

"We will find out, but yes, we think there's a good chance it will work. Just as importantly, we don't think the old way is sustainable. We know you were arrested again and things can only get worse if we carry on, so we have decided to deal with it ourselves. Poppy, this is partly for your safety."

She did not know what to say. It felt like they were stealing her idea, taking away her power, even though she knew the real power had always been theirs.

"Do you want me to help?" she asked after a moment.

We think it would be safer for you not to. We understand your commitment to this, and we know you have researched these men for years. So perhaps you would suggest which of the remaining indicted men we should start with. Send us an email with a list."

She considered this, it was at least something and she did not want to let go. "OK, I will do that."

There was a pause before Paul continued more quietly, "We probably won't speak again after this, Poppy, but we will not forget your dedication to justice. Without you, none of this would have happened, so if we can, we will recognise that somehow. When it is safe. OK?"

She had no choice and was close to tears, and in the end, she could not speak and disconnected the call. A moment later, she was quietly sobbing into her hands, the tears falling in her lap.

***

The following day, after the weekly meeting, Callum was in Sania's office listening to her explain what she and Paul were doing with the new All-Seeing Eye website. Unusually, Paul had not been at the meeting.

"I thought you knew all about this." Sania seemed surprised at Callum's lack of knowledge about what they had done, but after a moment's introspection, she added, "Actually, Paul never said that; I guess I just assumed."

"We talked about the idea that it could be used for something better, and I know Paul has a bee in his bonnet about this sortition thing, so I guess he ran with it," Callum explained.

Sania asked, "Don't you think getting associated with the site could be dangerous after all that's happened? Those men were killed, probably murdered. They might have deserved it, but what's in it for you and Paul? For us?"

He did not reply, was it rhetorical? He was trying to gauge how much she already knew, remembering that she had not been involved in any of their original conversations about Poppy. Now it seemed that Paul had rather casually included her.

She abandoned the question and typed the domain name into her browser to display the main page for him, "So the idea is to have a proposition which people will vote on, and then you give them both sides of the argument to consider. Paul is already assembling experts on both sides to do this. I haven't seen him for days; he's running around like a madman." She focused on the screen again, "I have no idea how you put together an argument to keep supporting a brutal dictator of a small African country; the devil you know, maybe, but that's not my problem."

Callum saw she was rather enamoured of the whole thing and let her carry on explaining it to him.

"We have to ensure that people engage with the material on both sides of the argument, so we ensure they watch the experts' videos and then they have to answer questions to demonstrate an understanding of what they have seen. There's all the usual Frequently Asked Questions stuff, and people can send us their own questions, which get added to FAQs. Anyone who wants to vote has to watch all the evidence and answer questions to demonstrate that they have understood it before they can vote."

"So what's to stop someone doing that lots of times and voting again and again?" Callum asked.

"Only that everyone has to register and each account can only vote once; so someone could register twice, but then they would have to watch hours of videos again and answer the questions. You can't skip through the videos, and the questions change each time, so you can't even leave it running and then try to answer the questions later because the software checks for activity on the computer or phone and will stop the video if there is none. But there's another reason why even if some people do that, it will not affect the outcome, which is the final sortition bit."

"Choosing the final voting sample from everyone who participated?" he checked.

"Yes, everyone who registers has to tell us a few basic things about themselves; gender, age, country of residence, highest education level and a few other things. So when all the responses have been made and people have voted, we create a representative sample of them for our final count. We need a statistically valid sample, so we create the biggest sample we can, which reflects the people who are eligible to vote, which I guess means everyone in the world in this case. So, we're trying to match our sample as closely as possible to the global population statistics. We can't guarantee people in every nation respond, so we have to group the nations a little, but we obviously need about half male and female, and these days, some non-binary, the right number from each age group and so on. The software creates a sample group of voters which matches these statistics. And that's it, we count the votes from that sample and display the result." Plus, we can do that multiple times if we have enough people. We can see how robust the outcome is with different random samples

"So if not enough people respond for a valid sample you don't publish a result?" Callum checked.

"Exactly."

Callum asked, "How easy would it be to link the site back to us, to Cyber Futures?"

"The domain is owned by a company that Armando set up a while back. If someone searches, they can easily find out who's hosting it, which is one of the big web hosting companies, but they won't be able to find out who ultimately owns it. We had to buy the domain from the previous owner, which was someone registered in Zambia. We offered them, I think, about ten thousand dollars, but you'd have to check with Paul or Armando; they dealt with that."

Callum shrugged, disinterested in that detail.

Sania concluded, "It's a private registration held by one of these proxy web companies so it will be almost impossible to find the company that owns the domain. And even then, knowing Armando, you won't be able to find out who owns the company."

"At the moment it's mainstream news, so I guess we'll see it coming if someone decides they want it taken down. But hard to see who would do that or what legal argument would persuade the ISP to take it down."

Sania nodded her agreement.

"That's good work, Sania. Who will maintain the site?"

"No idea, you'll have to ask Paul, it's his baby." She added as an afterthought, "He keeps coming to me for more money, I assume that's all OK."

"Yes, whatever he needs. It's not as though we can't afford it."

Three weeks later Paul's baby hit the headlines again. Ahmed Gweri, the previous head of the Libyan Internal Security Agency, who had been indicted by the ICC in 2013 for crimes against humanity, was displayed on the ASE site. Gweri was believed to be living in Cairo, but the Egyptian government denied his presence and so avoided the extradition demands on the basis that he was not within their jurisdiction. Almost every news item showed the domain name, **theallseeingeye.org,** driving millions of people to the site. When they displayed the page, they saw the proposition:

The accused, Ahmed Gweri, while head of the Libyan Internal Security Agency presided over Imprisonment, torture and other inhumane acts and the war crimes of torture, cruel treatment and outrages upon personal dignity. He should turn himself in to the ICC or face the sanction of the All-Seeing Eye.

The Land of the Blind

It was broadly a restatement of the ICC's indictment, and the site contained the evidence documents gathered by the ICC during their investigations into Gweri as well as videos presented by lawyers. There were four sets of videos, with a total duration of a little over two hours. The videos were in English but with subtitles in a growing number of languages. Paul's team had started with the next nine most popular languages, Mandarin, Hindi and down to Indonesian, but soon requests were coming in for others, and now three or four new language options were being added every day.

Attempts had been made to contact Gweri or anyone who represented him. Eventually a lawyer, while denying knowledge of Gweri's whereabouts, had been persuaded to produce a defence case in the same video format. His original video was in Arabic but again translated into the same growing list of languages as the prosecution videos. Neither lawyer was paid for their work, but the translators were. Paul suddenly had a team of twelve people working full-time on the project. They worked remotely and did not know who they were ultimately working for, but it was clear that this now had its own momentum and whatever Paul and Sania had once thought, they all believed it was only a matter of time before people found out who was behind it.

***

Lisa returned from work that evening and shouted her welcome to everyone. The children were upstairs in their bedrooms, engaged with their homework, and Paul was in the kitchen, cooking.

Before even removing her coat, she asked, "Have you seen it? You must have. It's all over the news; it's your Sortition people, isn't it?"

Paul knew immediately what she was talking about. "Yes, I've seen it, and no, it's not my Sortition people, at least not directly. We don't have the resources to do something like that."

"We've all, including three of the partners, just spent the last hour at work talking about nothing else. Well, if it's not you, you must know who it is. They are using your algorithms, or whatever you have; it says so on the site, plain as day."

"Those are public domain algorithms; we developed them along with Stanford University, and there are links to the code on our Sortition website; anyone can use them; that's the whole idea."

"So what do you think about them using this, using your name?"

"They aren't using our name; they are just crediting us as the originators of the selection algorithm so that no one can question how it's done. What did the partners say? I'm interested to hear what the legal professionals think."

"One view is that whoever is running the site is inciting violence, but the problem then is under what jurisdiction. The assassinations, if that is what they were, would be illegal in each of the countries where they took place, but given who the victims were, where the countries are and with a complete absence of hard evidence of a crime having been committed, it seems unlikely that anyone will ever be prosecuted."

Paul nodded as he pushed the spaghetti down into the boiling water, "makes sense."

"Then there's the fact that it's all based on indictments by the ICJ. These have international weight, and it's described as 'The World's Court', so the idea that citizens of the world could try someone indicted by the court in their absence is interesting. The general feeling was people sort of liked the idea, in principle, but thought there's no way to do it properly, you know, like a real jury where people listen to the evidence and make a decision based on that. It's a website, so it's just a trial by social media, which is never going to deliver real justice. But it's certainly got everyone talking. They were still at it when I left. It's like a bloody game show." She finally had her coat off and went to hang it up, calling over her shoulder, "As long as you're not involved in any of it."

**

The novelty of the proposition and the fact that for a few days it was the main news story worldwide meant that The All-Seeing Eye was everywhere on social media. As a result, more than seventeen million people registered over the first three days, and the number kept rising. The site was slow at times, but it did not crash, and Paul, Sania, and Callum watched in disbelief as the responses grew. At the end of the first week, when sufficient people had watched all of the videos, answered the questions and voted, they ran the Sortition Alliance's algorithm for the first time on the initial hundred thousand responses to see if it would generate a statistically valid sample. The software selected twelve thousand respondents in what it reported was a ninety-eight per cent fit against their demographic criteria. The system was working and it would produce several valid samples when they closed the site and ran it against all the responses. Now, they had to decide when to draw a line after which votes would no longer be accepted. They opted to allow three more days.

When the deadline passed at midnight, Coordinated Universal Time, on the tenth day, there were a little over sixty-three million people registered on the site, of whom almost seven hundred thousand had listened to all of the arguments on both sides, answered the questions to demonstrate their understanding and voted. They ran the selection software, and it generated three samples each of sixty-five thousand respondents, and they averaged and posted the results on the website at six o'clock. There were two sets of colourful bar charts, side by side. It was hard to display data for almost two hundred countries on a web page, but it worked. One set showed the breakdown of the global population in each country by gender and age group, and the second set showed the breakdown of the responses across the same countries. Side-by-side, the charts looked almost identical; it was obvious that they closely represent the world population based on these simple criteria. Above the charts, the site repeated the proposition and then stated:

The proposition is passed as follows: 86.2% in Favour, 13.7% Against, 0.1% Abstained.

The result was perfectly timed for the morning news round in Europe, and every outlet led with this story. The arguments were rehashed in miniature about the legitimacy of the method and the desirability of allowing citizens to decide on something as serious as this. Tellingly, many broadcasters had dropped the prefix 'uninformed' to describe the citizens who voted. They interviewed the academics who had been trying to integrate deliberative assemblies into the democratic process for decades. Until recently, these people were almost unknown except in their own field and were suddenly in high demand. Paul, Sania, and Callum slept through all of this, completely drained by the process, having only slept for a few hours in days.

Callum woke early-afternoon and switched on the BBC news

channel as he made himself a cup of tea while watching the scrolling headline:

'Ahmed Gweri hands himself in to the ICC following global citizens Jury Verdict.'

He phoned Paul, but the mobile rang out. He phoned Sania with the same result.

Sitting with his tea, he waited for the story to come around again and learned that Gweri had handed himself in to the Egyptian authorities, who claimed to have been unaware that he was living in Cairo. There was footage of a bearded, haggard, slightly stooped man. He was unrecognisable as the hard-faced military man pictured less than a decade earlier that had accompanied the story until now.

Half an hour later, the news was being repeated almost verbatim when Callum's phone rang.

"Have you seen the news?" Paul asked, almost shouting down the phone in excitement. "He's handed himself in."

Callum could not suppress a grin, "You did it, Paul."

There was a cheer from the other end of the phone before Callum continued, a little more quietly, "I'm not sure exactly what you've done, but this is potentially huge."

"Have you spoken to Sania?" Paul asked

"No, I assume she's still asleep. I rang earlier." Callum paused and then, "Paul, about Sania, I've been meaning to ask, how much does she know about the previous incarnation of The Eye?"

Paul was about to respond when Callum said, "Let's do this face-to-face. We need to decide what to tell her."

Callum dressed and walked slowly over to Waterloo Station. They had coffee this time, sitting in the same seats in the corner of the bar as their previous meeting.

The Land of the Blind

"So what exactly does Sania know?" Callum asked wearily.

"You don't seem as pleased about all this as I thought you would," Paul observed

"I'm just tired, I think. There's a lot going on." He paused, staring without seeing out of the window at the station departure boards. "Do you remember how set against this you were at the outset?"

"Hmmm, I was, wasn't I? I'd sort of forgotten." Paul said.

"Well, hang onto those thoughts because this might seem like a big win; well, it is a seriously big win, but we can't forget this is all built on …" He lowered his voice and turned back to Paul, "… the murder of five people."

Paul considered this, "But I think something's changed here, don't you?"

Callum equivocated, "Sort of. It seems the world, for now, has decided that citizens can pass judgment on international criminals and, in doing so, sanction their murder. The big problem is that, at the moment, we are the murderers. If it was state-sanctioned, the United Nations could send in marines to make good on the verdict. But that's not likely. So if the next person on the list decides not to roll over, then what?"

Paul looked down, "And have you heard the rumours about Gweri? Terminal cancer, months to live, perhaps a year. So an ICC cell with visits from his family and the best healthcare might seem like a win for him in the circumstances."

"Really?" Callum shook his head wearily but continued, "Still, this is a big moment. When we first met back at Leith Hill, and I talked to you about politics being one thing that needed to change, well, this was not remotely what I had in mind, but I think it could be hugely helpful. The problem now is what to do next. But first,

Sania."

"Ah, yes." Paul thought back, "I presented this All-Seeing Eye thing as your idea, but at some point, she seems to have realised it was me."

"That would be when I told her it was not me," Callum said with a thin smile.

Paul rolled his eyes. " Okay, I should probably have run it past you, but I didn't have a plan after we discussed it. There was no way to keep Poppy involved, and I just sort of came to the idea over the next day or so and talked to Sania about how we could run a website on that sort of scale. I didn't think she would have done it just on my say-so, so I let her think it was your idea."

"It's not a big deal." Callum agreed, "I've had enough to deal with. But back to the question…."

"I'm pretty sure she does not remember our interest in the original All-Seeing Eye website when we were first trying to find out who was behind it; she had one of her analysts find the site owner. Her concern is that this is completely unrelated to anything they do at Cyber. I just invoked you to avoid saying anything to her to justify it. I thought she would come back to me about it, but she hasn't."

Callum thought about this, taking a mouthful of coffee. "Well, as we know, nothing evades Sania's scrutiny for long, so we need to decide how to include her and how much to tell her."

"It's not complicated, is it, Callum? You either tell her about the killings, or you don't. But if we continue, you may need to do the same again in the future, and then she will put two and two together anyway if she hasn't already done so."

"How would she react to being involved in something like that? Like This?" Callum wondered.

There was a protracted pause while Paul considered this, "Honestly, I'm not sure. She's pretty black and white with moralistic stuff, but whether she would consider this rightful justice or vigilante killings…" he shrugged.

Callum was about to say something when Paul continued, "But now we have Grace to think about, too."

"Grace? Why? She's not involved in any of this."

"I assume you know Grace is in and out of the office all the time now. None of my business, but Sania said they are working on a joint project unrelated to work, something to do with asylum seekers." He raised his eyebrows, "I didn't ask."

Callum nodded sheepishly, "Yes, it's a thing Grace got involved in …"

"Whatever. Anyway, I'm guessing you've not seen the two of them together recently; based on how often Grace is in the office at weird times, I'd be surprised if you've seen much of her at all. Anyway, they get on like … well, I don't know exactly, but they are close. Grace is constantly flirting with her, too, which Sania clearly does not know how to handle, but equally clearly, at some level, rather likes. You, of all people, know what it's like when Grace gives you the full treatment."

Callum responded with a quiet, slightly uneasy laugh. "Yes, it's …" He didn't know what it was, let alone have the words to describe it.

Paul nodded. "Anyway, you know Grace, just a heads up."

Once again, the disquiet that flowed below the surface bubbled up. The fact of his constant deceit dragged at his heart, and he remembered her crying in his arms. How long could he sustain this, and how much damage was he doing to both of them?

26.

Some news stories flare, demanding attention, but are quickly forgotten; others begin quietly and gather momentum. The BBC's Panorama program about the development of nuclear reactors in China, based on the possible theft of plans from the United States, was the latter.

A typical Panorama audience of around a million watched the BBC programme as it was broadcast, with as many watching later, on 'catch-up'. Two days later, it was the leading story in every newsroom worldwide, and billions of people were reading and hearing a version of the story. In China, their technological breakthrough was being hailed as a master stroke only possible in a managed economy where enormous resources could be brought to bear on a problem vital to all mankind. The Chinese Communist Party reacted quickly to the unplanned exposure of their new technology. They immediately pushed a narrative positioning China as the world leader in carbon-free energy, claiming that they would save the world from the worst of global warming and climate change. Simultaneously, the petrostates were portraying the technology as an existential threat to humanity; a nuclear reactor in every city across the world could only lead to disaster. They were confident that when the first nuclear explosion took place, killing millions, common sense would prevail, and reliable, safe fossil fuels would continue to drive perpetual growth in the world's economies. Meanwhile, the same countries were desperately trying to acquire the technology themselves.

Russia was strangely quiet. The Kremlin released a bland statement recognising the Chinese achievement while intimating that Russia was on the cusp of a similar announcement. Externally, the United States condemned the Chinese government for stealing technology, and they attempted to corral the European Union and the United Kingdom into a similar stance until it became apparent that Europe had their own well-advanced design in development. Internally, the US government was apoplectic. Diplomats, scientists, their security services and their military reached across the world looking for answers and for someone to blame for being blindsided so successfully and dramatically by the Chinese.

At this early stage of the media frenzy, little attention was being paid to some of the less headline-grabbing parts of the Panorama report and the accompanying material published by Jamie Jones, the journalist at the centre of the story.

Jones had been conducting almost non-stop interviews for nearly thirty-six hours and was completely exhausted. He had managed only a few hours of sleep and became increasingly irritable. He finally snapped during a news briefing with NBC in the United States, where he threw a mild, very British fit. You cannot swear on American television, so when Jones, on a live prime-time news show, stopped the questioner and said, "Is nobody fucking listening to me?" he finally got the attention he was looking for.

"Stop blaming the Chinese for this; it is not their technology. They were deceived into believing it was stolen from the United States to guarantee its credibility and to ensure they took it seriously. Whoever did this, it worked brilliantly. The CCP has spent hundreds of billions of dollars on this technology over the last five years and has developed working reactors that could finally give us a chance to mitigate the worst effects of climate change. That's the real story."

The interviewer was about to ask another question when Jones ploughed on, "The Russians have the technology, the Europeans have it, and the Japanese have it. Everyone except the US has it, and I have the original schematics that were leaked to everyone, except you guys. Someone has played everyone, apparently, for the greater good. So governments, particularly yours, need to stop this pathetic squabbling and start catching up with the Chinese unless they want the CCP to run the world."

The clip went viral; a day later, half the world had seen or heard it, and that was when people started looking closely at Green Futures. Jones linked Green Futures' behaviour over the past years with the scheme to develop the nuclear technology. While he mentioned other companies that could have been involved, he identified Green Futures as possibly the company that was trying single-handedly to save the world from global warming. Now, everyone was asking what was in it for them. If this was true, why give away such powerful technology? Their various joint ventures in the renewable sector were spot-lit, and suddenly, people were simultaneously praising them while speculating that their plan might be to take over the world. A journalist obtained a list of the salaries for the senior management at Renewable Futures, and the press was surprised to see how modest they were. In an unprecedented step, Lorraine King, the group's CEO, did an interview with the BBC where she revealed that her annual salary was around half a million pounds, a little under six hundred thousand dollars. This, she agreed, was a lot of money. For

The Land of the Blind

context, the news anchor pointed out that the group of which she was CEO was currently forecast to be worth more than double the world's second most valuable company, and their CEO had taken over two hundred million dollars in salary and bonus the previous year. Given what she did, did she not think she was worth more than six hundred thousand dollars?

The clip of her response quickly eclipsed Jamie Jones'. "No one is worth more than half a million pounds per year. How arrogant would I have to be to think I was the only person who could do this job? There are millions of people out there who could do it. Some better, some not so well, I'd guess. Over the last decades, corporate and personal greed has blinded us to what's important and has led us to where we are today. Green Futures invests in people and technologies that we believe will make the world safer and more sustainable for everyone; we aim to be part of the solution, not part of the problem."

The social media clip of this segment finished with a still of the news anchor staring directly at the camera, a look of awkward surprise on his face. A caption beneath showing his annual salary at a little over three-quarters of a million pounds.

Politicians on the right branded King as naïve, trotting out the usual line that you needed incentives to hire the best talent in a global marketplace. Groups on The Left in the UK began campaigns calling for a limit on corporate salaries to half a million pounds. None of this would change the way capitalism worked, at least not in the short term, but it provided a distraction from the enquiries into the origin of the nuclear designs, which everyone continued to state had not come from them.

***

The timing of the Panorama broadcast could scarcely have

been worse for Carlsen Olson, and the river of news around the story gained another tributary when the Russians arrested him. The Kremlin statement was accompanied by a picture of a frightened-looking Olson while the commentator spoke about the theft of their nuclear plans by the British and Chinese states. It was patent nonsense like so many stories that the Kremlin promulgated when events jarred with their preferred narrative. Both China and the United Kingdom flatly denied their account, and the UK produced convincing evidence that on the contrary, Olson had been providing the Russians with technical help with their nuclear generation programme for years. Alice Robinson, the UK's Foreign Secretary, demanded Olson's immediate release, completely refuting the idea that he was a spy. She suggested the Russians were only blaming him to distract from the failure of their scientists to compete with the Chinese. Journalists across the world were now investigating their own governments' responses. It appeared that the Japanese were close behind the Chinese in their research, but they had done nothing to move the science towards production. Their long-standing fear of nuclear power apparently preventing them from acting in their own long-term interests. The Europeans were in a similar position, with arguably a better design than the Chinese. They were hamstrung by internal politics and a reluctance by many countries, foremost Germany, to embrace nuclear power. It was unclear why the United States were so far behind the others. If the unfolding narrative was to be believed, Olson had given the other nations the technology and had specifically kept it from the Americans. No one was sure why, and with Olson detained somewhere in Russia, no one knew where the original plans had come from.

A week after the story broke, the scale of the Chinese

commitment to the project became apparent. Twelve of the reactors were already supplying power in large Chinese cities and the rumour was that they would soon be producing one reactor per week from the vast plant shown in satellite images. People in the Chinese cities had been in the dark about deploying the new modular reactors so close to their homes. Some were outraged and frightened; others believed it would mark the point where China became the world's leading economy. Most were more pragmatically resigned to the fact that their government would do whatever it liked anyway, and their opinion counted for nothing.

It was amongst all this fevered speculation that Renewable Futures quietly announced their recent investments in plants to develop modular reactors in India and South Africa. Both plants had been under construction for almost a year. Carefully crafted announcements at the time they were announced had allowed everyone to assume that these were extensions of the company's battery production facilities. The company announced that they were in discussions based on the European reactor design to start production in both factories and that within a year, they hoped to produce four reactors per month from each facility.

In the business world, the Future Technologies group were the new rockstars. They were being touted as the new face of capitalism and the future of responsible global business. Everyone wanted a piece of them, and Lorraine King had become the most sought-after business Leader in the world. Because she was American by birth and mixed race, she could not have been more interesting to the American audience. The fact that she was a brilliant communicator and quietly religious but refused to proselytise worked perfectly for the heavily polarised Americans. Both sides claimed her as theirs and she had spent the last week on speaking engagements and doing television interviews across the United States. At every engagement where she had been paid to speak, which was most of them, she began her talk or interview by telling the audience how much her fee had been and which local homeless charity it had been donated to. She was a sensation.

Back in London, Callum followed her progress and its portrayal on social media. He knew her husband, Mike King, having eaten dinner at their house in Lausanne on several occasions, along with their four noisy boys. She respected Callum's desire that he not be part of the narrative, unaware of why he sought anonymity. She spoke about the culture of the organisation and the need for shared values, and she praised, as truly exceptional, the leaders in each of their businesses, so that Rupert Beder at Renewable Futures, Vivien Cazinski at Genetic Futures and Sania Hussein were name-checked again and again.

Everyone loves a success story, particularly when the people who have made it are likeable and modest, so each of the three business leaders attracted huge media attention. Rupert was more than happy to receive the plaudits, and Sania strenuously attempted to hide from it, which only made the press more curious and determined. In the end, she did a few interviews with high-profile publications and then made it clear that she would not be doing any more. She did not mention Callum at any point.

Something rather different happened with Vivien Cazinski. Callum was not certain it was intentional, but he believed it was probably driven by the guilt he knew she harboured about her stellar status in the science world. Everyone believed she and her team would get a Nobel Prize sooner or later and Callum knew that he had forever poisoned this accolade for her. In several interviews, when pushed about the source of her genius, she mentioned Callum Moorcroft as the one who deserved the credit.

A rather uninteresting, middle-aged Englishman did not improve the narrative or the overall story, so most of the journalists dug a little, and when it was clear Callum was not interested in talking to them and, more importantly, seemed rather dull, they moved on. But there is always someone who sees the story from a different angle. Jamie Jones, enjoying the enormous professional kudos as the man who broke the Chinese Nuclear story, followed the ripples as they spread. He was keeping an eye on everyone involved because, in his mind, there was a gaping and infuriating hole in his story to which everyone else was paying no heed. He now thought he understood the rationale behind the complex strategy which someone had followed so carefully for many years. Olson could not have acted alone, and as the global nature of the deceit became apparent, his curiosity and irritation grew in equal measure. Something or someone was missing, and then Vivien Cazinski credited this unknown man, Callum Moorcroft.

Three days after Vivien's final interview with Al Jazeera, she phoned Callum to tell him that Jamie Jones, had just turned up unannounced at their office. Callum advised her to speak to him because avoiding him would not help. Vivien called back barely half an hour later. She said she had told him nothing, but that he was convinced Callum or someone Callum was protecting was involved in some way behind the scenes. Callum could tell that Jones had got under Vivien's skin and was sure that was intentional. Jones was an experienced journalist working for the BBC, not a hack working for a tabloid. He was headed Callum's way, and it would be interesting to see what route he took.

The Land of the Blind
27.

Shanghai Chemical Industry Thermal Power Station is situated in an industrial area southwest of the centre of Shanghai, close to the flat coastline of Hangzhou Bay. Running on natural gas, each of its two generators was capable of producing three hundred and twenty-eight megawatts of electricity. This is a tiny part of the generating capacity of the city, dwarfed by the older coal-fired power stations and some of the more modern gas-fired plants. It had been chosen as a site for one of the new Modular Nuclear Reactors because there was grid connectivity and, running on gas, the turbines could be quickly cycled and brought back online if there was a problem with the new reactor. People live and work around that industrial area, and had they known, many would have been deeply concerned about a new, relatively untested nuclear reactor being placed on their doorstep.

The reactor had run faultlessly for the best part of a year at the test facility where it was built in Shidao Bay. When the engineers and scientists were happy with what they had seen, it was loaded onto a transporter and driven under heavy security the fifteen hundred kilometres south along the coast to Shanghai. Despite the story having broken months earlier in most countries, few locals were aware of the new reactors that China was building and deploying in their cities. Those who had seen the images of their scientists building these ground-breaking reactors believed China was leading the world in fighting global warming, leaving the increasingly divided and sclerotic Western democracies in their wake. For once it was broadly true. Rumours had spread that there was at least one in Shanghai but few knew where this device might be. A huge advantage enjoyed by the Chinese Communist Party over democratic administrations is that when they want something done, it happens. Taking account of public opinion and consulting with citizens to build a consensus was not something that constrained the CCP.

The inconspicuous plant has been running perfectly for six months in its new location, guarded at all times by troops who were starting to become rather blasé about the container-sized device that they were protecting day and night. It sat, inconspicuously, looking like a small storage container, in the shadow of the gas turbine plants and their chimneys. Connected to one of the turbine halls, the energy to drive the turbine now came from the nuclear plant and not from burning gas. Otherwise it was hard to tell there was anything unusual taking place.

The explosion in the small hours of the morning shook the whole site, the gout of flame blazing into the night sky, visible for miles. Anyone watching closely would have noticed two simultaneous explosions, one at a nearby liquid petroleum gas storage tank and one directly at the nuclear reactor's site. Three guards were killed and two injured in the explosions. Europe woke to the Russia Today television channel broadcasting news of a nuclear explosion at a power plant in Shanghai. They did not have photographs, due to a media blackout enforced by the CCP, but they were reporting a massive radiation leak and thousands killed. All the other news outlets scrambled to get reporters to the scene, and as with many breaking stories, the early reports were long on opinion and short on facts.

Callum was in bed stealing a few moments of calm before the day began. The gently rising alarm was playing classical music as his lighting system mimicked a slow dawn. Light suddenly flooded around the phone, face down, on the bedside table, the bright light bleeding across the surface to catch his peripheral vision.

"Paul, Hi. What's happening?" In seconds he was out of bed, standing naked in the living room in front of the BBC news, watching the journalist tagged as 'Joy Hand - Live from Shanghai'.

"… about three miles from here, and the radiation must have travelled in another direction because our instruments are not picking up anything."

"Thanks, Joy, that's Joy Hand, our foreign correspondent there in Shanghai, where there is confusion and fear surrounding a nuclear explosion at a power plant on the southern edge of the city." Darren Davies, normally the BBC's evening news anchor, had been drafted in to deal with what appeared to be a significant global story. "We have no photographs of the scene and no reports of casualties other than the reports earlier this morning from Russia Today and Al Jazeera, but I must stress these are, as yet, unverified reports." Davies' calming tone seemed to say that this was all under control, but clearly, he knew next to nothing about what was happening in Shanghai.

An hour later, Callum was barely any wiser but had showered and dressed as the coverage repeated itself. The United States confirmed that its satellites had not picked up any radiation or signatures of a nuclear explosion. There might have been an incident at one of Shanghai's nuclear generation facilities, but it appeared to be a relatively small conventional explosion. The US satellite had, however, pinpointed the site and there were overhead pictures showing that something had happened. The images showed clear damage at two distinct explosion sites close together.

Callum phoned Paul who answered instantly.

"What do you think? How bad is it?" Paul asked.

Callum was cautious, "I don't think it's anywhere near as bad as the early reports were suggesting, but it is one of the new reactor sites they deployed a few months ago. I think they might have had an accident with one of the LPG storage tanks and perhaps that affected the new reactor." He paused, "There's no way they would let journalists anywhere near the site if there was any radioactivity, and it doesn't quite make sense, because there's nothing combustible or explosive in the new units. We know they subjected them to some serious physical testing, and short of a cruise missile strike you're not going to breach the internal containment vessel."

"So it might end up being a good thing if there's really no radioactivity?" Paul suggested. "A demonstration of how robust they are?"

"Yes, I guess; could be."

"I don't get why Russia were so vocal about this, it's starting to look like their initial assessments were way wide of the mark."

"Yes, odd?" Callum agreed. "It's possible, and I've got to say it's pretty hardcore, but do you think they could have done this?"

"What, attack a Chinese nuclear reactor?" Paul was incredulous.

"Well, they sent those men to spread a nerve agent around Salisbury, here in the UK not that long ago. They clearly believe they can do anything they like now and deny it ever happened. I mean, if you can do that …"

"But a strike on another country's nuclear power plant?" Paul was unconvinced. "That's an act of war."

"Long odds I guess. They would have to be pretty desperate to go that far out on a limb."

"Unless, of course, the reactor had been breached, and there was now radiation all over Shanghai, in which case everyone would just assume it was an accident."

"But they have the schematics," Callum countered, "more or less the same ones used to build those reactors. They would know what you have to do to cause a breach. Maybe it's not the Kremlin; maybe they are being co-opted somehow. Perhaps there's something we're all missing here."

"Okay, well, we're not going to get much sense from anyone in Shanghai for a while, so I need to get the kids off to school," Paul replied.

So, like most people seeing the news worldwide, they gave it their attention for long enough to check it wouldn't ruin their day and resumed their reassuring, quotidian routines.

Callum wanted to speak to Olson; it would have been his first call, but he was still in Russia, at least that was the working assumption. The weird thing was that no one had officially missed him. The initial Foreign Office demands for his release had come to nothing. He was estranged from his family, or at least on such distant terms that a lack of communication for months caused no alarm. Callum knew that there was a case for him feeling some guilt at Olson's predicament, but he felt none. Olson knew what he was doing and had been warned about what was coming, but for some reason, he had chosen to stay in Russia. Callum thought he knew the reason and understood the weakness; the man had made his own choices.

Callum frittered away the hours moving between the television, from which information seeped at a glacial pace, and his computer, where he dealt with a list of annoying administrative tasks that could not be delegated. He was staring at the computer screen again, his mind wandering when he recalled something his father often related about his grandfather. It was not an original thought, but it had acquired weight through its use by someone close to him, 'It's the journey that's important'. Suddenly, while far from redundant, the things he had set in motion had gained their own momentum, and he had become more passenger than driver. He wondered afresh at the mind's ability for self-deception. He had known this for months and knew it to be the cause of his seeping discontent. Why had he taken so long to acknowledge it?

He did what he often did now when he needed to think; he walked. From the flat, he followed the embankment across the Hungerford Bridge and on through Trafalgar Square. He had no destination, choosing where he went at each intersection without a plan. There were lots of people on the streets, reassuringly old streets, some traversed for millennia. People were shopping, sightseeing, a study in normality; he was just one among many. He bought a sandwich and coffee, sat on a Green Park bench, and watched the people pass. It was ridiculous, but he finally allowed the ludicrous acknowledgement that he was bored. He also knew that the one thing he craved more of was Grace. It was preposterous, he had a possible nuclear incident threatening to derail his energy strategy, there were probably several state security services investigating the source of the livestock viruses, he had as much money as anyone could ever need or want, and he was bored. It was unanticipated and utterly ridiculous. He laughed out loud at himself and then smiled at the disconcerted woman who veered across the path away from him and hurried on.

The Land of the Blind

Taking a circuitous route home, he messaged Grace to see what her plans were. He kept checking the phone every few seconds, irritating himself with his impatience. She messaged him back a few minutes later. He'd forgotten she was training tonight, going straight from work. She would be late, but she would come over later. Halfway through typing a message to say he missed her, he stopped and stared at it for a long time before deleting it.

Back at the flat, he worked through more of the dull tasks he had been putting off and, by early evening, felt the satisfaction and mild surprise at having easily finished the work he had allowed to assume the proportions of a mountain.

He set about making himself a salad and poured a beer while keeping one eye on the news coverage. Things had moved quickly in Shanghai, where the Chinese, in sharp contrast to their normal behaviour, had invited everyone to see the explosion site. There was now detailed analysis from a legion of foreign correspondents, and the recurring images were of scientists in hazmat suits with Geiger counters testing for radiation leaks. This was becoming the big story, and as Callum watched, he realised just how big. There was no radiation leak. Somehow, someone had contrived to blow up a nuclear reactor without breaching the containment which protected the core material. It was later discovered that the shaped charges intended to penetrate the many layers of the fuel containment vessel had been placed incorrectly. The external connection layout that the Chinese used had been modified late in the design process, and whoever had placed the charges had misinterpreted where the internal reactor components were in relation to the external casing. The accidental effect was to demonstrate that the design was inherently safe. The nuclear fission reaction, which drove the reactor, had died away and stopped when its power supply had been cut. Sometimes blind luck was as important as the best-laid plans.

28.

In the days that followed the bombing, the world's media descended on Shanghai, and the Chinese Communist Party put their vast resources into attempting to find out who had attacked their country. As the most surveilled state in the world, they had a trove of video footage which allowed them to scour the physical area around the power station for evidence. Almost all the relevant surveillance cameras within the power station site were blank for the duration of the attack. The attackers had systematically disabled them, but a few cameras in obscure places had not been found. At the edge of the field of view of one camera, a few frames showed a hooded commando. He or she was clad in matt black, carrying an automatic weapon, and darting between shadows; it was the only direct evidence found, but it was telling. The enlarged grainy image became the one which accompanied the news reports from that point onwards. The sequence and location in which the cameras were disabled allowed the Chinese analysts to guess at where the commandos had landed. They must have come ashore somewhere along Haiwan Avenue, eschewing the simple but too visible route along the nearby dock where raw materials were delivered to the chemical plant. They would easily have scaled the low sea wall that runs for miles along this featureless flat bay, and whatever equipment they brought with them to get to the shore, they must have taken with them when they left. The search of the area, conducted for nearly a week between each high tide, revealed nothing of interest. If, as it appeared, they had arrived from the sea, they had returned without trace.

For a few days, the trail and the story went cold until the Chinese Foreign Minister appeared on state television to accuse Russia of the attack. Such an accusation could not be made lightly, and a lack of hard evidence until this point had prevented such a definitive statement. In a completely unprecedented move, and at a significant tactical cost, the United States government had provided the Chinese with the location of a Russian submarine and its track over the crucial twenty-four-hour period around the attack. The news machine exploded. The US president gave a press conference where he talked about extraordinary circumstances, an attack upon the world order, and working with the 'Great Chinese Nation' to defeat the powers of evil. The Russians, along with everyone else, believe their nuclear submarine fleets are undetectable. World peace, in a real sense, rests on this assumption. The inability of one nation to determine where another's nuclear weapons are has played a significant, possibly decisive, role in maintaining world peace since the Second World War. It now appeared that, at least under certain circumstances, these submarines could be tracked. The Americans were also revealing that they actively monitored the Chinese coastline, but that was hardly news. The submarine had moved into Chinese waters to a point some fifty kilometres from the entrance to Hangzhou Bay, where it waited and, a few hours later, moved back out to sea. The Americans even identified which Russian submarine they believed it to be.

The incident was now being treated by much of the world as an outrageous, unprovoked attack on another nation-state, effectively an act of war. The Russians protested their innocence more loudly than ever, accusing the Chinese and Americans of colluding in a plot to destabilise the Russian State, the 'fake' track of a Russian submarine, yet another fabrication of the Western Alliance. Almost no one, including a sizeable proportion of the Russian people, seemed to believe their president, but that had no obvious effect on the occupants of the Kremlin. Taking a portion of Ukraine by force was one thing; attacking, so blatantly, a sometime ally against the West was another. Despite the public grandstanding, there was intense diplomatic activity between the Russian and Chinese governments, and those who understood these machinations knew the Chinese would exact a heavy price when it suited them.

***

Russia had inadvertently succeeded in guaranteeing the nuclear technology's success and acceptance. In doing so, many commentators argued that they were consigning Russia to the status of a bit-player on the global stage. Their humiliation in being caught, despite their ongoing, alternative narrative, was thought by many to be sufficient punishment. Then, social media caught light and people across the globe began clamouring for President Kosegin to be added to the defendants of the All-Seeing Eye; demanding he top the fugitives list.

Although completely unplanned, the All-Seeing Eye had been one strand of Callum's life that he believed was under control. Now, this illusion was shattered. When Callum saw the demands, he felt physically sick; it was not remotely what he had envisaged when they took on Poppy Xaba's simple, powerful idea. The hastily arranged meeting with Sania and Paul had been brief. Callum argued strongly that without the protection and legitimacy of an indictment by the United Nations through the International Criminal Court, the All-Seeing Eye was little more than a modern vigilante group. They disagreed and felt that it was a powerful way to demonstrate that citizen of the world wanted their leaders to act for the greater good, providing a way to censure them if they did not. In the end, Callum lost the argument. His only stipulation was that for the result to seem credible, Russian citizens had to convict their own President with a strong majority in addition to the rest of the world doing so.

Sania and Paul had a well-tried process to follow and set about it with enthusiasm. It took a little over three weeks for the material for and against the proposition to be brought together, and having read all of it, Callum had to agree that it was even-handed. It included lengthy statements in the form of video recordings and transcripts of the Russian Foreign Minister and several Western academics about the danger of undermining the democratically elected head of a sovereign state. There was compelling evidence of the Russian state's hand in the attack, and few would be convinced by the Kremlin's assertion that they were not involved and had no idea who was behind it. As he read and listened to all of the material, it occurred to Callum that ordinary people were effectively being asked whether there should be a higher authority than the nation state. This had never been a consideration, let alone an intention in his plans. In theory, such organisations already exist, but the UN and ICC have proscribed powers, the mechanism of a veto all too easily deployed.

Callum reflected that the actions of a single determined South African woman were at the root of this. Once more, he understood how fragile his plans were, how easily a random action could resonate and undermine them. The establishment, everywhere, was resolutely set against the idea behind the All-Seeing Eye and the UN and the ICC initially refused to participate in any way. However, around the world, people registered on the site in their tens and then hundreds of millions, and it became obvious that this citizen process would take place with or without the existing global organisations' sanction. Eventually, both the UN and the ICC made submissions, but both warned that their legitimacy would be undermined by citizen interventions of this kind.

Over seven hundred million people consumed the initial content, and in the feedback process, it was clear that the argument to protect the legitimacy of the United Nations was resonating. A further submission from the UN was requested; if the organisation was effectively claiming jurisdiction over the attack, what would it do to punish the Russian government and dissuade it from acting similarly in the future? The response from the UN talked about the obligations of nations to behave in the interests of all and pointed to economic and cultural sanctions that might be brought to bear. In the face of a Russian veto, they could go no further; ultimately, their entreaties seemed toothless.

The global significance of the attack and the fact that so many people had become aware of the All-Seeing Eye following the surrender of Ahmed Gweri guaranteed that, for weeks, this was one of the top items of news across the globe. Curiously, for a brief period, even the Chinese Communist Party allowed its citizens access to the site. This bizarre democratic dispensation lasted only days before the Great Firewall of China fell decisively back into place. The site soon claimed close to eight hundred million individual users. What constituted a user was unclear, and relatively few were sufficiently engaged or had the time to follow the process. However, over half a million people devoted a minimum of four and, on average, nearly eight hours to reading and watching the arguments, demonstrating their understanding and casting a vote. The representative sample of more than forty thousand individuals, which the Sortition Alliance's software selected from over half a million responses, resulted in a vote of eighty-three per cent in favour of the proposition and seventeen per cent against. The proposition was;

President Kosegin of Russia has deliberately targeted a foreign state with the intention of causing a nuclear incident. He should surrender himself immediately to the International Court of Justice.

Paul, Sania and Callum had argued at length about the explicit threat of what would happen if Kosegin ignored the jury's verdict, as he surely would. In the end, Callum, the only person who could deliver on the threat, was resolute in his opposition, and no specific sanction was proposed. Ambiguity allowed room to decide what the censure might be, but the problem was, they only really had one sanction at their disposal, and that, to Callum at least, felt like a step too far.

Hours after the verdict was posted, Callum, Paul, and Sania met in the Cyber Futures office. Before their discussion, they watched various interviews and news reports from around the world. The global media machine was in an uproar, and people were discussing it on the streets, in restaurants and bars, everywhere. A special session of the United Nations was called to discuss the matter, and various governments, foremost Russia and China, were calling for the site to be taken down. There had been constant 'denial of service' attacks from the outset, the servers being bombarded with traffic from networks of hijacked computers around the world. But the site was widely distributed, and the software to mitigate these attacks had done its job.

The more thoughtful commentators, while almost unanimously condemning the implied threat to the Russian President's life, were astonished by how the phenomenon, being referred to simply as 'The Eye', had caught people's imagination.

While the Russian, North Korean, and Chinese states were doing whatever they could in cyberspace to shut down the site and find out who was behind it, none of the other jurisdictions that might have acted did so. It suited the United States and Europe to condemn the use of vigilante violence but to do nothing to prevent it in this instance. There was also the fact that the site was not being hosted in a single location; some of the servers were in Russia, and it was unclear whose jurisdiction it fell under.

***

Days became weeks and then a month, and it was clear to everyone that Kosegin would never take the threat seriously. African dictators in poorly resourced nations might have been assassinated, but his security and paranoia put him in a different league. Press speculation ebbed and people sensed that this was just one more case where the Russian president would somehow emerge stronger from an impossible political hole.

In London, the waiting was over. The conversation had been heated, Callum argued that assassinating the Russian president was a disproportionate response and they did not have any other option. Paul and Sania were implacable and, of course, had public opinion decisively on their side. They pointed out that Kosegin could still submit to the ICC and that over sixty per cent of the

The Land of the Blind

Russians who had used the site had voted for the proposition against their own president. Ultimately, Callum, given little choice, had accepted their decision. He was the only one who could actually make this happen; the only one with access to the technology that would produce the deadly proteins. In theory, he could defy them, but Sania had turned his own, oft-repeated aphorism about deliberative assemblies back on him, 'if you trust the process, you cannot question the outcome'. He was skewered, knowing he had no choice but unwilling to act.

That meeting had taken place three days earlier, on Friday morning, and now, as the new week was about to start, Callum lay awake watching the pale light from the street, four floors below, pucker across the ceiling. Unable to sleep, he had opened the bedroom door and blinds, the darkness, for once claustrophobic. Occasionally, the refracted light rippled above him, the coded distortion of a pedestrian or cyclist traversing the embankment. Even at four in the morning, London was not still. He had slept for an hour or two, but once awake, his brain would not submit again to the freedom of his dreams. This felt too much like a 'moment', albeit, for the first time, a decision that was not his alone; in fact, not even a decision he supported. What was now his inner circle had considered and decided to accept the will of millions of ordinary people around the world. Callum wondered how each would feel when they realised that, in a small way, they had been responsible for someone's death.

Sania had surprised him with her willingness to deliver this vengeance. Callum knew little about the Muslim faith and less about how Sania observed it. If it were anything like Christianity, there would be ample precedents to justify retribution, but whether religion informed her attitude at all, he had no idea.

The Land of the Blind

Following The Eye's verdict, Callum had argued that the Russian people would turn against Kosegin, and they did not need to act immediately. The others agreed to a pause, allowing that planning his demise was not something to be done quickly in any case. But Callum's last argument had become untenable as the days slipped by and the Kremlin dictated the Russian narrative. He could not dispute that, once again, the Russian President was openly laughing at the rest of the world, and no one was willing or able to do anything about it.

Assuming they were successful, Kosegin would die, more or less, in the same way as the others had, and in the circumstances, it was likely that there would be doctors close to him who might be able to keep him alive. Even if they failed, they would almost certainly discover how he was killed. So far, none of the other deaths had resulted in a detailed medical examination of the victims. Those who benefitted from the deaths had been happy to perpetuate the idea of divine intervention. That would not happen this time and Callum knew he was already on borrowed time with this weapon. As Arthur C Clarke pointed out, what he possessed might appear to be magic but was simply advanced technology. Eventually, others would learn how to control it.

Accepting the impossibility of sleep, he stood in the kitchen with the lights off, waiting for the kettle to boil. He always slept naked, now and often walked around naked, an indulgence he had acquired from Grace. The under-floor heating permitted the luxury of being barefoot and unclothed without discomfort. He looked along the street towards the river, standing far enough back from the large windows so that he could not be seen from the flats opposite. A slim, dark line parted one set of curtains across from him, and he imagined a slight movement in his peripheral vision;

it was absent when he looked directly. The dawn would soon begin to reflect once again from the choppy river to light London's familiar facades, and he would sit and watch the people return as they always did. Deep down, he had already made his choice, or had it made for him, so he now just needed to make his peace with that and begin his plans. He retrieved his dressing gown, sat with his laptop, and began searching for an event that the Russian President would be guaranteed to attend.

29.

The World Holocaust Forum in Jerusalem was an event that the Russian President would attend, even with the faint echoes of the Chinese Nuclear attack still reverberating. Failing to turn up might be seen as an implicit acceptance of guilt. It was scheduled to take place in a little over four months, long after The Eye's verdict would cease to be news. Significant international events such as this are always held under tight security, and, in Jerusalem, it would be tighter than ever. The event took place every year and had to be organised like any other large gathering of international leaders. A small, invisible army was required to ensure the delegates were safe and that the venue was spotlessly clean. The people who do this work, cleaning, wiping the seats and polishing surfaces, are innocuous and anonymous. They are always poorly paid, a commodity, and it is easy enough to ensure that they are not carrying weapons or planting bombs, so they represent no threat.

Dora Gini had been a cleaner at the Yad Vashem Remembrance Centre for over five years. She was known to the local businessman, Yitzhak Sabhan, because she occasionally worked privately for him. Sabhan was paid one hundred thousand dollars to give Dora Gini the small bottle of liquid to use as her final cleaning spray. He did not tell her what it was, only that it was not dangerous. If she used it for the final cleaning in the main auditorium, he would pay her one thousand dollars, and ten thousand dollars one week later. He gave her a story about smart water and tracking people, but she was not interested in the details. This was a huge sum for Dora, and while she did not know what Sabhan was up to, she had worked for him for years and knew him to be just a greedy businessman, not someone who would be involved in anything dangerous or criminal.

Callum had never met Yitzhak Sabhan and had communicated using the encrypted messaging app Signal after the initial email to tempt him. He had explained he needed the liquid he would supply, liberally spread around the main hall in the Yad Vashem remembrance centre, immediately before the Holocaust Forum. He had assured him that the liquid was harmless and not a poison. As a measure of goodwill, he would pay Sabhan one hundred thousand US dollars when he took possession of the liquid. If it were used in the centre as requested and did what Callum wanted, he would pay Sabhan another four hundred thousand dollars.

Yitzhak Sabhan made money trading goods and services all over the Middle East. He was trusted by the people he worked with and ran legitimate businesses. Despite Callum's assurances, he did not like the idea of handling this bottle of liquid, which he still believed might contain poison. Callum had told him it was smart water and that, through it, he could track the subsequent movement of the attendees as they travelled around the world. Sabhan's greed permitted his acceptance of this unlikely fabrication, and he sent Callum the account details for where the initial one hundred thousand US dollars should be deposited. He reasoned that he might decide to do nothing more, keep the money and flush the liquid down the toilet as Callum told him he could if he did not want the other four hundred thousand dollars. Callum gambled that he might get nothing for his initial payment, but after researching Sabhan as much as he could, he believed there was a good chance the liquid would be delivered to the auditorium.

Callum buzzed the courier in at the front door of Shaw House on Chesterfield Street and waited for him in apartment six. He was sitting at the desk in the apartment, facing away from the courier, the door slightly ajar, and the package waiting on the arm of the small sofa just inside.

"On the sofa there, mate," he said without turning around, waving his mobile phone to indicate he was on a call. The courier grabbed the parcel and scanned it. His handheld device beeped once and spat out a receipt. He placed it where the parcel had been and, without speaking, was gone, leaving the door open. Callum watched from the window as the van disappeared towards Curzon Street. This time tomorrow, the parcel would be in Jerusalem, and with luck, within a couple of days, the contents of the bottle it contained would be spread around the main auditorium of the Yad Vashem remembrance centre.

Callum left the apartment, closing the door quietly behind him. No one was on the stairs, and he was at the front door before the receptionist even looked up from the video he was watching. The one-bedroom apartment was rented by a company based in Geneva, and there was no way to trace it back to him or any of their companies. Callum pulled on his baseball cap as he stepped out, turned left and started walking briskly towards Curzon Street. He would be home in his flat within the hour, having enjoyed a walk across Green Park and St James's Park in the weak October sunshine.

The Land of the Blind

***

Yitzhak Sabhan met Dora Gini as arranged, on her way to work. He had seen the cleared funds in his account and had done nothing more than look at the water bottle he had taken from the package. It was an unlabelled, clear, plastic water bottle, about two-thirds full of what appeared to be water. The seal on the blue plastic top was broken, and it looked exactly like any partially drunk water bottle, found in their millions, almost anywhere on Earth. He lifted it from his jacket pocket and dropped it into the bag Dora was carrying, pulled an envelope from his breast pocket and passed it to Dora's adult daughter, who had accompanied her. Sabhan had advised Dora not to take the money to work because she would be searched before being allowed into the centre. Her daughter took the envelope and peeked inside, looking surprised despite knowing what it contained. She smiled nervously, kissed her mother on the cheek and turned and walked back the way they had come. Dora carried on towards the remembrance centre as she did most days. As she walked, she reached into her bag, took out the innocuous water bottle and sloshed the clear liquid around. She could not prevent herself from glancing around as she returned it to her bag, but today was like any other day. No one paid an unremarkable, middle-aged lady in a headscarf any attention.

Sabhan told her to ensure the liquid was spread around as much of the main auditorium as possible after the cleaning was complete, so she arranged with her fellow workers to do the final checking of the seats. The soldiers at security had made her drink some of the liquid before letting her take it inside, and her heart had raced as she did so, but it had no discernible effect on her then or later. Despite the event's importance and the principal guests' status, the

278

auditorium's front rows were temporary seating. Dora had replaced the cleaning product in her spray bottle with the liquid and went around a final time, squirting the fine mist and wiping it across most of the seats and seat backs. As she did this, she was watched, half-heartedly, by the four permanent guards who, as part of the security team, would maintain a permanent, watching presence in the auditorium until the ceremony. She ran out of liquid before the end, but she had done what was asked of her. She chatted with her friend from work about the price of food and the latest gossip as they walked home together. By the time they parted company half an hour later, she had not thought once about the bottle and its mysterious contents. She did think about it again the following evening when she saw the pictures of their prime minister addressing the dignitaries at the Holocaust Forum and the small clip of the Russian President giving his speech. She hissed gently at the screen when his image appeared and changed the channel, wondering whether she would ever get her ten thousand dollars. Whatever happened, she was already more than happy with the arrangement she had made.

The liquid in the bottle was mostly water, but it also contained microscopic, lipid-enclosed packets of the same flu virus that Callum had deployed several times. The liquid's contents had to remain viable on the auditorium's surfaces for about twenty-four hours. As a result, the process required to produce the active particles had been slightly different, but the core technology was the same: a carefully engineered version of a highly infectious, very mild variant of the common flu virus.

The room was seeded with this modified virus, and around ten per cent of the forum attendees ingested sufficient virus particles to become infected. The Russian president was not one of them.

The Land of the Blind

He was as fastidious as always about cleanliness, and his retinue opened doors and smoothed his passage through the world, insulating him from mundane physical contact. As a result, he touched none of the surfaces in the auditorium with his bare hands. However, three members of his entourage did, including two of his close protection team who inspected the venue before the president set foot inside. It was not until two days later that they infected their president.

Callum had added a slight twist to the virus payload, making it sensitive to human circadian rhythms. He wanted the proteins only to be expressed overnight to lessen the chance that the doctors could intervene and save the president. When Kosegin went to bed that night in his Novo-Ogaryevo residence, he put down his slight light-headedness to the second glass of vodka he had had with dinner. Kosegin's aide of fifteen years, Dimitri Levtan, knocked nervously on his president's bedroom door at six o'clock the following morning. The president would typically have been up and in his gym for half an hour by now, but no one had been sufficiently brave until then to intrude. The lack of a response was unprecedented; the aide gave up after several attempts and went for reinforcements. Alexei Magodov, the president's chief of staff, spoke briefly with Levtan over the phone and gave him the permission he needed to wake the president.

Kosegin was lying, unmoving, in bed when Levtan finally opened the bedroom door. He called repeatedly, and as he walked nervously towards the large bed, he began to panic. He knew the moment he saw the president's face that he was dead and collapsed to his knees, hyperventilating, unable to process what he was seeing. When he regained enough control, he scrambled to the emergency button on the wall above the bedside table and pressed it, holding it down, unable to move any further. Within seconds, the sound of shouting and running feet filled the hallway outside the door, and a moment later, it burst open, and two armed men crashed into the room. Levtan passed out and fell to the floor, tearing his cheek on the corner of the small table as he fell; dark blood oozed into the soft pile of the pale carpet.

Twenty-four hours later, the world's press had still not been informed about the president's passing. The cancellation of his duties for the day had caused barely a ripple, but this was a major news story and could only be contained for so long. Too many people knew, and rumours were beginning to circulate. Inevitably, given the recent level of interest and the international friction the All-Seeing Eye had generated, social media was soon buzzing with speculation that the president was its latest victim.

***

The Russian Security Council, led by the Prime Minister, Yegor Baltov, were seated around the table in the Kremlin listening to the report of a terrified chief coroner. The cause of death appeared to be suffocation, but in the strangest of ways. The president's blood appeared as it would if he had been poisoned by carbon monoxide. The president's doctor, seated beside the coroner, hands trembling, emphasised repeatedly that the president was in excellent health. For the third time, he told them that the most recent blood test, just before the trip to Israel, showed no signs of abnormal red blood cell levels. The doctor kept to himself the raised levels of Prostate Specific Antigen that he had discussed with the president. The Federal Security Service, the FSB, had tested the president's room, and no source of carbon monoxide had been found. They were out of ideas, and no one had a plausible explanation for the President's sudden death. The only thing tacitly agreed upon by everyone sitting around the table was that the president had not died from natural causes.

Baltov waved the doctor and coroner away without speaking, and the men at the table waited for the heavy doors to close behind them before anyone spoke.

Nikolai Baruskov, Director of the FSB, began, "This is the work of the Americans. That website must be theirs. It has always been their plan to do this. No one else would dare perpetrate such a naked act of international aggression. It is a declaration of war."

Felix Dzerzhinsky, Director of the Foreign Intelligence Service, the SVR, leaned forward in his seat, glancing at Baltov at the head of the table before he spoke in a more measured way.

"I have spoken with my counterpart in America," almost everyone reacted to Dzerzhinsky's opening, and he immediately raised both hands palm forward and stared them down. When there was quiet, he continued, "I did not, of course, give the reason for my call, but I alluded to something relating to President Kosegin. I am confident that she is unaware of what has happened. But with all the recent coverage and that All-Seeing Eye site, she must be wondering. Perhaps she is a better actor than I believe her to be, but I do not think this was the Americans. This is too provocative an act for them." He leaned back in his chair. "Given what has happened recently, surely China is responsible?"

Seven of the twelve men around the table nodded their agreement, and Baltov cleared his throat.

"Gentlemen, comrades, this is a dark day for our country. We have lost a leader who has made us once again a force to be reckoned with in the world. I agree with Director Dzerzhinsky about the Americans, but I do not believe another state would contemplate such an act against Russia. Therefore, until we have evidence to the contrary, I believe we will assume this is the work of the terrorist group behind the All-Seeing Eye. We must allow our intelligence service to determine who these people are." He nodded, looking at Dzerzhinsky.

"Whatever resources you need, Director." He paused, placing both hands on the table and looking around at the solemn faces. There was no dissent, and he continued. Now we must prepare the Russian people for this tragic loss and tell the world what has happened to our President."

As he spoke, every person around the table heard the words, understanding that any reckoning for the president's death was, for now, beyond them. More importantly, each was already calculating furiously what their next move would be in the dangerous game of political chess in which they had just become pieces.

Before they could rise, Dzerzhinsky coughed slightly, and all eyes turned to him. "Gentlemen, I do not think we should underestimate what has just taken place, and I do not think the Americans will welcome this outcome." He paused, sweeping his formidable gaze around the faces, imposing absolute silence. "Someone has just enabled the citizens of the world to try, convict, sentence and execute the elected leader of a sovereign nation." His dark eyes challenged them, but no one spoke. "If you are not very concerned by this, you have not fully understood it."

There was a shuffling around the table as everyone took in his words.

Baltov's heavy brow was deeply furrowed as he asked, "You are not suggesting that we collaborate with the Americans in some way? This is a matter for the Russian people."

"I am merely saying that this goes much further than the

assassination of our president. This directly threatens democracy and the rule of law worldwide, and I believe the Americans and all other nations will take the same view. We may see the world differently, but we need everyone to condemn this as an outrage and to mobilise every resource to find the perpetrators."

"Do you know how many Russians participated in this and voted for the proposition?" someone asked quietly, "I understand the figure is available on the website."

There was an uncomfortable murmur, and all eyes turned back to Dzerzhinsky, who nodded imperceptibly, "That is almost certainly propaganda, yet another lie."

No one, including Dzerzhinsky, believed this, but they all nodded in agreement.

"I can only repeat that this is perhaps the most dangerous moment for our nation for a century. Others will come to the same conclusion; whoever is behind this must be stopped at all costs."

30.

The All-Seeing Eye site had crashed repeatedly in the days after the Kosegin judgement was posted, and it crashed again after the assassination. Wave after wave of concerted denial of service attacks. On each occasion, Sania and Paul watched the large threat analysis screen, occupying half of one wall in the office, seeing the source of the traffic swamping the servers. The assumption was that the attacks were Russian in origin, but the ownership of the massive botnet was unknown, and it was a futile gesture, a protest, given that the site was effectively dormant. The millions of hits per day quickly subsided when nothing further was posted.

The dominant political response to Kosegin's assassination had been vehement condemnation. However, it was not long before commentators reflected on the stark disconnect between the citizens' judgment and the politicians' disquiet. Much of the press sensed a moment of significance. Without anyone to blame for the killing, the narrative shifted to whether The Eye represented a new form of democratic expression, closer to the original ideals of democracy, rooted in citizen participation. In temporary accord, academics and politicians began by lamenting that this could never be truly democratic because one needed internet access and a computer or a smartphone to participate. They pointed out that the so-called democratic tool instantly disenfranchised around forty per cent of the global population, even before one considered China's embargo. This analysis was soon shown to be flawed; videos and stories began to appear of villages in Asia, Africa, and South America, with groups of people watching the evidence videos and discussing the issue. Reality and the academic claims were imperfectly aligned.

After the assassination, enormous pressure and criticism were brought to bear on the web services company that hosted the site. Their CEO defended their right to host it while distancing them from the death of President Kosegin. Because they were an American company, the inevitable lawsuits alleging inciting terrorism began. The legal battle would run for years, but in the meantime, the site would remain available, albeit now dormant. It was unclear where the leak originated, but it was probably inevitable that Cyber Futures would eventually be identified as the website domain owners. Two days after this information became public, someone attempted to firebomb their London office. The man, quickly caught, was a disaffected loner, managing only to set fire to the entrance doorway with a crude petrol bomb thrown from a moving vehicle. No one was injured, but the offices were closed for two days, and when they reopened, it was with obvious security at all times.

Sania was interviewed by the BBC and explained that while, strictly speaking, it was a different company supporting the site, it was indeed ultimately owned by Cyber Futures. She reiterated that they were engaged in a democratic exercise and had no desire to see anyone hurt, including President Kosegin. She denied that they had any hand in his assassination. Russian scientists continued to search for the cause of their president's death. There was virus RNA in his blood, but nothing they identified as likely to kill anyone. A group within the Russian Cabinet were deciding what to do with the little information they had. At this stage, they knew that a virus had been used as a vector, but their scientists did not yet understand the mechanics of its effect on Kosegin. Speculation was rife, and many continued to point the finger towards Cyber Futures despite their denials. Callum, Paul and Sania avoided any discussion of their fears, but they all believed it was only a question of time before the Russians discovered how their president had been assassinated. When they did, it would bring them a step closer. No one had, so far, managed to find a link between the livestock viruses and Callum, but with each use of the technology, the risks and the stakes for all of them grew, and each felt the shadow growing and darkening.

***

Although Cynthia had come over at Grace's request, Grace was asleep when she emerged from the shower. She stood by the bed, looking down at her friend, wondering what was happening in her world. As she slid gently under the duvet, Grace shifted unconsciously, pulling her knees up against her chest. Some six hours later, Cynthia switched off the alarm and, leaning across, kissed Grace's face until she woke.

"Oh, babe, what time is it? I fell asleep." Grace mumbled, eyes closed, making a half-hearted attempt to curl the duvet around her.

"It's morning, I'm afraid," Cynthia responded quietly, gently prising the duvet free and sliding her body against Grace.

"Can't be, no alarm yet," Grace muttered, eyes tightly closed.

Cynthia circled her with her arms and pulled her close. "What's going on? You were out for the count last night in two minutes. Now it's time to get up again."

Grace squinted and saw that it was indeed daylight. "Oh fucking hell, what time is it?" She groaned miserably.

The Land of the Blind

"Six thirty. I'll make coffee, you shower."

Grace fumbled her arms free of the duvet, eyes closed, and groped to find and hold Cynthia's face and kiss her. "Thanks, babe. Sorry."

Cynthia rolled from the bed, drawing the duvet with her as she went to prevent Grace from falling asleep again. Hitting the light switch on her way to the kitchen, she heard Grace grumbling but moving and, moments later, the sound of the shower.

Grace appeared in her knickers with a towel around her head about ten minutes later. The kitchen was filled with the aroma of fresh coffee and slightly burned toast, a slice of which, buttered, was cooling on a plate.

"What's going on, hon?" Cynthia asked.

Grace bit greedily into the toast and slurped the coffee. Between mouthfuls, she said, "I'm just knackered. We've had a big case at work that's about to go to trial, tomorrow in fact, plus two others that keep turning up new leads. I've not been to training for two weeks I've not had a fuck for weeks and I never see my best friend." She looked mournfully at Cynthia.

"Why don't you take a break, go away for a few days. You must have so much annual leave owed. When did you last have a holiday?"

"Too much to do." Grace pondered her last holiday. "You know, I think my last holiday was that weekend away with you in Brighton, at the end of last year or whenever it was."

"That's what I mean, that was over a year ago. You're behaving like an idiot, Grace. You need a holiday. Get that rich boyfriend of yours to take you somewhere they don't have mobile phone coverage and go and fuck each other in the sun for a week."

"I'd settle for a week's sleep."

The Land of the Blind

"I'm serious honey, you look like shit and you should treat yourself better than this. Know what, I'm gonna phone Callum and order him to take you away."

Grace rolled her eyes, pushed the toast into her mouth, and went to dress, but she did not take her phone.

Callum answered the call on the second ring; she never phoned him early in the morning. It was Cynthia. After their brief chat, reflecting on the fleeting panic he had felt on hearing someone else on Grace's phone, he sat in bed for a while, thinking about what Cynthia had said. She was so protective of Grace and had accused him of being a shit boyfriend. It made him smile, but she was right, their lives had gradually become so one-dimensional; work, work, occasional sex and more work. As Cynthia said, the MET would not collapse if Grace took a week off, nor would the companies in the Green Futures group if he took some time away. The international political pressure and press scrutiny over the All-Seeing Eye had ebbed over the last months. Christmas and the dark of Winter had passed, and there was no news of any progress in identifying Kosegin's assassins. His paranoia had ebbed, now barely perceptible most days. What did he spend all his time doing? he suddenly wondered; mostly just worrying. Paul, Sania and Armando were more than capable of dealing with whatever came up in his absence. An idea he would not have entertained moments earlier was now too obvious to ignore.

He checked his calendar and, having stared at his phone for minutes, racking his mind for a reason not to do it, sent Grace a message, 'Holiday 12 to 19 May?' He saw that she had seen the message, but there was no response.

Grace encountered no resistance from her boss at the idea of a holiday, and the same was true of both of the Inspectors on whose cases she was working, even at such short notice.

"Got anything planned?" DS Hardman had asked.

"Sleep."

And so, at four o'clock that same day, Callum received a response to his message. 'Leave booked. This had better be good'.

**

Two thousand miles away in his office in Moscow, Nikolay Grigoryev was staring again at the oximetry results from the blood samples he had tested months earlier. Grigoryev was one of the scientists involved in the autopsy of their deceased President. When he carried out the original tests, something had not made sense, and the puzzle remained. The oxygen saturation of the blood sample was low, below forty per cent, which clearly killed Kosegin. The rumours were that it was carbon monoxide poisoning, but the levels of carboxyhaemoglobin were too low. The anomaly was that the analysis showed deoxyhaemoglobin, blood not carrying any oxygen, at almost sixty per cent. If carbon monoxide had been present, this unoxygenated blood would have taken it up. The overall profile appeared as it would in someone who had drowned, but that was not what the autopsy findings reported. He knew he would probably be better leaving this alone, but picked up the phone to speak to the head pathologist who had carried out the post-mortem. After the conversation, he was no wiser. The pathologist, confused as to why, after all this time, he was opening this dangerous can of worms, confirmed, with considerable irritation, that, as stated, there were no signs of carbon monoxide poisoning in the tissues. The President had died of acute hypoxia, a lack of oxygen, not an excess of carbon monoxide, and no, he had not drowned. The blood profile also reminded Grigoryev of something he once read about suicide through breathing helium, but the autopsy report did not mention helium or any other inert gas in the lung tissues. In theory, someone could have flooded the President's room with an inert gas and then flushed it away after he had died. That was too much like a far-fetched film script; their President was not well-liked, but he had a fanatically loyal group who protected him and whom he rewarded lavishly for doing so. Grigoryev re-read his original toxicology report. He might now make a few minor changes, but, along with everyone else, he and his report lacked a firm conclusion as to what had killed the President.

Week after week, this small, open sore sat at the back of his mind and irritated him as he tried to work on other things. He was missing something. This morning, once again tortured by his inability to solve the riddle, he left his desk and wandered along the corridor to see who was around. His friend Sasha was more than happy to join him for coffee.

Sasha Antonov had worked in forensic science for nearly thirty years, twenty for the Directorate of Internal Affairs, the Moscow Police. He had a reputation for being rather pedantic and dour, and Nikolay had never seen him laugh, a thin, mildly amused smile being the height of his emotional repertoire. He was also renowned for his tenacity, and stories about his persistence in prosecuting cases where the initial evidence had been sparse and difficult to interpret were well known in the institute. Over coffee, he listened to Grigoryev's description of the blood work results. It was clear that hypoxia was the cause of death, but this was at odds with the President having died overnight, in bed, without trauma or any unusual substances found in the room. Antonov made Grigoryev go through, in detail, each of the haemoglobin derivative levels he had found and agreed that there was an

291

anomaly. For some unexplained reason, there was almost no oxygen in the samples, and they could assume that the levels in the room had been normal. Antonov suggested that there had to be something else in the blood that none of their tests had detected. Something that prevented the cells' ability to transport oxygen. Grigoryev knew he had successfully infected Antonov with the same intellectual irritant that this puzzle was causing him.

The following day, Antonov arrived at Grigoryev's office carrying two coffees. Together, they re-read first the toxicology and then the virology reports. There was a detailed RNA profile for the flu virus, but it was clear that this had not caused the president's death, and neither man was sufficiently knowledgeable about genomics to interpret the analysis. Once again, they almost failed to follow this clue, but Sasha Antonov's reputation for thoroughness and tenacity was well-founded. After a brief phone conversation, they set off to find Professor Turgenev.

Ludmilla Turgenev worked in the adjacent building, and they had to leave theirs and walk the short distance along Bolshoy Spasoglinishchevskiy Pereulok to see her. Judging by the quality of the equipment in her laboratory and her large office, the two older men had to assume that Ludmilla Turgenev was well connected or perhaps that genomics was the future and the Russian state was investing heavily in it.

She welcomed them and went through the analysis they had brought her of the blood and tissue samples. The virus was a common flu, but it contained one novel sequence. The analysis had failed to identify the protein the sequence coded for, but it was not flagged as toxic. Now, being asked to consider this again by these two older scientists, she agreed to have one of her team look in detail at the unknown protein. This would take time; her team would have to first synthesise the protein and then analyse it. She sent them away and told them to come back in a week. They did as asked, but the analysis was still a work in progress when they returned. Her assistants had fabricated the protein, but all they had was a small molecule, and still no idea what effects it had on human biology.

***

Their seven-day timeout was over. Grace and Callum barely spoke on the flight home, reading or staring at the words on the page, slowly re-engaging with the complex puzzle their lives had become. The peace and simplicity of their week had restored a veneer of calm elegance, and fellow travellers saw a tall, striking couple moving easily together, bound by an invisible synchronicity. The train from the airport to Victoria Station submerged them further in the busy city, and a sense of certain surveillance and growing danger.

***

In Moscow, Nikolay Grigoryev conversed with Ludmilla Turgenev, the two of them standing awkwardly in front of her desk.

"Sasha Ivanovic phoned me after your visit and asked me to check the new protein's affinity for haemoglobin." Turgenev was saying. "His intuition was correct; it appears to bind about four hundred times more strongly than oxygen. I think this is what killed our president. I think he was assassinated."

She spoke quietly, and he could barely hear her despite being so close. They both understood how sensitive this information was.

"Are you sure, Ludmilla Dimitrova?" Grigoryev whispered, "Have you detected it in the blood samples?"

The Land of the Blind

"We are waiting for the diffraction analysis, Nikolay Igoravic, which we will get tomorrow or perhaps the next day, but I am confident it will be there."

They stared at one another, both unsure of what to do next.

"Well, we must be certain." Grigoryev said, "Before you put this in your report, Ludmilla Dimitrova."

She instantly understood him. He wanted nothing to do with this revelation and would not be adding it to his original report. The fact that her laboratory had unearthed this difficult fact now made it her problem. In theory, she had completed an excellent investigation and demonstrated strong diagnostic skills, but that assumed the result was welcome. The trick now was for her to decide who received this information first. With care, this could provide another boost to her already rapid ascendance within the party.

"Comrade Grigoryev, you can be assured that I will be confident of my findings before I publish the results."

He left her, happy for her to take whatever advantage she could of the situation, knowing that to miscalculate amidst the febrile political wrangling might produce lethal consequences.

The Land of the Blind

31.

Bradley Forbes handed the USB memory stick to the technician, who glanced at the CIA logo as he hurried from the office.

Each in their mid-forties, and both senior figures in their respective foreign intelligence services, Brad Forbes and Robert O'Dowd had met many times over the years. The CIA had taken the lead on what they were framing as a global terrorist attack on their nation. That millions of Americans could no longer consume vast quantities of beef, pork and chicken as a core component of their diets would, to the citizens of many countries, not seem like an existential national threat, but no one was saying that out loud. The effects of the virus had initially been more limited in Britain, and the British Government had been slow to react to the idea that this was a terrorist attack. When the domestic dairy industry began to fail, they had been forced to reconsider. MI6 had been cooperating fully with their American counterparts for over a year, but they had developed no active leads, and their resources were gradually reassigned to more pressing and tractable issues. Now, Forbes was in London to press the case for surveillance of a suspect, a United Kingdom resident.

There was a file on Director O'Dowd's desk and he flicked it open, read and summarised the findings out loud, "Spanish citizen, domiciled here in the UK, lives just a stone's throw away, across the river here in London. Presents as a low-profile businessman, works for the Green Futures group, so he's connected with some rather formidable technology, including their Bio-Tech lab in Berkeley; from where, it appears, Cazinski will win the next Chemistry Nobel." He looked at Forbes, "Do you really think this chap is involved in terrorism?"

Forbes straightened his tie, nodding, "Bob, we do. We now have him at four separate locations on different continents, commensurate with our epidemiologists' timelines for the infection spread. We think he might be the source."

"Intentional, or is this one of those bio-tech laboratory fuck-ups?"

"Oh, intentionally, no question."

O'Dowd scanned Callum's bio again. "How extraordinary. Seems such a boring fellow. Not exactly a big hitter, paid about a hundred thousand, give or take, but does live in the company flat. Never takes holidays as far as we can see, not at all ostentatious, and apparently in a relationship with a junior detective in the metropolitan police." A carefully elevated eyebrow portrayed his scepticism.

"Well, Bob, he was there in the right time frame, and their bio outfit, Genetic Futures, has the technology to do something like this. So we're preparing to hit their lab in Berkeley and find out what really goes on there."

The desk phone rang. "O'Dowd." He listened for a moment and then responded, "Thank you." Tapping his keyboard, he logged in to search for the case where the technician had loaded the files Forbes had brought.

There were four short clips and some stills, all obviously processed and enhanced. Each showed Callum Moorcroft casually walking with the same small rucksack over one shoulder.

"Beijing, Rio, Houston and Frankfurt. You can see the timestamps," Forbes said.

O'Dowd watched all the clips again carefully. "Could he have a plausible reason for being at each location, at each of these events?"

"Unlikely. He's the investment group's technical advisor, but no specialist, and the group has no interest in livestock breeding, so we need eyes on him. He's dirty, I know it."

"Rather dramatic, Bradley," O'Dowd responded evenly. "And motive? He is not acquisitive, and this confers no obvious financial benefits to him or the group he works for. I assume you'd posit ideology?"

"Bob, the group he works for are all about climate change mitigation. It fits."

"Cyber, Bio-tech?" O'Dowd interjected, one eyebrow raised.

"Side shows, Bob, look at where the real money is, and I mean real money. These guys dominate the renewables scene. When they monetise, when we're all hooked into their tech, they will own the planet."

"How does destroying the world's major livestock industries play to their advantage?"

"The guy's an eco warrior, plus shaky background; we're having trouble putting together a profile and history for him. Apparently, early education in Spain, we believe, but no records we can find. Bob, trust me on this, there is something off about this guy."

O'Dowd regarded his visitor thoughtfully. "Why now, Bradley, this is old news, surely."

"A few things. The Kosegin assassination, for one. All the paths keep leading us back to Green Futures. You know one of their companies hosts 'The Eye' site, right?"

O'Dowd nodded, but did not respond immediately, staring across the Thames towards Victoria through the layers of thick glass from his office on the tenth floor. "Talk to me about the technology, this virus. Not my thing, but I've read our analysts' briefs and it's puzzling, is it not?"

"Not mine either, Bob, but yeah, Moorcroft's team have come up with some stuff that none of our guys or yours have seen before. Chemistry and biology that no one else seems to have. And they were ready for all our vaccines and released variants that defeated them. It's a very sophisticated operation, Bob. Someone in that organisation is into some leading-edge stuff, and we don't think it's Moorcroft; this is too technical for him. We need to get across this before someone else does."

"Intriguing. A biological weapon that none of us has access to. Could this be directed at humans? Perhaps already has; have you heard anything from our Russian friends?"

"No, nothing, but our guys all say yes, it will work in humans too, in principle." He paused dramatically, "One theory is that there is already a human version responsible for the falling birth rates in the developed world."

O'Dowd steepled his fingers, just touching his lips, "Mmmm. You don't strike me as a conspiracy theorist, Bradley; is there any evidence behind that?"

"Not yet, Bob. But let's get ahead of this before these people blindside us again."

O'Dowd considered this in silence for a while, "And you believe a targeted version, aimed at one man, Kosegin, might be how they got to him?"

Forbes was nodding, grim-faced, It's possible."

The Land of the Blind

O'Dowd stared at the open folder on the desk for some time. "I'm far from persuaded that this is our man, Bradley, but in the circumstances, and given the paucity of alternative leads, I think we have no option but to pursue this."

"We have spent a ton of time on this, Bob, analysts trawling the world for CCTV footage searching for common links. We found plenty, of course, in all that data, you'll get correlations everywhere. But we've tracked them, talked to thousands of potential suspects, and we still have a few loose ends we're running down, but nothing solid. Except this guy."

O'Dowd was unimpressed, "Hardly what I'd call solid, old chap. I'd be underwhelmed if one of my analysts brought me this after a year of work. However, the precautionary principle suggests we should take this seriously. Let's find out all we can about Mr Moorcroft and his associates."

32.

Everyone seeing Callum after his return from holiday, commented on how well he looked. The week began with a visit to the group's Financial Director, Armando Castillano, in Switzerland. Callum flew to Geneva and stayed overnight with Armando, Constanza, and their twin girls at their home overlooking the lake in Morges. Armando was happy with pretty much everything in their world. Funding had ceased to be a problem; they could not make and sell their batteries fast enough across all their production plants, which were, at least for now, all running smoothly. The money was cascading in and was being deployed as fast as possible, building new nuclear reactor fabrication facilities on every continent. He was also pleased to hear that the word in the science community was that Vivien and her team were all but certain to win the next Nobel Chemistry Prize. Their development teams and partners continued improving their hydrogen generation and storage technologies, and a new industry was developing around hydrogen production, storage and transport. Perhaps the most directly positive change following Russia's attack on the Chinese nuclear plant was that the United States was pouring billions of dollars into their own nuclear production facilities. With the advantage of access to the same plans the other nations had been unwittingly sharing through Carlson Olson, they were making rapid progress. When America puts its mind to something, it can change the world faster than anyone, and the threat of China dominating global energy production had proved the best possible stimulus. Their internal domestic focus was now on developing nuclear energy generation as an economic imperative.

Callum was back in London by Wednesday and had dinner with Paul and the family. They were delighted to see him and quizzed him in detail about the holiday, chastising him for not having a single photograph to show them. Paul was clearly delighted that he looked so rested and relaxed, and they all demanded that he bring Grace to meet them soon.

As he left the house to walk to Wimbledon station, something about a man on the opposite side of the street felt odd. Unsure what had unsettled him, Callum tried not to react. Had he seen him before? He racked his memory but found nothing. He realised that his unconscious paranoia had been cataloguing anything unusual for some time, and suddenly remembered a moment of feeling watched as they were preparing to leave the harbour in Skiathos just days earlier. And the flat opposite his always had the curtains just parted, never quite closed. He made a mental note to check when he got home.

The curtains were exactly as he remembered them, parted just off centre with a gap of perhaps a hand's width, an impenetrable void reflecting nothing from the street lights. He stood for some time at the window, tea in hand, looking along New Globe Walk towards the river, watching the pedestrians while his peripheral vision monitored the dark line. Nothing.

Working at home all day on Thursday he avoided looking directly at the flat opposite and the featureless slit. His mind filled the room behind with numerous ridiculous possibilities; it would be the perfect place to watch him from. Grace came over after work, and they ate sitting at the kitchen island. He created as closely as he could the Greek salad they had eaten for lunch on the first day on the boat. It was delicious, but divorced from the original context, a pale imitation.

When they finished eating and chatting about her day, Callum casually flicked on the tap in the sink. Over the sound of the running water, he said quietly to her, "Don't look now, and I might just be paranoid, but I'm concerned that flat across the way with the gap in the curtains would make the perfect place to watch us from."

Grace did not turn; her raised eyebrows pulled closed to a slight frown, "Why would anyone do that?" and after a moment, added, "Shall we go for a stroll along the embankment?"

They walked, arm in arm, onto Bankside and past the Tate Modern gallery. The embankment was busy, and they leaned on the railings close to the crowded Founders Arms, loud voices washing over them. Looking out across the river towards Baynard House, the ugly rectangle of city-streaked concrete and glass squatting on the north bank at Blackfriars, they spoke quietly.

"I was at Paul's yesterday, and felt that I might have been followed when I left. Nothing definite, you know, just that feeling." He said.

She nodded, retying her hair, "But why, and what makes you think the flat might be bugged? What are they after? Is this something to do with your business stuff that you can't talk about?

He had to tell her something. "That nuclear reactor that the Russians blew up was our technology."

Her alarm and scepticism were twinned, "You think the Russians are after you?"

He shook his head, trapped again, desperate to confide in her, knowing he could not.

"Not likely, but you just never know. And that flat opposite might be nothing, but recently the curtains never move, and it would be the perfect place, wouldn't it?"

"It would. You could get your place swept." She said with little enthusiasm, clearly thinking he was being paranoid. "Do you have someone?"

"Sania will know somebody. And I guess I should get my phone and computer checked."

The background tension, which the holiday had all but banished, was building steadily back, the closeness of their week together eroding.

"Unless you're into some other serious shit I don't know about, you're being paranoid." She looked at him, watching closely.

He felt the weight of her gaze and needed to give her something. It was now public knowledge, even though she seemed too busy to hear about it; "Well, there's the thing with the global assembly and Cyber Futures.

"What thing. Sania didn't mention anything to me."

"When did you last see her or talk to her?"

"A couple of weeks ago, I guess. I've been under the cosh at work."

"Well, Cyber Futures owns the website that hosts the assembly, or the domain at least."

"Why would you be involved with that?" She stared at him, her curiosity growing.

"It's a long Story. You know Paul works with Sania - "

She rolled her eyes. "Nothing gets past me, call me Sherlock."

He smiled weakly, "Well, it's been a bit of an obsession with him. He's been involved with this citizens' assembly stuff for years and wanted to ensure the assembly was done properly."

"To convict and kill Kosegin? Paul?"

She was incredulous, dismissive.

"No, obviously not, it's just the process; it needed doing properly, and they ensured it was."

"Paul and Sania?"

He felt her eyes searching his face and wondered how long this could go before it all blew up. "It's just a process," he repeated.

"So we're confident that Paul and Sania did not kill Kosegin?" The words, awash with sarcasm, retained a razor edge.

"Don't be ridiculous."

"And you?"

"And me what? Kill Kosegin." He prayed his pulse was not visible in his neck as she watched him like a predator.

She didn't reply, waiting.

"How on earth would I do that?"

"I have no idea, Callum, but did you?"

"You're overreacting." He could not bring himself to lie to her directly, and alarms were blaring across his mind.

He watched her jaw clench, but she just turned, inscrutable and walked on, and he walked beside her.

After a moment, she asked, "The flat opposite, do you know how long it's been going on? When did you first notice the curtains?"

He shook his head, "No idea. I use my laptop in the bedroom office. It's not in line of sight, but do they have the ability to read any of that? There's nothing on it anyway, just business stuff."

"If they are listening, they'll have a lot of silence interspersed with us occasionally having sex. They don't need to have the place bugged, you know, to hear conversations inside. There are laser devices that will pick up sound waves from conversations that hit your windows, and all that glass is perfect for it."

"Well, there's nothing to hear so …"

They walked on in silence.

"I'll get Sania to have one of her people sweep the flat." He said. Grace did not respond.

***

Sania best summed up Callum's less fraught demeanour: "It's good to have you back, Callum. The other version was getting to be a bit of a waste of space. I'm seeing Grace tomorrow for the first time in weeks, so I hope she looks as well as you do. I'll just say, it's about time. You need to be nice to that girl."

Over the following days, the two properties and the Cyber Futures office were swept, and no devices were found. All Callum's and Paul's devices were checked, and all were clean. Two discrete cameras were installed at Callum's flat, facing the building opposite; one trained on the window with the parted curtain and one on the main entrance door to track who was coming and going. The same contractor managed to enter the building and planted a tiny camera in a corridor ceiling light to cover the door to the flat from where they suspected Callum was being watched. By the next weekly meeting, they had more than three days' footage from all the cameras. No one had entered or left the flat, and they were starting to think that perhaps it was just empty. They needed certainty, so they arranged for the contractor to enter the flat and check.

Callum was now convinced that he was being followed. On several occasions, he feigned having forgotten something and abruptly changed where he was going and was sure he had seen people hesitate or make sudden phone calls. It was nearly impossible to tell if someone was communicating with others as part of a well-coordinated tail or simply chatting to their mother or girlfriend on hands-free. Everyone, it seemed, walked along talking to themselves now. If Callum was being followed, it was by someone skilled and well-resourced. It required manpower and experienced operatives to successfully tail someone alert to that possibility.

Whoever had been watching Callum from the flat across New Globe Walk, no longer was. The contractor showed them pictures of marks on the carpet where a large tripod and a chair had stood. Someone had been there recently and had slept on, but not in the bed. The evidence, from many tiny food particles, suggested someone had spent a long time sitting in the chair beside the tripod. They were now trying to find the flat owner to see who had been using it. The game had changed. Someone was suspicious of Callum, and they needed to find out who it was and what they knew. Callum told Grace about the surveillance from the flat; at least she would not think he was paranoid, but he could sense her edging away, emotionally.

***

All the raids were timed for the same moment. It was five in the morning in London and ten o'clock in the evening in California. Local law enforcement officers arrived at the Laboratory in Hearst Avenue as others knocked on the door of Vivien Cazinski's family home on Grizzly Peak Boulevard. The armed officers, led by a man and a woman wearing bulletproof vests with the large letters CIA on the back, escorted a distraught Vivien away, leaving her panicked husband trying to find a lawyer to call.

Grace woke to a knock on the flat door and pulled on a

dressing gown to look through the spy hole. Four firearm officers were in the hallway. She flicked on the living room light and opened the door immediately.

"Step back into the room, please." The female officer commanded. Grace stepped back and almost fell over a chair as the officer and two large, armed male officers strode into the flat. One officer went through to check the bedroom and returned, giving the female officer a quick shake of the head and then stood facing them in the doorway.

The female officer looked at Grace, "Grace Sommers, I am arresting you on suspicion of aiding the commission of a terrorist offence. You do not have to say anything. But it may harm your defence if you do not mention, when questioned, something which you later rely on in court. Anything you do say may be given in evidence."

Grace had only used the words once herself, and although they were familiar, she was instantly disoriented. "What the fuck are you talking about?" She stared blankly at the officer.

"I need your phone; now," the officer demanded.

"By the bed. Terrorist offence? I'm a police officer." Grace said.

The officer at the bedroom door turned and returned a moment later to the doorway facing into the living room, sealing her phone in an evidence bag. The tiny flat seemed full of bodies. It felt, as Grace knew it was supposed to, overwhelmingly intimidating.

Grace tried to assert some control: "My laptop is on the table, there, and the bag on the chair contains work material. There's nothing else."

"Get dressed, please, DC Sommers."

The Land of the Blind

There was nothing as civilised about the raid on Callum's flat. He woke to the sound of the door being smashed in, heavy feet thumping across the living room and the bedroom door flying open. He was blinded, with bright lights in his face, and people screaming for him to show his hands.

The images of the footage released after Osama Bin Laden was killed flashed into his mind, and he thought he was about to be shot. He registered a curious lack of emotion at the notion, immediately followed by overwhelming regret that he would never see Grace again.

The duvet was pulled back, and although he was naked, he did not move to cover himself; he just lay perfectly still with his hands in the air, eyes closed against the blinding lights in his face. Someone switched on the light, and he squinted as a towel was thrown over his waist. The men were all armed and all wearing masks.

Someone read him his rights and told him he was being arrested for terrorist related activity and finished with "Get dressed."

Callum found clothes and dressed himself, and was handcuffed and marched out of the flat to a waiting car below, which, flanked by two others, drove smoothly away.

Grace and Callum, ignorant of each other's location, were in separate cells at The Lavender Hill Custody Suite in Battersea. They had been there for two hours, and Grace had been given breakfast. Grace was the first to be led from the cell to one of the interview rooms. She sat at the desk appraising the two officers sitting opposite her. They were both women, which for some reason surprised her. One obviously older than her and one younger, her hand resting lightly on a closed file on the desk. The older woman appeared to Grace as she imagined a career detective would. Her complexion told of too many ready meals eaten in front of the television, and not enough green vegetables or sleep. The woman's regular features somehow failed to add up to their parts. The younger woman was thin-faced with pale shoulder-length hair. She looked rather frail, but Grace's eye was drawn to her immaculately painted nails. Her elegant hands did not belong to a detective.

Grace finished her appraisal of the women and stared past them at the reflective glass behind, wondering who was watching. She was on the wrong side of the table; it was so familiar, so alien, and so disconcerting.

The older woman spoke first, "Good morning, DC Sommers. My colleague and I are with the Security Services."

Grace registered surprise. They were not detectives, which meant this was not a standard interview. In that moment, she knew that they had simply wanted to search her flat and get hold of her devices, and she was certain that Callum would have been arrested at the same time. How had they been allowed to arrest her? There was nothing to arrest her for; someone very senior would have had to authorise this.

"Although you have been arrested under section five of the Terrorism Act of 2006, this is not a formal interview. That may follow, but at this time we simply want to ask you a few questions about your relationship with Mr Callum Moorcroft. As you can see," she indicated the familiar recording device on the desk, "we are recording this interview."

"My relationship?"

The Land of the Blind

"Mr Moorcroft is a person of interest in a terrorist investigation, and some of his activities took place at the time when we understand you and he were intimate."

"Intimate?"

"Were you? Are you?"

Grace paused, looking from one to the other before replying, "Yes."

"Our enquiries suggest that few of your previous relationships have been long-term. Would you say that was an accurate characterisation?"

Grace looked bewildered at this question and then smiled. "Great question, ladies. Are you trying to suggest that I have had a lot of short-term sexual partners?"

Grace focused on the older woman, who did not flinch. "We are suggesting that this relationship is unusual for you based on a previous pattern of behaviour. Possibly even important."

Grace took a moment but acknowledged, "That's fair."

"And we also understand that you are in a same sex relationship with Cynthia Gordon."

"Oh, for god's sake; she's my best friend."

She tried again, "Would it be fair to say that you are in a sexual relationship with Cynthia Gordon?"

"Mostly not, but occasionally, yes. Let me check something." She grabbed the older woman's phone from the desk before they could react, and pretended to check something. "Ok, just ensuring we hadn't time slipped back to the 1980s."

The older woman rolled her eyes in exasperation, and the younger woman suppressed a smile.

"Is Mr Moorcroft aware of this relationship?"

Grace frowned at both women. "Seriously! Ladies, where is

this going? If you want details of my sex life, we'll be here a while. If you think trying to shame me with some pathetic innuendo is going to be effective, then you don't know what you're doing. What exactly do you need to know?"

The older woman was about to respond when Grace added, calmly, "Callum and I fuck each other a lot. It works for both of us."

The younger woman reacted to Grace's profanity, but the older officer was inscrutable.

"Grace looked up at the glass and went on, If there are any gentlemen back there, when you interview Cal, you could do worse than get tips on how to make a woman feel good. He could teach you a lot."

Now the older woman did react, she was visibly irritated, "DC Sommers, we are investigating serious allegations and you do not seem to be taking this at all seriously."

Grace fixed her with her gaze and held it, "Is that so, and yet all you've done is ask me whether I'm fucking Callum Moorcroft."

The woman returned her gaze. "That is not what I asked you, DC Sommers. If you recall, and I am absolutely certain that you do, I asked whether you were in an intimate relationship with Mr Moorcroft. We believe that to be the case, and if it is, he is likely to have confided in you in a way that he might not have done were the relationship more superficial."

After a moment, Grace smiled at her and nodded, "Yes, I'm in an intimate relationship with Callum Moorcroft."

"Thank you, DC Sommers." The woman responded with a tight smile before continuing, "Mr Moorcroft travels a lot on business. Is that correct?"

"Varies; he's often at their office in Geneva, I believe, every week or two, and he travels at other times. But I've never asked where."

"And he's never told you where he goes."

"No, why would he?"

"It's the sort of thing that couples often - "

"Couples." Grace interrupted her instantly, "Why are you conflating an intimate relationship with the idea that we are a couple? Can I get a definition? Couple?"

The woman hesitated, watching Grace closely, "Perhaps I've mischaracterised your relationship with Mr Moorcroft, DC Sommers, in which case I apologise. I'm looking at a pattern of behaviour which leads me to believe that you are a couple. However, that is not material, so let me rephrase. It's the sort of thing one might tell a partner in an intimate relationship."

"No."

"No, he never told you where he went?"

"Correct."

"And you were not curious?"

Grace looked away and pondered this, "No, never." She said, slightly surprised.

"When did your relationship with Mr Moorcroft begin, DC Sommers?"

"April, just over a year ago. We met by chance as part of an investigation."

A peripheral movement or reaction from the younger woman pulled Grace's focus. She watched her carefully, and the woman looked away.

"The specific dates we are interested in are rather earlier than that, DC Sommers."

"OK." Grace switched back to the older woman and waited.

After a pause, the woman asked, "What sort of man is Mr Moorcroft, DC Sommers? Is he politically motivated and passionate about things, such as climate change?"

Grace considered this, "I don't think of him as a passionate person. He's calm, rational, and the only man I've ever met who has been completely, emotionally honest with me."

The words were carried on a conviction that neither of the women could doubt. There was a prolonged pause before the older woman said, rather quietly, "You're lucky, DC Sommers. But just because he is emotionally honest with you does not mean he's honest with everyone or that he is honest in every aspect of his life. We all divide up our lives, don't we?"

Grace nodded gently, suddenly all too aware of the myriad things she sensed Callum hid from her. Could he conceal something as big as this? It seemed inconceivable; he was a businessman ...

"Has Mr Moorcroft ever said or done anything which has given you cause to believe he has committed something you know to be a criminal offence?"

"In what context? I assume you're not talking about speeding. Although he doesn't have a car."

"Any non-trivial context."

Grace stared unfocused at the glass, willing herself to remain calm, dredging her memory for what he had told her, conscious of the plethora of tiny signs she could unknowingly give off at this point. She shook her head, keeping the movements as small as she could. She had to be very careful; lying would end her career. The words she would use were the truth, but deep in her heart, a dark seed she had chosen to ignore was growing despite all her efforts to wish it away.

The Land of the Blind

"No, Cal has never said anything which makes me believe he's committed an offence."

"Are you sure of that, DC Sommers? You seem uncertain."

"I'm certain. I was trawling my memory for anything that he might have said that would have made me suspicious."

"Well, DC Sommers, it's not my place to give people advice, but we believe there's rather more to Mr Moorcroft than first appears."

Grace fixed her, "No, it's not your place. And I don't need your advice. I am quite capable of making my own assessment of Cal. I know him and he is a good person." That she believed this, completely, was plain for all of them to see.

The older woman returned Grace's gaze for some time in silence, but eventually looked past her, "We will need to keep hold of your phone and laptop for a day or so, just to complete our investigations, but you are free to go, DC Sommers."

Grace was on her feet in a second, "Well that was pure bullshit, wasn't it ladies." She left the room before the two women had moved from their seats. A minute later, she was in the street.

Callum remained in the cell all day, being brought food twice. He was given no information other than that he could legally be held for up to fourteen days without being charged. He was offered the chance to make a phone call, but responded that he would do so if necessary when he was told what he was supposed to have done.

***

At the Genetic Futures lab in Berkeley, the staff arriving at work were met by police officers who escorted them to various meeting rooms. Everyone was being interviewed, in turn, by CIA agents and then sent home, told not to discuss this with anyone.

The Land of the Blind

The agents asked them questions about their work and any interaction with Callum, and for most, this was easy, as only a few had ever met him.

The interview with Vivien was, of course, the most important one for the CIA. She was interviewed in her own office, where they asked her to log on to her computer and to allow them access to her email and other messages. She was frightened, and in her heart, she knew this was all about Callum. She also knew she and her staff had done nothing wrong. Inevitably, the conversation quickly focused on Callum and her relationship with him. In particular, how she had managed to secure such a lucrative and prestigious position running her own lab with so little experience. Again and again, she said they would have to ask Callum about this or that, and they slowly closed on the line of questioning that she knew was coming.

Yes, she did think he was hiding something from her and the staff; she knew he was, because she had challenged him about it. She described, in detail, the meeting where he had flown over simply to hold the conversation face to face when she accused him of stealing information from another lab.

***

It was late in the evening when they brought Callum to the interrogation room and sat him down with the same two women who had earlier interviewed Grace. Again, the interview was framed as an informal conversation before the police interviews were conducted. Callum, tired and increasingly irritated, simply shrugged.

As before, the older woman asked the questions, and the younger one observed him.

"Can you tell us where you were on the third of June 2023?"

The Land of the Blind

Callum looked blankly at her, but immediately knew. "Not offhand, but if you get me my calendar, I can tell you; it's all in there. Just get me a laptop; it's all online, like most things these days."

The older woman seemed to freeze momentarily and listened to something in her earpiece. He could not understand why his response had produced this reaction.

He could not see the violent reaction his words had caused in the five people behind the one-way glass. They had only seized his laptop earlier that day, and for some reason, no one had thought to cross-reference the dates they had placed him in the foreign countries with his online calendar.

"One minute, please," the older woman said tersely. "We'll get one now." Her face barely concealed what Callum took to be fury.

All three remained silent, avoiding each other's gaze for the excruciating minutes it took to find a laptop. The two women stood behind him as he logged in to his online calendar and then asked for the date again.

There it was, plain as day, the 16th China International Meat Industry Exhibition in Beijing.

"One moment, please," the older woman said before leaving the room. The younger woman and Callum could distinctly hear raised voices nearby, but they could not understand what was being said. Callum said quietly, "Woops, someone's not happy."

The younger woman ignored him and looked down at the file on the desk, visibly embarrassed. After a few minutes, the older woman returned and sat down as if nothing had happened. Impressive self-control, Callum thought.

"So Mr Moorcroft, could you explain what you were doing at that exhibition and the others you attended, all over the world, around that time?"

"Well, I'm sure you know we have a successful bio-tech facility in Berkeley run by Vivien Cazinski. One of the applications for the gene editing technology she and her team have developed is selective breeding in livestock, so I was doing the rounds to see what other people are doing, looking for opportunities to improve the industry."

She had clearly expected something along these lines. "You are not a biologist, unless I'm mistaken."

"No."

"So what would you gain from being there?"

"It's just an industry, I was looking to see where the trends were."

"With that in mind, what do you make of the disaster that has since befallen the global livestock industry?"

"It is undoubtedly a disaster for the local producers and the industry, but taking a wider view, it was a very destructive industry in terms of its impact on the planet. So I have mixed feelings about that, as do many people."

"The fact that your technology seems to be at the core of this disaster, does that worry you? You must be aware of the impact this disaster is having on food distribution and global food markets."

"Our technology?" He said.

"Genome editing, your facility in Berkeley, California."

He nodded, "Ah, okay. Well, technology is neither good nor bad; it's what people do with it."

She stared at him, clearly trying to read him, and after a pause, he continued calmly, "The progress already being made in human medicine as a result of Vivien's great work is truly impressive."

317

The Land of the Blind

She was unimpressed: "The timing of the release of the various animal viruses suggests to the experts that this was all a carefully planned campaign to destroy the industry. Someone intentionally did this. Was that you, Mr Moorcroft?"

The direct question caught him off guard. "Why would I want to do that?" he deflected.

"Why, was not my question, I asked whether you were responsible."

"No, I'm not responsible for any of that." He said clearly. "Why would I do that? What do I possibly have to gain?"

"That's a good question, Mr Moorcroft."

"Vivien Cazinski believes you are hiding something from her related to their work. Are you aware of this?"

Callum nodded, "Perhaps it's a form of impostor syndrome, I'm not sure." Callum disassembled, "Vivien seemed certain I was getting information from other laboratories, stealing information. She accused me of that directly once, but it's not true. I tried to reassure her at the time, but it seems she still does not believe me. It's a shame; the work she and her team have done in the last few years is remarkable. I wish she could take the credit that everyone else knows she deserves."

The two women opposite were watching him carefully, and he felt the unseen gaze of whoever was behind the glass.

They asked Callum further questions about the lab and his involvement in the detailed work, but he could see they were going nowhere. They must have believed he had made clandestine visits to the trade exhibitions. But that was circumstantial evidence, at best, and they had failed to imagine that the information was in plain sight in his calendar. He found it hard to believe this was sufficient evidence to hold him. At least he now knew he was not being paranoid about being followed.

They kept him in the cell for another three hours while they shouted at one another, and of course, MI6 blamed the Americans. It was acutely embarrassing, and everyone except Bradley Forbes thought it was a monumental waste of resources. He was convinced that Callum Moorcroft was responsible and was not about to give up trying to prove it. He was also far from out of cards to play, and he called the head of the US Homeland Security. Forbes needed evidence against Callum before the British police released him. They now had access to all Callum's possessions and fourteen days to unearth what they needed to charge him.

Grace now knew the security services were surveilling them. It was freeing; she no longer needed to worry about whether this was Callum's paranoia or who it might be. But a malignant dread had seeped across her mind, forcing all other thoughts aside. She had always known Callum was concealing things from her, but on this scale? Could he possibly have done this? Why would he? She called Paul on an open line, and then Sania. They made plans to sweep each of their houses, and the London office immediately and then every week, in future, for listening devices. They also decided to install permanent CCTV coverage around each building to check for anyone attempting to enter. Making it plain to the security services that they knew they were under surveillance was the best insurance, and they did not try to hide any of this activity.

Grace was unaware, but Paul and Sania had far more reason than she had to be concerned about eavesdropping and surveillance. All conversations about their clandestine activities now had to take place face to face and in a controlled location. With directional microphones and lip reading, their discussions could be heard from a considerable distance away, and with laser-based devices, an external window or even a wall through which sound vibrations travel were points of vulnerability. They had the office windows covered with film to reduce the possibility of reading radio frequency signals from outside, and the glass-walled boardroom inside received the same treatment. They made their plans and waited for Callum to be released.

33.

Callum had no idea where they were taking him. He was escorted from the cell at Lavendar Hill in handcuffs in what felt like the middle of the night and chained in a windowless van. The drive took about an hour. When he emerged, he was clearly in a secure facility. The guards wore uniforms with only the designation 'HM Prisons Service', and there was nothing between the enclosed vehicle reception area and the cell to which he was taken that provided any more information. The cell was not unlike the one at Battersea, but it immediately felt more permanent. As well as a single bed, it had a plastic chair, a steel toilet, and a hand basin fitted into the floor and wall. It had no window. The CCTV camera wedged like a malevolent bug in a top corner showed a constant bright red light. Callum lay on his bed in the harsh glare of the single, unshaded fitting at the centre of the off-white ceiling. He involuntarily glanced at the camera now and then. A sense of time was created only by the arrival of a tray of food, clearly breakfast, pushed through the slot in the door. The porridge was almost tasteless, but there was plenty of it, and he ate it without hesitation, along with the sweet pot of yoghurt. He did not try to communicate with whoever delivered the food. They would talk to him when ready.

Some hours later, he was led from the cell wearing his temporary prison slippers, having to occasionally hitch his beltless trousers. The standard interrogation room was empty, and they seated him on one of the two chairs so that he could see himself in the reflective glass. One of the prison guards remained in the room, standing beside the door for the brief time it took for his interrogators to arrive.

The two men arrived carrying their files and three cups of tea between them, one of which they placed in front of Callum as they sat opposite. They arranged their papers on the desk, and one of them pressed the record button on the device on the table and waited for the sound to stop.

The first man gave the date and time and then they confirmed their identities, "This is an interview with Mr Callum Moorcroft, conducted by myself, Detective Chief Inspector Quentin Hunte …"

"And Detective Inspector Duncan Roberts."

DI Roberts appeared to be in his forties; he was small and looked fit, a sense, perhaps exaggerated by the tailored black leather jacket which he had hung on the back of the chair to reveal an expensive-looking shirt and cufflinks. His hair was close-cropped, cut with almost military precision. He was conventionally good-looking and clean-shaven with a slight tan, which contrasted sharply with his colleague's almost translucent complexion. DCI Hunte appeared rather older, but Callum suspected much of the difference was in his weight and thinning hairline. He seemed to care little about his appearance and did not remove his crumpled suit jacket. He peered over his rimless glasses at Callum, whose eye was drawn to the roll of flesh escaping his shirt collar.

DI Roberts said, "This interview is being recorded both for audio and …" He indicated the four cameras, one in each corner of the ceiling, "on video. Would you please state your name for the record?"

"Callum Moorcroft."

DI Roberts then repeated the arrest charge and asked if Callum understood.

Callum nodded in response and remembered the recording, "Yes, I understand." And went on immediately, "Is it possible for you to notify someone that I'm here? Is that one of my rights?"

DI Roberts picked up his pen, "It is, who would you like us to contact?"

He hesitated, suddenly unsure that his instinct was sound, "Grace Sommers. I'm sure you have her details."

DI Roberts nodded and wrote Grace's name on his blank notepad, "We will let her know."

"And you will tell her where I am, wherever that is? And will you do this immediately?"

"It will happen shortly, and yes, she will be told where you are, which is Belmarsh Maximum Security Prison." He paused momentarily, adding, "It is also your right to have a solicitor present for this interview. Do you have one, or would you like us to appoint a duty solicitor?"

"No, I don't believe a solicitor would be helpful at this stage. But can I request one at any stage if I change my mind?"

"Yes, you can; that is your right."

Callum nodded, drank a mouthful of tea and sat upright in the chair.

DCI Hunte opened one of his files and said, "Mr Moorcroft, you have been arrested for committing a crime under the terrorism act." His manner was relaxed, as if they were chatting, perhaps deciding what to order for lunch."

Callum reciprocated, "Can I ask what that crime is?" he asked, with affected calm.

DCI Hunte glanced down at one of the sheets of paper before responding with, "We believe you have created or caused to be created and disseminated a disease-causing organism or toxin to harm or kill humans, animals or plants."

Callum raised his eyebrows.

The two men glanced at one another briefly before DCI Hunte continued. "Mr Moorcroft, we have compelling evidence that you created a biological weapon using a human virus as a vector."

"I think the accurate term is anthroponotic."

DCI Hunte's eyes narrowed fractionally, and his raised eyebrow invited an explanation.

"A human virus that will infect animals."

"Ah, quite." DCI Hunte said, "Mr Moorcroft, you obviously know what we are referring to. We believe you have deployed a virus which, amongst other effects, has destroyed the global livestock industry. The Biological Weapons Convention covers such a biological weapon. I assume you are familiar with that." His small eyes, magnified by his glasses, focused unblinking on Callum.

"You believe I've destroyed a whole industry with a biological weapon. Well, someone did, but I'm not sure why you think it was me or what evidence you have."

"The collection of evidence is ongoing, Mr Moorcroft, but you clearly have the motivation and means, and we have established that you were in the locations at the appropriate times where these viruses originated. Everything points to you, Mr Moorcroft."

They both waited, watching him closely as he regarded them in turn.

"And that's your evidence?" He asked, eventually. "This is not my field, gentleman, but I know that circumstantial evidence is rarely sufficient to get a conviction; particularly in something like this, where thousands of people could be responsible for spreading a virus."

"In terrorist matters, where the risks are deemed sufficient, there is a precedent for long-term preventative detention."

Callum did not understand what he was being told. "What, you can keep me here without any evidence, for as long as you like?"

"Not here, Mr Moorcroft, not under UK legislation, at least." DCI Hunte said quietly.

"Where then?" Callum asked, concern edging into his voice.

"This is a global matter, Mr Moorcroft, and our American colleagues, amongst others, are pressing for your extradition."

Callum looked from one to the other. "You'd give me to the Americans even though you don't have enough evidence to convict me of anything?"

DI Robert shrugged and said, "Politics."

There was a long silence while they let this sink in. Callum said nothing, but they could see he was unnerved.

"Of course, if you were to be convicted here in the UK, you would serve your sentence here." DCI Hunte offered.

They watched him, seeing the thoughts flash behind his eyes. And after a moment, DCI Hunte said, "Why don't you think about that, Mr Moorcroft, and we can talk again."

They terminated the interview, and the guard led him back to his cell, which already seemed smaller. Could they really extradite him to America? The image of hooded men in orange jumpsuits, chained to the ground in Guantanamo Bay, came to him, and he felt the rising panic. He focused on his breathing to dilute the fear. There was nothing to do except think and stare at the claustrophobic walls and ceiling, and the hours dragged by, marked only by the arrival of more food. It was a meat stew of some kind. He wondered if they knew he was a vegetarian, but he ate it without complaining, along with the ludicrously sweet sponge and almost cold custard. He drank the bottled water and refilled it from the sink, keeping it when the guard collected the tray some time later. More hours passed, and his thoughts seemed to escape his mind to swirl around him, confined only by the mass of concrete and brick. How much did they know? Would they find the evidence in his possessions? It was there if they knew where to look. Would it be better to admit what he had done and serve a sentence here? What sentence would he get if they convicted him of using a biological weapon? Where was Grace? Where was Grace?

***

He had fallen asleep, and the metal door creaking open woke him. Instead of a guard to lead him for another interrogation, he was astonished to find an attractive, immaculately dressed woman standing in the corridor. She looked entirely out of place, dressed in a pale grey suit, knee-length skirt, and vivid, almost iridescent blue high heels. She was carrying a slim, pale leather briefcase and exuded an expensive authority as she stepped without hesitation into the cell and waited for the door to be closed behind her. Callum had difficulty guessing her age, not young, but her skin had a cared-for perfection, and her glossy, black shoulder-length hair framed her face and emphasised striking pale blue eyes.

Callum realised he was staring at her in astonishment, suddenly wide awake, and the woman suppressed a smile at his candid appraisal.

"Acceptable?"

He flushed bright red. "Oh, I'm sorry, that was so rude. I

wasn't expecting someone …." He ran out of coherent words.

"Grace sent me." She smiled.

The complex chain of emotions that these three simple words triggered was surprisingly powerful. He laughed, but it wasn't amusement, rather a swirling mix of gratitude, relief, and hope. His eyes teared, and he blinked quickly as she stepped forward with her hand out: "Gail Bailey-Royce. I'm here to act as your legal counsel if you want me to represent you. Please call me Gail." She was watching him carefully, unable to decipher the strong emotion her presence had obviously created.

He took her hand, "If Grace sent you, then I'd be an idiot to refuse."

She took the chair, and he faced her, perched on the edge of the bed. She twisted to look up at the camera in the corner behind her, and Callum noticed that the red light had been extinguished. She took out a contract, resting on the briefcase on her knee, which he signed without reading anything except the first sentence.

"Good, so Callum, may I call you Callum? Tell me why you are here."

"And you need the truth, and it's confidential."

She nodded, "Client privilege."

"And we can't be heard or seen?" He glanced up at the camera.

"No, Callum, this is between you and me. If they did listen in, it would be inadmissible, gained illegally."

He gave her a brief history of setting up the companies in the Green Futures Group and pieced together everything about his campaign to stop the global trade in livestock. She listened and made notes, seemingly unmoved by what he told her. He guessed that she had heard some remarkable things in her line of work. It was not until the end that she asked. "And your motivation for doing all this is to mitigate climate change?"

She seemed to have accepted what he told her as facts to assemble as they fit.

"Where did you get the formula, if that's the right term, for the active part of the virus? How is it that no other scientists have been able to work out what it is? We are, after all, talking about the best biologists in the world."

He looked at her, weighing up his options. This was in confidence, but some truths were too heavy to share. "I can't easily explain that. Does it matter?"

She considered this, "It suggests the involvement of other parties, which you will be asked about, but that would be supposition. In short, you do not have to say where it came from or identify any other parties."

She asked a few more technical questions about how the virus had been administered and disseminated. She was mildly shocked to learn that they were both almost certainly carrying some of it around in their bodies, or at least they were carrying antibodies, their body's defensive record of a previous exposure to it.

After probing what he knew about the prosecution case and how strong their evidence was, she finished by asking him, "Are you aware of the CIA's interest in this matter?"

He nodded, "They threatened me with extradition."

She nodded, "Interesting. I understand that pressure has been brought to bear at a high level. I know the current Director of Public Prosecutions well, and I have reasonable access to the Home Secretary. My sources tell me the Americans are extremely upset by this and want someone to convict and incarcerate—or at least incarcerate."

The Land of the Blind

"They will be grateful when their new plant-based diets reduce all that heart disease."

She failed to suppress her momentary amusement, but counselled, "Callum, I would advise strongly against being flippant with these people. No good will come of it, however good it makes you feel in the moment."

He accepted her gentle admonishment, "Understood."

"Given the political weight employed by our American friends, I anticipate they will keep you here for every moment of their two-week time allocation. In addition, unless I'm mistaken and they have evidence we have not anticipated, the Home Secretary is unlikely to grant an extension, so they will either have to charge you in another twelve or so days or release you. I would bet on the latter, but prepare yourself for a long stay in this unappealing cell. I will arrange a timetable with them for questioning, but my strong advice is to refuse to talk to them in my absence. Will you do that?"

"I will."

She put her pad away and stood up, smoothing down the expensive skirt.

"That's quite a thing," Callum said, looking at her left hand. "Is that an engagement ring?"

"It is." She studied the huge stone as if surprised to see it there, straightening it on her finger with her thumb beneath.

"Love is a hard thing to measure, isn't it?" Callum observed.

She looked at him, surprised and unsure of how to respond.

"But it appears that someone is rather fond of you, Gail."

She raised her eyebrows and acquiesced silently before adding, "Yes, it appears so. And speaking of such things, do you have a message for Grace?"

He shook her hand, "Tell her I'm very impressed indeed with

her choice of lawyer."

Gail blushed slightly, acknowledging the compliment and turned to rap on the door, which opened immediately.

"I'll see you tomorrow, I suspect," she said as she left the cell and walked away, her heels ringing against the hard floor and resonating off the unyielding surfaces in the confined passageway.

***

The night in the cell was uncomfortable. Not particularly physically, but the prison was never silent, and a fine wash of light beneath the door spilt across the floor, occasionally accompanied by voices and footsteps in the corridor outside. The darkness between these intrusions was almost the same as he experienced in his bedroom, except for the red light on the camera, which seemed disproportionately vivid and intrusive in the dark, representing their ability to watch him constantly. He closed his eyes and remembered Grace arriving in his dark bedroom and the sound of her undressing and getting into bed with him. He could deal with his current situation; it was not that much of a hardship, but the strength of his desire to see Grace was unexpected. He desperately wanted her beside him, their legs intertwined, her arms around him. He missed her strength, or at least the strength he felt when she was with him. He buried the idea of never seeing her again; he could not deal with that now."

Morning brought a novel visit to the showers, which he was informed would occur every second day. After that brief interlude, he was returned to the cell and an identical breakfast.

When they took him to the interview room later, Gail was waiting for him.

"Good morning, Callum, how was your night?" She asked.

He shrugged, "Passable."

The Land of the Blind

There was nothing except a folded broadsheet paper on the desk. She opened it and showed him the headline, remaining seated while he stood reading the article.

The headline read 'Mastermind millionaire of Green Futures arrested on terrorism charges.'

There was a slightly grainy picture, clearly taken from above in low light, of Callum being escorted, handcuffed, to the police car outside his flat. He knew immediately where the photograph had been taken from—the flat opposite his with the parted curtain. So the security services had not been watching him from there after all.

"How do they know I was arrested on terrorism charges?" He asked.

"Money changes hands, people talk, the usual." Was her dismissive assessment. "Do we need to talk somewhere less public about these accusations of industrial espionage and the link to this nuclear business?"

Callum read the article and knew immediately that, despite it being someone else's byline, it had to be the work of Jamie Jones, the BBC journalist he had leaked the nuclear story to. He was being accused of espionage and endangering the life of Carlsen Olson, using him to sell nuclear secrets to the Russians and Chinese. Now, Olson was rumoured to be 'entombed' in the notorious Butyrka prison in Moscow. According to the article, Callum had been playing multiple nations against each other to drive up the price of the information, Olson, his hapless pawn.

He looked across at her for a minute, considering her earlier question, before responding, "Possibly, but there's nothing criminal in any of this. The basic story is true, but they are way off with some of the details. I guess their version makes for a better story, but it's not true. What is true is that I put Carlsen in harm's way, but with his informed consent, he understood the risks."

"It's the first thing they will ask you about today, I would guess, so if there's anything I need to know before that happens, we should talk.

He thought hard again, slowly shaking his head and gazing off. "No. I'm confident there's nothing in this." After a moment, he added, "Are they going to charge me under the Chemical Weapons Act if they can't make it fit under terrorism?"

Gail gave a curious smile and replied, "Let's see; I doubt it." She signalled to the glass, and the camera lights blinked on. A moment later, the two detectives entered the room.

They performed the standard routine, announcing themselves for the recording.

DCI Hunte spun the paper on the desk and looked at the headline. "You seem to have your fingers in quite a few pies, Mr Moorcroft."

Gail and Callum watched the two men carefully, waiting for a question.

"Have you been involved in this nuclear thing, Mr Moorcroft, as the article suggests?"

He nodded, "Some years ago, I engaged the services of Carlsen Olsen to speed up the development of new nuclear energy generation technology."

Both men were surprised by his candour. "So you have dealt with this man, given him classified documents?" DI Roberts asked.

"That's not what I just said." Both Callum and Gail fixed him.

DCI Hunte raised an eyebrow, "Carry on, please, Mr Moorcroft, you were saying."

"I gave him plans to pass to the Russians, Chinese, and

whoever he thought would do the most with them. He knows that world far better than I do."

"To give or to sell?" DCI Hunte asked.

"I gave them to him and strongly suggested that he give them, not sell them, to whoever wanted them. I paid him well for his services, so he would not have to take money. I wanted him to appear as an idealist who wanted the plans to be developed and the technology to be delivered. As far as I know, that's what he did and was happy with the arrangement. If he took money from anyone for the plans, I am not aware of it."

"And how did you come by these plans?"

Callum hesitated and sensed the two men lean in slightly. "I obtained them from another party who did not want to be involved in any of this. They were not stolen. In fact, if you ask the UK Atomic Energy Authority, I would not be surprised if they have a copy. But if they do, it will be from Carlsen."

"So you are claiming that you gave away the plans for these new nuclear reactors that everyone is talking about. Like the one the Russians blew up in China." DCI Hunte was openly incredulous. "Why?"

"Look at all our work. It's all about climate change. If we don't quickly build a huge amount of nuclear generation, we have no chance of stopping the worst of it."

"So you say."

Callum raised his eyebrows and added, "OK, then, find an energy expert who thinks this is not a good idea in mitigating climate change, or can give you a credible plan without nuclear."

They stared at him, and he watched both men decide to duck his provocation. DI Roberts asked "Do you know where Olson is?"

The Land of the Blind

"Not for sure, but the last time I spoke to him, some months ago, he was in Russia."

"So he could be in Butyrka as the article claims."

Callum nodded and added, "I warned him, told him to get out before it all became public, before the Chinese made their announcements. But he seemed to have other priorities."

No one spoke for almost a minute. DCI Hunte shuffled papers in his file, but he was clearly organising his thoughts rather than the sheets of paper. Callum glanced at Gail and then watched the two officers, as both, unfocused, listened to whoever was behind the glass. Finally, back in the room, DCI Hunte shifted himself in his chair to rest his arms on the desk. "OK, Mr Moorcroft, we will look into this further, as you might imagine." He tapped the paper with his index finger, "But we now need to return to your involvement with the livestock virus.

Gail leaned forward, "If I may, Gentlemen. I believe we are all in the same boat here. What I mean by that is there are forces in play way above our heads dictating the shape of this investigation. However, you have several significant problems other than that. The first, a rather important one, is that I see no compelling evidence that ties my client to livestock viruses. Placing him at events involving thousands of people in that industry will get you nowhere. He may have the means and the ideological motivation, but I will be amazed if that gets you a conviction. However, as I believe you know, that is moot; you have a far bigger problem." Gail turned to Callum, momentarily to include him in the audience for her following remarks, "This has come as a surprise to almost everyone, I believe, myself included. Even if you had evidence of his involvement, you cannot charge him under the Terrorism Act. What has been done to the livestock industry is the result of a biological weapon. As you know, their development and use are prohibited under the Biological Weapons Convention. However, despite that, their use is not currently a criminal offence in this or any other country, provided that no humans are harmed."

Callum stared at her in astonishment. "What?"

She kept her gaze on the two men opposite and quieted him with a tiny movement of one manicured finger. He turned his focus to the two detectives.

They watched her impassively.

"Gentlemen, I understand that you will not release my client until the deadline in something over eleven days, no matter how persuasive my legal arguments or how poor your evidence against him. However, I am confident that when that deadline comes, you will have no option but to release him. I believe the United States Government will apply for extradition, but this is likely to be denied."

"Get to the point, Miss Bailey-Royce." DCI Hunte said, unable to contain his irritation.

"My client will not be answering any more of your questions. We will, of course, be happy to indulge in wasting everyone's time over the coming days if that is your wish. But I suggest you house Mr Moorcroft at Her Majesty's Pleasure for the remainder of his time here while your investigators attempt to find evidence to build a viable case against him, which, in any event, is not an offence in any jurisdiction."

DCI Hunte repeatedly clenched his jaw and was about to speak when an instruction was delivered into his ear.

After a moment, he looked at Callum and said, "My instincts tell me there's something else going on here, Mr Moorcroft. You seem to be the brains behind some of the largest companies in the world, and yet you live in a nice but ordinary flat in London and are in a relationship with a detective constable in the MET. You don't spend money on anything as far as we can tell, other than a relatively inexpensive holiday recently to Greece, which you flew to on a charter flight. And then there is your past, Mr Moorcroft. It's odd. You have a Spanish Passport, although I understand you have permanent leave to remain here after we left the European Union. And we can find nothing of your past before about ten years ago."

Callum and Gail listened carefully to this impromptu rant. DCI Hunte seemed to be inviting a response without asking a specific question, but Callum did not oblige.

"We asked our Spanish colleagues to do a little research, and they have provided us with a birth certificate which suggests you were born near Salamanca, in Spain, in nineteen eighty. Could you tell us where you went to school, what your parents, Dr Robert Moorcroft and Claudia Santi, did for a living?"

Callum was about to answer when the finger rose again.

"I don't know where you are going with this, DCI Hunte." Was I not clear? My client will not be answering any of your questions."

DCI Hunte looked at Gail as if he wanted to punch her. Which they all knew, he probably did. He addressed Callum again, "There's something here, Moorcroft, I can feel it. Whatever your lawyer is telling you, the people we work for are seriously considering just handing you over to the CIA. Their definition of terrorism seems to be a little broader than ours, and, at the very least, the legal process will keep you in one of their maximum security prisons for years."

Callum glanced at Gail, but her attention was firmly on DCI Hunte.

The Land of the Blind

"And then there's your little notebook. What a curious item that is. Clearly written in your own sort of code. Would you care to explain the contents of that to us?"

Callum controlled his breathing and did not attempt to answer.

DCI Hunte leaned across the table. He began quietly, his voice rising steadily as he spoke, "Many important people are demanding that you be punished for what you've done to the livestock industry, regardless of why you have done it. You have ruined countless lives, and there has to be a price to pay for that." He paused, warming to his rhetorical assault, "But there's more. I understand our scientists cannot determine how you have done this; where you got the knowledge and information to make that virus. They believe others are involved, much smarter than you, and we will keep digging until we find out who they are and what they want. And eventually, we will decrypt that little book of yours. We have time on our side, so you'd better make yourself comfortable here because I predict that you'll be at Belmarsh for quite a while, expensive lawyer or not.

34.

"How is he?" Grace was waiting in the car park across the thin strip of well-tended grass at the prison entrance when Gail emerged. The squat ornamental box hedge beside them was a pathetic attempt to soften the brutal brick façade and forbidding concrete walls that stretched away.

Gail Bailey-Royce was the senior partner at the law firm Anders, Jones & Royce, who represented, at significantly reduced rates, the trafficked girls who ended up in any of the five Elira refuges, which Grace had helped establish. She was highly regarded and had recently defended several high-profile terrorist suspects against the Home Office. Her long career included representing clients before international courts, being appointed to several international human rights investigations, and advising the United Nations. She was as close to the perfect person to represent Callum as it was possible to find.

"Surprisingly well. He's not overly enamoured with spending twenty-three hours or more daily in a cell by himself, but as you know, he's a self-contained and resourceful man. He asked me to tell you that he's doing an hour of exercise each day. That seemed to amuse him for some reason."

"An old joke we have. And their case against him?"

Bailey-Royce was clearly encouraged; "One of the detectives became rather agitated towards the end of the interview, and we gained a little insight into their thinking. But they have hit upon a rather unexpected problem unless this becomes political. What Callum has allegedly done is not proscribed in any jurisdiction. The use of a biological weapon against livestock is not covered under any terrorism act, either here in the United States or anywhere else. It's a surprise to all of us."

The two women were standing behind Grace's car now, but Grace could see that something else was bothering the lawyer. She stopped, faced her, and waited.

"They are convinced there are dimensions to this which Callum will not reveal, and they are continuing to hold the threat of extradition to the United States over him, even though there is no way that will happen." She paused, looking Grace in the eye, "Are you aware of what he might be hiding from them, and why?"

Grace shook her head slowly, "No." She looked down and then back up at Gail, "I know his life is complicated and there are things he will not share with me, and we are dangerously honest with one another."

Gail frowned at Grace's peculiar description of honesty.

"Perhaps client-lawyer privilege …"

Gail shook her head and saw the tiny pull at the edge of Grace's lips.

"Are you complicit?"

Grace paused, thinking. "No."

Bailey-Royce narrowed her eyes, "You don't seem entirely confident. Is he protecting you?"

"Only by not telling me everything."

"You were arrested in relation to this current charge, I understand."

"Complete bullshit. They wanted to search my apartment, but

would never have got a warrant. I was in and out in hours. Absolute bollocks, they had nothing. I'd have been embarrassed if I'd been on their side of the table."

Bailey-Royce regarded Grace carefully, "I understand that the financial support for your Elira refuge initiative came from one of Callum's companies. Is that correct?"

"Yes, Cyber Futures. Why?"

"I'm just curious about your relationship. A detective in the Metropolitan Police, and this man who is alleged to be guiding the activities of the world's most valuable company. You are an odd couple to say the least."

Grace was suddenly aware of Bailey-Royce's extremely expensive suit and fabulous shoes. And then there was the enormous diamond ring, which everyone knew was a gift from her fiancé, the frontman of one of the best-known music bands in the world.

"Neither of us is particularly interested in material things, I guess." She said, after a moment. "Callum is, theoretically, wealthy, although I don't know who owns Green Futures, but if it is him, he's got no interest in the money other than as a means to his ends."

"And that really is to mitigate climate change?"

"It really is." Grace nodded.

"Is that a cause you've always been passionate about, too?"

Grace laughed briefly, "I never even considered it before I met Cal. Should we get going? We can chat in the car."

As they pulled out of the car park, Gail glanced at Grace. "I'm surprised you haven't asked whether he's missing you."

"I don't need to."

***

The Land of the Blind

For the next ten days, Callum was held in a cell in Belmarsh while the British and American security agencies and governments traded back and forth on what they would do with him. Throughout, Gail made ever more insistent demands of the Crown Prosecution Service to release or charge him. She left them in no doubt that they would lose the case should they attempt to characterise what he had done as terrorism. The United Kingdom government's problem was that no one had envisaged the scenario that had come to pass. Callum's actions had not directly caused the death of any humans, and the United Kingdom, in common with every other jurisdiction, had never legislated to criminalise the use of Weapons of Mass destruction. Until now, everyone had assumed that only state actors would have access to and use such things. The law would catch up, but at the moment, Callum's crimes appeared to fall between the legal cracks, and this depended anyway on them finding hard evidence to link Callum to the deployment of the virus.

***

In the days after Jamie Jones' article, Sania and her team saw the number of cyber attacks on their systems increase dramatically. It was impossible to tell where the traffic was coming from, but every employee was warned to follow their security protocols to the letter. Even so, there were several breaches at their manufacturing plants caused by people opening emails or following links that appeared to be legitimate. All were contained, causing minimal damage. Her team assessed that it was the work of a state security service, although they had no way of knowing which.

The police held no further interviews with Callum and released him an hour before the fourteen-day limit was reached, which was, of course, in the small hours. Grace was in a deep sleep when her doorbell rang. It took her a moment to wake and realise what was happening. The sepia image on the door camera was of a grim-faced Callum. Nevertheless, her heart skipped when she saw it and buzzed him in.

It was a curious, tense greeting. She opened her door and let him in, and instinctively they held onto one another without speaking, leaning against the closed door to keep the world at bay. He released her, and she eased away, and he knew, instantly, that something had changed.

"You don't smell great. Why don't you shower and change, and I'll wash your clothes. Are you hungry?"

"Starving."

Callum dressed in a combination of his clothes, which Grace had purloined over time, and hers that fit well enough. He sat at the small table watching her make him breakfast, saying nothing, grateful to be free and with her but dreading what was so obviously about to happen.

She placed the food and the tea on the table and sat across from him.

He stared at his plate for a long time, smiling. "Postponement of gratification."

He ate the scrambled eggs on toast, and they silently drank their tea. For Callum, it was easily in the top five meals he had ever eaten, and he savoured each mouthful. Finished, leaning back, he placed the empty tea cup on the table.

"More?"

"No. That was unbelievably delicious. It would be impossible to repeat." He closed his eyes and tipped his head back.

"Cal,"

The Land of the Blind

He could not look at her, his heart accelerating so fast he was dizzy.

"Cal, calm down. We have to do this."

She was unnaturally calm, her arms crossed, her dressing gown tight around her, and she looked so beautiful.

He looked at her and had to look away again. "I know."

"I know you did it, all of it. You couldn't lie to me the other morning on the embankment, before they arrested you, when I asked you directly." Her words fell like slabs of stone, emotionless, paving the way to a place of abject misery.

He nodded gently and watched the silent tears overflow her eyes, and the pain he felt was appalling; it tore through him, reminding him of that visceral slicing the words had caused when they told him his wife and daughter were dead. He couldn't see her clearly for his tears, and like her, he held himself tight and waited for the pain to become manageable.

"I have my reasons, Grace."

"I should fucking hope so." it was almost a plea, "But it's hard to imagine what that could be."

The room seemed too small to contain so much pain and the pitiful sound of two people sobbing.

After an age, he asked, "Will you trust me just once more? Can I show you something and take you somewhere to help you understand?" He looked up, blinked away the tears, and brushed his palms across his face. "Please, Grace."

Her face was like stone, and he could see how desperately she wanted to strike out at him and how her heart would not let her while there was still the slightest hope.

"You fucker."

She stood and left the room and closed the bedroom door

behind her.

He let himself out quietly and found himself walking the London streets as dawn began to spill light into another day, and he tried to find hope in that new light.

***

Grace had become a curiosity at work; her situation could hardly have been more complicated. She was in a relationship with someone arrested on terrorism charges and had been arrested herself. Her superiors debated suspending her from work, but they had no real grounds to do so, other than their unsubstantiated suspicions that she would bring the Metropolitan Police Service into disrepute. On the other hand, she continued to be a highly effective and now decorated officer after her pivotal contribution to dismantling a prominent London trafficking gang. In the normal course of events, she would have been promoted to Detective Sergeant in the next round. Now rumours were circulating that her 'terrorist' boyfriend was responsible for the collapse of the global livestock industry, but that there was no way to charge him with a specific offence. As if her reputation and standing were not already precarious, someone had leaked a brief audio section of her interview following her arrest, where she appeared to suggest that anyone interrogating him could take sex lessons from her boyfriend. Someone had taken this further, and she received an anonymous gift-wrapped parcel delivered to the office. It turned out to be a large dildo with a card that read, 'Until My Release, Callum'. She had thought it was quite a witty line. The dildo stood prominently on her desk for a few days until DCI Bailey spotted it as he passed through the office. When he asked her why it was there, she replied that it was a thoughtful gift from her colleagues at a difficult time. The brief meeting that followed in DCI Bailey's office had been a weird mixture of his obvious concern about her well-being and the fact that this was beyond office banter. She had reassured him that she had not interpreted it as anything other than workplace banter and had made him blush when she suggested it would be a welcome addition to her collection.

A number of her male colleagues disliked Grace. They had tried to undermine her when she first arrived, and she still received an unacceptable, but tolerated, level of quiet racist and sexist bullying. Nevertheless, over time, their dislike had been leavened by a grudging respect. She never, ever, complained, and had turned out to be very good at her job. Her female colleagues had mixed feelings about her. They envied her self-confidence and loved socialising with her because they never had a dull evening in her company. She openly traded stories about the physical attributes and sexual preferences of the men she had sex with, a few of them police officers. On the other hand, she was both physically attractive and good at her job; professionally and socially, a threat.

DS Andrew Morris was the one person who was resolutely, always, in her camp. Her direct superior never treated her as a subordinate. Grace knew that this partially stemmed from his attraction to her. She also knew that with a young family, their second child due in four months, he would never act on this attraction. No one else in the office seemed to know how to interact with Grace now, but DS Morris came over to her desk as she was logging in to the computer. "Morning, Grace. Are you OK?" He could see she was upset about something. "I assume he got out?"

Grace gave him a tight smile. "Yes, I'm fine. Thanks, Andrew. How does everyone know so much about this? None of it is public knowledge."

"You know the MET and MI6, too many old mates. Nearly impossible to keep anything secret, particularly at Belmarsh; might as well livestream the interviews. I hear he has a good lawyer; they say Baily-Royce tied the CPS in knots."

Grace frowned, "It's ridiculous, how can this all be just out there?"

"Have you read the press, seen the news?"

"You know I don't do that."

"Your boyfriend, usually accompanied by a gratuitous and rather flattering picture of you, by the way, has been everywhere in the last couple of days. Word is, it's pressure from the Americans trying to get him held for longer and that they are still investigating."

Grace frowned deeply now. "How did I miss this?"

DS Morris shrugged, "Search." He nodded towards the computer.

An avalanche of images and headlines filled the screen. She was the glamour. The tabloids' favourite image was of her in a cocktail dress at a reception, held soon after the opening of the first Elira refuge. Her hair was tightly tied, and she wore a close-fitting white dress. Even she thought she looked attractive in it. The reports fell short of a direct accusation that Callum was responsible for 'The Destruction Of An Entire Industry', but the inference was everywhere. The media had gratefully added a 'Female Metropolitan Police Detective in a 'Highly Charged Sexual Relationship' to help sell the story. Despite having good photographs of Callum from the same reception, they used grainy pictures of him in handcuffs while being arrested.

Grace closed the browser in disgust.

The Land of the Blind

When Callum arrived at the Cyber Futures office, having walked for almost two hours, only Sania and the early starters were there. She rushed to him, hugging him fiercely, taking him completely by surprise. There were tears in her eyes when she released him.

"Oh, Callum, we were so worried." She was still holding both his hands. "Was it dreadful, did they treat you badly, did they interrogate you, did they … "

"It was fine, honestly," Callum reassured her, laughing, telling her of the added benefit of losing weight and the uninterrupted hours of thinking time. Taking their inevitable cups of tea, they sat in Sania's office. Before they talked, Callum checked when the office had last been swept, then explained to her what he had not told the security services. Sania was not as shocked as he had imagined she would be to discover he was behind the livestock virus.

"I assumed it was true. You should have told me."

Once again, he saw that her trust in him was unshakable and felt a wave of gratitude, washed away by the guilt of not having trusted her. It took him a moment to respond. "There was no reason to tell you, Sania, the less you knew the better for your own safety."

"Except, I know enough about more damming things. Does Grace know? Have you seen her? Did you tell her?"

He nodded but could not manage the words as the emotion, already so close to the surface, swept over him again. He drank a mouthful of tea.

"But they let you go, so is it over?"

"I'm not so sure, and because they didn't charge me in the end, we don't know exactly what evidence they have."

"The thing about the CIA is they are like a dog with a bone," Sania said, heavily.

"A big, rather scary, dog." Callum agreed.

"I'm afraid there's more," Sania added, "This is a bit out of left field, but we think Olson may have been released. If not released, then maybe no longer in prison, maybe house arrest. He's been using his laptop again, and he seems to be cooperating with the Russians, and it's all about you and Green Futures. He only used the laptop once before they found the software, but we have audio, and they do not appear to be coercing him. He was retrieving all the documents you've given him, and they were talking about where you met him and what you wanted."

Callum considered this before asking, "Anything about Kosegin?"

"No."

He stared into space, trying to see how this might play to the Russians, and seemed unaware he was speaking quietly, but aloud, "It won't be obvious how it all fits, but .... I mean they won't have any direct evidence and I don't see how they are likely to be able to get any, but maybe, if they could tie it all together then, then ... But I've been careful, so careful, but you just never know what you've missed."

He stopped and returned to the room. "Sorry. There's a lot going on."

"More than a lot." She said, grim-faced.

35.

Despite the painstaking work undertaken by Brad Forbes and hundreds of agents working on the animal virus attacks, the breakthrough emerged from an offhand remark made by a researcher at one of the bio-tech labs where the FBI was interviewing everyone. The routine was the same at each facility, and while most people recognised it as a box-ticking process, it was nevertheless being done diligently. The Agency intended to leave no stone unturned, but that is demoralising when it feels like you are working on a pebble beach.

Rosie Crantz, a young FBI agent still in training, had been questioning a researcher, and the young man had laughed and said something about not filing all the requests in his brain like a database. "I'll just check my logs," he had said, theatrically staring into the middle distance for a few seconds before saying, "Query returned zero records."

Rosie had stared at the irritating, gangly young man with his unwashed ponytail and had almost said something she should not. She was about to continue when he added,

"If you're looking for old data, you should be looking at emails; no one ever deletes them. Whoever requested the sequence will have emailed it to one of the labs."

Rosie's pulse spiked; it was so obvious. How had everyone missed this? Hundreds, possibly thousands, of companies offered these services worldwide; in theory, they would have to subpoena and search all of their email records. However, if they assumed that their suspicions about the suspect in London were well-founded, and by looking only at manufacturing labs in the UK when the query was made, they could narrow the search dramatically. If whoever had requested the RNA sequences had used an overseas lab, they were back to square one, and the task would take months, but it was a logical place to start. Rosie found that only three facilities were offering the service in the UK at the time, and she passed this information up the convoluted chain of command, where it eventually reached a delighted Bradley Forbes. His phone call to Robert O'Dowd requesting, in the strongest terms, his assistance in accessing the mail records of these companies was never likely to be denied.

When the CIA and MI6 decide something needs doing, their combined weight will persuade most Attorney Generals that it is worthwhile. The three companies were visited within twenty-four hours, and their computer records and backups were seized. Because they had a specific pattern to match, the technical experts took less than twelve hours to find what they were looking for. The data preparation took most of this time, and the disk search for the sequence took less than an hour. And there was the email containing the file matching the genomic sequence in one of the animal viruses.

If Callum had set up a generic email account and sent the request from there, he would have escaped, but every organisation requesting the fabrication of an RNA sequence has to be registered. Callum had been forced to send his email from an authorised domain, in this case from a fictitious laboratory. A court order allowed the bank account used to pay for the domain registration to be found, and it belonged to Green Futures. Callum had been careless. The trail was convoluted, and the chance of it ever being found was slight, but the smart, flexible thinking of Rosie Crantz and the belligerence of Bradley Forbes had finally paid off.

36.

Callum could not free himself from the web of catastrophising in which he found himself enmeshed. He had managed no useful work and had barely slept for the four days since his release and the conversation with Grace. In one world, Grace understood his reasons and forgave him, and the CIA unearthed no evidence they could use to obtain an extradition warrant. In another, far more likely reality, he was in chains wearing an orange jumpsuit and would never see, speak to or touch Grace again. He was quietly, grimly sure that either of these outcomes would be more than he would choose to bear. His options had narrowed, and he was faced with something he had vowed never to do.

She was impossible to read, but as he met her at Wimbledon Station, she could see his anxiety writ large and said to him, "It's just lunch. Don't be weird. Show me what you need to, and that's it, OK?"

Five minutes from the station brought them to the square of Victorian houses around South Park Gardens. It was a perfect late spring day, white cumulus clouds dotted across an azure sky. The trees in the park wore their new, delicate, pale foliage, the planted beds bright with flowers, and Grace seemed to Callum to be an elemental part of the day. Her bright yellow dress was a cruel taunt, so at odds with the dread that filled him. Wearing only modest heels, she stood almost two meters tall with her hair in a full afro.

The Land of the Blind

He sensed it was a graphic display of the strength she needed to deal with whatever was coming. Her flawless, dark skin against the bright yellow dress and matching nails drew the attention of the few people they passed. It was exquisitely painful for Callum; he loved just being with her and found the simple act of walking the streets beside her thrilling, cleaving to her radiance. The possibility that this would be the last time made the brief walk excruciating. He steeled himself for what was to come, knowing there was nothing else he could do. For the next few hours, he would pretend it was just lunch, and then she would have to decide about the incredible things he would tell her afterwards, and his fate would be sealed.

The houses around South Park Gardens are not particularly large, but most have been extended as far as the planners and common sense allow. After their lottery win, Paul, Lisa and the two children had moved there from one of the nearby terraced streets. Callum rang the bell and could immediately see movement through the frosted glass. Lydia opened the door and gawped, speechless at Grace.

"Lydia, this is Grace." He stepped forward and kissed the girl on each cheek.

Lydia did not move; she just stared at Grace. To a sixteen-year-old girl, she looked impossibly glamorous and intimidating, and Lydia was clearly unsure how to greet her. Grace offered her hand, and as the girl took it, she said, "That's a lovely necklace, Lydia."

Lydia's hand jumped to her throat and touched the silver fern, "From my godfather in New Zealand," she said, blushing slightly.

"It's really pretty; suits you," Grace said.

"Are we going to be allowed in?" Callum asked with a smile.

Lydia blushed further. "Sorry, yes, come in." She stood back to allow them to pass as Paul stepped from the kitchen to meet them.

Callum assumed Grace and Paul had at least been introduced in the office, but, curiously, he had never checked. "Paul, this is Grace."

Paul was almost grinning, "Yes, we've met. But I've not seen this glamorous version before."

Grace stepped inside, ducking slightly under the door frame to take Paul's hand and to kiss him on both cheeks. "Well, it's a pleasure to finally meet you, properly, Grace."

Paul and Callum embraced briefly, watched by Cal, now standing at the end of the hall.

"Hello, you must be Cal," Grace said, offering her hand for the boy to take. They all saw his eyes dance over her, his mouth slightly open.

"Hello." He managed and held onto her hand, unsure of what to do next. Grace smiled at him, saying, "Well, there's a problem for me right away. I call Callum, Cal, so how will we know who I'm talking to?"

Callum ushered them through to the large, bright room that spanned the rear of the house. It was the fashion, and everyone who extended had a large combined dining, living room and kitchen with glass doors opening onto the garden. The doors were folded against the walls, and the room and garden felt like one space, exactly as the architect had promised it would.

Callum kissed Lisa on each cheek. "Lisa, this is Grace."

Lisa gazed in open admiration at Grace, "Finally, he never stops talking about you, now I see why. Oh my god, what are you doing with this fabulous woman, Callum? There's clearly been a mistake. What a lovely dress. Grace, come and have a drink, let me get you a glass of wine or something." She took Grace's hand and led her into the kitchen. Grace surrendered to Lisa's direction and laughed with nerves and genuine delight at the welcome.

"Garden's looking nice. Enjoying your man cave?" Callum asked Paul.

"Yes, I love it. But these days, I'm hardly ever here." Paul headed towards the fridge. "Beer?" He turned to Cal and Lydia, who were talking quietly in the doorway. "You two can sort yourselves out for drinks?" he asked, and they nodded.

They had a traditional Sunday lunch sitting at the large table. Grace quizzed the children about their respective schools, the exams looming over them, and their social lives, interested in what teenagers were up to. She asked them about drink and drugs in the clubs and bars, and Callum watched Lisa and Paul staying intentionally quiet, finding out more about their children's social lives in just a few minutes than they had managed in total to date. Lydia had soon forgotten any shyness she might have had and was talking about consent and the difficulty in dealing with boys who thought that pornography was normal sex. Eventually, Cal asked Grace if it was true that she was a detective, and from that point on, Grace's job monopolised the conversation. Hers was usually the most interesting in any gathering, and she was practised at revealing just a glimpse of that intriguing world of human behaviour. During the conversation, Callum also learned that she had done some firearms training, initially in the United States as a student, and then after joining the MET. He remembered her breaking the man's nose that evening on the embankment and wondered what other skills she might have that he was unaware of.

After lunch, for once, the children did not leave; they remained and chatted with the adults, happy to listen and watch what were, clearly, more interesting conversations than usually played around the table. When the time came to leave, Lydia kissed Grace and hugged her, as she might have done with her school friends. Cal kissed her on the cheek and blushed deeply, as he did. As the front door closed, Callum slowly and deliberately removed several of Lydia's stray hairs from Grace's shoulders and put them in his jacket pocket. Grace watched him, expressionless.

Grace said nothing until they reached the end of the street, lost in thought. And then it started.

"Ok, Cal, what's going on? Who are those people? Oh and by the way I'm pretty sure that Lisa is fucking around." The words were delivered provocatively, and she watched Callum's reaction carefully.

His alarm was evident: "Did she say that, did she tell you?"

"No, of course not, but there's something about how she talks about the men she works with. Something I recognise. She's an attractive woman and seems pretty ambitious, and I think the men represent opportunities to her."

"Wow. OK, that's not something I was aware of. I mean, I think they're going to stay together…. They seem happy, don't they? Did she say anything about them, the two of them?" He was talking too fast, off-balance at her revelation.

"You seem rather heavily invested in them," Grace observed, watching him as they walked.

"They're close friends, I wouldn't want to see anything happen to them, that's all."

"You haven't, have you? You and Lisa, at some point?"

"Oh my god, no, no, nothing like that."

He felt her insistent gaze and knew his reaction would appear disproportionate.

"Interesting. I'm not saying she wants to trade Paul in; she obviously loves the whole family thing. I suspect this is just her way of getting on. But you know how that shit works, don't be surprised if there's collateral damage along the way."

Callum was quiet, digesting this until Grace asked, "Are you related to them? I know Paul works at Cyber, but there's some other vibe going on here, right?" She looked at him curiously, "Is that boy your son? Did you have an affair with Lisa?"

Callum laughed awkwardly. "No, Grace, I really, really have not had an affair with Lisa, no, he's not my son. What made you say that?"

"Because he looks like your son. It's so obvious. He looks more like you than he does Paul. You have the same eyes, and there are odd little things he does that you do. Speech patterns. I can't quite …"

"Can we wait till we get to your place to finish this conversation?" Callum asked. "Because it's complicated and I'm not sure how you're going to react when I explain it all. I'm not even sure you're going to believe me."

Grace set her face.

**

The District Line Tube took them back to East Putney, where they walked the back streets to Wandsworth and Grace's flat; they did not exchange a word. Inside, Grace peeled off the dress, leaving it lying across the bed, tied back her hair and changed into comfortable clothes. Callum made them tea, and they sat opposite each other across her kitchen table. His hands shook slightly as he put the mugs on the table, and Grace picked up on it instantly.

"Ok, Go." She said, looking straight at him across the table.

Callum was beyond nervous, and it was clear Grace would not

reassure him. He imagined this was how it would feel to be in a police interview room confronted by DC Sommers. He attempted to hold her gaze but had to look down, convinced that his pounding heart must be audible. He shut his eyes; could he actually do this? Did he have a choice?

"Cal, whatever this is, just tell me." His nerves were unsettling her.

He tried to speak and had to stop and control his breathing before he managed to say, "I honestly don't know how to start with this. I've thought about little else for weeks, maybe months, and it's been eating me up."

"I just need all of it; one shot, Cal, the whole thing."

"Oh, you'll get everything! Whether you believe it or not …. It's going to be hard to believe, Grace, it's as strange a truth as you'll ever hear."

"Just start." She frowned, taking her tea in both hands, and watched him consciously relax his shoulders as if shaking off a loose garment.

"I've told you some of this before, but imagine being woken one day by a police visit to be told that your wife and daughter have just been killed in a car crash. I spent the first years not dealing at all with losing them, angry and then hopeless. Lost. But I had friends and time helped, and eventually I was sort of OK again, able to function anyway. On the outside, I look like the same Callum, but losing a child breaks something that can never be fixed." He stopped, controlling his emotions.

Grace was nodding, his pain was real and visible, but she did nothing to reassure him; he could see how tense she was.

"I did what lots of people do when something life-changing happens. I looked at my life and the world around me and decided

The Land of the Blind

I needed to do something more useful, more meaningful. At the time, I was working at a spin-off from Cambridge's Cavendish physics laboratory. We were doing some pretty speculative high-energy physics." He was following the narrative in his head, and the words began to flow. "When I say we, I was the commercial director and my friend, Graham, was the lead scientist. He's a proper full-on genius and had a team of very smart people working for him. The work had some military links as well as purely commercial ones." Callum smiled at the thought of his friend. "Anyway, at the centre of the work was a device which, Graham believed, would be able to move objects through space. Teleportation, if you like."

Grace inclined her head slightly, eyes wide, incredulous.

"Sure, mad scientists, sci-fi and all that. Until we demonstrated it was possible."

"Teleportation; seriously?" Grace asked, her words laden with scepticism.

"There's more, I'm afraid. You might have heard scientists talking about space-time; so if you can move an object in physical space, it should theoretically be possible to move it in time."

A deep frown betrayed her incredulity, "Now you're telling me there's a time machine in Cambridge?"

"I did say it would be hard to believe."

The frown deepened, "There's hard to believe and there's full-on fantasy."

"Well, you're going to have to make up your own mind, detective. Just let me tell you the rest of it." He took a breath, "So, you have me, a man with nothing to lose, and a team of scientists who believe they can move an object through time."

She straightened. This was too much. "What? You're saying

you went back in time?" She was irritated, openly incredulous, now.

"Imagine everything I've told you took place in the last decade of the twenty-first century."

"In the nineteen nineties?"

"No, twenty-first century, in the twenty-nineties."

There was a long, long pause, and her eyes never left his. "In the future, at the end of this century?" she asked, very slowly.

He nodded and waited. Her face relaxed, and she looked at him now not as Callum but as a problem she needed to understand. He waited, determined that she should exhaust the impossibilities herself.

Finally, carefully, she said, "So you're suggesting to me that in the future, some seventy years from now, there will be a time machine built and you'll hop in and come back to now, our present. Or whenever you arrived."

"September 2014."

Her eyes flared momentarily, and then she stared at him again, expressionless, her mind racing. "Except that if you lived until the end of the century that would make you ninety something, so that's clearly bollocks." She said loudly.

"Almost one hundred now, actually."

This was too much, "So the machine reversed your ageing, too?" she said sarcastically.

He could see deep concern creasing her face; had he lost his mind? He carried on as calmly as he could, "Not exactly, but in that future life, I was involved with a company called Telogen. It was the first company to commercialise a drug that stops ageing. I started taking it when I was about forty. It reduces some effects of ageing and then pretty much holds it there as long as you are taking the drugs."

"Just a minute." She held her hands up, "Just wait. So now you are telling me you were born when?"

"Tenth of July two thousand and three."

She seemed reluctant to utter the words, to give any credibility to what she was thinking. "So you are now -" She stopped and stared at him

"Shit! That boy, Cal, you are telling me it's you?" She said the words because they fit the narrative, but he could see she did not believe it.

Callum nodded.

The thoughts tumbled from her, "Oh my god, this is a complete mind fuck, because that would make Lisa and Paul your parents?"

He nodded again.

"And Lydia's your sister. Do they know?" There was a brief pause, and she raised her voice, "No, no. That's not a question; this is impossible. This …"

She was momentarily lost; logic had deserted her. He saw her slowly regroup and focus on him, searching for the lie.

"Paul knows." He said.

She shut her eyes and he waited, watching her, hands in the air just above the table, trembling.

"Do you believe me?" he asked quietly.

"Fuck No!" she opened her eyes, and then as though she could not cope with seeing him she shut them again, "Yes. No. I don't fucking know! How can this possibly be true!"

He replied, "You're the detective, you have the facts, you tell me. Am I lying?"

She did not respond, but some moments later, her hands

settled on the table, and she opened her eyes again, returning his gaze and weighing his words. "So that's why you kept some of Lydia's hair. So I can prove whether she's your sister." She was regaining her balance. "So I'm fucking a pensioner."

He laughed out loud, a flood of relief and amusement at how her mind worked. The tea was going cold, and Callum reached for his, giving her time to think. She stared out the window and back at him several times, sifting through what she had just heard. She stood suddenly as if to go somewhere, but just took a few agitated steps around the room, pausing several times, about to speak, but then retreated to her thoughts and sat again. "If this is true, why did you come back, and are there others with you? Is there an invasion of time travellers hiding amongst us?"

He smiled at the idea, "No, it's just me. At least I think so. The amount of energy needed to move my mass through time was absolutely enormous. In a few seconds, we used more energy than the world currently uses in a decade." He paused to let this sink in, "We had to do it in secret, so only a few people knew what we were doing. It would have taken them years to store enough energy to make another attempt, even if they wanted to, which I doubt. The thing is, they don't even know whether I survived. So I'm not expecting company."

She was watching him, searching for the slightest flicker of inconsistency. "So this is like a suicide mission, or something?"

"Well, I survived, as you can see, so Graham was right, as usual."

"But you're all alone here."

It was a statement of fact, but it stopped him. "After a pause, he said, quietly, "There's Paul, but yes, I was until I met you."

He watched her anger, confusion, and agitation grow.

The Land of the Blind

"Why did you do it. Are you trying to save your wife and daughter, to stop them from dying?"

He smiled, bleakly, "It doesn't work like that. Well, at least I don't think it works like that, and my wife won't even be born for another thirty years. Even Graham didn't know what effect my being here might have on this flow of time versus the original. This version seems separate from the one I lived through before, but that might not be true either. Perhaps we are just erasing the previous version with this new one. In the end, it doesn't matter. I'm here now; this is our reality."

"I can't get my head …" Grace shook her head, staring blankly into space until the next question appeared. "Why come back to now, or rather, 2014?" Before he could answer, she added, "And what were you doing before I met you?"

"Why? Well, the world I came from, the world we are heading for, was in a really bad way. Things started to unravel in the late twenties, so in just a few years from now. It was all so, stupidly obvious looking back, but all you really need to know is that global warming got out of control and we passed some tipping points; the permafrost in the northern latitudes began to thaw and the Amazon collapsed, most of it disappeared in a decade and that was when everyone knew we were in deep trouble. It's not such a big deal, you might think, if you live in the UK or Europe and some other parts of the first world, but losing most of the Amazon disrupted the planet's established water cycle. Much of the Middle East and, more importantly, sub-tropical Africa became uninhabitable unless you were wealthy. Big parts of the Indian sub-continent were below sea level, and millions died of heat stroke there. The immigration we have today is just the start, a trickle that will become a full flood. There was a brief nuclear war in the forties. Just two devices, if you can call that a war, but tens of millions of Iranians and Israelis were killed in just a few hours. There was civil unrest across the world. A number of the American states formed their own government and seceded from the US. There was widespread famine, and over the forty years from the mid-thirties, about three and a half billion people died."

The words seemed to tumble from him, and Grace was stunned. "Three and a half billion? I mean, isn't that like half the world's population?"

He nodded, but could see that she was elsewhere, her mind grabbing at the tangle of loose ends. "But why now? Why not go back further, you know, before the world got too hot, before coal and oil got properly started? Go back then and stop it all happening in the first place."

"Leverage and energy. Graham and I ran thousands of simulations with the best artificial intelligence, powerful AI models. We couldn't find a way to make it work. Nothing we modelled prevented the world from using fossil fuels when they were discovered; they are just too good, and make human life so much better. Also, the further back we went, the less influence I could have. The models showed that after 2010, it was our best option because of some of the technologies that became available around that time. Unfortunately, it's too late to stop some pretty horrible things from happening, but we thought we could do just enough to prevent the worst of it. We needed certain technologies to be emerging so we could develop them and have the impact we need."

"What technologies?"

"Well, that's what I've been doing for the last seven years, Grace, developing the technologies we need as alternatives to oil and coal. It's all been in the news. But just as important is the internet and social media. This is the first time in human history that it's possible to communicate with a significant chunk of the world's population in almost real time."

She weighed this, "Can't wait to follow @timetraveller."

He smiled, grimly, "We're trying to build the tools to give us all a fighting chance this time. Our companies have already developed technologies revolutionising battery storage and hydrogen generation. You remember that little rechargeable battery pack thing a few months back?"

"Oh yeah." She nodded, remembering DS Morris and his dusty old fan.

"It's only one little thing, and we're already producing millions of vehicle-sized versions of those batteries, but the big thing, the game changer, is nuclear power. Ultimately, that's the only thing that will save us."

She was only half-listening. "But why not tell people, show them you've come from the future to warn us. If you can convince me, you can convince others."

He equivocated, "That was our original plan, sounds obvious, but when we ran the simulations, we couldn't make it work. Humans are weird, and the idea that we do things based on rational self-interest is one of the fundamental errors everyone makes when working out how to run the world. That's just not how people work. We're masters of self-delusion, and cognitive dissonance is our default state." He knew this was her territory and that she would understand him, and she did, and he watched her adding this to the mental picture she was constructing.

"So, sounds like you've done what you came to do then?" she said.

The Land of the Blind

He laughed, grimly, "Oh, if only." He shook his head, "The idea that if you build a better mousetrap the world will beat a path to your door is only half the story. You have to show the world you've built it, but that only works if they need a new mousetrap."

"Enough of the mouse thing, spell it out."

"We have to massively reduce our use of fossil fuels, as fast as possible, and to do that, there has to be an alternative. People will never forgo their current lifestyles. Also, there are vested interests, powerful groups, and they will do everything they can to slow down any reduction in fossil fuel use. The energy companies have been doing this for decades. It's just too profitable. In fairness, this is an existential threat for the petrostates, so there's no way they will go quietly; for them, it's the rational thing to do; fight to the end."

"I don't know anything about world energy or any of that stuff," Grace shrugged, "but I can see there's no easy way to force a country like Russia to do anything they don't want to do."

"Exactly."

"So, how do you deal with that?"

"On a global scale, we can only use the market. We have to make the alternative cheaper. So that's what we are doing."

"I don't see much happening on that front. Not that I follow the news that closely. Am I missing something?"

"We're not quite there yet, but we're getting close."

The logic and his narrative had carried her along, but suddenly, she put her hands to her face, elbows on the table. "Stop. This is all too much."

He waited, and they sat motionless, silent for over a minute.

"It all just seems …" She stopped again. "Don't you have some super weapon from the future or something?" She looked up at him now, "You're telling me it's just you fiddling around trying to save the entire planet. It all seems a bit lame."

"Sorry to disappoint you. Sadly, we don't have any magic powers; it's just me with what I can carry in my head. But in seven years, we've built the world's most successful group of companies. From scratch."

She nodded reluctantly, sensing his irritation.

"And we've removed an entire, horribly polluting, global industry."

It took her a moment, but she already knew this: "Yes, you killed all the livestock. How did you do that?" Her words were heavy.

He carried on without meeting her gaze, talking into the room, as if to hear the justification himself, again. "A few years ago, some smart scientists, Jennifer Doudna and Emmanuelle Charpentier, discovered a way to find particular genes and to change them by swapping bits of DNA. Their tools were a bit clunky, but with my future knowledge of how this developed, we set up a lab which developed the necessary refinements. We have a better version that does exactly what you want it to."

"Which is what?" She was wary now, almost reluctant to ask.

"To reliably edit DNA."

"And why do you need to be fiddling with DNA?"

He carried on quietly, carefully, "So, as an example, we can make a virus containing genetic material that significantly alters a female's ability to implant and carry a foetus."

Grace looked horrified. "What?"

"I'm not talking about people, Grace. Cattle, livestock, that's how we did it. Do you know how big the carbon footprint is for the livestock industry? Or was." He added quietly. "Obviously, the industry didn't know why this was happening, but they identified the original virus and created a vaccine. It's not even that unusual; animal viruses have always done this sort of thing from time to time, and they thought it was just another one. But they were wrong this time, it wasn't, and it just kept getting worse from their perspective."

"So why didn't their vaccine work?"

"It did, but we changed the virus RNA multiple times, and the new versions evaded their vaccines each time."

"But all of those people, all of those jobs."

He met her gaze. "Give me an alternative."

She did not flinch, and he knew that while it was the last thing he wanted to say, he had no choice about what he was about to tell her. She probably knew somewhere in herself, but he would have to make it real.

"There's another thing, I think you may already …. "

She sensed the change and drew her arms in, crossing them tightly.

He looked down at the table as he spoke, "So, as I explained, we can easily put whatever RNA we like into a virus. That RNA can be constructed so that it has a minimal effect on anyone other than one person on the whole planet. Assuming I had a sample of that person's DNA, of course."

"You could make the virus infect just one person? Give them flu, or whatever?"

"Well, it infects everyone the way viruses do, but you choose a mild one, and then when it's in the body, the RNA allows the virus to do something specific to only one person. For example, produce a particular protein that stops haemoglobin from absorbing oxygen. Suffocate them."

The Land of the Blind

Grace could not prevent the look of horror from briefly crossing her face, and then she tightened her jaw. "You killed those men."

He could not speak and just nodded, barely.

"What the fuck! Cal, Assassinating people? What good is killing a few people going to do? Who are you?" She stood up now and stared down at him.

He did not lift his gaze and asked quietly, "What would you do if you knew for a fact that someone would be responsible for the brutal murder of, say, half a million innocent people?"

He looked up now, challenging her. "That's not a rhetorical question, Grace. Tell me! What would you do if you knew for an absolute certain fact?"

She stared back at him, jaw clenched, unwilling to yield.

He waited.

Finally, she broke his gaze and rolled her head slowly back to look up at the ceiling. "I can't, I mean I …"

"There were a number of unpleasant individuals, responsible for millions of deaths, whom I found, quite by accident, while I was doing my research. All three were African dictators, alive when I arrived."

"Stop, stop, stop, stop, stop!"

He stopped talking.

Her anger filled the room. "Get out."

"What?"

"You heard me."

"Grace, we need to talk about this."

"I can't. I'm sorry. You've lied to me. From the very start, every single day, every single time. You lied."

He stared at her. Whatever he thought she would say or do, he had not envisaged her just rejecting him. Paul had believed him."

"Get out now."

He did not move.

"Please."

A minute later, she shut the door behind him, and he could hear her crying. It sounded like she was leaning against the other side, and he stood with one palm pressed against the door, desperate to go back in and fix everything. Her distress was too much to bear, and after a moment, as his own tears started, he crept away and tiptoed down the stairs.

37.

Grace asked Cynthia to come over. Having returned late from work herself, she was nursing a second glass of wine and staring out of the window when the door buzzer derailed her circular thoughts.

It was rare now that Grace asked Cynthia to stay over. They understood that each was available to the other when they needed it emotionally and occasionally physically. They barely spoke when Cynthia arrived, showering together before sliding beneath the protective carapace of the duvet. Grace curled her arms around her friend's warm, soft body, her almond, pale skin in stark contrast to Grace's. They lay together in the darkness.

"So, babe, what's going on?" Cynthia asked quietly, holding Grace's arms around herself. "Cal?"

There was a long silence and then Grace rolled onto her back and put her arms above her head. Cynthia curled under her arm and stroked her stomach. "So tell me."

Grace gave a huge sigh. "Oh babe, it is so complicated and there's stuff I can't tell you, because it's, … it's, … well it's just crazy. But the long and short of it is that I have a choice."

"Is this something you've done or Cal has done?"

"It's Cal, but now he's made me an accessory to things he's done."

"As in, he's committed a crime, accessory?"

"Yes, but it's so much more complicated, and although he has, it was for a reason. Possibly a good reason."

Cynthia continued soothing Grace, her palm moving gently across her stomach.

"So the choice is, I either walk away, turn him in for what he's done, or join him in what he's doing."

"Join him in something criminal?" Cynthia was shocked. "Grace, that's just not you. What are you saying?"

Grace stared up at the ceiling, "Oh god, I know. But …"

"I know you like the bloke, but it's not as if you can't get that whenever you want."

Grace gave a hollow laugh. "Oh, Cyn. I don't believe there's just one person for everyone; that's bollocks, but I know that there will not be many people, men, who I meet who will make me feel the way he does."

"Oh no, you're in love with him." Cynthia was equally delighted and horrified.

Grace turned and smiled at her, "Oh, if only it was that simple." She thought for a minute, "The real problem is that he genuinely wants me to be happy. He just …" her voice wavered, "He calls it something else, but I know he loves me in a way that I'm never going to find again and I don't want it to stop."

Her silent tears ran freely down both cheeks, and Cynthia pulled her towards her and held her.

"Why are you crying? That's beautiful."

Grace drew gently away and wiped away the tears with the heels of her hands. "I don't understand." She wailed quietly, "I don't even like men. Now this fucker is asking me to compromise on everything. If I carry on with this, I will break the law. There's no way around it. I've promised to …"

She broke down in tears again, sobbing onto Cynthia's shoulder, the tears running between their bodies as Grace clung to her.

When the sobs subsided, Cynthia asked, "Is that what he's asking, for you to join him, help him with whatever it is?"

Grace shook her head, rocking slowly against Cynthia's shoulder. "No. That's the worst of it, he's not asking anything of me, he just told me what he's done and explained why. And it's some serious shit, honestly, babe you would not believe it." Grace looked up and smiled, back in control. "It's a real burden, and it's getting too much for him, and I think he wants me to share it."

"Are you going to get into trouble at work if you do this?" Cynthia asked.

Grace laughed, properly, ridiculously amused at the depth of her dilemma, and then groaned a long, drawn-out plea that morphed into tears. The silent tears returned, and Cynthia took her face in both hands and kissed her cheeks, absorbing her sorrow.

After a moment, Cynthia sat up, decisively and put her hands on Grace's shoulders, "Only one thing at a time like this, you need tea."

Grace dried her face with the duvet and pulled it around her. Cynthia made tea while Grace calmed herself, sitting with her knees pulled up to her chest in the safe, warm bed.

38.

Three days later, Callum had heard nothing from Grace. He checked their usual messaging app, but could not bring himself to initiate the conversation. He lay awake for hours each night, triggered by the thought of losing her and having to stare again into the hopeless darkness of loneliness and emotional loss. Only now, with her gone, did he truly realise how much he needed her. Each night, lying in the dark, he resolved to contact her the following day, and each day he found he could not. As long as she had not finally rejected him, there was hope.

He had to tell Paul what he had done and warn him in case, as now seemed possible, Grace could not bring herself to compromise. They arranged to meet at the Waterloo Station bar.

Paul was in a buoyant mood. "It was Great seeing you and Grace last weekend. We should do it more often. I met her in the office a few times, but she is just fabulous. She dropped in yesterday for a cup of tea on her way home. She was in Wimbledon for something. Late afternoon, she spent ages chatting to Lydia and Cal. Lydia is obsessed with her; she talks about her all the time."

Callum attempted to keep his tone neutral. "Oh, that's nice. How was she?"

"Same, glamorous, force of nature." Something in Callum's manner alerted Paul, "Are you two OK?"

"Fine, yeah. We've not spoken since that day, actually, too busy."

"It's nice you have someone now." Paul probed, "Particularly someone so …"

Callum smiled again, almost reluctantly. "Yes, she's …"

Paul raised an eyebrow. "You two seemed remarkably close. How long have you been together? Where did you meet her?"

"So many questions, do I detect Lisa's hand here?"

Paul smiled sheepishly, "I am under instructions to find out more, but honestly, I was just so happy to see you with someone."

"I'm as surprised as anyone about this; I certainly wasn't looking; it was just chance. We clicked from the moment we met."

"Love at first sight?" Paul smiled.

"Something like that." Callum's smile did not quite work.

"And you're OK?"

Callum nodded.

"That's great, Callum, really. You deserve another chance after what you've been through."

Callum nodded and took up his beer.

"But," Paul began carefully, "Isn't it going to be difficult to keep what we're doing away from her. She's a detective, for gods sake."

Callum looked steadily at Paul and then closed his eyes, "I told her," he said quietly.

It took Paul a moment to understand, and then he sat back, his mouth open, shocked. "What, everything?"

Callum nodded, "Well, not quite everything, but …"

"What did she say, I mean, did you talk about that thing with the Italian guy, the mafia…?"

"No. we didn't get that far. She was pretty upset; she threw me out."

Paul had his head in his hands. "What will she do? Will she turn you in?" They were whispering.

"I have no idea." Callum sat back and stared, unseeing, across the bar. "You know how it sounds, it's crazy. She listened for a while, but then she was just angry, really, really angry, and upset. I think I've hurt her, Paul, by lying to her. Well, I know I have."

Paul blew out his cheeks. "Why did you tell her, Cal? What possessed you?"

Callum just looked at him, and Paul understood.

"I thought her seeing all of you would make her understand I was telling the truth."

"Oh, so that's why she came back. Do you think she believes you?"

Callum shrugged, "Maybe."

"Well, she hasn't turned you in yet," Paul said.

Callum was staring at the table. "I don't want her to …"

The almost pitiful longing caused Paul to shut his eyes for a moment. They were silent for minutes, each sipping their beer, lost in their thoughts.

"I guess we have to decide what to do if she …" Paul said, slowly. "I wonder, I mean, will they arrest me? What evidence do they have?"

Callum was shaking his head. "I don't know, but think about it. There's no way they will believe the time travel stuff, so it's about finding evidence of any crimes, and I'd say you're completely in the clear. I suspect they won't even be able to find anything directly implicating me, but I do keep thinking about what you said about the laboratories. They have the animal viruses, obviously, and …." He tailed off.

376

"There's nothing we can do, is there?" Paul said quietly.

"Honestly, Paul, I'm sure you and the family are going to be Ok."

They sat quietly again, each catastrophising their futures for a moment until Callum asked, "Are you and Lisa Ok?"

His discomfort in asking the question was evident and instantly infected Paul. "What makes you ask that?"

Callum saw Paul's gaze slide away, and his heart fell. "Nothing, none of my business." The following silence begged to be filled, and Callum could not resist: "It was just something Grace said."

"Which was?" Paul looked at him now.

"No, nothing, I mean, it's none of my -"

"What did she say?"

Callum shut his eyes as he spoke, unwilling to see the words land. "She thought Lisa might be having an affair, but I've no idea why, Lisa didn't say that."

Paul was staring at the table when Callum summoned the courage to look.

"Oh, Paul. I'm so sorry, this is my fault."

"Don't be ridiculous, it's not your fault, Callum, these things happen."

Callum knew Paul would not ask, but could not help but say, "Well, it didn't happen before."

It took Paul a moment to realise what Callum was saying.

Paul gave a short, mirthless laugh. "Well, if it did happen before, you were unaware of it. Do you think Cal knows? I doubt it?"

"Do you want to talk about it?" Callum asked.

"Not really, not now."

"Well, when you do, if you do ..."

377

The Land of the Blind

Paul nodded, and they drank their beers.

39.

Walking back along the embankment, Callum passed the place where Grace had assaulted the drunk racist. He remembered the warm evening and the potent combination of fear and lust that suffused the memory. The blood on the pavement, her vomit on their feet and the feeling of her body as they clung to one another in the shower. He was staring at the spot in the near dark, people moving past him, and he was suddenly aware of the cool wind off the river and the trees in their new foliage reading themselves for summer. He thought again about the conversation he had just had with Paul. But Paul had no idea how close he had been to the emotional precipice. He understood that his dangerous relationship with Grace made no objective sense—his weakness, his astonishing, almost pathetic need, verged on embarrassing. But now, the idea that he could have continued alone, without the emotional support she provided, astonished him. It had all seemed so logical when he had planned all of this years earlier. Reality was so much harder. He was weary, playing with fire and knew that only a few things needed to misalign for him to lose control. On impulse, he phoned her and to his surprise, she answered immediately.

"Hi."

"Oh, I didn't expect you to pick up."

"Why phone then?" she said.

379

The Land of the Blind

He took his time to answer. "I miss you, Grace."

"Fucker!" She cut the call.

He stared at the phone, and physical pain suffused his heart. He was close to tears, too many things crowding in on him. He closed his eyes and breathed away the hurt, steeling himself.

The phone rang and he dropped it. He scrabbled on the ground and turned it over. The screen had a diagonal crack distorting the caller's name, 'Grace'.

He held the phone to his ear and waited. It took a few seconds for her to speak.

"We need to talk. Meet me at the pier at nine tonight."

***

It was dark, but only city dark. A ferry had just arrived, and a knot of people disembarked. Callum and Grace waited in silence, and as the ferry pushed off, they walked down to the end of the pontoon.

Standing side by side, a little apart, out of the wind, looking towards Blackfriars Bridge, they leaned against the shelter wall, barely above the water which bounced and scattered the city's lights at them.

"Have you told me everything?"

"Paul said you went back to the house?"

She turned her head to look at him. "I took some of Lydia's hair; I needed to do it myself."

"And what did you test it against?" he asked.

She gave a short, grim laugh. "I live in a soup of your DNA, Cal, finding a sample was not hard."

"And?"

She looked away, "And I am forced to believe that, however unlikely, you could be telling the truth." She stopped, held her hands to her face, and leaned forward as if in pain.

He waited until she straightened, desperate to reach out to touch her, knowing he could not. "So what happens now?" He asked.

"You tell me all of it, every sordid, criminal fucking part." She was struggling to contain the flaring anger. "You do know what you've done to me, don't you? I hope you fucking understand." She could not look at him.

He was staring at his feet, beginning to realise how deeply he had hurt her, stunned at how little he had considered the effect this would have on her. He could barely speak, "I'm so sorry, Grace."

"Don't!"

He was trying to remember what he had already told her, unsettled by her rage. "I explained why I was compelled to do all this."

"Yes, climate change; and that while you were here, destroying the livelihoods of a few million people, you thought you'd assassinate a few dictators too."

"I asked you what you'd do if you knew what crimes they would commit. You never answered." He said, the challenge clear in his voice.

She turned to look at him, her face hard, her lips a compressed line. "Fuck off."

"No, Grace, you can't do that; you know as much as I do now." He watched the fury flare in her eyes, but before she could answer, he said, "I understand your anger, I'm beginning to see what I've done to you, and you are right, it was, is, grossly unfair. But I did not set out to hurt you. I honestly believed I could carry on with what I was doing and keep it all separate. You are the most perceptive person I know, Grace, so I think you know exactly how I feel about you, don't you?"

She didn't answer.

"Don't you?"

She shut her eyes momentarily and turned away.

"So, the thought I would intentionally hurt you, you must know I would never knowingly do that. Ever."

"And yet, you have." Her voice was flat.

"Yes."

"Just tell me, Cal. Tell me all of it, and then I will decide whether I can live with this or whether I have to walk away to save myself."

He could barely speak and had to breathe through the emotion for almost a minute before he could start.

As he was about to begin, she asked, "Who else knows?"

"Just Paul."

She nodded but did not say anything, and he began, "Building a multi-billion-pound company from scratch in just a few years is difficult. Seems simple now, looking back, but we needed to finance everything, and I arrived with nothing. When Graham and I planned all this, we searched the archives for winning lottery numbers around this time. That was how I got started. But you can only do that a few times before someone starts to smell a rat. Even so, winning lotteries around the world netted me hundreds of millions of dollars."

"Netted! You mean you stole several hundred million dollars?"

"Explain how that's theft?" he challenged her again. "It might be immoral or unfair, but theft?"

She was unhappy but had no answer and continued staring along the river. "I want to see the tickets. Do you still have them?"

The Land of the Blind

"Yes, I do, and you can." He picked up his rehearsed sequence, "One major advantage we had was in your field, cyber. You know what a zero-day exploit is?"

She recited the definition, "A flaw in software that only a hacker knows about, so the exploit works before anyone can patch it."

"Well, I have a list of them; some in code that hasn't been written yet. So we started by buying a small cybersecurity company, and 'discovered' a few of these exploits before anyone else, and made a name for ourselves. We also used a couple for our own purposes, along with some malware that is not easily detected by any of the current security tools."

"Sounds like that's breaking the law. Again. Why did Sania go along with this?"

"It was. Is. You'll have to ask her that yourself."

"And you're still doing it?"

"No, we no longer need to, and it was only ever used against criminal organisations, which I think is why Sania …"

She turned, suddenly and cut across him, "The HSBC exploit."

"Yes."

She was about to let him continue when something occurred to her. "Don't your people know about this? How much does Sania know?"

"Actually, she's one of the few people who know most of it, just not who I really am. She helped develop the exploits."

Grace's mouth dropped open, and a smile edged the anger aside. "Lying bitch! Nice work, sister."

He watched another thought dawn on her. "Oh, of course. That evening at the Oxo Tower. I told you about his mistress. And you didn't know and flipped out." She was replaying the scene in

383

her mind.

She paused, something nagging. "I don't quite get it, how did you, or how did Sania, hack all those accounts, thousands of them, along with the two-factor authentication each time? We never worked it out." She was distracted, her emotions temporarily displaced by the puzzle.

Callum was impressed with her ability to find the loose thread so quickly but was more grateful that her analytical mind was beginning to assert itself. "Ok, so there's one more thing to do with encryption."

He waited to see if Grace would put it together, and after a few moments, she did. After all, it was a topic of speculation across the entire cybersecurity world. She stared at him, her eyes wide. "No!"

He nodded.

"You broke encryption?" she whispered.

He nodded.

"The keys to the kingdom. You own the whole fucking internet the banking system, everything, the whole lot." He could see that she was truly shocked, but equally impressed.

"Yes, we just syphon off the network traffic from anywhere we have our software, …"

She interrupted, "HSBC. You're hacking your own Cyber Futures Clients."

"Not exactly, but sort of. We temporarily store the network traffic for analysis. It's encrypted, so as far as everyone is concerned, that's not a problem. Except, we can decrypt it, and it doesn't take a genius from that point."

Grace looked away again, staring without seeing, absorbing the real implications of this revelation.

"So where did all that stolen money go?"

"It all went to fund the expansion of our businesses, developing new energy technologies, and setting up factories for manufacturing. All from the proceeds of organised crime."

She turned back to him, serious again, "You do know that people died because of that, don't you. Directly because of you."

He spoke quietly, nodding gently, "I didn't know as such, because I've not looked, but yes, I knew that people might die; would die." He paused, thinking, "Actually, I did know about one. I read about Kosegin having Navalny Kolotsev killed -"

"You who stole Kolotsev's money?"

He nodded.

She was shocked, but suddenly wary, "How many more of these are there?"

"A few, but only one large one, other than your friend Bontempi, which you know about. The Sinaloa cartel lost a lot of money a couple of years ago; that was us. I'm guessing people lost their lives."

"Oh, Good guess, Cal." Her voice had a hard, controlled edge again, her anger palpable, "In fact, I think quite a few did. And of course, as I keep reminding you, Bontempi's mistress died too; those people always have a younger mistress? Remember how she died, Callum?"

He waited. She had already told him, and it was not an image he could ever remove.

She was seething and told him again, "She had her left breast cut off while she was alive, and she was thrown out of a fifth-floor window."

He looked away. "Yes, you told me."

"It's always the innocent women who pay, not the fucking men who exploit them."

The Land of the Blind

The outburst was sudden, evidence of how close below the surface her anger was. He waited as her breathing slowed. Eventually, she said heavily, "One more question about the HSBC thing and you and me. Did you somehow engineer to meet me because I was investigating the hack? Am I part of the collateral damage?"

"No, absolutely not."

She considered this carefully, "So our meeting really was just chance? Sania set us up, remember."

He nodded, "Yes, but that was because she sensed how lonely I was and she noticed how I reacted when we met."

"Smart woman." Her relief was palpable, but then she fixed him with her brown eyes and asked, "And you are telling me all of this, putting your master plan at risk, putting yourself forever in my power, because?"

'Forever in my power', he stared at her. Suddenly, he knew what she would do, and waves of relief and fear washed through him. She was watching him with complete focus. "You want me to say it?" he said.

"I want you to tell me why. I need to understand, and you telling me all this doesn't make sense from your perspective. It's weak, stupid, pathetic, and a needless risk."

"God, you're a hard case sometimes." He responded bleakly.

He had rehearsed the narrative so many times about how he had time-travelled, the progress they had made to get to where they were now, the businesses and technologies, all of that he knew. But now he had to explain his emotions to her. He started slowly, uncertain of his own mind. "One of the things I've learned, being over one hundred years old, is that I'm not the same person I was when I was twenty or fifty or even seventy. And I don't mean that you learn along the way and become wiser. You change, your personality changes, and you become a different person. I'd be irritated by the insecure, brash twenty-year-old me; disappointed by the complacent fifty-year-old me; but maybe I would be friends with the seventy-year-old me. Usually, you're ageing physically too, and it's hard to separate the learning and emotional changes from the physical deterioration. But imagine having the same energy and drive as you had in your thirties when you are a hundred. We only have a relationship now because I'm as old as I am. The twenty year old me would have been terrified of you; the fifty year old would just not have understood you but would have wanted you and would have pursued you, obsessed about you and the seventy year old would have liked you and been impressed by you, but would not have dared entertain a relationship. The hundred year old version of me, this me, understood from our first meeting how attracted I was to you and was smart enough not to fuck that up. So my current obsession with you is my problem and delight, not yours.

He paused, "I have this theory that the word Love is at the heart of many relationship problems. The Eskimos are supposed to have many words for snow; so how does our society have only one word for every type of strong emotional attachment? You've never heard me say I love you, Grace, and you never will, because the word is utterly inadequate, does not get close to describing my complicated feelings for you. Think about it; the feelings I had, that I still have, for my daughter do not intersect with my feelings for you. The feelings I had for Maria when I met her were not the same as those I felt in the days before she died. People who say they love someone just as much after decades as the day they met are either delusional or have poor memories. They mean something else; they just don't have the vocabulary. Oh, and people are told to learn to love themselves; it's stupid to use the same word."

He lapsed into silence, but she knew he had not finished and waited,

"Telling you was never my plan, Grace; you were never in it. I thought I could do this alone, this whole project, my obsession to save the world from itself. I lived it alone for so long, lying to everyone around me, choosing not to see the toll it took on me. Sharing it with Paul helped, but as time went on, it weighed on me more and more heavily. I closed myself off emotionally after losing Maria and Rachel; initially, as self-defence, not ever wanting to risk something so damaging as that loss. You get used to the slightly numb feeling and accept it. And then I met you, and you crashed through my defences. There it was again: the best feeling in the world. I was shocked by my initial, almost overwhelming animal need for you. Perhaps there's something to be said for a decade of abstinence. That infatuation is how humans bond, but it's chemical, a form of madness, and eventually it dwindles. There has to be something that binds people over a longer period. I don't quite have the words to describe what you do to me. Sometimes I believe I'm the luckiest man alive when I'm with you. It happens when I'm just walking in public with you, when I kiss you, it's the most glorious delusion. My seventy-year-old version would have been frightened of losing you, and it would have, slowly, eaten him up. Of course, the idea of losing implies I ever 'had' you, that you were ever somehow mine. The hundred-year-old me, this me, knows that's not true, that it's impossible. I want to spend as much time with you as I can. However much or little that is, it will never be enough and more than I could ever have hoped for. And none of this would be possible if I were to carry on concealing a large part of me, deceiving you." He gave her a moment before continuing "So that's why I've had to drop you in this shit and that's the way I feel today. It will not be the same in a month or a year, but today that's how I feel about you and why you had to know."

Grace had her eyes closed and Callum had no idea what she was going to say as the silence lengthened.

"Why couldn't you be just a wealthy businessman, nice and simple, loads of money and a high sex drive?" She paused, opened her eyes, and turned to him. "I think this might all end in tears; that's what I really think. On one hand, you have said some of the nicest things a human could say to another, while in the other hand, you're holding a grenade with the pin out. It was so much easier when we were just fucking each other, Cal." The words were weary, but she forced a smile. "Obviously, I see your emotional …" She paused searching, " dependence on me, and now I understand it better, but I can't respond now, because I'm just too confused and angry."

"You don't have to respond, it's not a competition, my feelings are my feelings. You telling me to fuck off and never speaking to me again would honestly be like an ice-pick through my body, and you saying you'll join me on my journey would be fabulous. But my feelings would not change in this moment."

"Ice-pick? Interesting choice. I have to think about this, and I can't do that when I'm with you. It's too much." She stared at him hard, and he waited. "You understand the moral dilemma I have now. Are you sure I won't turn you in?"

"My best guess and my hope is that you won't, there's a lot still to do."

She raised her eyebrows.

"I remember you said you thought I was a good person. I believe I am, despite what I've done and have to do in the future, because the greater good really is being served."

"You fucker." She said, quietly, her jaw muscles tight, lips compressed. "That greater good depends on me believing you have actually seen the world falling apart. That you are a time traveller, I can't believe I'm saying the words." She was shaking her head.

There was nothing he could say.

"Impossible fucking mind fuck. Fuck! If I believe you I'm fucked, aren't I? If I don't believe you I'm fucked too." Her anger blossomed again, and as Callum raised his hands, she shut her eyes and screamed at the top of her voice. She was rigid, fists clenched with her face to the sky and as the long, vicious howl of frustration and outrage at what he was doing to her poured forth.

He instinctively stepped away from her against the guard rail and looked up at the embankment above them, seeing the faces turning towards the source of the dreadful sound.

Finally, she stopped and faced him, her face a mask, and he was trembling. "Grace …" he started, but he had no idea what to say.

"You fucker." She said, again.

"There's nothing else I can say, Grace. You need to do what's best for you now, whatever that is. I'll be here whatever you decide. I'm in Geneva the rest of this week, so take your time."

"Independent, neutral Switzerland? We have extradition treaties, you know?" She turned abruptly and walked quickly away.

He watched her ascend the walkway and, without turning her head, stride away along the embankment as he tried to control his racing heart and the very real fear he had felt at her violent anger.

The Land of the Blind

What had he done?

40.

The Metropolitan Police came for him, as before, in the early hours. They did not plan to break down the door this time; they knocked and waited. MI6 had him under surveillance and knew that he was alone in the flat, but there was no answer. After a few minutes, they had no choice but to force entry again. The flat was empty. The bed had been slept in, but it was cold, and now, for the first time in weeks, they had no idea where he was.

***

The Signal call woke Callum several hours before the MET arrived at his door. It was not a number he recognised, but he answered anyway, blind in the dark room, groping for the table lamp. She said, "They are coming. Leave now, and remember, they are watching."

After his first arrest, at Grace's insistence, he had a bag ready to grab, containing a few essentials and cash. When they discussed how he would escape, if it ever came to this, it had seemed melodramatic, but Grace had been insistent. Her paranoia saved him. Ten minutes after the call, with the small rucksack cinched against his back, he slipped quietly through the fire door onto the flat roof of his building and crept, crouched to the rear edge away from the prying eyes at the front. On the south side, furthest from the river, was an office building, and they had decided that if it came to it, he could jump the gap from his building roof to this adjacent one. From there, he could climb down one of the rainwater pipes at the far side of that building. Standing on the roof in the dark, the gap had doubled in size. His mind told him this jump was impossible, and the fall, if he did not make it, would kill him. But the human mind is pliable, and he found himself walking back along the roof to where he needed to sprint from. He closed his eyes and wished he were in Grace's body. She could have jumped this with ease, and in his mind's eye, he saw her standing, hands on hips, on the far roof patiently waiting for him to catch up. Afterwards, he could retrieve no memory of the next few seconds. He sprinted as fast as he could to the sound of his feet striking the roof and then silence as he launched himself into space. Had the two roofs been level, he would not have made it, but his building was one floor taller, and he cleared the lower roof edge by almost half a meter. As he jumped, he had no thought for the landing and, unprepared, crashed forward, sprawling onto the abrasive surface, removing the skin from both palms and forearms and one of his knees. He lay dazed, one cheek against the rough, cold surface, panting uncontrollably even though the whole thing had taken only five seconds. He was sure he had broken something and lay still, waiting for his extremities to report the dismal news. Nothing. Cautiously, he moved his feet, legs, and arms and realised he had survived intact, at least for all practical purposes. He knelt, cautiously stood in a crouch, and shuffled across to the far corner of the building, where he knew there was a rainwater downpipe. His left foot felt odd, but there was no pain. The building had been renovated recently, and for continuity, the planners had insisted on using certain external materials, including cast iron rainwater pipes. Callum inched his legs over the low parapet and tried to wedge his feet between the pipe and the wall. As he lowered himself over the edge, the pain from his skinned palms made itself felt. When they came to find how he had escaped, they would not have to look far. As he grasped the coarse, cold pipe with his bleeding hands, he thought for a moment that he would not be able to hold on; the fire across his palms was unbearable. But his body knew better, and as the adrenaline surged and the endorphins dampened the peak of the pain, he lowered himself, leaving a smeared, bloody trail on the pipe. It took several agonising minutes, and his arms were beginning to shake as, twisting to look down, he dropped the final few feet to the dark ground. For an instant, he thought that he had been electrocuted or tasered. A white hot bolt of undiluted pain exploded in his left leg, and he collapsed on the ground, whimpering and clutching his ankle. He lay there for a little while, waiting for the pain to become bearable, leaking pathetic sounds. Eventually, his breathing calmed, and the edge of his world expanded beyond his own body again. There was no sound, no one running to apprehend him, but he was wet on one side, lying in water of which he had been unaware until then. It was disgusting. He was beside a row of large refuse bins, industrial-sized with pivoting lids, and the water must have leaked from them. He considered climbing inside one and curling up, but his rational mind gradually reasserted itself. He rolled onto his knuckles and knees and immediately regretted doing so, whimpering again at the onslaught of pain. After a moment of self-indulgence, his mind allowed that the pain was a manageable eight or nine out of ten, a pale imitation of the twenty out of ten he had experienced and survived just seconds earlier.

He heard himself whisper, "Pathetic," and forced himself to his feet, or at least his right foot, balancing with just the toe of his left on the ground. There was no way to walk on his damaged ankle, and he hopped and limped awkwardly around the bins in the lee of the building and into Bear Gardens. He could feel the swelling in his ankle without looking, as his body immobilised the joint and numbed it. The uneven cobbles drew whispered curses until he emerged on Park Street, and then, slowly, heaving on the cold handrail, mounted the steps onto Southwark Bridge Road. On one knee, he leaned against the damp brick at the top of the steps and, hidden from the road, he waited; there would be a taxi along, eventually.

He waited for fifteen minutes, during which time his body went into shock. He was sick on the pavement and began to shake uncontrollably. He missed two taxis, unaware of their existence in the grim, swirling haze he was immersed in. Gradually, he emerged, shivering with cold, and stumbled onto the pavement. Attempting to appear in control, he managed to flag down a black cab, its glorious, bright, yellow beacon surely there to save him.

He had the presence of mind not to tell the reluctant cabbie the exact address while negotiating the hundred-pound tip and promising to sit on the floor. His claim that he had fallen in the river seemed plausible to his addled brain. The driver assumed he was drunk, stoned or both, but a hundred quid plus the fare, in cash, on a quiet night and a trip back into the centre of town was not to be sneezed at; as long as the drunk really did stay off the seats.

Callum lay in a foetal curl on the floor, marvelling that, thirty minutes earlier, he had been perfectly comfortable in his bed, lost in deep sleep.

***

His last visit to the apartment in Shaw House had been to send the package to Yitzhak Sabhan in Jerusalem; the contents of which had ultimately killed the Russian President. Then, he had wandered over from the nearby tube station in minutes. Now, the shorter walk, from where the taxi dropped him at the entrance to the Washington Mayfair Hotel on Curzon Street, took fifteen minutes, all endured in considerable pain. The two large Ibuprofen tablets he had swallowed, with difficulty, while lying in the back of the cab, were finally beginning to have an effect as he stood in the lift enveloped in his stench of vomit and refuse. He realised now why the cabbie had scoffed at his initial offers of twenty and then fifty pounds.

When the Metropolitan Police broke down the door of his flat in New Globe Walk an hour later Callum was just a few miles away in the bath surveying the damage to his body, gently removing the blood and grit from his hands and forearms, his grossly swollen and increasingly colourful ankle propped on a chair beside the bath.

When the water cooled and nothing more could be done to soothe his lacerated palms, he hauled himself upright and showered away the blood. Wrapping himself in a towel, he hopped to the bed and, before he fell asleep, checked that the small laptop and two modified mobile phones Sania's team had prepared for him were intact. Their careful padding and the toll he had paid in skin landing on the roof had ensured their survival. Starting the laptop, he connected to a Virtual Private Network before emailing Gail Bailey-Royce, 'Please tell Grace I'm safe. Callum.'

***

He woke five hours later, and for a moment, he had no idea where he was. He moved, and the recent events slammed into his consciousness with a sickening jolt. One arm and knee were stuck to the sheets, and a hand was oozing blood and plasma onto his stomach. His left foot was numb, not communicating, as though it had been amputated. He gently, painfully, freed himself, inspected his wounds and lay quietly wondering what his next move should be; certain that, for now, everyone he knew would be under surveillance. His friends would attempt to communicate with him via the phone he had left on the bedside table in his abandoned flat. For now, the only safe communication was with Gail. In theory, any interaction with his solicitor was subject to lawyer-client privilege, but he had no illusions about how little protection that might offer in his circumstances. The security services would be listening. They might be unable to read or hear what was said, but all they needed was his location. There were tins of food and dried goods in the flat so that he could eat, but more urgently, he needed bandages and some basic medicines; he had to avoid his wounds becoming infected, and the flat contained only a basic first aid kit. He agonised over sending the list of things he needed, plus a delivery address to Gail, but his options were limited. Could the security services track something her law firm sent to him? He decided it was unlikely. They must courier parcels to people all the time, and there would be no way to track all of them. Despite this rationalisation, he was extremely uncomfortable with the idea of delivering something right to his door.

Finally, he eased out of bed and dressed himself as best he could before sending encrypted emails to two different people. Breakfast was baked beans, warmed in the microwave. He settled, in discomfort, in the armchair to wait and was soon asleep. Pain from his ankle dragged him back to consciousness several hours later, for as long as it took to swallow more analgesics and retreat into sleep again. The delivery arrived four hours later, and a knock on the door woke him. Callum remained quiet, knowing that the instruction would be to leave the parcel if there was no response, but the courier did not even wait to check and left immediately. He now had what he needed to allow him to hide quietly for days.

41.

Grace played no part in Callum's escape, finding out about the new arrest warrant through a circuitous route long after the dramatic events of the previous evening. It was to Sania's planning and foresight that he owed his tenuous freedom. Sania still had access to Jamie Jones' pwned phone, the messages from which Callum had started to review over recent weeks in an attempt to find who Jones' contacts were in the press, police and security services. They still had no answers, but Sania was capturing all his messages and had put a watch on several key words; 'warrant' being one of them. The alarm had been triggered by a message to an unknown number about three hours before the raid on Callum's flat. The software alerted Sania at around one o'clock, and after reading the full message, she immediately called Callum. Too agitated to sleep for the rest of the night, she had started reading the message feed from the pwned phone and listening to the recorded calls. The mundane drudgery of another's life would ordinarily have induced sleep in short order, but now it felt like she was panning for gold amongst digital dross. She learned nothing useful, and by morning had no idea what had happened to Callum.

Grace received a WhatsApp message from Gail Bailey-Royce to say that Callum was safe. The message was disturbing because she had not known he was in imminent danger; although, given

399

what had been happening recently, it was not wholly unexpected. She phoned him and was mildly surprised when his phone rang. He did not answer, and she left a message asking him to call her. On her way to work, she made an encrypted call to Sania to see if she knew what was happening, and the pieces fell into place. The fact that she had not had a visit from the security services was puzzling; evidence that they were monitoring her communication and watching her, and knew that she was not involved. She smiled to herself, thinking that his luck was holding. They had talked about what to do if the security services did find sufficient evidence to re-arrest him. Gail was adamant that, even if there were compelling evidence, the United Kingdom government would still fail to convict him under terrorism legislation. The highest risk was that they would take the easy route and turn him over to the Americans. Callum was equally adamant that he would not allow this to happen; they had only spoken about it briefly once, but she could not remember him being so resolute in his opposition to an idea. He refused to debate the options.

They were waiting for her at Wandsworth Police Station, allowing her to walk directly to them. When she arrived, the desk sergeant told her she was required in one of the interview rooms. Despite knowing exactly what was coming, as she stepped into the room, she had to lean back against the door and close her eyes for a second, composing herself before glaring at each of them, in turn, fists clenched, her jaw set. She closed her eyes again, breathed deeply, and relaxed her hands, shaking them loose. It was time, she was about to be asked to choose sides, and in that moment she realised she had made up her mind.

"Good morning, gentlemen, how can I be of assistance?"

The older, balding, slightly overweight man introduced them,

"I'm DCI Hunte, and this is DI Roberts." He saw by her reaction that the names were familiar, and she pre-empted him.

"Ah, you are with counter terrorism, aren't you? You interviewed Callum at Belmarsh. Wow, sending in the big guns right off."

DCI Hunte ignored her lack of deference. "DC Sommers, you are not under arrest..." The inevitable pause: "At this time … and you may leave at any point, but we would like to ask you some questions about Callum Moorcroft and your relationship with him."

"Sure," she smiled grimly and took one of the chairs, "Can I ask who's back there?" She nodded at the mirrored glass.

The two men sat opposite her, "There is no one observing us, DC Sommers, and this interview is not being recorded. Should we deem that necessary, we will make further arrangements."

She nodded her understanding and took a close look at DI Roberts. She felt that DCI Hunte would be entirely impervious to her emotional influence, but DI Roberts was altogether more interesting. The fact that they had illicit access to his phone and some of his most intimate interactions gave her a tiny, almost sexual thrill and a sense of advantage over him. He was sharply dressed and groomed, and she examined his eyes and mouth closely until she sensed his discomfort. Holding his gaze, she saw him compose himself and affect a look of casual indifference. She smiled and turned back to DCI Hunte. "How can I help?" adding quickly, "Sir."

"Do you know the whereabouts of Mr Callum Moorcroft?"

She surfaced a plausible reaction. "At home in his flat, I assume. Unless you arrested him, but then we would not be having this conversation." Her eyes widened, theatrically, "He's escaped?"

The Land of the Blind

DCI Hunte could not suppress his irritation. "Mr Moorcroft is not in custody, and we have a warrant for his arrest on serious charges. Facts we believe you may have already been aware of, DC Sommers."

She paused before replying, "In which case, you must have new evidence with regard to the terrorism offences you believe he's committed."

"As you might imagine, we are not likely to discuss that with you. All I can tell you is, we have a warrant for Mr Moorcroft's arrest, and he seems to have fled."

"Well, I think you know I've no idea where he is. You've been watching me closely enough for some time now. You know he was not at my flat last night, and I'm pretty sure your intercepts will tell you that I've been trying, unsuccessfully, to contact him this morning. He's not answering his phone, and he usually does when I call. Now I know why."

"Could you answer the question, DC Sommers?"

"Sorry, too busy joining the dots as it were, old habits. No, Sir, I do not know where Callum is." And then, despite herself, added, "But I'm glad you lot don't have him."

"You lot? Don't we work for the same team, Detective?"

With half a smile, Grace said, "Sometimes, sir, yes, we do, and sometimes our lives are a bit more complicated."

DCI Hunte's tiny reaction acknowledged the kernel of truth in this.

"Help us out here, DC Sommers. It seems you know Moorcroft better than anyone. I've listened to your recent interview at Battersea. Yours is not a casual relationship, is it?"

"No."

"If I were not an old, cynical copper, I'd say that you and he are in love, at least you are in love with him."

She fought to suppress the unexpected blush and failed.

"That's what I thought. So I'm guessing you would do a great deal to protect him."

She stopped herself from the impulse to shift in the chair and answered truthfully, "Yes, I would."

"To the point where you lose your job, your career?"

She remained still, and it took her a moment to respond, but again, it was the truth: "Possibly, yes."

"Well!"

DI Roberts's verbal smirk caught her off guard, and she turned to him but controlled herself just in time. She held his gaze until he dropped his, which took several seconds. Then, she turned back to DCI Hunte, who was watching her carefully.

"It's a powerful emotion, true love," he said, quietly, a slight wistfulness in his tone. "Now where were we?" he asked rhetorically, "Ah yes; perhaps from your vantage point you could give us an insight into what's driving Mr Moorcroft."

Perhaps she had misjudged this detective; there was something or someone familiar hiding in that myopic, overweight and deeply unattractive body, and her prejudice had not allowed for this. What would she be asking if the roles were reversed?

"This is all about climate change, sir. What do you know about the subject? Unless you have an understanding, nothing will make any sense."

"Interesting you should ask, DC Sommers, because after our previous interviews with Mr Moorcroft, when he spoke about this, I followed up with a little research, so I think you could say that I now have a reasonable grasp of the subject. To the surprise of my daughter, I might add."

The Land of the Blind

"Callum is convinced that the problem is much worse than most people appreciate. He believes that unless we act far faster than we have been doing, the costs to the whole world will be vastly greater than anyone can imagine."

"He seems to be going about this rather differently from most of the tree huggers, wouldn't you say?"

"Ever since he's understood the problem, he and the companies he works for have been developing technologies to reduce our greenhouse gas emissions, and the livestock thing is just one of them."

DCI Hunte reacted imperceptibly to what appeared to be a tacit admission that Callum was responsible for the virus attacks, but continued, "He's made either himself or their investors, or both, a great deal of money in the process."

"And where is all that wealth, the flash cars and yachts?" she countered.

"A fair question, DC Sommers. But the fact that we can't see it doesn't mean it's not there."

"Believe what you will, but if you think he's motivated by money, you're barking up the wrong tree."

"OK, then what does he get out of this?"

Grace considered this. "Have you ever been at the scene of a serious accident, DCI Hunte, or seen someone hurt or in danger? I have, and there's a human instinct to help. It's hard to understand, logically, but people do it all the time. They put themselves at risk and do, as we say, 'the right thing'. That's what this is. He's watching a slow-motion crash on a planetary scale and doing what he thinks is right."

"And part of that, 'doing the right thing' is destroying an entire industry, millions of jobs and livelihoods? Blighting countless lives?"

She held his gaze, "That's what he believes."

"He obviously holds that the ends justify his means. But the problem is we don't know what these ends are, so we don't know what he's saving us from; in which case, is he not on shaky moral ground? Isn't he just the same as every zealot with a passion, a religion to sell?"

It was a reasonable analysis, but Grace just shrugged, "I can't help you there, DCI Hunte, I can only tell you what he believes."

"And what you believe too, DC Sommers?"

"I'm prepared to believe him."

"And you're a reliable witness?"

"We all have to believe in something."

DCI Hunte paused, "Really. I thought our job was to weigh the evidence and reach a conclusion based on that, not believe what we are told."

"Facts are slippery, DCI Hunte. In our line of work, we soon discover that, and in the end, there's more belief than we usually acknowledge."

He regarded her carefully for a moment, nodding imperceptibly.

"In this matter, DC Sommers, you can have no evidence, there is none, so I am forced to conclude that your willingness to believe Moorcroft has more to do with your feelings for him than anything more tangible."

"Sir, all I can tell you is what I believe his motivation is. I'm a bystander in this. What he or someone else did to the livestock industry took place before we met, and it was only recently that I discovered what that was."

"And rather than come forward with this information, you

chose to keep it to yourself. Or perhaps it gave you some leverage with this rather wealthy businessman."

She did not react to the provocation.

"You have a reputation for being highly manipulative where men are concerned, DC Sommers. Is that fair?"

"Ha! Not that old trope again, the manipulative slag with loose morals. Not for me to say, Sir." She replied shortly and fixed him.

He paused, long enough to acknowledge the accusation, but continued, "If I put it to you that you acquired the funding for your refuge project because of the leverage you enjoyed over Mr Moorcroft. Is that such a ridiculous suggestion? Surely that's plausible?"

"Plausible, but wrong."

"We only have your word on that, don't we, DC Sommers?"

"Yes, sir, you do."

There was a long pause as DCI Hunte stared off into space while DI Roberts kept his attention on Grace, and it was her turn to feign casual indifference. Eventually, DCI Hunte resumed. "So, DC Sommers, how do we track down Mr Moorcroft?"

"I have no idea, Sir."

"For example, what would his reaction be to an appeal by you to give himself up?"

Grace's surprise was evident: "He would ignore it. We've spoken about this. For whatever reason, he's not prepared to give himself up if the result is that he ends up in the hands of the Americans."

"Interesting. Our American friends are the bogeyman, rather than us?"

"Let's say he has more faith in British justice than American. But it seems that's part of the problem, too. His solicitor is pretty confident that you will not be able to convict him of terrorism. Apparently, for reasons only our government can explain, it is not illegal for an individual to deploy a biological weapon in the way you believe Callum has. Who knew?"

"Indeed, that is something of a surprise to many of us." DCI Hunte was not being facetious.

"So it's a fair bet that if we can't convict him of anything, the Americans will not just let him go free, regardless of the fact that they have only motive and means and thin, circumstantial evidence. As usual, they need their simple narrative of goodies and baddies to play their modern version of cowboys and Indians, this time with Callum in the role of Sitting Bull. And don't tell me you're sure we won't roll over and hand him to the Americans, I'm not that naïve."

He replied with a conviction she recognised, "We will eventually find him, you know, DC Sommers. Sooner rather than later, probably, so the question is how do we make that as painless as possible for everyone?"

***

They let her go and when she walked into the office and sat at her desk, there was complete silence and ten pairs of eyes turned to watch her.

"You still got a job then Polly? You're like a cat with nine lives." DC Hinkley called across the room.

She looked across at Jane Hinkley, "Seems Callum's done a runner, but since I've been under surveillance for weeks they know I don't know where he is. So for now it's business as usual."

"It's not going to end well." Was Hinkley's summary.

Grace called Sania and arranged to come to the office after work and then tried, with mixed success, to focus on her job as a detective.

It was late when Grace arrived at the Cyber Futures office to find Paul and Sania the only people still there. They had waited for her. The three of them sat in the shielded glass meeting room, and more cautious than ever, they played a recording of background noise while they talked. They had no idea where Callum was.

"He'll still be in the UK, I assume, because there's a watch on all ports of entry," Grace informed them. "I believe the company owns or rents more than one flat in London and possibly elsewhere, but fortunately, I have no idea where or how to find out."

"Armando might. You know, follow the money as they say." Paul said.

"He won't tell them, and there's no practical way to force him. We've no jurisdiction in Switzerland, and there's nothing to tie the company or him to what Callum's done."

Sania was visibly upset and close to tears. "I can't see how this can be fixed. They will never stop looking for him, and then they will lock him up forever, won't they? I mean, how long can he hide for?"

Grace shook her head, "It's not even that simple, I'm afraid." She explained the likely result of them catching Callum, being unable to prosecute him under UK law, and the Americans insisting on his being handed over. "All of which would take many months, possibly years, to play out. We have resisted American extradition requests in the past, but this is so high profile I can see them forcing the issue, eventually."

There was a grim silence to which Grace added, "And I'm pretty sure he will not let the Americans take him, whatever happens." It was her turn to stem tears, and when Sania took her hand, they both failed.

They composed themselves and then Paul said, quietly, "You know what he has to do. He does have one final card. He convinced us; if he convinced them, they would never surrender him."

Grace looked at him, thinking and nodded, "You're probably right, but would he do that?"

Sania was watching them, confused. "What are you talking about?"

Paul and Grace exchanged a long look. He nodded to Grace, who turned to her, "Sania, there is one thing that Callum has never told you. Only two other people know this, Paul and I, and I only found out recently."

She told Sania how Callum had travelled from the future to attempt to stop the worst of climate change and that he was Paul's son. Both Paul and Grace had been through this moment, and they took their time. They understood it would not be quick. Sania refused to believe their explanation, resisting the outrageous fabrication as strongly as either of them had done. But as she directed question after question at them, she gradually realised that they were telling her the truth. Suddenly, breaking encryption made sense, and eventually, after more than an hour, the sheer weight of small things overwhelmed her scepticism and disbelief.

"All those zero-day exploits we found, it was always him." She stared at them, reluctant acceptance taking hold as it had for each of them.

"And so," Grace finished, "Paul means he has to tell them who he is and why he's done everything, to convince them that he had no choice."

"But it also gives him leverage. Our Government will never

The Land of the Blind

hand over someone with his knowledge to the Americans, he would become a prized asset." Paul added.

"They would have to accept this narrative without making it public," Grace added. "There is no advantage in the rest of the world knowing who he is and what he knows."

"But, there are two things we've not discussed." Paul interjected, "They absolutely can't know about our ability to break encryption or the full details of our involvement in the All-Seeing Eye."

The implications of what they had been doing all this time seemed to close in on them, and their thoughts turned inwards, the only sound in the room, the incongruous background sound of a tropical forest.

Suddenly, Sania blurted, "But that's the answer, The All-Seeing Eye." She had always liked this idea in a way the others failed to appreciate, and now she thought she had a way out for them. Her childish delight was infectious, and she drew them in as she explained how she thought they could save Callum.

42.

Grace contacted DCI Hunte the following morning and asked to see him. He told her to come to Scotland Yard and he would meet with her as soon as she could get there.

She knocked on the door bearing the designation 'Detective Chief Inspector Hunte', and wondered momentarily whether a similar door would one day have her name on it. The realisation that this future no longer existed for her, that even if it had only ever been a dream, it could never happen, caught her unawares. She stared at the letters as the tide of anger rose and fell back as resignation and hurt before she was called to enter.

Sitting opposite DCI Hunte, she took in the small, slightly untidy office, the picture of a woman and two young girls at the edge of the desk. She had rehearsed what she would say on her journey over and was about to begin when he pre-empted her, "You look tired, DC Sommers."

"Sir, yes, long night."

"I can imagine. So, have you considered your position regarding Moorcroft?"

"Well, sort of. The first thing to say is that I do not know where he is. However, I understand that he can be contacted via his attorney, I believe you know her, Gail -"

"Bailey-Royce, Oh yes, I know her."

She could not read him, but it was irrelevant, and she

411

continued, "I don't think she knows where he is either, but they are in contact."

DCI Hunte just nodded, watching her.

"I believe we might be able to persuade Callum to give himself up."

"That's good to hear, DC Sommers, because we believe he may be injured." He ignored her alarm and continued, "We found blood on the adjacent building to where he lives; it was how he escaped. Quite a reasonable amount of blood, I understand. So perhaps the sooner we find him, the better."

Grace was about to speak when he continued, "Do you have any idea how he was alerted to his impending arrest?"

She paused, then spoke carefully, "It would appear, Sir, that there are people within your organisation who have relationships with press members. My understanding is that he found out as a result of that."

DCI Hunte was unamused, and one of his fingers began tapping the edge of the desk until he realised he was doing it.

"And how exactly …" he began, before continuing in a resigned tone, "That's rather disappointing to hear; can you provide any more details, DC Sommers?"

"No, " she said slowly, "But it's something that I might be able to follow up on if it would be helpful. I mean, there are people I could ask."

DCI Hunte was irritated now. "DC Sommers, I do not pretend to understand your role in this, but you are a police officer charged with upholding the law. I hope that has not slipped your mind in all the excitement."

"No, Sir, it has not," Grace replied firmly. "I take my responsibilities as a police officer very seriously indeed." She paused and added, "But, Sir, I find myself in a position where it is far from clear where my moral responsibility lies."

His eyebrows shot up, and then he frowned. After a moment, he said, "OK, Sommers, go on, tell me how we resolve this."

"Well, Sir, I'm afraid this is the bit you will not like. I need to talk to the Commissioner."

He stared at her, brow furrowed, "The MET Commissioner?" She nodded.

"There is no way we are going to see the Commissioner, Sommers."

After a moment, looking directly ahead and not at him, she added, "I need to see her, sir, on my own."

She had never head him swear but he did now, laughing he said "Fuck off Sommers." and then after a moment, shaking his head in disbelief, "That's not the way it works, Constable. If you have information pertinent to the arrest of Callum Moorcroft, it is your duty as a Police Officer to reveal it."

"In that case, sir, I do not."

He was furious and suddenly stood; she automatically stood too, knocking over her chair.

His voice was controlled, but he spat the words at her, "Consider very carefully what you say next, DC Sommers, because it could end your career as a police officer."

She did not speak, looking straight ahead, trying to stop her hands from shaking.

"I will ask you once more: what information do you have concerning the whereabouts of Callum Moorcroft?"

She was breathless, but said quietly, "None, sir."

He picked up the phone, hit a button hard and almost shouted, "Duty Sergeant, security, my office, now!"

The Land of the Blind

Within seconds, the door opened, and two firearms officers, one crouching, weapons in hand, found DCI Hunte and DC Sommers standing immobile, staring past one another in silence.

"Lock her up."

The two officers glanced at one another but immediately shouldered their weapons. One stepped up behind Grace, saying simply, "Hands." She put them behind her back, and the cuffs closed on her wrists. They were considerate enough to do it with a minimum of force.

"Follow me."

She was escorted through the building to the basement, one officer in front, one behind, and placed in a holding cell without another word being spoken.

***

Only a few miles away, Sania and Paul were having a far more productive day. They had been updating the All-Seeing Eye website and had transferred ownership of the domain to a Subsidiary of Cyber Futures. They intended it to be visibly their project. They created a holding page, a teaser for the new question they would ask the world to debate. The new page, **theallseeingeye.org/livestock**, was posted across all social media outlets. Following the press outrage at the death of Kosegin, nothing on the site had changed, and people's interest had waned; it quickly re-ignited. The headline image was of three cows, on the canvas of a vast, otherwise empty, pasture.

As the likes and forwarded messages spread and people began to find the new site, interest flared. They watched all day as the story began to unfold, and by that evening, it was the second item on the UK's national news and headlined worldwide. This time, no one was being threatened; the new question being asked of people was whether the use of a virus to destroy the global livestock industry was justified. It was an emotive global story, and news outlets everywhere competed for experts to opine on both sides. Some cited the gravity of climate change and the impact the livestock industry had been having as justification, and others thought it was terrorism ruining lives. In parallel, a debate was taking place about whether one of the world's largest IT companies should be hosting the site on its platform. Once again, the company's position, set out by their Chief Technical Officer in San Francisco, was that as long as the site did not advocate violence in the way that the original had, it would not be taken down. Further, their press release stated:

'The model the site's owners are using to assess public opinion represents a novel and potentially beneficial way to reach trans-national democratic decisions, and we will continue to support the project. '

Given that Sania and Paul had sought no assurances from the hosting platform, this statement was a fantastic endorsement. As the CEO of Cyber Futures, Sania posted on the company site, thanking them for their support of popular democracy. The press and social media gobbled up the controversy and spat it around the globe

***

After holding Grace in a cell for several hours, DCI Hunte, accompanied by one of the security officers, brought her a drink. She was asked again what information she had and threatened with a charge of perverting the course of justice. She refused to change her mind and, for the second time, found herself charged and under arrest. DCI Bailey seemed to take a perverse delight in cautioning her himself. As soon as this happened, she had the right to a solicitor and phoned Gail.

Gail could not get to her until the end of the day, and it was after eight in the evening when they let her into the cell. Grace spent fifteen minutes outlining what they needed to do without revealing the key piece of information which would justify all the effort. She would only tell Gail that Callum possessed something the state would find compelling and that he would be able to use it as leverage to prevent his arrest and deportation. Gail probed hard for details, reluctant to accept that there could be anything so valuable it could bestow this sort of protection. Only their personal relationship, developed in working together over many months on the Elira refuge project, swayed Gail to trust Grace's judgement.

Finally, she agreed in principle. "OK, but why the Commissioner?"

"She runs the MET. Who else can I go to with this?"

"If whatever revelation you have carries the weight you say it does, perhaps we should go higher."

"Higher, who?"

"I may have mentioned before that I have access to the Home Secretary."

Grace's eyes widened.

"But," Gail was emphatic, "I absolutely cannot go to him with something half-baked; my credibility is on the line at this point."

"I promise he will run with this if you can get me to see the Home Secretary for ten minutes."

"Get you to see him?"

Grace looked embarrassed, "I'm sorry, Gail, I know this sounds so … "

"You can't trust me with this, Grace? Really?"

The Land of the Blind

Grace held her face in her hands and, after some time, looked up. "You're right, that's not fair. I can't exclude you. But when you discover what this is, I hope you will forgive me for being so disloyal."

Gail was hard to read. She looked hard at Grace, thinking about all their interactions over time, and then stood and pulled out her phone. There was no signal, and she had to leave the cell to send the message. A few minutes later, she returned.

"Well, he's seen it, but so far no response."

"What did you ask him?"

"For two minutes on a secure phone line. So I need to go now, in case he calls, and as soon as I have anything, I'll return. Whatever time it is."

It was almost midnight when they came to get her. She was temporarily released into the custody of her solicitor but would be returned to her cell immediately after their business was concluded. Grace had no idea how something like this could happen, but she climbed into the large black car with Gail, and they were driven a short distance from the Embankment to the Home Office on Marsham Street. Ten minutes later, they were being escorted into a surprisingly plain, functional office to find Jonathan Cooke sitting at his desk, with the classic red briefcase open to one side. He was reading some papers, a gold pen poised in one hand. Without raising his head, he held up one finger and continued reading the page before him.

Grace and Gail stood where they were as the door closed behind them and waited. Grace was aware of her heart beating and tried to still her hands to prevent them from repeatedly smoothing her trousers. In contrast, Gail seemed completely at ease, taking in the room calmly. It was rather austere, with frosted glass

417

cupboards, pale wood, and a dark carpet. The blinds were closed, and the uniform light from the ceiling tinged everything sepia.

Cooke tossed the papers into the red briefcase, closed the lid, stood up, and stretched his arms upwards. It seemed such a normal thing to do, but Grace registered surprise. He was dressed in a classic suit, the jacket over the back of the chair, and his red tie matched the colour of his ministerial briefcase. He seemed so familiar; she had seen his image countless times and on television. As he came around the desk, smiling at Gail, he was much smaller than Grace had imagined.

As Cooke approached, Gail stepped forward. They took each other's hands and kissed on both cheeks. This simple action could barely have made Grace more uncomfortable. Here was one of the country's most senior politicians and its highest-profile human rights lawyer, and they might have been meeting casually in the supermarket or perhaps one dropping by at the other's country home.

"Gail, it's been too long. How are you? You look just fabulous, as always."

Grace watched the two of them wearing their power and privilege so lightly. She waited as they discussed Cooke's son, who was studying at Cambridge. Gail closed the conversation, "You and Audrey must come over for dinner. Curtis is recording at the moment, so he's around. We can have a proper gossip then."

Gail turned to Grace, "Jonathan, this is Grace Sommers. I've been working with her for some time on a project she initiated to support trafficked women. She's a DC, as I think you know. She's a remarkable young woman." She smiled at Grace as she said this, and Grace could tell that her affirmation carried weight with Cooke, who extended his hand.

The Land of the Blind

"Home Secretary, it's nice to meet you, thank you for allowing us some of your valuable time."

Cooke indicated the two chairs at the desk, behind which he returned to sit and face them.

"It was a rather curious request from Gail, I must admit. Why don't you explain how you contrived to get yourself arrested. Again."

Grace could not prevent herself from blushing. Her hands fidgeted, suddenly acquiring an independence they did not usually enjoy. "This is so weird, I'm not sure where to begin, but …"

"Perhaps if I explain what I've been briefed on so far, that will make it easier for you to complete the picture?" Cooke offered.

Grace nodded, grateful for the lead.

Cooke's precise, Southern Counties accent made him sound like a newsreader from fifty years earlier, "There is an outstanding arrest warrant for a Mr Callum Moorcroft, who stands accused of creating the viral infections in livestock which have devastated the industry across the globe. Gail has explained the curious position in which we find ourselves concerning the current legislation and the difficulty in securing a conviction were he to be tried in our courts. The whereabouts of Mr Moorcroft are currently unknown despite a considerable effort underway to locate him. It has been suggested that you may know where he is, but for personal reasons, will not provide that information."

Grace was finally able to think more clearly and answered carefully, "I do not know where Callum is, but, yes, I believe he was involved in the creation of the viruses, although I don't have any direct evidence of this." She added quickly. "But whether it was him or not. It's just part of a much, much bigger plan of his to address climate change."

The Land of the Blind

"Ah, climate change, again, it seems all roads eventually lead there these days," Cooke interjected wearily.

Grace carried on, "I'm sure you know that Callum has invested a huge amount of time and money in building the Green Futures group of companies and has probably done more than anyone on the planet to help stop global warming. The livestock thing is a part of that. The Amazon will be destroyed if something isn't done."

"Well, I've seen some of the science and I understand that we are making progress."

"Callum has actually seen it happen." She had not intended to say this, but she sensed that the Home Secretary was not taking her seriously.

"Many people have visited the Amazon to see these things for themselves. What makes you believe Mr Moorcroft is any more qualified than the other scientists to assess the future impacts?"

"I mean, he's seen what will happen in the future."

The resulting silence filled the room, and Grace suddenly felt Gail's nervousness; this was not playing out as she had expected. She looked from one to the other. "I'm serious. He's travelled from the future."

They were now both visibly unnerved, and Grace ploughed on before either could speak. "How do you think he's single-handedly managed to revolutionise renewable energy technology and get everyone, including the Chinese, to build these new nuclear generators, making cheap hydrogen, those new batteries that charge instantly, and all that stuff? Because he knows what technology works; he's seen it already."

Silence. They exchanged glances, trying to decide whether Grace was delusional or unwell or both. Before they could recover, she pushed on, trying hard to keep the edge of desperation out of her voice. "Let me tell you where he got the money from to start the businesses. He won several lottery jackpots. I think he won six or seven times; here and in the US."

Their concern was morphing into incredulity.

"I don't have them, but I know Callum still has the tickets." She challenged them. "So if he does have the tickets, what are the chances of him winning all those jackpots within a few months. How could he do that, unless he already knew the numbers because he had travelled from the future?"

Gail opened her mouth as if to speak, but nothing emerged.

Grace's words came even faster, "He's come back because he's seen the planet being wrecked, and," she stressed the words heavily, "literally billions of people dying." She remembered something he had said. "He was in tears once, describing the boats in the English Channel and the piles of bodies washed ashore on our beaches."

At last, here was an image that resonated with Cooke, and he raised his hand to stop Grace.

He was shaking his head imperceptibly and slowly said, "Let me be clear. You are suggesting that Callum Moorcroft has travelled from the future to save the planet from Global Warming and has killed most of the world's livestock to save the Amazon Rainforest, as a part of that plan?"

Grace nodded.

Cooke leaned back in his chair with exaggerated calm, lacing his fingers in front of himself as if erecting a barrier against this madness. He dragged his gaze from Grace to Gail, "I'm not sure what to say. Did you know any of this? Did you know what she was going to say?"

The Land of the Blind

Gail seemed more composed, "No. I was unaware of these revelations until now. But," she paused, "As implausible as this sounds, it would explain Mr Moorcroft's actions and if these lottery tickets do exist, they would, as Grace says, constitute compelling evidence."

Cooke was openly incredulous. "You think this confection might be true?"

Gail remained calm, entirely in control of her emotions. "Oh, certainly, it might be true. Whether it is or not, that's what the evidence might tell us." Gail looked at Grace carefully before returning her attention to Cooke, saying, "I have worked with Grace for a while now, and I have never had any sense that she is unstable or easily deceived. Quite the opposite. I've always found her straightforward, pragmatic and extremely perceptive." After a pause, she continued, "I think we can safely assume that Grace believes what she is telling us. The implication being that if it is not true, then Mr Moorcroft has been deceiving her for some time; to what end, I am not sure. I have only spent a short time with him, and had no sense of him being manipulative, at least personally. I would say the things he needs and gets from Grace are emotional and physical, and I can't see an obvious rationale for such a preposterous deceit."

She turned to Grace, "Do you have any other evidence?"

Grace faced her, unwilling to take the next step, knowing she had no choice. "He shares his DNA with someone else." She said quietly.

"What does that mean, exactly? He has a twin?" Cooke asked.

"No, there is a child alive now who will grow up to be him in the future, so they have the same DNA."

There was a prolonged silence while they thought this through.

"You tested their DNA, the two versions of him?" Gail asked. Grace nodded; it was almost true.

"I don't know what to say." Cooke was shaking his head. "How do we resolve this. And if it is true, what does it mean?"

"What it means," Grace responded instantly, "Is that Callum is potentially very valuable. I don't know how much more he knows, but look what he's done with the technology he's developed so far. I don't think it would be a smart move to let the Americans get their hands on him."

Cooke sat forward at this and focused on Grace, "Do you know where he is?"

"No." Grace shook her head emphatically and looked at Gail, "But I believe Gail knows how to contact him."

Gail nodded, "We have exchanged emails, but no, I don't know where he is, although I think he may still be in London somewhere. He asked me to send some things and gave me the address of a courier. I assume he contacted someone else to provide the courier with the final delivery address."

"What did he ask for?" Cooke asked.

"Some basic first aid equipment and a few food items."

"Is he badly injured?"

"He said not, but I don't have any details," Gail said.

"Does he know you are here?" Cooke looked from Gail to Grace. They shook their heads.

"So this is not his plan? To save himself, I mean."

Despite his initial scepticism, Cooke's questions continued, and he quizzed both of them about their dealings with Callum, his businesses, and how he and Grace had met. When he finally assimilated what he could, there was a prolonged silence before he summed up.

The Land of the Blind

"I am going to give this more thought tonight, but it goes without saying that we need to see the evidence and in the end we will need to speak to Mr Moorcroft in order to make a proper assessment. I suggest you contact him and find a way to provide the evidence we need. We will speak early tomorrow morning."

They left the Home office to return Grace to her prison cell. As soon as they got into the waiting car, Gail said, "Grace dear, I'm not one for hyperbole, but I have never in my life heard anything quite so extraordinary as the idea that your boyfriend is a ..." She didn't finish the sentence, glancing at the driver.

The car moved slowly from the kerb, and Gail watched Grace carefully. "Are you alright, dear?"

Grace nodded and reluctantly broached the subject that had been eating away quietly at her. "Gail, there is one possible problem." She began tentatively, glancing at Gail before averting her gaze, "He might not go for this."

Gail continued to stare at her, "I'm not sure he has that many options." And she suddenly realised that Grace had tears on her cheeks.

"Oh my dear, what is it?" She took Grace's hand.

Grace quickly wiped the tears away with her sleeve, but with her other hand held tightly to Gail's. In a tight voice she said, "I can't believe how fucking emotional I am at the moment." After several more deep breaths, she continued. "He said he would never allow the Americans to take him. I didn't understand what he meant at first, but I think, no, I know ... " Her voice cracked, and she put her arm across her face, stifling the tears.

"Oh, Grace."

After a few moments, she managed. "I think he might take his own life." Then the words tumbled out, "He's lived for a hundred years, his wife and child were killed. He's already lived two lifetimes, and I don't think he would mind if it stopped now." She was sobbing into her sleeve, and the driver glanced nervously in the mirror at Gail.

Gail asked the driver to stop. He pulled over, set the hazard lights and stood by the bonnet, distracting himself with his phone.

"Grace, I'm sure he wouldn't. I think he loves you; I rarely see people like you two. If I'm honest, I'm jealous. I can see it in both of you. I don't know why you're both pretending it's not happening. Why would he leave you?"

Grace had controlled herself now. "You're right, we call it something else, but I know what it is. We both do. Part of me knows that this will be the most important relationship of my life, but I won't grow old with him. Another part can't bear the idea of being abandoned by him." The tears started again. "And I hate that he has turned me into such a weak, snivelling child."

Gail responded instantly, firmly taking both hands and pulling her to face her. "Don't mistake what you're feeling for weakness, Grace, that is not what it is." After a moment, she continued, "We must take one step at a time and see what happens. Why don't I contact Callum and see if he will consider it, and under what terms? At least I have a better understanding of what's happening now." She laughed, "There I was, thinking you needed a lawyer, and it seems a therapist might be more appropriate. 'Man saves the World, but his love for a mad detective proves too much to deal with.'"

Grace forced a grim laugh between deep breaths, "Hard to see a happy ending though."

"We'll see." Said Gail, tapping on the car window.

43.

Over the next hours, despite getting only three hours of sleep, Gail managed to arrange a virtual meeting between Callum and the Home Secretary. The agreement was that there would be only Gail, Grace, and the Home Secretary on the call. Gail was surprised Callum had agreed to it being a live phone call until Grace explained that on an encrypted Signal call, he could make it through a VPN, which would be impossible to track. It was scheduled for the following morning.

Until now, the Metropolitan Police and MI5 had been doing all they could to find Callum. When he first evaded them, they were hampered by a lack of CCTV footage of him escaping the area of his flat. Among all the spurious sightings from the public, one line of enquiry assumed that he could have hailed a cab. In addition to the public appeal, they made a specific one to any Black Cab driver who had picked up an unusual fare in the area late that evening. Callum's image was on every news item, everywhere on social media and public screens all across the United Kingdom. It was only a question of time before the taxi driver came forward, but it took more than thirty hours. Their search was immediately focused on the Washington Mayfair Hotel on Curzon Street, where the driver had dropped Callum. A nearby camera revealed a dishevelled man limping slowly west after the taxi departed. These were the only images they could retrieve from the public cameras, and they began systematically working their way along the various restaurants and shops on his potential route in search of whatever footage they could find. At this point, over one hundred people were actively involved in tracking Callum, and they were making progress. By the afternoon of the second day following his escape, they were confident that they had narrowed down to just two blocks of Mayfair in which he must be hiding: Chesterfield Gardens on the west side and Queen Street on the East, Charles Street to the North and Curzon Street to the south. Roadblocks were set up, and they went from building to building, showing everyone pictures of Callum and viewing any camera footage they could find. They had barely started this door-to-door search when the call came down from above for them to stop. Everyone involved on the ground was mystified, and rumours soon began to circulate of a political deal that would allow the Americans to render him out of the country. There were some angry people in the MET and MI5, but for now they did as they were told, held the roadblocks around the perimeter and waited.

***

Despite the visible police activity, Callum was much more focused on what Grace and Gail were doing. He acquired a small parcel containing two new mobile phones through the same process he had used to obtain the bandages and food. The final email confirmation from Gail about the call with the Home Secretary included a cryptic note from Grace that he should not make himself too comfortable. With little else to do while waiting for the phones to arrive, the hours passed slowly, the mental confines more imposing than the physical constraints. He had evaded them so far, but they were close, and they would find him soon. He either had to keep moving or to make a deal to protect himself. Gail was hoping for a permanent way out, but however positive he tried to be, his predicament felt bleak. The dreadful, dead weight which had descended and enveloped him when Maria and Rachel had been killed was stealing back, and he would not have believed how desperate he was now to be with Grace. He had told her he did not want to continue if that meant he could not be with her, and he had meant it; but there is a difference between acknowledging a fact and having it soak into every cell in your body. He diverted his mind with more pressing practical problems. Browsing on the phone Sania's team had prepared for him, he searched for the location of nearby mobile phone towers to double-check how quickly and how accurately they would be able to place him when the call started. Could he trust the British Government and the Home Secretary? He would know soon enough. It was time to change the dressings on his hands and knee again and take more anti-inflammatory tablets for his swollen, kaleidoscopic ankle.

***

Gail collected Grace from New Scotland Yard for the short journey to the Home Office. This time, she was leaving for good. At Gail's request, the Home Secretary had decreed that she was doing whatever she could to assist their enquiries and that any charges against her should be dropped. Gail and Grace had to wait, and when they were finally shown into his office, it was uncomfortably close to the appointed time for the call. A slightly fraught Jonathan Cooke was waiting for them.

"I'm Sorry, but our American Friends are increasingly agitated about this whole matter. I've assured them we will have something concrete for them soon, so I hope you ladies can deliver that for me."

The Land of the Blind

Gail produced a mobile phone and switched it on. The informality of their first meeting was long forgotten. She passed the phone across the desk, saying, "Home Secretary, this is the phone he will call. It will be on the Signal app so the call will be encrypted, and only we can hear it."

Cooke placed the phone on the desk in front of him. The clock on its face showed nine fifty-eight. The three of them, still standing, watched in silence as the seconds ticked by in slow motion. Despite the fact that they were expecting the call, all three jumped at the ringtone as the app lit the phone screen. Cooke tapped the green icon to accept the call and then the speaker icon. He slid the phone towards the centre of the desk to allow the others to hear clearly.

"Good morning, who am I speaking to?"

It was a man's voice, and Cooke could tell by Grace's controlled but unmistakable response that it was Callum.

"This is Jonathan Cooke, the Home Secretary, and I have with me Gail Bailey-Royce and Grace Sommers. Ladies."

"Good Morning, Callum, this is Gail."

"And it's me, Cal."

"I assume this is Callum Moorcroft."

"Yes, it is."

"Just to confirm this, Mr Moorcroft, would you mind if I had Miss Sommers ask you a question only the two of you are likely to know the answer to?"

There was a pause. "Of course, go ahead."

Grace was caught by surprise, and the Home Secretary asked her to think of a suitable question and write down the answer on the pad on the desk. After a moment, Grace did this, and then she asked, "What was our favourite meal on our recent holiday?"

The Land of the Blind

She stared at the phone, and they could see her stress: her hands in constant fractional motion and the fast pulse in her neck.

"Greek Salad, " came the instant reply, and all three of them sensed that it was said with a smile.

"Well, it would appear that we are talking with the right person then, Mr Moorcroft, thank you." After the briefest pause, the Home Secretary continued, "Mr Moorcroft, I assume you know that Miss Sommers has made some rather startling assertions on your behalf. If they were true, it would alter how your case is handled. To put it bluntly, it would alter the calculation as to whether to grant the extradition request from the American Government, which I understand they are in the process of preparing."

There was silence. "Can you hear me, Mr Moorcroft?"

"Yes."

There was a delay on the call, an artefact of the encryption and the connection through the mobile phone system and the internet.

The silence continued, "I won't repeat everything that Miss Sommers has told us, but would it be possible to get your reaction and, in particular, whether you can provide any hard evidence as to the veracity of her claims?"

"My reaction is one of disappointment." There was a pause. "I never wanted this information to be known by anyone. I don't think any good can come of it. For any of us."

Grace placed her hands on the desk and tipped her head forward, staring down, unmoving.

"Mr Moorcroft, if what you claim is true, the British Government would do whatever it takes to ensure your safety and that of those close to you. We could find a way for this to benefit all of us."

The Land of the Blind

"In answer to your question, whether I have evidence to support what Grace has told you depends upon exactly what she said and how strong you want the evidence to be. There is nothing I can do to prove who I am conclusively. But I think it would be beyond reasonable doubt, to use a phrase you'll be familiar with."

"Mr Moorcroft, time is short. It will not surprise you to hear that every effort is being made to find you through normal police enquiries. I do not believe you will evade them for long. I understand you are in possession of a number of jackpot-winning Lottery Tickets; if you can provide these quickly as evidence, we might be able to prevent this all from getting out of hand."

"Let me think about it. I'll call on the same number in two hours."

He disconnected the call.

Just minutes later, Grace and Gail stood outside the Home Office. Grace was free but refused to speak about what had been said; her emotions were held tight. Gail hugged her and climbed into her car, leaving Grace alone on the pavement. After a moment, glancing around the mundane London street scene, she turned quickly and headed for St James's Park tube station.

***

Before the two women left the Home Office, thirty armed officers spread through Shaw House. The security services had installed equipment in the next office to the Home Secretary's before Gail and Grace arrived. This equipment identified the unique ID of the phone she brought as soon as it was switched on. With that information, they could route the phone's connection through their software rather than directly to the mobile network. This was a component of the delay in the connection. When the incoming call arrived, they identified the device Callum was calling from and, within seconds, the mobile phone cell to which it was connected. That cell was on a mast on the roof of the London Hilton Hotel, some five hundred meters from Callum's flat in Shaw House. With only this information, there was no way to find the exact location of the calling phone; it could be almost anywhere in a square mile with one corner at the cell tower. However, other data searches quickly identified five other cell towers in the same part of London with which Callum's phone had briefly negotiated before it was connected to the one with the strongest signal. Knowing the location of each of these other cell towers and the signal strength at the phone from each, it was possible to identify where the calling phone was positioned within a few meters. Within thirty seconds of the call starting, five vans dotted around the area converged on Chesterfield Street. They were slowed briefly by the roadblocks the metropolitan police had in place. The police were in the dark about what was happening and had taken a moment to clear the way for the blacked-out vans. Callum was disconnecting the call as the officers assembled quickly and efficiently on the street outside Shaw House. The triangulation from the phone towers in an area of such high building density left some uncertainty about the vertical height of the phone in the building. It appeared to be some seven meters from the ground, which implied the second floor, but to avoid any risk, three teams of armed officers swarmed into the building, up the stairs and into the corridors on each of the four floors. They lined up on either side of the appropriate door on each floor in identical formation, and at each one, an officer stepped up, poised with a ram. They waited in silence, listening for activity in each flat. They could hear nothing, and on a shared signal, seconds later, they smashed open each of the four doors simultaneously and swarmed into the rooms in a cacophony of noise and shouted warnings. The elderly couple on the ground floor, in the middle of a late breakfast, were terrified to see masked, armed men screaming and pointing weapons at them. The old lady fainted and slumped from the chair, her panicked husband trying vainly to prevent her from slipping to the floor. All three flats above were empty.

Two MI5 agents had been listening to the call in the office beside the Home Secretary's. The Home Secretary joined the agents, and now the three men watched a live video feed from a body camera on one of the officers. It was loud and confusing, with dark uniforms moving in and out of focus. On their headphones, they heard a series of shouted commands and people calling 'Clear'. An ambulance was summoned for the old lady on the ground floor, and it took a moment to confirm that Callum was not in their apartment or any of the other three. All of the neighbouring flats were checked. Two doors on vacant flats had to be forced, but it was soon clear that Callum was not in any of the apartments in the building. Another video feed appeared on the agent's laptop from a different officer's body cam, and they realised they were looking at a mobile phone lying in the middle of a dining table. Suddenly, the call's delay and odd acoustics made more sense. Callum had not been in the room; he had somehow routed the call through that phone from wherever he was. A gloved hand appeared in the shot and tapped the blank face of the phone, and the screen lit. An application was running and it had a simple interface with two sections, one titled 'Outbound', which read 'Call Disconnected' and the second titled 'Inbound', which read 'Data Connection Active'.

"I think he may be hearing this, Sir." One of the MI5 agents said.

"Shit!" Cooke exclaimed in frustration, his excitement of a moment earlier gone in an instant of dreadful realisation. He threw his headphones onto the desk, turned on his heels and marched out of the room. "Find that man. Now!"

When Gail phoned Grace several hours later to tell her what she was hearing from her contacts in the security services, Grace was at home, having called in 'sick'; something she had never done before. She listened as Gail's explained what appeared to have happened; there were a few gaps but they both understood the gist and when Gail had finished Grace gave her succinct verdict, "That slimy wanker."

"Not how I would have put it," Gail replied, clearly disapproving of the language, "But I do share the sentiment."

"And do they have any idea where he is now?"

"Apparently not. The connection he used for his call into the apartment was made via the apartment's Wi-Fi, and, of course, he used a VPN so they can't trace where he connected from. He clearly expected this or something like it; otherwise, why use a mobile phone for the call? He knew it would give them his location. In retrospect, it seems obvious, I can't believe Cooke went for it." There was a deep sigh, "I suspect our lunch date is off and I may not be getting a Christmas card from him this year; time to start sounding out my contacts to see who the next Home Secretary is likely to be."

There was a brief silence and then, with half a thought for whoever else might hear this, Grace added, "Stupid fuckers, all they had to do was trust us and do it right. They won't find him now, you know. Not if he's got this far." Then she added, "The things we discussed with Cooke in our first meeting, do you think

434

he passed that on?"

"Hard to be sure, but I suspect not. I think he found it a bit far-fetched." She paused, "As do I, Grace."

Grace ignored the comment, "So he would have given Cal to the Americans, you think?"

"That's my guess. Jonathan was never overly sentimental."

"No shit. Slimy, two faced, wanker, then."

There was a short silence, and then Gail asked, gently, "Have you heard anything about your position at work?"

"Not yet, I'm at home, just getting my head straight, but tomorrow will be an interesting day, that's for sure."

Grace lay on the sofa, staring at the ceiling for a long time, wondering what to do next. It felt like her world was collapsing. How could they keep her in her job after everything that had gone on? But how could they sack her? What would she do with herself? Would she ever see Callum again? How had that sneaky bastard wormed his way into her heart and undone her so easily? She felt like she had trained most of her life to prevent something like this from ever happening, and with his gentle smile and handsome face, he had slipped through her defences as if they did not exist. She needed to make things simple for a few hours, to turn her brain off, so she called Cynthia and asked her to come over. Her friend sensed it was important and promised to be there after her shift. Grace donned her running kit and jogged to Clapham Common, where she spent the next hour immersed in a training session as mindlessly savage as she could manage. Many people saw the crazy woman on the common sprinting back and forth over various distances with her loose hair streaming behind her. Finally, she could do no more and lay on the cold grass her body heaving with the effort, gulping down oxygen to repay the lactic debt. No one saw her on her knees, curled tight to compress the sobs as her tears ran into the earth.

Cynthia had never seen Grace like this. She showered and dried her and held her close until she eventually fell asleep in her arms. It was after five in the morning when Grace finally jerked awake after almost twelve hours of dreamless sleep.

Her violent movement woke Cynthia. "Babe, babe, It's fine; I'm here." Cynthia stroked her cheek in the half-light and kissed her gently.

"He's gone," Grace said quietly.

"Who? Callum, where? Why?"

"He's just gone. It's not his fault. It just is."

"He loves you, babe, he wouldn't leave you."

"Oh, Cyn." Grace held on to her tightly. "Please don't ever leave me. Promise."

"I promise, I promise."

Just a few minutes later, sleep recaptured her, and Cynthia slipped from the bed and sat in the kitchen with a coffee, wondering what on earth had happened to her best friend and the woman she could not help but love.

44.

Grace agreed with her boss, DCI Bailey, to take a couple of weeks' vacation to 'let the dust settle'. Neither of them knew what this meant, but neither wanted to deal with the current situation in which Grace found herself. She avoided being alone, spending the days in the office with Sania or with Cynthia; in her flat, volunteering with her at the church in Balham or walking to and from the Windmill for her bar shifts. Suddenly, she was a presence again at her athletics club in Enfield, and they welcomed her back with open arms.

In the middle of the second week of this lacunae, Sania waved her into her office and handed her the phone. For as long as it took to unthink it, she imagined it was Callum, and the adrenaline spike made her momentarily dizzy as she refocused on Armando's calm voice. Without saying Callum had contacted him, he made it clear that whatever she was worrying about, she should not, and went on to ask her for some personal details without explaining why. She had avoided asking Sania about Callum, but after the call, she did, and Sania showed her the TOR messaging app that they were using to communicate with him. Later that day, Sania beckoned her over again, and she had seen the words appear on the app as Callum 'chatted' with Sania. No one had any idea where he was, and he had given no clues, other than to say he was well and getting plenty of sun. His unspecified wounds were healing well, and Grace smiled at the image of yet more scars, more evidence of life etched on his already well-worn body. Thinking about him upset her more than she was prepared for, and from then on, she avoided being in the room when he was online. With the distraction of the All-Seeing Eye, her running and Cynthia, her days and nights were full, and as the end of the two-week vacation approached, she knew what she would do and made her peace with it.

The meeting with DCI Bailey, where she resigned, was highly amusing. She had arrived smartly dressed but, for the first time at work, with her hair in a full afro. Everyone in the station gawked at her in disbelief, and she smiled happily and defiantly back. DCI Bailey had been unable to mask his relief when she announced that she was resigning. Grace liked him and felt a little sorry for him, suppressing her amusement at the politically correct knots he found himself tied in. Her colleagues, seeing her return from his office, had no idea what to make of her amusement. Her presence filled the office for the last time, and they watched, mesmerised, as she said goodbye to everyone, promising to have a drink with them sometime; promises they all doubted would ever be kept. Except perhaps for one. Her last words were with Andrew Morris, shortly to be Detective Inspector Morris. She thanked him for being such a good bloke and being kind to her. Not long ago, she would have indulged in some graphic sexual innuendo or pretended to reveal a fact about her sex life, but, without noticing the change, she had stopped doing this over the last months. Instead, she hugged him and they kissed on both cheeks. The rest of the office looked on in surprise.

"I'm going to miss you, Grace; this place will be far less interesting without you."

The Land of the Blind

She blinked rapidly, unwilling to allow anyone other than Morris to see how much this meant to her.

***

And so, Grace suddenly began a new life as she joined Cyber Futures to work for Sania alongside Paul and all the young geeks. Nobody, including her, knew where this was going, but it was exciting, and she certainly changed the atmosphere in the office. She flirted outrageously with everyone, and, other than Paul and Sania, they were all equally thrilled and terrified by her. She dived into the world of deliberative democracy with a passion, and Paul introduced her to the people at the Sortition Alliance, which was expanding like crazy and busier by the day as the idea of citizens' assemblies started to grab people's attention. She joined the team assessing the material the experts were compiling for the forthcoming livestock virus assembly. Ten people were working full-time in the office, collating the material, and many others in academic institutions and associated companies were fact-checking the data, ready for release. The oversight panel, consisting of four ex-politicians and four internationally renowned academics from six countries, met online twice a week for an hour to monitor progress and to ensure the process would deliver a balanced view for both sides. There was a real buzz about what they were doing; it felt new and relevant, and they were making the news. When people realised that Cyber Futures was, now openly, behind the All-Seeing Eye concept, the world's media came knocking. Film crews from across the world were calling Sania, and for several days, she was unable to deal with anything else. It caught them all by surprise, and they quickly shifted responsibility to Paul, who was now effectively running a new business within the existing one, negotiating more office space and hiring staff.

The Land of the Blind

They kept Grace away from the media. Links between Cyber Futures and Callum's recent arrest and release, rumoured to be related to the livestock virus, made for good headlines and every interviewer asked the question. Sania initially, and now Paul, responded by saying they were an information technology company with nothing to contribute regarding Callum Moorcroft's rumoured involvement. It helped that the Metropolitan Police put out a statement to confirm they no longer had an active arrest warrant for Callum, that he had answered their questions about the matter, and that the case was now closed. It was also an open secret that Jonathan Cooke's tenure as Home Secretary was effectively over as a direct result of the case. He was a 'dead man walking', and would be replaced as soon as sufficient time had elapsed for the Prime Minister to deny any link to the failed terrorism charges or rumours of a highly controversial extradition to the United States. What was also understood by those on the inside was that SIS, under pressure from the CIA, were continuing their search for Callum. The Americans wanted their pound of flesh, and they would not desist until the political pressure moved elsewhere or someone else stood in their dock or, more likely, was chained in an obscure rendition site. Sania monitored Carlsen Olson's pwned laptop, but it did not come back online. The thought of him conspiring with the Russians was a tiny open wound for her, but she could do nothing.

The last Friday of October marked a turning point for Grace. Callum had been gone for almost a month, and her life had changed in a way she could not have foreseen. So many things she thought defined her had dropped away, yet she was still here, still Grace. The call from Armando came out of the blue. Her initial reaction was to say no, it was too much, but the words were never formed. The papers were couriered to the office less than an hour later, and she signed them and became the owner of the flat in New Globe Walk and everything that it contained. She still had her door keys.

Later that evening, as closing time approached in the Windmill, Grace was nursing a large Gin and Tonic. She had arrived late, walking from Clapham Common tube station after taking the Northern Line from the office. Cynthia was pulling the last pints, and the bar was quiet. Grace had been perched on her stool for the best part of an hour, in what she thought of as her corner. Everyone left there was drunk to some extent, and three men had already tried to engage her in conversation in a way she recognised and part of her craved. But something in her had changed, and she let them all down easily and kindly. Lost in thought, her subconscious glimpsed a man's profile in the bar mirror. She looked away, quickly, but instantly knew his name. The last time she had seen him was after a night of sex, the details of which she had not recalled even then, and she remembered waking that morning not knowing his name. The memory and his name, Karl, came to her unbidden and made her blush. She watched him for a while in the mirror, talking and laughing with a blond woman at a table behind her. The compulsion arrived swiftly and was irresistible. She walked over, hands in her jeans pockets, arms tight at her side, making herself small.

"Excuse me, sorry to interrupt."

They looked up at her, and she saw his instant recognition and watched his jaw set and eyes narrow as the memory surfaced. Pre-empting him, she said, "Hello Karl, You might not remember," she switched her attention briefly to the woman, "We had a … well it was a while ago now but we spent the evening together, and

The Land of the Blind

I was… well I was rude." Karl was staring at her, nodding imperceptibly. She rolled her eyes, "Who am I kidding. I was a complete shit, and I'm sorry, you didn't deserve it, you were nice." Her hands came out of her pockets, and she opened her palms. "That's it. I just wanted to say sorry." She turned away and sat at the bar with her back to them. Cynthia had watched the whole exchange and came over to see if Grace was okay. Karl and the woman finished their drinks and left without looking at Grace.

An hour later, as they set off, arm in arm across the common towards Wandsworth, Grace was lost in thought. They walked in silence until Grace asked Cynthia, "Babe, when did I become such a ball breaker. I've been thinking about all those men. That bloke in the pub was one of them, and I was just so unbelievably mean to him, to most of them."

"I guess you took what you needed from them, sort of getting your revenge, it felt to me."

Grace nodded and then suddenly stopped walking. "Oh, I was on autopilot; I nearly forgot." She smiled broadly at Cynthia and turned to her right, gently pulling her along. "I've got a big surprise."

The taxi dropped them outside the apartment block in New Globe Walk. Grace let them in, and they took the lift to the top floor. There was new plaster around the door frame, awaiting a decorator, and the door had been repaired.

"Why are we visiting his flat? Is he here?" Cynthia asked.

"We're not, we're visiting my flat. He gave it to me." She pushed open the door.

Cynthia stared, open-mouthed in delight and astonishment. "Babe, oh my god, babe, it's fantastic. He just gave it to you?"

"Best sex of his life, what do you expect?" Grace smiled as

some of the memories returned.

"Is he coming back?" Cynthia had managed not to ask this question for weeks, but she wanted to know.

Grace looked straight at her, "He's gone, he's not coming back, he can't."

They moved inside the doorway, and Grace had to stop as the memories overwhelmed her. She put her hands to her face, and Cynthia crooked her arm. "We don't have to do this now, babe. Come back on your own, another time."

Grace said nothing for a moment, immersed in an orgy of memories; the smell of onions cooking, the feel of his body against hers, the two of them walking around naked and the way he looked at her when he thought she was not watching. The tears seeped between her fingers and dripped to the floor, and Cynthia wrapped her in her arms and held her until her tears stopped.

Eventually, Grace lowered her hands. "He's gone, so I just need to deal with it. Come on, come and see." She took Cynthia's hand and walked across to stand in front of Zania Tariq's canvas, remembering being in the gallery with Callum and her excitement when he had bought two of her pieces. "Don't you love it?" They looked at the bright colours and felt the movement they created. "We're in there, somewhere, Cal and me."

Cynthia had no idea what Grace was talking about, but she sensed a profound happiness, which was enough. They moved slowly around, taking in the office and the spare bedroom. Everywhere, drawers were open, and things were clearly missing. The apartment's last role had been as a crime scene, which felt deeply familiar to Grace. She absent-mindedly wiped the fingerprint dust from a door frame, missing the excitement, the challenge of looking through a blurred window into someone else's life, trying to pull it into focus.

The flat was warm, the heating had been left on, and they dropped their coats on the floor and kicked their shoes off to stand and look through the glass wall towards the Thames and St Paul's across the river. "Fuck, this is cool babe," Cynthia said.

Grace noticed the small, blue leather jewellery box on the kitchen worktop. The ribbon had been removed and lay beside the box. Still attached to the ribbon was a small card with just her name, written in his handwriting. She stared at it, started to reach out, and stopped herself.

Cynthia sensed her mood shift. "What's that?"

"They opened it," Grace said. "Nosey fuckers."

"What is it?"

"I don't know, but it's for me from him."

"Open it. What's the matter?"

"It's just …"

"Grace, what's the matter?"

"I think I know what it might be and it feels like something …" She put one hand on the worktop, "something he might do if he thought something bad was about to happen."

"You don't know that." Cynthia stepped over and took Grace's hand. They both stood and stared at the small blue box.

When Grace lifted the lid, silent tears slid down her face.

"Oh my god, it's so beautiful," Cynthia said. She looked up at Grace, who was now resting both hands on the edge of the worktop, her eyes closed, her cheeks wet with tears.

"Does it mean something?"

Grace nodded, and a small sob escaped.

Cynthia lifted the necklace from the box and held it out. It was silver with six pendant gems strung along it. The gems sparkled, each stone a slightly different colour.

"Wow," Cynthia said.

Grace opened her eyes and looked through tears that made the string of tiny dancing lights blaze. "Memories," she said.

Cynthia looked to her for an explanation, but Grace smiled and wiped the tears away. "It's fine, it's just something we …."

"Do you want to put it on?" Cynthia asked.

"No. I'll wear it when …." The simple sentence filled her eyes again, but she pushed the tears away with both hands.

45.

The global assembly went live at midnight in London, three weeks after Grace moved into the flat. Hundreds of moderators were online to answer questions and to guide the discussions. After participants watched each evidence video, the site required them to join a small, live discussion group to discuss what they had just learned. Each group was moderated, controlled by someone, or something. With the help of one of the world's leading Artificial Intelligence companies, they were trialling AI moderation. Some of the moderators were people, some were AI systems, and part of the project was to assess how well each worked. When participants clicked to join a group in their chosen language, they were connected with up to seven other people who could be anywhere in the world. They were linked by video or, if they preferred, just audio, with a moderator in each group always present in audio only.

Strict rules were in place about behaviour, and the moderators encouraged everyone in the group to speak and ensured that no one dominated the conversation. It directly mirrored the in-person methods used in most citizens' assemblies. This process repeated for each topic and evidence set, so that to join a discussion group, everyone had to watch the full video and then answer several questions to test their understanding. In this way, the system tried to ensure that people were truly engaging rather than simply ticking a box that reflected their initial, probably unconsidered, opinion. Participation at each stage demanded the completion of the previous one, until, after hearing all the evidence and having participated in a discussion about each, people could finally vote on the four questions being posed by the assembly. Everything was recorded and was publicly available online.

The commitment required to listen to the experts and participate in the discussions was significant. There was over ten hours of recorded evidence, and on average, it took a little over thirty-five hours for each person to work through it and participate in the discussion groups. An overall time limit of one month was set, and people took it at their own pace.

Within days, millions of people worldwide participated around the clock, and for days, it dominated the news agenda in the same way that the indictments of Ahmed Gweri and Konstantin Kosegin had done. Now, the world's governments and ruling regimes were being forced to take this seriously with the creeping realisation that it could represent a direct threat to their usual way of doing democracy. In the United Kingdom, the Government reshuffle, in which Jonathan Cooke lost his job as a minister, went almost unnoticed.

One of the criticisms being levelled at the process was the expense. All the costs were made public, and the teams on each side of the argument had been given ten million dollars to create whatever content they deemed appropriate to promote their argument. In this case, both sides were backed by huge constituencies and had far more money than this at their disposal, and there were no rules as to how much they could spend. There were arguments that the side with the larger financial backing would dominate, but in this instance, the opinion was that both sides were equally well-resourced. Regardless of how much they spent, all the content was reviewed by the group of experts overseeing the process to ensure it reflected the best available knowledge.

In addition to recording their video evidence, both sides made short films to summarise their positions, each enlisting a Hollywood 'A-list' celebrity to voiceover and endorse their stance. The livestock industry showed abandoned pastures, outrageously priced meat and dairy products on supermarket shelves and scrolling images of ranchers and farmers who had committed suicide in the aftermath of the disaster. Part of the delay in the assembly going live was that the oversight committee insisted on a biography and documented evidence that each suicide had likely been caused by the virus destroying that person's livelihood. Some could not be proved and were dropped, but many remained. The costs of subsidies to the farmers from various governments were listed, totalling hundreds of billions of dollars.

For the environmentalists, the images of unbroken rainforest transforming, in time-lapse, to dusty, open savannah over just a few years were just as emotive, and the data about falling rainfall and the increasing frequency of natural disasters were becoming well known.

The assembly ran for a month, and unexpected things began to happen; people from distant places around the world who met online, expressed their opinions and argued their positions in a civilised, respectful way, chose to meet in real life. Sometimes they were from different continents; others lived just a few miles apart. These assembly friendships burgeoned; most were brief novelties, but some would go on to last, and a few people met their life partners through the assembly. A subtle but real effect emerged as people realised the world was, perhaps, not quite as big as they had once thought.

The new website coped easily with the traffic even as the end of the month approached and participants scrambled to complete their learning and to vote. People cared about this issue, and the numbers were remarkable. The highest number participating at any one time peaked at nearly six hundred million, and when the assembly closed, well over nine hundred million people had voted. It was second in size only to the Indian general elections as the world's most extensive democratic process.

For weeks, the leaders of the democratic countries had been criticising China and North Korea for not allowing their citizens access to the assembly. Grace, Sania and Paul particularly enjoyed watching the American President squirming in an interview on CNN, caught between allowing American citizens to participate in a supra-national process that might usurp his administration's authority, while demanding the same democratic opportunity for Chinese citizens.

When the polls closed, they ran the selection software. It created a representative sample of almost two hundred thousand respondents and displayed the results at midnight in London. Rather than a simple proposition, several questions were asked of all the participants, and there was no simple, single analysis to be had, except perhaps in the response to one of them.

Sania's initial reaction on seeing the results was disappointment. When she first conceived the idea, she was certain public opinion would fall heavily on Callum's side, justifying the use of the virus. That was not what the world thought.

The first question posed was;

'Was the use of a biological weapon justified to target the

livestock industry to preserve the Amazon Rainforest and to mitigate global warming?'

The assembly returned 36% justified vs. 64% unjustified.

However, people soon started arguing about the demographic details because, for people under thirty, this was reversed, with almost 60% believing it was justified. In the age group of over-seventies, an even more decisive 78% believed it was unjustified.

As if to prove how complex the issue was, the response to the second question surprised many;

'Should coordinated efforts be made to reinstate the livestock industry?'

Only about a third of participants across the whole sample supported this. In other words, two-thirds of the world's people thought no effort should be made to reinstate the industry. Support for doing nothing was strongest in the younger age groups.

The third question received almost the same response. To the question;

'Should governments be doing more and acting faster to reduce the use of fossil fuels than they are now?'

A little over two-thirds agreed.

However, the standout result of the assembly was the response to the final question;

"Should citizens' assemblies be used widely at national and international levels to make democratic decisions?"

Sania had been insistent about adding this question despite opposition from the others, and it was clearly not a distraction. The response was an astonishing eighty-nine per cent in favour, and it was this that caught everyone's imagination, with the questions of the virus and climate change relegated to a distant second.

***

During the following days, everyone at Cyber Futures worked on autopilot, as if sharing an emotional hangover after the excitement and frenetic activities of the previous weeks. The technology advisory group continued to investigate the fake accounts set up in an attempt to affect the assembly outcome. In total, they identified around eighty thousand accounts where software was being used in an attempt to mimic the actions of a real person. However, for each account, whoever set it up had to find a human to participate in the discussions. They did not have to be seen, but they had to participate at a basic level, and the moderators, both human and AI, had flagged many people they did not believe were true participants. After adjusting the results for the relatively few fake accounts that survived to the end of the process, it was clear to everyone that the numbers were too small to have had any material effect on the results. There were too many 'real' participants for the fake ones to matter, and the obvious conclusion was that the process was hard to subvert.

***

Grace and Sania wanted more. They were unsure exactly what they wanted, but the profound sense of agency they experienced with the project was intoxicating. That was how the two of them, along with Paul and Gail, came to be sitting around the dining table in the flat, now Grace's flat, in New Globe Walk.

They stood around the worktop together, chopping, chatting, preparing the food, and drinking. As the large pan of risotto took up the last of the stock, they sat to eat their Greek salad starters. Grace laughed that someone else would have to host the next meeting, as she only had two meals in her cooking repertoire.

The Land of the Blind

Before they started, they had a simple toast, 'To absent friends'.

Gail tasted the salad and reminded Grace about their meeting with the then Home Secretary, "This was the answer to the question you asked Callum, wasn't it, when we were on that call with Jonathan Cooke?"

"Or as I call him, the slimy two faced wanker." Grace added sweetly, to loud laughter.

They toasted 'the slimy two faced wanker and all those like him'.

Gail asked Grace, "Where did you and Callum have the salad?"

"We made it on the little boat we rented for a week, on the first day, for lunch."

They could all see the memory was still strong, and her eyes shone.

"Oh, Grace, I'm sorry that was insensitive of me."

Grace held a napkin to her eye, and Sania placed one hand on hers on the table.

Grace smiled at them, "That week was one of the happiest of my life, and it's a memory I can't get enough of. Lying on the deck of that boat in the sun together, that's my happy place."

Now they all had tears in their eyes and Grace laughed, "Oh for gods sake, this is not a wake, the bastard is out there somewhere, probably lying on another boat taking things easy while we deal with all the shit he left us."

The mood lifted, and Gail mused, "I've thought a lot about Jonathan Cooke. I can't decide whether he believed what you told him about Callum?"

Grace and Gail looked at one another across the table, and after a moment, Grace said, "We never really talked about that, did we?"

The Land of the Blind

Gail shook her head and looked at the other two. "You know?"

They both nodded, inscrutable, watching her reaction.

"It's not an easy thing to believe."

They simultaneously made a noise of agreement with this glorious understatement.

She looked at Sania and asked, "Do you really believe him?" There was silence, and everyone was watching Sania.

"He knew so many things that he could not have known," Sania said. "I can't think of another explanation, no matter how outrageous the truth seems."

Gail seemed to accept this and looked to the other two to see them nodding their agreement.

"As for Cooke, hard to say what that shit-bag believes," Grace said. "I doubt he believed it. He was happy to say whatever was most likely to trap Cal. But even if he did, his credibility is shot now, don't you think? Imagine him trying to tell people; he'd come across as desperate or mad."

Paul stood and collected the plates. "That was delicious. Despite being a Greek salad, and it's the middle of winter."

"You can fuck right off" Grace said happily, walking over to stir the Risotto for the last time.

"Why does everyone in London use such profane language?" Sania asked.

"I think you'll find that Grace is significantly raising the average all on her own," Gail replied. "It's her way of keeping people slightly off balance, or perhaps it used to be, but now I think she just likes it. There's something rather delicious in using some of those words for those of us who never do, don't you think?"

"Certainly not," Sania said, laughing, "Some of us have to maintain standards."

The Land of the Blind

Grace and Paul served the risotto, and as they started to eat, Paul said, "Time to be serious for a moment, I think." He took a sip of wine and carefully placed the glass back on the coaster. "None of us has seen what Callum has," he began, "and I don't know exactly what he told you, Grace; everything I assume, and maybe more than me about some things, but as far as I know neither of you know anything except the basic fact of him being here."

He looked at Gail. "He's my son."

All three watched her shaking her head, trying to absorb this.

Paul paused momentarily before continuing, "The same, but different to the teenage boy at home with his mother in Wimbledon. Or more likely out with his mates with a false ID, getting drunk."

Grace smiled, but felt the edge in Paul's words and wondered what Lisa was doing this evening.

"Your son!" Gail echoed.

"He has to be someone's son." Paul smiled.

"Did he come to you first when he arrived?" Sania asked.

Paul nodded

"Does your other Callum know?" Sania was fascinated.

"I don't think so. I assume Callum has not told him, but I can't be certain. I've never had the conversation."

"I'm pretty sure he doesn't know," Grace added.

Gail looked at Grace, "You did a DNA test?"

"Yes, with his sister, actually. It flagged her and Callum, the older one, as siblings."

"I thought you did it with the young Callum?" Gail said.

"No." Grace paused. "I said that when we were with Cooke because it sounded like the obvious thing to do, but imagine the lab doing the test. There are age markers in DNA, and I have no idea how they would have interpreted the two otherwise identical samples, so I decided the sibling match was enough. It was flagged as a sibling match with a large age gap. Also, I have no idea how the drugs have affected his DNA."

Sania looked confused. "Drugs?"

"So, turns out, I've been fucking a pensioner. Sorry." Grace looked mildly contrite and continued, "If you count the total years he's been alive, he's about one hundred years old." Sania and Gail were dumbstruck.

Grace continued, "Some time in the next twenty years or so, I can't remember exactly, but in the near future, someone will develop a drug, which was called Telogen in Callum's world. He was involved with the company that developed it, and he took it from the age of about forty, and it stopped him from ageing. Usual shit of course, personalised medicine, only the beautiful, wealthy people could afford it, but that's by the by. Long and short, he stopped ageing for about fifty years until he came back in time here, where we've not invented it yet, so now he's started ageing again like the rest of us."

"Science fiction." Gail mused. "You can see why we would not want the Americans to get their hands on him. I wonder what else he knows."

Paul picked up again, "One of his rules from the outset, and he never compromised on this, as far as I know, was not to discuss any of our futures. He would not say a word about what happens to us."

Grace nodded, and Paul continued, "He said the only point of his being here was to change what happened, so it was pointless to speculate anyway."

The Land of the Blind

"And I assume the Lottery tickets exist?" Gail asked.

Paul smiled at the memory. "Oh yes. The first time we met was a Sunday morning. He'd given me a jackpot-winning ticket for the Lotto draw of the night before, "

"What, you already knew him?" Gail asked.

"No, this stranger just handed it to me in the street outside my office and walked away. But as well as that one, he had two other jackpot tickets, for the previous week's Euro Millions and the previous week's Lotto draws. I remember it like it was yesterday, searching on the lottery website for the winning numbers of the previous draws and that 'hairs on the back of your neck' moment when they all matched. But even then, I don't think I truly believed him."

They watched Paul relive the memory.

"There was something so weirdly familiar about him. From the moment I first saw him when he gave me the ticket, and then our meeting on Sunday at the tower at Leith Hill." He was looking at each of them in turn, "It's hard to explain, you know something deep down is true, but you absolutely cannot accept it; then there's that instant when you just know."

All three were nodding, smiling, remembering the same point of inflexion, the revelation, an impossibility becoming reality. They went back to their food and Paul began to explain to Sania and Gail some of the things Callum had told him about what climate change would do to their world; had already done to his world. Grace contributed some of the more upsetting things he had told her and Gail recalled her description to Cooke of bodies floating in the Channel and washing up on British beaches.

As they finished the risotto, Grace said succinctly, "So he felt we'd fucked things up and deserved another chance."

"Still, it's quite a thing he chose to do. He abandoned another life in the future to do this." Sania observed

Grace did not explain, just nodded, saying, "He had his reasons."

"So the question is," Paul said, standing to collect the plates, "Do we think his work is done or has he left us more to do?"

They talked for hours and were still talking after one o'clock when Cynthia returned from her shift at the pub to find Paul stacking the dishwasher and wiping down the surfaces. She joined them for a final drink.

They were all, except Sania, a little drunk and Gail, perpetually fascinated by Grace and her relationships, asked Cynthia, "Have you ever met Callum?"

There was silence as they all turned to Cynthia.

"Twice."

"I'm sorry I didn't mean to pry," Gail said.

"Oooh, you liar, you definitely want to pry," Grace said, but her tone did not admonish.

"Really, don't answer." Gail said, "That was insensitive."

"I've met him twice, for a total of about three hours," Cynthia said, turning to Grace as she spoke. "I know how much he means to Grace, so I felt I had to meet him. Although I didn't really want to."

"Oh, Cyn," Grace said quietly, guilt and concern writ large.

"But, as you all know, he's a quite delightful man; it's hard not to like him."

They could not read her.

"Of course, he's still in our lives," Cynthia said, without emotion.

There was a hard silence.

The Land of the Blind

"He's pink and about six or seven long, and Grace keeps him in her bedside drawer where she thinks I won't see him."

Grace rolled her eyes and put her hands over her face. Cynthia smiled now as they howled in protest or laughed. Minutes later, they grabbed their coats and hugged one another before filling the resonant stairwell with their too-loud voices and clattering feet.

Something shifted for all of them that evening. Each had shouldered a little of what had been Callum's burden. The world was changing, slowly, but it was clear that they could do more, and if they could do more, they all agreed they had to. It was trite, but Gail used the oft-quoted and misquoted, *If not now, when? if not us, who?*

They all knew the answers.

46.

Gail left the Cabinet meeting and found Grace in the small office in Number 10, where she had been waiting for barely twenty minutes. Grace had never seen Gail so angry. She radiated fury, unable to speak as the two women stepped out through the famous door and climbed into the back of the waiting car, ignoring the inane questions thrown at them by the journalists across the narrow street. The car had barely moved when Gail screamed at the top of her lungs. Grace banged her head on the inside of the car roof as she jumped in fright, and the driver stamped on the brakes. He turned in alarm to see Gail, both hands covering her face, shaking with anger. After several seconds she finally dropped her hands and looking straight forward said loudly and clearly said, "Wankers!"

She and Grace fell into hysterics as the bemused driver looked on, mystified. Gail waved him on, and by the time the car had negotiated the famous black Downing Street gates onto Whitehall, they had composed themselves enough for Grace to ask what had happened.

"They are completely in denial. I can't ever remember speaking to a group of educated people who are so caught up in their groupthink. It has become an impenetrable carapace; no amount of rational thought can pierce their delusion."

"But they must see what's happening in France, the

459

Netherlands, Colombia, Australia, it's starting everywhere."

"Oh, they will not see. They are telling themselves it will not last, that it's a fad. They believe that 'the people' will soon see that nothing ever changes and that they need enlightened leaders with vision. Just like themselves. You really could not make it up."

Grace was about to ask another question, but Gail was not finished. "They were so patronising. Talking down to me as though I were one of those influencers or data analysts they seem to give so much credibility. It's so narrow-minded."

Grace smiled broadly, enjoying Gail's passion. They were driving past the Houses of Parliament, and Grace looked past Gail at the famous façade, "Well, you know what I think."

Gail looked at her, "Sadly, my dear, I think you might be right after all."

"Seriously?"

Gail followed Grace's gaze out of the window just as they passed the Emmeline Pankhurst statue. She asked quietly, "Did Callum say how it happened in his time?"

"No, just that it took decades," Grace said.

"And how much did he tell you about his plans?"

"A little, but I know he and Paul discussed it in much more detail. I think he wanted to have started it by now, but you know, only so many hours in a day."

"Paul's always rather retiring about this subject, don't you think?" Gail said.

"I'm not sure it's that, he's been busy too, and then there's the distraction of his domestic thing at home; it's hit him hard. Did I tell you, Cal, I mean his son, the young… you know. He's been staying over with me off and on, just when he needs to get away for a night or two, and of course, Lydia was quick to follow. I've had to put up a small bed in the office for her."

"I had no idea. Are they OK, the children?"

"Oh yes, I think so, they're old enough that it won't be too traumatic. I've defended Lisa a few times when I probably shouldn't have, but the sisters have to stick together."

"Mmmm, up to a point," Gail replied, unconvinced.

"Well I'm hardly going to be the one casting stones at someone fucking around, am I. I think it's my job to make sure that both parents are seen to shoulder the same amount of blame. It's always shades of grey when you dig deep enough."

"If you say so," Gail replied. In the way she moved as she asked the next question, Grace sensed her embarrassment in its obvious prurience, "It must be slightly odd having him, the boy, in the flat, living with you."

Grace could not prevent a wicked smile. "Odd doesn't begin to cover it. I mean, what can I say? A young fit version of the man who I've spent the last couple of years fucking whenever I got the chance. And I can see him looking at me. He's all hormones and longing at that age."

"Oh my god, Grace. You can't really be considering, I mean, you haven't, have you?"

Grace shook her head "No, absolutely not, it would be just too weird."

Gail suddenly remembered the driver and pulled a face while glancing at the back of his head.

Grace shrugged and rolled her eyes. "Modern parenting. Bloody minefield. How did this conversation start anyway?"

"Paul, and him being quiet about the democracy 'thing'."

"Ah, yes, a bit off track. Let's talk to him properly if you're serious about us doing this now."

The Land of the Blind

Gail was decisive, "Grace, I am absolutely serious. It is time those dinosaurs met their comet, and we are the people who can deliver it."

"In which case we will need to visit Armando. The one thing I do know is that it will require a shed load of money, and for that, Armando is our man."

47.

Callum closed the novel, lowered it to his lap, and shut his eyes. He had chosen the book impulsively from Armando's home office and spent the previous afternoon and most of the morning sitting in the early winter sun, ensnared by the bleak narrative. He remembered reading it as a young man and thought he might have seen a film version in his teens or twenties. 'The Road' had become a cult novel in the forties, rediscovered by a generation who feared that the apocalypse, envisaged by Cormac McCarthy at the start of the twenty-first century, might be their fate. He wondered once more at the author's skill, his ability to convey so much with so few words. It was a work of genius, so vivid and toxic, he wondered why he had carried on reading it. The protagonist's relationship with his son reminded Callum too painfully of his lost daughter, and at one point, he had sat, shedding quiet tears. Now, closing the book, he felt a tight band across his chest again. Opening his eyes and breathing deeply, he focused across the lawn to the lake in the middle distance, drawn closer by the Alps beyond, their white peaks concealed in cloud. The quotidian beauty of the scene was a balm, cloaking the fearful images that McCarthy had reawakened. He remembered the despair of that time, the late forties, and the spate of suicides, lasting months, when a madness had seized thousands of young people around the globe. Humanity had seemed to teeter on an existential precipice. There were many theories about why it happened, but Callum believed it was the final realisation of the damage humans had wrought on the planet and all its sentient inhabitants. Guilt so profound that it threatened to undermine our species' right to exist. The moment had passed, but the mental scars remained in anyone who endured that time.

He shook off the morbid thoughts and as he did, was suddenly aware that his self-deception, confected over the last weeks, could not stand. He had almost convinced himself his work was done; at least safely in the hands of others. The illusion had already been fraying; perhaps that was the subconscious motivation for picking up the book. The next thought, about Grace, was wreathed in a particular guilt. Could his motivation to re-join the battle be so basic as a desire to be with her again? He longed to see her face, hold it, kiss her, and feel the softness of her lips. The sexual images of her, which he returned to so often, were visceral and powerful. He wanted her so badly that he discounted her dangerous power over him. He knew the lie he had told himself at the start was just that. The rapturous animal response, which time would inevitably blunt, was already leavened with something far deeper. He closed his eyes again and chose different memories to dull his need for her. There was still so much to do, and they would be so much less effective without him. The furore over the livestock virus was already fading, and people, as they always did, were accepting a new reality and getting on with their lives. The British justice system no longer wanted him, and as long as he stayed clear of American jurisdiction, they were unlikely to pursue him. The world remained unaware of some of the other changes he had put in train, but when these emerged, he hoped he could stay one step ahead of those who would undoubtedly try to stop him.

For a few moments, he allowed himself a dispassionate assessment of what he had achieved so far. The crucial development was nuclear power, which had always been the only practical option for any realistic chance of success. The world's nations had failed to grasp this the first time, and were failing now. Despite his efforts over a decade, there was still no possible way to reduce carbon emissions without massive investment and the adoption of nuclear power. He knew that history would wonder how almost everyone had been so blind on this point, how societies had failed to recognise the true role and scale of fossil fuels in our lives. The narrative that fossil fuels powered the global economy was a convenient fantasy. The reality was that practically our entire economy, our way of life, was fundamentally built upon them. They *were* our economy.

Now, the Chinese were building their modular reactors at an impressive rate, and the Americans and Europeans, fearing the economic dominance this would confer on their competitor, were attempting to catch up. But the fossil fuel industry was still the largest on the planet, and they were far from down and out. Despite twenty years of developing renewable energy before Callum arrived and all his recent efforts to date, more than three-quarters of global energy still came from fossil fuels, and that industry was unconcerned about renewables replacing them. They had calculated that other technologies would take several lifetimes to impact their bonuses and profits. By then, the current raft of business leaders would have retired in affluent luxury. The sudden development of the new modular nuclear reactors posed a direct threat to their business model, and they were lobbying hard to slow down their deployment. With almost unlimited funds to shape elected representatives' behaviour, they would likely succeed. Callum knew he had to change the game. Although nobody other than Paul knew it, democracy was his ultimate target. He needed a revolution. He had the resources and knew precisely how to start it. He stood, testing his ankle while taking a final look at the view before turning towards the house. He would be here in self-imposed exile for several more months, but he knew he had to return to the fray and Grace. It was time to break the silence. He knew she had made her choice, and he had to let her know he would be back and would never break his promise to her. Change was coming to the world, like it or not, and his small group would deliver it. Many would not like what he was planning.

*****

The Lands of the Blind - Book 2 Sample

27 May 2089

The fens were quiet and still, the line of gold that had breached the horizon moments earlier bleeding colour into the darkness. The last stars were fading to the west as the wide tyres hissed across the road surface, tearing the silence. In the low, sleek car that curved away from Waterbeach onto the long arrow-straight towards Ely and the dawn, the young driver glanced at the controls and then fixed on the empty ribbon of tarmac that stretched away to a distant point. One deep breath; he floored the pedal and was pinned by the acceleration as electrical energy poured through the howling motors, hurling the car forward with brutal efficiency. Thanks to the G-suit, he remained conscious under a force eight times the Earth's gravitational pull. In two seconds, he was travelling at almost three hundred miles per hour. Adrenaline flooded his body, overwhelming his mind as the fens stretched to a blur in his peripheral vision. Euphoric, immersed in the moment, he neither saw nor heard the car's proximity warning.

Maria and her drowsy teenage daughter were listening to music as their car carried them towards the main road. It was a regular journey; Maria to Cambridge airport for the early hop to Madrid; Rachel to a friend's house on the outskirts close to school. Approaching the junction in the half light, neither saw the blood red car closing fast. Their vehicle's systems had, of course, 'seen'

1

it and suddenly braked hard as they approached the junction. The slowing car logged the event in the transport databank, including the approaching vehicle's lack of an identifier and its unlikely speed of two hundred and ninety-four miles per hour. A police drone would arrive within minutes.

Reaction times for living creatures are predictable. Just as one cannot dodge a bullet in flight, the hare that hopped lazily across the road could not react in time to evade the speeding car and was obliterated. Had his vehicle been controlled by the software used in every road-legal car, the impact would not have caused it to deviate; not that a car under Vehicle AI would ever have been travelling at that speed in the first place. However, the software controlling this highly customised machine was the young man's nervous system, and the instinctive, fractional twitch of his hands on the wheel was sufficient to unseat the tyres from their tenuous grip. The car twisted, and the laws of physics, expressed now as aerodynamics, delivered the inevitable outcome. In a human time frame, the sequence lasted little more than the blink of an eye; for the collision avoidance system in the reversing car, there was time for many thousands of calculations to be made and the outcome foreseen, but insufficient time to prevent it. The speeding car's wheels lost contact with the road in three milliseconds. It covered the forty meters between the two vehicles in just three hundred and sixty milliseconds. Maria and Rachel would never know why their car stopped and reversed. The speeding car, rising on a layer of air as hard as stone, had become a missile, and in that sliver of time, the lives of all three people ended.

27 May 2090

27th May 2090 fell on a Saturday, and Callum woke naturally a little after nine. He had silenced his comm before sleeping, forestalling the need to communicate with anyone, either real or a construct, on this day. As his conscious mind reasserted its flimsy control, a lance of pure grief impaled him, as it had done without fail on each of the last three hundred and sixty-five mornings. He was alone, they were gone and the black hole where his heart used to be threatened to swallow him. His hand slid across the cool bedsheet to the void beside him, as if to prevent his slide into the abyss, and the absolute silence of the house settled, suffocating. He lay like this, unmoving, fighting the ache in his chest until the anger flowed in to replace the cocktail of pain and self-pity. He waited again for the numb resignation to descend, as it usually did. He wanted to hide from the world, but knew that today, friends and family would not allow this feeble indulgence.

Resigned, he thought, 'Internal comms on' and sensed the thrill of the warm static seeping across his mind. He could not remember starting to vocalise his side of the conversations, but with so much time spent alone, the physical sound reassured him and served to slow his tripping thoughts. He habitually returned to silent communication when in public, even though many engaged audibly with unheard voices.

"Who called?"

He listened to the roll call of names. Of course, his sister had left a message of support; Lydia, her husband and their two children, his niece and nephew, were now his only family. After skipping all the messages and listening only to his sister's, he said, "Reply to all; Thanks. I appreciate you thinking of me today. I'll be in touch soon."

All sent. What are you going to do today? The AI, which interfaced with his subconscious, asked.

"I'll visit them, say hello. Then … not sure."

You should see someone, Graham would want you to call.

"Mmmm, we'll see how I feel. I might walk or ride somewhere. What's the forecast?"

Thirty-six, thirty-seven.

He glanced out the window at the arid, barren landscape, and a memory surfaced of him walking through a wood as a child. He remembered cool shade beneath vivid broadleaf trees and bracken up to his waist, his hands held out, palms brushing the soft, curled fronds. The image was trailed closely by his dangerous anger. If he walked today, it would be across a pale, desiccated landscape, stunted hedgerows rustling their death rattle above the hardy succulents, European floral immigrants, now ubiquitous. "Why am I even bothering? What's the fucking point."

You know. The crazy idea; it might just work.

"Work. Whatever that means, we've already trashed the planet."

But it wouldn't feel like that; it might feel like saving the planet.

He stared at the bedroom ceiling. "It might." The idea was growing daily, an indulgent delusion, sunrise to overwhelm the darkness. He was gradually immersing himself in the past, reading, researching, and forcing meaning back into his life. He avoided examining the sensation, but he knew what it was: hope. It might kill him, of course, but that was barely a consideration; either way, the pain would stop. He swung his legs and sat on the edge of the bed, head in hands. "Let's start with breakfast, I suppose."

August 2090

Callum tapped on the clear ceramic wall and indicated his backpack. Graham turned, nodded, and continued talking as he picked up his lunchbox and cap from the desk and waved the air display off. By the time he reached the office door, he had disconnected from whomever he had been speaking to.

They walked in easy silence down the wide stairs to the entrance lobby and out through the sliding glass from the cool building into the intense summer heat and brilliant light. Both men automatically pulled on their caps and slid their sunglasses into place, pausing momentarily as the heat enveloped them and their clothes responded, adjusting their porosity to minimise moisture loss. The brittle air birthed tiny vortices in the dust on the almost empty car park and the baked ground beyond. They moved quickly to the walkway and then sauntered in the shade that led to the stand of eucalyptus a few hundred meters away. The circle of newcomers had been planted around the hull of a massive oak, and their pale, smooth simplicity emphasised its complex, ancient skin. It was the last old-growth tree in Cambridge, famous, but dead now for over two decades; a brutal monument to forces that had passed beyond human control. For miles around, the slim leaves of the interlopers provided the only natural shade beneath the relentless blue.

Half-heartedly, they brushed the dust from the seats and sat opposite one another under the awning of one of the empty picnic tables. Few ventured outside during the summer, and no one could overhear their conversation.

Graham looked at his friend and half smiled, "You've decided, haven't you?"

Callum shrugged, "I've got nothing to stay for."

"Thanks a lot, mate."

"You know what I mean. It's just …"

They started on their sandwiches, listening to the wind rattle the leaves in the gums above them, the fallen, skittering around their feet.

"Do you really think it can do any good? Look around you, it's done, you can't change what's already happened." Graham said, gesturing across the arid fens towards Cambridge in the distance. The heat shimmered the air over a patchwork of browns and ochres stretching away, not a trace of green in sight.

"Let's not have the same conversation again, Gra," Callum said wearily. "You're the one who says other realities exist."

Graham frowned, "In theory, yes. But how would you achieve anything useful? You won't understand the technology; it's stuff from museums. None of the tech we have now will work."

"I've a pretty good idea what I can use. I've been thinking about this for a while, you know."

"Oh, I know." Graham nodded, grim-faced. "But you'll be all on your own, mate. It's going to be almost impossible …."

"It's all about the timing," Callum said, becoming animated. "You know what it's like looking back at anything; you see when the opportunities were missed, when you should have acted, what you should have done. That gives me a huge advantage. I'm not saying I'll get it 'right', there's no right, but I might be able to prevent the worst …" He looked up and scanned the landscape.

"… stop it being quite so catastrophic."

"Perhaps." Graham conceded.

Callum snorted, "It's a pretty low bar. Even if I only manage to save a few hundred million or a billion lives, surely that's got to be worth a try?"

Graham rolled his eyes. "In theory, I guess. But I still don't know what big advantage you think you'll have, and even if you do, how will you force people to do things differently? If I remember my history, it wasn't just the fossil fuel companies. Whatever the popular narrative these days, it was just about everyone."

"I know that, but I'm sure I can find a way. I've done some basic modelling, which is promising, although I can't make it work the way I want it to, so I could do with your help."

"Make what work?"

"The big problem, back then, was that they, we, started too late, just didn't have the technology in time to make a difference so we were screwed. But we know what tech did work in the end; it's just that it was too late. So I need to create those solutions faster, in time to make an impact."

Graham nodded, "Makes sense."

"So, I tried setting up some models to see what might work, but even with the lab's best systems, I don't seem to be able to create a model where people move away from fossil fuels fast enough to make any appreciable difference. The best scenarios result in three, maybe four hundred million fewer deaths."

"You're using the labs' modelling arrays for your little project?" Graham's eyebrows slid slowly upwards. "Which framework are you using?"

"The latest IIM models."

Graham nodded, "OK, interesting." He took a bite of his lunch and stared off into space.

Callum waited for the result.

"Likely to be the intrinsics." Graham offered when he had emptied his mouth. "Those models are built for a different world and sensibilities; people now don't behave as they did a hundred years ago. Drop me access and I'll take a look." He bit into his sandwich again and eventually continued, "I was wondering, don't you think you'd be lonely. You wouldn't know anyone. I mean, imagine it."

"I can't be much lonelier than I have been for the last year or so, mate," Callum replied quietly.

"That's grief, not loneliness."

"Grief and loneliness."

They ate quietly again for a few minutes, both lost in thought.

Finally, Callum looked at Graham and asked, "So if you think this is such a bad idea and I've got no chance of success, and you know how dangerous it is, how come you're so keen to help?"

Graham shifted his gaze away and failed to stop himself looking sheepish, "I'm not keen, exactly."

"You could have fooled me." Callum taunted him gently, grinning at his friend, "It's not like you can even win a Nobel these days, so as things stand, you're not even likely to be famous. One of the greatest scientists of the age dying in obscurity."

"Yea, Yea." Graham glanced back and smiled, "It would be quite an achievement. But proving that it worked is the big problem, as you know. Short of you returning to tell us of your temporal exploits, with photos of the early twenty-first century."

"I guess we both know it's a one-way ticket," Callum said evenly.

9

The One Eyed Man - Sample

"In theory, there's nothing to stop us re-linking the identical physical space if it were possible to coordinate the timing …. But on a more practical note, you know what will happen when we pull this stunt. I'll be lucky if I've still got a job. They're definitely not going to trust me ever again, and even persuading them not to wind up the whole project is probably a long shot."

"I wish I could be around to see Campbell's face when they get the lights back on." Callum was smiling broadly, staring off into space. His attention returned as Graham started to shake quietly, his eyes shut. It happened to them occasionally, but this was the first time for as long as either could remember. Callum began to shake with the effort of subduing the laughter, and in no time, both men were racked with uncontrollable, suppressed, silent delight, tiny squeaks emerging from both of them. Graham just managed to squeeze out the words, "He's going to wet himself." And they were off again, clutching their sides against the fabulous pain. Eventually, exhausted, they wiped away their tears and finished the remains of their lunch without speaking, neither daring to catch the other's eye.

***

That conversation was a watershed. Graham had finally accepted what he already knew: Callum would not be deterred. Despite believing there was every chance his friend would not survive the journey, he decided to act as if that were not true. From that moment on, he set his formidable mind to analysing how this crazy project could work. The research and their elaborate preparations would take five years, but throughout, Callum was focused, craving the distraction from grief as much as the learning. He buried himself in the research, spending countless hours watching archive material. Starting from the beginning of the 21st century, he immersed himself in the culture, watched old films, listened to conversations, and attempted to understand the politics of the time. Much of what he watched and read had the potential to be unbearably depressing, like watching a disaster movie again and again from different perspectives, hoping it would end differently. The documentaries about the inundation of Bangladesh and Pakistan and the shrinking of the water flows in the Indus were shocking. He had lived through that time as an adult; where had he buried those memories? How could the knowledge of more than two hundred million deaths in just a few months not be part of him; he felt shame at the absence.

Most relatable and upsetting were the archive clips of the clashes in the English Channel when the United Kingdom closed its borders. Eventually, the waves of refugees stopped when it became apparent that there was no way to evade the navy boats with their sophisticated monitoring systems. One carefully buried memory resurfaced all too easily. The images of dismembered bodies churning in the wake of a British frigate forced him to stop watching a news report from 2044. At least by then, there was some positive progress, with the sharp drop in fossil fuel use as more nuclear plants came online. In retrospect, 2045 marked the beginning of the end of the contraction era. At the time, growth and prosperity seemed impossible, barely an aspiration even for those who lived in the new world of abundant cheap energy. Our technology fix arrived thirty years too late to save vast tracts of the planet from ecological devastation. And then there was the nuclear war between Israel and Iran in 2046; if the detonation of two weapons twenty hours apart could be deemed a war. It was over before it began, with some twenty million dead, most of them on the Iranian side. Why Iran chose that moment to attack Israel was never fully explained. The region had become almost uninhabitable, and the physical state of Israel would have soon, like that of Palestine a few years earlier, ceased to have any physical manifestation other than historical lines on a map. The Jewish diasporas in France and the United States had grown quickly over the previous decade, leaving only the most orthodox communities or those too poor to escape that cursed land. From the nadir around 2050, the world's economic fortunes began to recover, but it was a slow and painful process for those outside the nuclear energy states in the Global North. Around a third of the world's population, some two billion of the six billion who remained, managed to maintain the illusion of civilisation and prosperity even as people outside their borders starved to death in their millions each year.

There is only so much misery anyone can observe without taint, and there were times when Callum slipped back into the well of self-pity that losing his family had opened for him. It was Graham's constant friendship and strength that he clung to in these moments, and each time this happened, his belief that he had to change the ending grew stronger. In reflective moments, he wondered how he could possibly achieve what he was planning in the time he would have. One man, armed only with knowledge. He clung to an image, his version of the ancient quote credited to Archimedes some two and a half thousand years earlier. 'Give me a place to stand and with a lever I will move the whole world.' His lever was knowledge, and he and Graham were carefully choosing where he would stand.

About The Author

Peter Cross

Peter is an engineer, at least temperamentally if only somewhat professionally. He made stuff up (software) for a few decades and is now making other stuff up (stories and novels). Engineers like to know how things work and cannot avoid being offended when they work badly. It's hard to make things work better in our increasingly complex world, and plenty could do with an upgrade, but people don't want to be told how to change. Perhaps the best way is to tell them a story; try to infect them with that most virulent of things, a new idea.

Peter and his wife preside over an empty nest in South London, their two adult children fledged into an increasingly complex world. He has not abandoned the idea that, with some persistence and smart thinking, he could make the world a little less difficult for them and many others.

Printed in Dunstable, United Kingdom

65555755R00271